Enemies from this world . . . and the next.

Toshi Umezawa works for himself and cares only for himself.
A highly skilled ronin, he treads a lonely path. Across it come
a princess, fox folk, and a secret the Daimyo would kill to prevent others knowing. And amid it all, Toshi must guard against
attacks from the kami, spirits who have launched an all-out war
against the Daimyo's kingdom.

**Scott McGough begins an epic story of a ronin and a
princess and the strange alliance they must make to
discover the truth behind the kami's war.**

EXPERIENCE THE MAGIC™

Kamigawa Cycle · Book I

OUTLAW
Champions of
kamigawa

Scott McGough

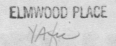

ELMWOOD PLACE

YA fic

OUTLAW: CHAMPIONS OF KAMIGAWA

Cover art by John Bolton
First Printing: September 2004
Library of Congress Catalog Card Number: 2004106767

9 8 7 6 5 4 3 2 1

US ISBN: 0-7869-3357-7
UK ISBN: 0-7869-3358-5
620-17750-001-EN

U.S., CANADA,
ASIA, PACIFIC, & LATIN AMERICA
Wizards of the Coast, Inc.
P.O. Box 707
Renton, WA 98057-0707
+1-800-324-6496

EUROPEAN HEADQUARTERS
Wizards of the Coast, Belgium
T Hofveld 6d
1702 Groot-Bijgaarden
Belgium
+322 467 3360

Visit our web site at **www.wizards.com**

Dedication

This book is dedicated to my father-in-law, Dr. C. Herbert Schiro,
for his years of support, his boundless eloquence, and his keen
appreciation of a good fantasy tale.

Acknowledgments

This book would not have been possible without contributions
from the following exceptional individuals:

Elena K. McGough, who makes it all worthwhile
Peter Archer, who made this book better
The staff at Wizards of the Coast,
who brought this novel to colorful life
The crew of the BeBop: Spike, Ed, Jet, Faye, and especially Ein.
See you, space cowboy.

The Daimyo's child was born at sunrise. Lady Pearl-Ear of the *kitsune-bito* looked at the wailing, red-smeared newborn and then to the first spears of daylight streaming in from the open window. Which omen would prove more powerful, she wondered—a baby born in concert with the dawn of a new day, herald to an age of light? Or a dire warning that the Daimyo's legacy would be drenched in blood?

Amid a cluster of bustling servants, the midwife wrapped the infant in fine Towabara linens. She handed the child to Lady Pearl-Ear, then drew the bedclothes up to the mother's chin.

The unnamed baby went quiet in the fox-woman's arms. Lady Pearl-Ear's long ears stood up straight as she tried in vain to isolate the infant's aura. As a *kitsune*, Pearl-Ear's shallow muzzle had no visible nose or mouth, but her senses were still sharper than a real fox's. To her, a person's scent was inextricably bound to disposition—industrious people smelled of clean sweat and wood shavings while layabouts gave off waves of stale air and mildew. In this case, all she could sense was a normal, helpless infant in need of succor. She cradled the princess's head against her heart, the soft texture of her fur seeming to soothe the tiny child.

Pearl-Ear tried to relax as well. She had lived among the humans of Eiganjo for almost a decade, but their offspring still

1

struck her as remarkably small, too quick to cry, and distressingly hairless.

Nearby, the new mother lay exhausted. Lady Yoshino was the Daimyo's most favored concubine, and carrying his child was a special honor the bachelor ruler had bestowed upon her. The labor had been extremely difficult, and now Yoshino barely breathed as she slept among the sweat-soaked sheets. Pearl-Ear said a silent prayer as she looked down on her friend. She knew this appeal joined thousands of others, an entire kingdom beseeching the most powerful of the *kami* for the sake of their great leader's child and the lady who bore her. Pearl-Ear's own people in the woods honored the same spirits as the citizens of Towabara, and together their voices were a grand chorale that rang across the spirit world. The kitsune-bito knew the power of such prayer, and Pearl-Ear also knew that without them, Yoshino might not have survived at all.

The midwife's apprentice began cleaning up as the midwife herself bowed before Lady Pearl-Ear. "Mother and child are alive," she said. "Daimyo Konda must be told."

Pearl-Ear glanced down at the baby. "A child," she said, "but not a prince."

The midwife shook her head and smiled sadly. "Perhaps this princess will confound tradition and succeed her father." She glanced at the bustling servants, then added, "But no time soon, of course. Long live the Daimyo."

"I share your hope," Pearl-Ear said. She held the infant out with both arms, staring deep into half-opened eyes that had not yet learned to focus. "I would not put Lady Yoshino through another ordeal like this one for the sake of gender."

Pearl-Ear handed the infant back to the midwife. "Make mother and daughter comfortable. I shall inform the Daimyo." The fox-woman's ears folded back around her head and she gathered the sleeves of her voluminous robe around her. With a nod to the sentries outside the midwife's chambers, Lady Pearl-Ear stepped out into the storm.

It was a short walk from the rear corner of the Daimyo's stronghold to the main entryway, but the winds were fierce and the sky was a scowling mass of grayish-yellow clouds. From the great stone parapet that overlooked the lower courtyard, Pearl-Ear could see that only a few hundred of the faithful maintained their vigil, awaiting the arrival of the Daimyo's child. Eiganjo's citizens had gathered in their thousands the night before, but fatigue and the growing tempest had forced most to withdraw. She wished she could spare a moment to tell them the news they had been waiting for so patiently, but they were so distant and the storm so loud that they would never hear her words.

The retainers on the central level's main gate recognized her and waved her on. She had made many visits to the top of the Daimyo's tower over the past two days, even though she had never spoken to Konda himself. His advisors received her cordially, but they would not interrupt their master, who had given word that the future of the kingdom depended on his not being disturbed.

Once the great gate closed behind her and the wind was at bay, Pearl-Ear let out her ears and loosened her robes. She paused, sniffed the air, and rotated her ears towards the main stairwell. Satisfied, she folded her ears back and darted forward, scaling the seemingly endless steps so lightly that her padded feet barely made a sound.

She passed dozens of courtiers and servants on the stairs, but most were too busy to take a second glance. Those that weren't never got the chance. She ran easily, weaving around obstacles and darting between soldiers and shadows alike. She could run this way for a week if she had to, with scarcely any sign of exertion, and she made excellent time as she ascended to the upper reaches of the stronghold.

The higher she went, the more sentries Pearl-Ear encountered.

Twice she was ordered to halt and identify herself, but each time the Daimyo's symbol on a slip of parchment allowed her to go past. Thankfully, these sentries were all familiar with the kitsune-bito in general and with Lady Pearl-Ear in particular. They knew she was no threat and that she came bearing news from the midwife.

Pearl-Ear slowed her pace as she drew near the uppermost chambers of the tower. She smoothed wrinkles from her robes, hoping that this time she would receive an audience with Konda himself.

Lady Pearl-Ear opened the door, which led to a small ante-chamber crowded with armed retainers. She recognized some of the Daimyo's most trusted warriors, including Captain Nagao, hero of Konda's second campaign against the bandits that plagued the southern countryside. Nagao came forward and saluted.

"The child is born?"

Lady Pearl-Ear's whiskers twitched, and she bowed. "I would tell his lordship first, gracious Captain Nagao."

Nagao smiled. He was a lean, leathery man with a hard, square face. "Do you think me a palace gossip, O fox maiden?"

"Never, sir. But Daimyo Konda is most particular about how things are done. I would hate to be the cause of a shadow on his esteem for you."

Nagao jerked his head, and the sentries behind him uncrossed their spears, leaving the exit behind them clear.

"Deliver your news, honorable Lady Pearl-Ear." Nagao bowed. "I will hear it soon enough from the palace gossips anyway."

A small laugh rose among the retainers but died just as quickly under the captain's withering glare.

She returned the bow. "Thank you, Nagao. I will tell the Daimyo how safe he is in your care."

Nagao's face tightened, and Pearl-Ear sensed a mild surge of frustration. To her, it smelled of burning hair.

"If you are able speak to him directly," Nagao muttered, "I will thank you for your praise."

Pearl-Ear hesitated for a moment, but Nagao had already turned away. Her ears swiveled after him, but she said no more and went into the chamber.

The huge square room was lit by a single torch in each corner. Sumptuous bolts of cloth hung from the ceiling beams like sheets of silver spider's silk. Even in the dim light Lady Pearl-Ear recognized two of the three tall figures at the center of the room.

General Takeno, commander of the Daimyo's cavalry, stood alongside an elderly, white-bearded wizard named Hisoka from the Minamo Academy. Beyond them was a hooded person facing away from Pearl-Ear. From the haughtiness of his posture and the scent of cold, pure rain, she immediately placed him as one of the *soratami* moonfolk. The three turned as one to face her, standing between her and the darkened doorway beyond.

"The child is born," she said. She had been right: the hooded figure was a soratami, as they were known informally—one of the strange, ethereal denizens of the clouds above the Minamo Academy. Both the wizards' school and the soratami had excellent relations with the Daimyo's kingdom. She knew Konda took wizards and moonfolk into his confidence, but she hadn't realized that both were represented here, on the most restricted levels of his stronghold.

General Takeno grunted. "Long live the Daimyo, and his child."

"Most excellent news, Lady Pearl-Ear," said the wizard.

"Our lord must not be disturbed." The soratami frowned from beneath the folds of his hood.

"I bring most urgent news, soratami-san." Pearl-Ear assumed he was male, but the voice was a husky whisper and the heavy robe masked both scent and features. The "he" could well be a she—the moonfolk themselves drew little distinction between the genders.

"His lordship gave strict instructions not to be disturbed. The future of Towabara—"

"Lies asleep in her mother's arms." Lady Pearl-Ear's ears stretched out on either side of her head. "Surely a father would pause in his great work to learn that he is, in fact, a father." And to inquire about the health of the mother, she added privately.

The soratami shook his head. "Your news can wait." With a condescending wave, the moonfolk turned away from Pearl-Ear.

The fox-woman's brow creased, but Takeno placed a hand on her shoulder.

"Write it down," the general said evenly. "I will mark it with my own seal and it will be treated as a battlefield dispatch. I guarantee no one will read it before his lordship."

Pearl-Ear started to nod, her eyes still fixed on the moonfolk's back. Before she could answer, a powerful voice rolled out of the darkness beyond the far doorway.

"Send Lady Pearl-Ear to me."

"Sir!" Takeno and the wizard bowed, stepping aside for Lady Pearl-Ear. The moonfolk stood firm, facing the unseen speaker.

"Daimyo Konda, respectfully—"

"Now." The ruler of Towabara had a loud, ragged voice that had led a hundred campaigns. He was not used to repeating himself.

The moonfolk stepped aside but did not face Lady Pearl-Ear or even bow. She swept past the towering robed figure through the doorway and up another set of stairs.

Daimyo Konda was waiting for her at the top. The ruler of Towabara was over fifty years old, but he was as strong and alert as he had been at twenty-five. He wore his thin white hair long, and it flowed freely around his head from under his round skullcap. His mustache and beard both hung down past the center of his chest. He was dressed in a brilliant gold robe inlaid with rich red silk and dazzling gems. Though he seemed distracted, he was still brimming with the famous stamina that had conquered a nation. Shouldering the burdens of leadership for so many decades had made him stronger as he aged instead of weaker, seasoning him like hardwood.

Lady Pearl-Ear bowed. "My lord," she began.

Konda sat cross-legged on a raised platform, inches from the floor. He clutched the handle of a sheathed sword, cradling the weapon across his lap.

"You have news."

Pearl-Ear bowed again. "You have a child, my lord."

Daimyo Konda nodded. A strange, feral grin split his fine features and he croaked out a dry laugh. "A girl."

Pearl-Ear paused. "Yes, my lord. The princess sleeps soundly, alongside Lady Yoshino."

"Princess. Yes. But that no longer matters." The Daimyo either would not or could not focus his eyes. He stood facing Pearl-Ear from the center of his small chamber, but his rich almond pupils listed from side to side like a rudderless ship. In the dim light, it even seemed that Konda's eyes were floating outside the boundaries of his face.

The Daimyo smiled again, and let out a long wail, his voice rising and falling as his thumb worked the hilt of his sword.

Distracted, Lady Pearl-Ear's own eyes focused on the space behind the Daimyo. A small stone shrine had been built against the far wall, in the space usually occupied by the shrine to the Myojin of Cleansing Fire. Now the only representation of the Daimyo's patron god was the ornate mural that covered the northern wall, depicting Konda and the myojin leading the Daimyo's troops into battle, side by side as equals. Both wore expressions of righteous fury in the face of their enemies. Above them, the great sun spirit Terashi illuminated the heavens.

Now, a new shrine featured a square granite pedestal topped by a marble column. A rough stone disk hovered several feet above the column, smoking slightly in the cool air. A strange shape had been carved into the disk's face, something with the head and horns of a beast lying curled into a fetal position.

Konda stood, his vacillating eyes still straying across his face. He held the sheathed sword out toward Lady Pearl-Ear, its blade parallel to the ground.

"Don't look at that," he said. "It's mine."

Pearl-Ear shuddered. "Forgive me, my lord. I meant no harm."

"I am beyond harm now, Lady Pearl-Ear. I am beyond most of what you comprehend. But my will is still law in Towabara. Let my enemies tremble!"

Pearl-Ear bowed to hide her expression. "Long live the Daimyo." She looked up and said, "If I may, my lord, Lady Yoshino—"

"Has given birth, yes, yes, yes. So you have said, Lady Pearl-Ear of the kitsune-bito. But I have also created something this night. I have also given birth. I am father and mother to this entire nation. My children are legion, and will one day sit on the throne of this world and the next. You have noticed the changes to my shrine."

Pearl-Ear paused, thrown by the sudden shift in the conversation. The Daimyo was not asking; he was observing.

Lady Pearl-Ear lowered her head and bowed. "I have, my lord."

"Remember it well, for you will never look upon its like again. It is a monument to Towabara's hope. It is the doorway through which I will secure the future. It is the symbol of my divine destiny and of my people's good fortune."

"Wonderful, my lord." She was catching something strange and foreboding from the Daimyo. Something about his eyes and the nauseous excitement that came off him in waves had raised an almost overwhelming urge to bolt from the room.

"I have dared much, Lady Pearl-Ear. I have risked my life and all that I have accomplished for the sake of my people. And I have won."

Pearl-Ear raised her head. "If I may ask, my lord . . . what have you won?"

Daimyo Konda's vacillating eyes suddenly stopped and fixed on Pearl-Ear. "Lasting peace," he said, his face split by a mad, leering grin. "The rule of law, ensured by the power to enforce it." His wandering eyes began to glow softly in the dimly lit room. His mouth widened, revealing square, sharp teeth. "Permanent prosperity. The best of all possible worlds for my children, and their children's children." Konda's voice remained low and ragged, but Lady Pearl-Ear heard a sound like a kettle's whistle behind his words. She winced inwardly, careful not to let her discomfort show.

"Now, Lady Pearl-Ear, the glory of my beloved Towabara will never fade away." The Daimyo turned to face the marble column and the floating stone disk. He threw his arms out wide and cried, "Behold! The new spirit of my kingdom!"

Pearl-Ear stood and stared . . . at the Daimyo, at the shrine, at the unsettling figure scratched into the disk. On the north wall, the mural showing Daimyo and kami seemed to move in the flickering torchlight as the painted and etched figures relived a glorious victory.

Daimyo Konda still held his arms aloft. "You may go now, Lady Pearl-Ear. I will see my other new child presently. And you need not worry. Though my manner may be strange and my thoughts confused, I am finally at peace. Go, Lady Pearl-Ear. Tell the world that soon everything will change for the better."

"My lord." Lady Pearl-Ear silently backed out of the room with her head bowed until she reached the top of the stairs. As she turned to go, she stole one last look at the odd tableau.

The Daimyo stood, silently exulting. The stone disk floated and smoked over the new shrine. And on the north wall, the Myojin of Cleansing Fire wept, real tears sizzling as they splattered against the cold granite floor.

Pearl-Ear fled down the stairs, past the Daimyo's retainers, and back out into the storm.

PART ONE

OCHIMUSHA

Something big was happening on the outskirts of the old city. Toshi Umezawa stayed far behind the pack of ratfolk as they picked their way through the ruined buildings on the edge of Eiganjo, well out of sight and scent range so they would not realize they were being shadowed. The *nezumi-bito* were good at covering their tracks, but Toshi was better at uncovering them.

He could hear snarling little whispers as the two hindmost ratfolk conferred. The fact that they spoke at all told him they had no idea he was there.

"Smell anything?"

"Neh."

"Hear anything?"

"Neh."

"Me neither. We go?"

"We go."

Toshi listened to their slight scrabbling noises as they rushed to catch up to the others. He had counted almost a dozen nezumi-bito as they skulked through the debris. It was unheard of to see more than three or four at any one time outside of their territory in the Takenuma Swamp unless they were robbing your shack or cutting your throat. They were effective as thugs only when they had superior numbers, and as thieves only when someone else came up with the plan.

The rats were well-suited to following orders and bartering acts of violence for cash, though, so Toshi gave them plenty of room. Twelve or more nezumi on the streets before sundown meant they had a serious thing in the works. If he were sharp he could score a significant piece of the job without actually doing any of the work.

Toshi waited for a few more seconds to make sure the nezumi were well away and then followed. He was an unspectacular figure physically, of medium height and medium build, but he was as sinewy and lithe and moved with a powerful grace. Unlike the nezumi, Toshi made no sound and left no traces in his wake. His simple coal-gray cloak was topped by red and black scale-mail that protected him from edged weapons. His face was smeared with black mud and his bright green eyes gleamed in the dim light.

He had been told that he was disarmingly handsome in a boyish sort of way, but only by people he had bested and who were trying to explain how. Besides, to date, his face had never gotten him *out* of a dangerous situation.

To his mild surprise, the nezumi were not heading south, away from the Daimyo's stronghold, but north toward it. This meant they were not after salvage from the blasted cities and villages surrounding the stronghold but rather something that someone still owned and cared about. Toshi nodded to himself. Good. Maybe this job would be worth hijacking after all.

He followed the nezumi for another hour as they skulked across the wasteland. He began to feel more positive about his prospects—the nezumi weren't even searching for valuables among the broken storefronts and once-opulent manor houses along the way. Wherever they were going, whatever they were after, it was worth more than an average night's looting.

He also caught a glimpse of Marrow-Gnawer, a prominent rat with a small measure of respectability back in the Marsh. Toshi had worked with Marrow-Gnawer and against him over the years, and he was both smart and strong for a nezumi. Marrow-Gnawer kept to the head of the column, leading the others, and Toshi smiled. Marrow-Gnawer did dangerous work, but it was always worth the risk. As the leader of the party, Marrow-Gnawer was also the only one Toshi had to worry about impressing when it came time to assert his claim on the evening's activity.

Toshi slowly peered around a cornerstone before continuing. Ahead, the nezumi had stopped and were clustering together in the mouth of an alley. As the others disappeared into the alley, Marrow-Gnawer and an unfamiliar nezumi had a conversation that was quickly becoming an argument.

All the signs were there—they stood face to face, shoulders hunched, ragged teeth exposed, their strange, pointed faces jittering up and down. Toshi could not clearly hear what they were saying, but after a few moments Marrow-Gnawer swatted the other on the ear and shoved him into the alley.

Toshi was impressed at how quickly and quietly Marrow-Gnawer had decided the matter. Toshi had hired nezumi as backup for the odd job here and there, and he never got them to obey so readily without dire threats, blasphemous curses, and the occasional crippling injury.

He waited as Marrow-Gnawer scanned the area and led his brothers into the alley. If his own experience held true, Toshi knew that the nezumi would cram themselves into the smallest possible area and wait for the man with the plan to arrive and tell them what to do next.

Toshi stood up and crept out into the street. All he had to do was insinuate himself into the rat pack before the ringleader showed up and force Marrow-Gnawer to purchase Toshi's noninterference . . . or better still, Toshi could tag along for an equal share. The hardest part of any score was in identifying the opportunity, which in this case was already complete.

When he was close enough to hear their hushed, ragged whispers, Toshi cleared his throat. The sounds in the alley died away. Toshi drew his jitte from his belt, tossed it end over end, and whistled as he strode into the alleyway.

Toshi caught the spiked truncheon by the handle as the first nezumi attacked. The rat-man latched on to Toshi's free arm with his small, powerful hands, but before the dirty claws could cut Toshi's skin, the *ochimusha* casually clouted the rat between the eyes with the long end of his jitte.

The first nezumi fell and Toshi followed, dropping to one knee. Now at eye level with the ratfolk, he caught a filthy, rusted dagger in the hook of his jitte and snapped the blade off with a sharp twist. Reversing the weapon, he drove its handle deep into the stabber's midsection. The second nezumi let out a wheeze and fell onto his side.

"Quit, Marrow-Gnawer," Toshi hissed. "Or the next one doesn't get up."

"Be still!" Marrow-Gnawer's voice was like a rasp on glass. The other nezumi stopped where they were, red eyes blazing in anger. Marrow-Gnawer stomped up to Toshi and shoved the larger man off-balance before Toshi could rise to his full height.

"Get lost, stupid Toshi! You'll get us all killed."

"Hello, vermin." Marrow-Gnawer seemed more frightened than angry, so Toshi decided to overlook being shoved for now. He pushed the little rat-man aside and got to his feet. "I'll keep it simple, so you can explain it to your friends. You're up to something. I'm in."

"No, no, no. This is bad and you are stupid. Go away, Toshi."

Toshi paused. This was not standard nezumi behavior. No threats, no craven whimpering, no fleeing to round up reinforcements. Was Marrow-Gnawer bent on keeping tonight's score for himself?

"We deal," Toshi said. "And I'm in for one-tenth of the take. No haggling. A fair share."

Marrow-Gnawer sneered. "Fifteen of us. Sixteen, with you. And you get one-tenth?"

Toshi smiled, and his green eyes flashed. "I could kill a few of you to even things out. Or maybe I'll just make a whole lot of noise—rouse the go-yo squads so that nobody gets anything."

"No constables," Marrow-Gnawer snarled. "Big job, secret." His eyes were darting nervously.

"Think it over, then," Toshi said. "You and your pack get nine-tenths or you get nothing. I'm offering you a bargain."

"That's a fool's bargain, sir, even for a nezumi." The new voice was hollow but sharp, like a stage whisper. It echoed off the bricks and resonated in Toshi's ears.

"Stand aside, Marrow-Gnawer. I will attempt to renegotiate with this young entrepreneur."

The ratfolk leader locked eyes with Toshi, his expression woeful. "Oh, good. Now we die. You, me, we, all die. Thanks, stupid Toshi."

Toshi turned to the voice at the back of the alley. Two hooded, robed figures stepped into the quickly fading sunlight. They were tall and narrow-shouldered, with large, oddly shaped heads. Something about that cold, hollow voice and the nezumi's reaction put a lump of suspicious dread in Toshi's stomach.

"You must be the brains behind this endeavor," he called airily. "Allow me to offer my—"

"Your head?" The figure on the left reached up and pulled back his hood with his thin, white fingers. His pale face was small and angular, with a series of tattoos across the eyebrow ridges. His long, floppy ears were twisted around his head like a turban, and also tattooed. The markings on his head and ears moved and shifted like a line of tiny dancers.

"Because if you're offering your head, I think we can come to an arrangement very quickly. One less ochimusha lowlife will hardly be a blow to the community. Eitoku?"

Toshi swallowed hard. This shinobi was a soratami. No wonder Marrow-Gnawer was so anxious: working with them was as uncertain and as dangerous as balancing on the end of a poisoned blade.

The second hooded figure drew a long katana from beneath his robe and tossed back his own hood. This moonfolk was a *bushi*, a warrior. He was silent but visibly furious, and he clearly knew how to use his sword.

As the soratami bushi stepped forward, Toshi said, "Some other time." Then, he quickly dropped and punched the tip of his jitte down through Marrow-Gnawer's foot. He yanked it free immediately and then kicked the screaming nezumi into the center of the ratfolk gang, between himself and the soratami. The rats went wild in fury and panic, and the alley exploded into a mass of hissing, thrashing bodies.

With Marrow-Gnawer's blood still dripping from the tip of his weapon, Toshi scrawled a kanji symbol on the pavement stones.

"Smoke," he read silently, focusing both will and magic through the symbol, giving them form and substance.

There was a bright flash of light and a geyser of foul-smelling black ash. Toshi grabbed another ratfolk by the tail and slung him into the confusion. Then he turned and sprinted back toward the marsh.

Even as he ran, Toshi cursed his luck. What were moonfolk doing with nezumi in the first place? It was like the Daimyo's elite guard recruiting blind, legless madmen for the infantry. Times must be tough for them to come slumming among the ruins.

He'd heard some tall tales about the moonfolk in action, but no one he knew ever claimed to have seen anything first hand. The soratami were notoriously good at going unseen and undetected— so good that they were more like rumors than real people. Even if you did well for them, you were likely to wind up dead, just to sever any links between them and their crimes.

Toshi ducked around another corner, complicating his trail as much as possible while continuing to put distance between himself and the moonfolk. He sincerely hoped they weren't as good at seeking as they were at hiding.

A gleaming steel spike suddenly sprouted from the pave stone in front of him. Toshi stopped short, his eyes darting up. He caught a glimpse of a dark, two-toed sandal and a pale white foot before a forearm clamped around his throat and hauled him off the ground.

Make a note, he thought. They are good at seeking.

Unable to breathe, his vision rimmed in red, Toshi fumbled with his jitte. The iron arm tightened across his windpipe and his captor shook him, trying to dislodge the weapon. Toshi slit the gray cloth over his thigh as he tried to hold onto the jitte. The sharp tip scored angry red lines across his flesh.

With one final shake, the jitte fell. Toshi felt his sword belt being torn away, and then the cold embrace of the stone wall as his face slammed into it. The pressure around his throat vanished, but that same grip now held his head immobile against the wall. A practiced hand searched his body for any hidden weapons, and then a hollow voice whispered, "He is now unarmed."

The soratami shinobi spoke from overhead. "Thank you, Eitoku. Turn him to me."

Toshi was roughly spun around as Eitoku manhandled him into the center of the alley. The moonfolk warrior grabbed both Toshi's elbows and forced them to touch behind the ochimusha's back.

"Easy there, whitey," Toshi growled. Wincing, he struggled until Eitoku slammed him into the wall again, all the while maintaining the pressure on Toshi's arms. The soratami bushi dragged him into the center of the alley once more and held him upright.

The moonfolk shinobi floated down from above, both feet now shrouded in small silver clouds. His face was calm, almost amused. His eyes were wide and cold. "Marrow-Gnawer and his brothers have withdrawn, but we shall visit them soon. In the interim, I will ask you one question, lowlife, and ask it only once."

"Could you make it a history question? I'm good at those."

Eitoku squeezed Toshi's elbows together and the ochimusha winced again.

The shinobi floated closer. "What are you doing here?"

Toshi struggled for a moment. "Sorry, was that the question? I wasn't ready."

Eitoku sent him on another trip to the wall. Toshi left some of his blood on the jagged stones.

"He knows nothing," Eitoku said. "Kill him and be done with it."

Toshi spat blood, careful to miss the floating moonfolk. No sense in being overly rude. "I know you don't want to mess with me. It's not healthy."

The shinobi drifted back and rose slightly above Toshi. "Oh? And who protects you, ochimusha lowlife? What kami answers your prayers?"

Toshi smiled through a mouthful of blood. "I take care of myself."

"Then you'd best get started. Eitoku," the floating moonfolk began to rise, rotating so his back was to Toshi, "you may kill him now."

To Toshi's surprise, Eitoku turned him loose before administering the death blow. True, the moonfolk warrior had every reason to be confident. Toshi was unarmed, his arms weren't working well, and the left side of his face was swollen and bleeding. But in the fen society where Toshi and the nezumi lived, confidence killed many accomplished warriors.

Toshi didn't even try to defend himself. His shoulders were too sore and his arms too drained of blood to do him any good. He simply stood facing the soratami bushi, taking solace from the fact that even if the moonfolk had stabbed from behind, the end result would be the same.

Eitoku's sword was a gleaming whisper in the dark. It punched through Toshi's chest but did not come out of his back, even though Eitoku jammed the blade in all the way up to the hilt.

The kanji Toshi had carved into his own thigh flashed. The cold gray light was reflected in his eyes and on his chest, where Eitoku's sword was lodged. The ochimusha smiled.

"That looks like it hurts." He glanced down at the blade in his torso, then back up at Eitoku. "Does it?"

The soratami's mouth hung open and his eyes went glassy. His jaw bobbed, but no sound came out. A line of brackish purple formed in the center of his chest, and Eitoku clutched at it with one hand as his pulled the sword free with the other. Warrior and blade alike then dropped loudly to the ground.

Almost instantly, a silver spike sprouted from Toshi's forehead. Above him, the floating moonfolk gasped. Then he, too, came crashing down, landing in an undignified heap of robes and twisted limbs. A small, perfect hole adorned his forehead.

Toshi quickly retrieved his weapons. Both soratami were struggling to move, clawing and grasping at his ankles, but he carefully avoided them. Calmly, casually, he tied his sword belt, repositioned his katana and wakizashi, and sheathed his jitte. From sheer force of habit, he nudged both moonfolk over with his foot and scanned their bodies for valuables.

There was not much to choose from. Eitoku was wearing a stiff, hardened fabric under his robe, but beyond his own daisho swords that marked him as a samurai, the soratami bushi was unadorned. His partner didn't even have any extra silver spikes to steal, but he was wearing some sort of silver emblem around his neck. As Toshi reached for it, the soratami under him murmured.

A breeze kicked up and Toshi's well-developed sense of self-preservation kicked in. He hopped back just as a blue glow enveloped both soratami. With a quiet susurrus of sound and light, the two pale figures disappeared.

"Not that I'm keeping score," he called after the vanished moon-folk, "but right now the ochimusha lowlife from the fen is up on the snooty, whitewashed aristos two-nil."

Perhaps, came a distorted, disembodied whisper. *But the game is far from over.*

Toshi swallowed hard. He dabbed the blood from his thigh and checked the marks he had scratched into his own flesh. The kanji that had reflected the soratami's attacks would last only as long as the blood flowed, and the minor wound was already starting to scab over. It occurred to him that he was alone in the ruins, having antagonized two demigods and the most capable nezumi he had ever met.

Carefully, he slid into the shadows and quickly headed back to the marsh. If there was ever a prudent time for him to disappear for a while, this was it.

His mind worked furiously as he plotted out the details. He needed a few things from his hovel. He needed to make some small arrangements before he went. But once those minor errands were run, it was well past time for a change of scenery.

Silent as a shadow, Toshi slipped out of the ruins and into the darkness.

CHAPTER 2

Toshi climbed down the side of a rocky mud-hill that separated the Takenuma Swamp from the edge of the old city. The ruined buildings on the higher ground had been slowly leveled by twenty years of the Kami War, but his own home had been a wasteland for far longer. As his feet sank into the swamp, he looked out over acres of oily water and fetid marsh.

"Home sweet home," he muttered. He trudged through the watery mud, keeping a careful eye out for hostile spirit manifestations. They came most often to the ruins directly outside the Daimyo's stronghold, but lately the attacks had been spreading outward, increasing in frequency and scope.

Though now little more than a rotten bamboo forest struggling out of a thick, noisome ooze, the marsh had once been a thriving village. The story of its rapid slide into decrepitude varied depending on the teller. The nezumi said that the fen was a paradise for their kind until the Daimyo's human ancestors came and ruined it. The local cult of *jushi* wizards told of a spell cast generations ago by a handful of ogre mages—the intent was to construct a breeding ground and hunting preserve for the terrible demonic oni they worshiped, but the end result was just another cursed cesspit.

Still, Toshi thought, the fen provided a haven for people like him: the fallen and the forgotten. Most of the marsh residents were barred from the Daimyo's society, unwelcome in the wilds, and unwilling to take up the hard, violent, and frequently short life of a bandit. The swamp had its own society with its own rules and castes, but unlike the rest of the world, they were self-enforced and easy to circumvent with impunity . . . provided you had the wit and the power.

The old city vanished into the yellow, sulfurous mist behind him as Toshi marched on. His own shack was in the southeast quarter, on the edge between Boss Uramon's turf and a large nezumi village. If Toshi kept west and circled around, he would minimize the chances of meeting one of Marrow-Gnawer's people. This would take him into jushi territory, but he was on excellent terms with several of the cult's more powerful wizards. It would be relatively easy to negotiate his way past if they stopped him.

Up ahead, the mist parted and Toshi caught sight of a pair of armed sentries standing under a tall torch. The male sentry bore a huge *no-dachi* battle sword strapped across his back and crude plate armor over his shoulders and chest. He also sported a metallic, wide-brimmed hat and a black scarf over his nose and mouth. The female wore a heavy wrap over a colorful kimono, and a cowl that covered her face and scalp. Her long hair streamed out from under the cowl, reaching down past her elbows. It was a strange purple-black color, and to Toshi, the hair made it seem she was also wearing a cape. The cowled woman had a simple *fuetsu* axe on her belt and an vivid purple flower embroidered on her shoulder.

"Hey," Toshi called. "I'm coming through the fog. Don't kill me by accident."

The male stiffened and put his hand on his no-dachi. The woman unfolded a black and purple fan and gently waved the fog away from her face. Toshi peered carefully through the yellow haze and spotted metal gleaming on each of the fan's spines. It was a *tessen*, a disguised weapon that could either block an incoming sword or crack the arm that wielded it.

Toshi stepped out of the fog with his hands held open at his sides. He stared at the woman and the purple flower on her shoulder. He smiled.

"Kiku," he said. "I recognized your camellia. Please don't tell me you've been demoted to border guard. Not even your jushi masters could be stupid enough to waste your talents this badly."

The man stepped forward as he drew his sword, but the woman stopped him with a gentle hand. Her wide, vibrant eyes scanned Toshi. She stepped forward and stared down at his swords.

"Hello, Toshi," Kiku said. Her voice was languid and bored. "It's a bad night to come looking for work."

"Not looking tonight. I just need to get back to my shack without stirring up the rats."

Kiku shrugged. "Go right ahead. But the nezumi-bito are the least of your worries if you cut through our property. The kami are out in force tonight and they're looking for blood."

"Is that why you're dressed like one of Uramon's hatchet men? Where are the purple silks and slit skirts? Where's the glamour and beauty that make Kiku such a famously beautiful nightmare?"

"That is none of your business." She smiled, but her eyes remained wide and fixed.

Toshi repressed a shudder. Kiku was stunning but terrifying. She could kill ten people with her magic in the blink of an eye, but her bored expression rarely changed. She had the distracted, unsettling intensity of a well-fed cat in search of prey to torment. She was not Toshi's enemy, but they regarded each other with caution.

"So," he said breezily. "You don't mind if I just press on?"

"Not as long as you go quickly," she said. "And quietly."

"Done and done. I just—"

The male sentry suddenly choked and began to tremble. The fog thickened and began to swirl around them, creating a tall cone of wind and sulfurous fumes.

Toshi hastily backed away from the sentry. The ochimusha

recognized signs of a kami manifestation. Judging from the way Kiku also withdrew, she did as well. The swirling wall of fog expanded around them, giving them more room to put distance between the stricken sentry and themselves. Toshi tested it with his hand as he kept an eye on the emerging kami. The wall of vapor was dense and resisted his touch like a wool blanket. He did not relish the idea of getting mired in it with a hostile spirit nearby.

Kiku also tested the barrier, then snapped open her fan to cover her face from the bridge of her nose down. Toshi nodded to her and drew his blades to fight. The Kami War had come to the marsh once more.

There were several ways a kami could cross the barrier between their home in the *kakuriyo* spirit world to the *utsushiyo* material one. Toshi had seen them shimmer in and out of the air like heat mirages, or grow their misshapen bodies out of moss, wood, rock, and whatever else was nearby.

Priests and monks said there was a kami spirit for everything in the utsushiyo: rivers, battlefields, mountains, swords, graveyards . . . even one's ancestors. There were kami that embodied the spirit of entire cities and kami for the people who dwelled there. There were spirits of song and of sunlight, of death and darkness. Twenty years ago, common spirits from the farmer's field and peasant's well rose up against the people who prayed to them. Then, larger and more powerful entities draped themselves in flesh and began marauding, without regard to whom they killed or how pious the victims were. The kami of storms, fire, and lightning ceased to be random destroyers and began targeting the tribes of Kamigawa with focus and precision.

When these angry spirits came, they did so in shapes unfamiliar, even unrecognizable. It was as if the journey from spirit to flesh was so wrenching that it twisted them into monstrosities. Toshi knew some overly religious types who claimed that a kami's monstrous appearance was inevitable, since they were divine beings who now existed in a realm of gross physical forms. Whatever shape they took, they were always accompanied by a cloud of smaller aspects, floating in the air around the spirit like attendants to a king. These aspects were tenuously tied to whatever shape the kami had assumed—a battlefield kami might come with a flock of daggers, a forest kami with a swarm of leaves. In the Takenuma Swamp, there were soothsayers who would happily relieve you of your cash in exchange for their reading of what a hostile kami's form signified. For an extra charge, they would also tell you how to appease it.

Toshi didn't really know or care what made them so freakish, but he had battled kami as large as buildings and as small as butterflies. All in all, he preferred the butterflies. No one truly knew why natural spirits and household deities had become so vengeful. As far as Toshi was concerned, the only thing that was important was the fact that the kami's physical manifestations made them as vulnerable as anything else in the utsushiyo to blades or magic. The spirits could kill, but they could also be killed, and that put the entire situation into terms Toshi could manage.

He was ten yards away when the doomed sentry opened his mouth to scream. The man stood with his jaw locked and his throat moving, but the only sounds that came out were those of cracking bone. A dull roar rose over the vortex's howling winds, and then the sentry vanished in a cloud of blood and armor as the kami exploded out of his body.

It was a full thirty feet from head to tail, though Toshi would not want to wager on which end was which. A long, grasping arm with multiple elbow joints extended from the center of a squat, grub-like mass. It had a ghastly wound of a mouth at one end, full of sharp teeth that were bent at irregular angles and curved inward. It had a single red eye above its mouth, two yellow ones at the opposite end, and a mold-green one on the knuckles of its only hand. The kami's unwieldy body floated above the sodden ground while a cloud of small, glowing insects buzzed all around it.

It seemed somewhat disoriented by its journey from the spirit world to the fen, and it paused, sniffing the air and shaking bits of meat from its bulging eyes. Toshi circled around the gruesome spirit with both swords drawn. He considered reaching for his jitte, but decided to leave the killing magic to Kiku. It was her specialty, after all.

In twenty years of conflict, Toshi had seen only a handful of kami that were capable of speech and he had never heard one talk. Mostly they just showed up and started tearing everything apart. This one aimed most of its eyes on the ochimusha and grabbed for him with its long arm. He was well clear of its reach, but he stepped back and beckoned it in, keeping its attention on him. Clearly, it had determined that the bigger targets were the most dangerous and was saving Kiku for last. It wouldn't be the first entity that died for underestimating her.

The grub-like spirit made another grab, brushing Toshi's blades aside with its clawed fingers. Toshi backpedaled, and the kami pursued.

"Kiku? I've got its attention. Easy pickings, if you strike from the rear." He struck a finger from the kami's hand with his katana. The beast roared.

"Easy pickings? It's looking right at me," Kiku said. She crossed her arms, almost petulant, and snapped her fan shut. "And I don't like the looks of that eye."

"I'm the one it's after," Toshi shouted.

"And this concerns me how?" Kiku was smiling slightly, and Toshi cursed himself. He should have just inscribed a kanji and cast a spell himself. Better still, he should have circled behind Kiku and forced her to defend them both.

"Just kill it," Toshi spat. He dodged another lunge, but now his back was up against the whirling wall of fog. "If I die here, you know I'll come back and haunt you."

"Get in line. I've already got a parade of ghosts who march behind me, single file."

The kami slapped the katana from Toshi's hand. He lopped off another finger with the shorter wakizashi, but he was quickly running out of room to defend himself.

"Don't tell me the great and terrible Kiku is going to pass up a kill," he shouted. "Isn't this what you're out here for?"

"It is. But nobody said anything about saving freelance thieves."

"Or sentries, I take it." Toshi skewered the kami's hand with his short sword and threw his entire weight onto the hilt. He bore the kami's hand to the ground and pinned it there with his body. Positioned as it was, the kami could not maneuver its bulk around its own arm to get close enough to bite. It roared again in frustration, then sank into the muck, gathering strength and leverage to toss Toshi aside.

Toshi locked eyes with Kiku. "Besides," he said. "I'm not technically a freelancer. Remember?"

The powerful limb beneath him creaked, and Toshi rose into the air, riding the kami's hand. If he let go of the sword, the spirit beast would simply snatch him from the air as he fell. If he stayed where he was, the kami could pop him down and consume him whole like a freshly peeled grape.

Instead, a light purple flower blossom arced up over the kami's central mass and gracefully fluttered onto its back. He could see Kiku's lips moving as she chanted, the tessen fan clenched tight between both hands.

The small lavender flower sprouted roots that burrowed into the skin on the kami's back. The brute flailed, casting Toshi into the watery muck of the swamp. The dazed ochimusha felt the sword still in his hands, and he struggled to keep the tip pointing upward to ward off further attacks.

None came. The grasping kami was spinning furiously in place, clawing at its own back where the flower had taken root.

The camellia's soothing purple color darkened into a toxic black where it touched the kami's flesh, and the grotesque roots undulated as they dug in.

Toshi got back to his feet and quickly found his katana. The kami was still thrashing and revolving, its bellows of pain and fury echoing across the sodden landscape. Kiku stood clear of the melee, fanning herself.

"Throw the axe!" Toshi yelled. "It's still alive, still dangerous. What's with you, anyway? Are you being paid by the hour?"

Kiku sniffed. "Bladed weapons are so common," she said. "Would you ask a master carpenter to build with sponge instead of wood?"

"I would if he'd kill this big bug-thing faster than you are." Toshi waited, timing the stricken kami's revolutions. When its eye was facing away, he dashed in and chopped off its arm at the first elbow.

Maimed, the kami screamed and hurled its bulk at Toshi. The ochimusha dived clear, rolled, and came up alongside Kiku.

The fog behind them began to fade. Together, from a safe distance, they watched the appalling jets of blood and ichor foul the water. The kami wallowed in the swamp, still attempting to reach them, but soon its struggles slowed and then ceased altogether. One by one, the glowing insects dimmed and fell beside the larger mass. The grub-like spirit monster was still breathing, but the breath was labored and it was already starting to shudder in the final throes of death.

Toshi approached the dying spirit with his katana ready.

"It's already dead," Kiku called. "I killed it. Its brain just needs a moment to catch up."

Toshi stood over the quaking mass. "This thing gets nothing from me," he said, and then he plunged his sword deep into the kami's largest eye.

Black blood spattered, and the kami keened one last time. The vortex of wind dropped away and yellow fog dispersed. Then the kami slowly began to fade.

Toshi flicked the blood from his katana and then wiped the blade on a patch of swamp grass. Kiku's flower was still blooming on the thing's back, a gorgeous and fragrant corsage atop a monstrous heap of blood and meat. As the dead kami vanished into the fog, the bright lavender flower lingered to mark its passing.

Without a word, Kiku turned and headed back into the sulfur mist, toward her cult's headquarters.

"So," Toshi yelled. "You don't mind if I cut across your land?"

Kiku waved her hand dismissively, not even turning as she walked.

"Good," Toshi said. "That's really all I wanted."

* * * * *

Toshi reached his shack just before dawn. This was the dullest section of the fen, known as Numai because so many humans had constructed their houses upon great stilts of bamboo. Where rich and powerful people like Boss Uramon lived in restored manor houses from years gone by, common folk had to make do with far less. Toshi had even spent some time among the piecemeal cottages and community nests of the nezumi, and if not for the ratfolk themselves, he would have vastly preferred their homes to his.

Still, the southwest quarter provided all the privacy and anonymity he needed. Prying into others' affairs was dangerous, even suicidal in the main marsh, but it was unheard of in Numai. There was hardly anyone worth knowing and definitely nothing worth stealing, so Toshi could largely do as he pleased.

Now, it pleased him to collect the few belongings he treasured and to take a small vacation, far from moonfolk and nezumi and kami attacks. Perhaps he would head to the shoreline and feast on mussels and eel for a few weeks. Get some sun and enjoy the sensation of not being hunted.

There was no real entrance to Toshi's house; it was a feature that he had purposely omitted. No door means no visitors. His one-room ramshackle domain stood about twenty feet over the surface of the swamp, lashed and enchanted to some sturdy bamboo poles. The walls were a confused tangle of planks and joists salvaged from other homes, and the roof was a disaster of crude thatch and carelessly laid beams.

Toshi quickly glanced around to make sure he was unobserved and then shimmied up one of the bamboo supports. From the corner, he climbed hand-over-hand along one of the floorboards until he came to a trap door. He shoved on the hinged panel from below, then pulled himself up into the unlit room.

He moved quickly through the darkness until he found an old oil lamp. He lit the lamp with a stone and a piece of flint, careful to keep the flame low so as not to dazzle-blind himself. The small lamp threw out the barest hint of light, but it was enough for Toshi to see the room and everything in it.

Four soratami were lounging casually in the corners of his home. He recognized Eitoku and his shinobi partner from the alley. The other two were also moonfolk bushi, dressed like Eitoku with stiffened cloth armor and the traditional pair of samurai swords.

A fifth soratami sat smiling on the floor in front of him. All the moonfolk were slender and androgynous, but this one was the most feminine he had seen. She wore her long ears gathered at the base of her skull. Her legs were crossed and she was leaning back on her hands with a contemplative smirk on her face.

"Hello," Toshi said. "Have you seen Toshi Umezawa? He owes me money."

"Take him down," the woman said. There was a blur of motion, and Toshi found himself pinned, disarmed, and restrained, face down on the rough wooden floor. Someone, probably Eitoku, kicked him solidly in the ribs. Someone else grabbed a handful of hair and forced Toshi's face up.

"You embarrassed the soratami," the woman said. She did not sound angry, but rather distracted. "And worse, you spoiled our endeavor for the evening. These are remarkable feats for a lowlife such as yourself. Truly, the benevolent rabbit in the moon has smiled upon you this night."

Toshi blinked. "Who where did what when?"

The woman laughed, her hollow voice surprisingly warm and gay. "You've never heard of the rabbit in the moon? Shocking. To which kami do you pray?"

"He does not pray," said the moonfolk who had tried to spike Toshi's head. "He 'takes care of himself.'"

"I take care of my friends, too," Toshi added. Sweat ran down into his eyes, and he could feel his heart booming. "If you'd care to be my friend, I would—"

Eitoku silenced him with another kick. "Keep his hands pinned," the samurai said. "He uses kanji magic."

The female leaned forward, her face close to Toshi's. "Tell me about your friends," she said. "Do any of them know where you were tonight?"

"I lied," Toshi said instantly. "I don't actually have any friends."

"Hmmm," the woman said. Her eyes seemed to bore straight through Toshi's skull. "Is that loyalty, or candor?"

"Neither," he said. "Check the back of my left hand and you'll see."

"Don't touch him!" Eitoku snapped. "He's full of tricks, this one."

"Yes, I can see that." The woman stretched and then stood. She nodded to Eitoku's partner. "Check his hand, shinobi. He intrigues me, this arrogant ochimusha who does not pray. The rest of you, keep him still."

The shinobi from the alley took Toshi's hand and twisted the palm down. He motioned for the lamp, and one of the samurai brought it forward. The lamp-bearer, the shinobi, and the woman all leaned in to look.

"A triangle," she said. "Most impressive. Though the lines are a bit jagged. You might want to engage a tattoo artist who isn't shaking from narcotic withdrawal."

"It's not just a triangle," Toshi said. "It's a *hyozan*, an iceberg. See? There's a kanji and everything." He pressed his wrist forward, revealing more of the mark.

"It's a gangster tattoo," Eitoku spat. "He's one of Boss Uramon's reckoners. Muscle for hire."

"Ahh," the woman said. "So you are protected after all. But Boss Uramon isn't here, little thug, and we wouldn't care if she was."

"I don't work for Uramon," Toshi said. "Or any other boss. Haven't you heard of the hyozan reckoners? We work for ourselves."

"How formidable. And I imagine the iceberg is symbolic of your hidden strength? Attack the tip, and the rest of your gang surfaces to take revenge? That is what reckoners do, isn't it? Take revenge for money?"

"Sometimes. We also throw dice."

The female moonfolk laughed again. Then, her smile disappeared like a wisp of steam and her eyes flashed with cold blue light.

"I think we've wasted enough time on you, hyozan reckoner. I think the iceberg is a clever ploy to make people think you've got hidden depths. It's the perception of danger that keeps people away. You like to keep people away, don't you? Else why would you live in the most drab and awful place in the world? Seriously, even nezumi won't come here without a good reason."

The pinned ochimusha held her eyes. "I gave your stooges fair warning before, and now I'm giving it to you. Turn me loose and go away, or things will get ugly."

"Ignore him," Eitoku said. "There are no more kanji on his body, and he's incapable of drawing with his hands pinned."

The female soratami returned to her casual sitting position. "I think we'll hang your body somewhere prominent. To make a good impression on the locals." She nodded, and Toshi heard the sound of a sword being drawn.

Overhead, the moon slipped out from behind a cloud. Its light shone through a gap in Toshi's roof, casting a jagged shadow on the floor.

"You're right, big ears," he said loudly. "I can't draw any more kanji. But I can use the one I built into the roof."

As one, the moonfolk looked up. With the moonlight streaming through, the shadows from the rafters formed a clear symbol.

"Stay," Toshi read silently.

In response, a glittering purple breeze descended and crossed the room like a wave. The moonlight flickered as a cloud passed overhead. When it came back, the roomful of soratami were in the exact same positions. Their eyes darted back and forth, and some of them made low, moaning sounds, but they were otherwise frozen in place.

Toshi quickly began working his hands free. The soratami fingers holding him had enough give for him to twist himself loose, and he wriggled out from under their weight, kicking his ankles free as he went. Two of the moonfolk holding him toppled over as Toshi rose, and they remained where they landed, as still as stones.

The ochimusha quickly went to a loose floorboard and retrieved a bag of coins, his good jitte, and a small parcel wrapped in cloth and twine. He was very careful not to come into contact with the soratami. Incidental contact could disrupt the paralysis spell, and he didn't want to have to fight his way clear. He straightened his clothes and approached the female soratami where she sat on the floor.

"Here's where we all just walk away," he said, hoisting his pack over his shoulder. "I fouled up your score tonight and bloodied your noses, but I didn't kill you. Let's leave it at that. Do us all a favor and don't come looking for me again."

The woman's eyes were furious. *Run fast*, her voice rang in Toshi's ears, though her lips did not move. *Run far. It won't save you.*

He raised an eyebrow. "That was your voice in the alley, wasn't it?" He leaned down into her face. "This is twice now. See how well bothering me works out? If you want us to try to kill each other on sight from now on, that's your choice. But I can guarantee that you'll never see me coming."

Perhaps.

Toshi shrugged. "You keep saying that. It means nothing." He stood and strolled over to the trap door in the floor. He opened the trap, sat on the edge of the hole, and looked back at the two moon-folk who had fallen, each now staring helplessly up at the ceiling.

"You got off light," he called. "You should have seen the position I was *going* to leave you in."

Then dropped down into the fen and landed with a splash. As he took his first few steps, the moon slipped behind another cloud. When it emerged, it lit the entire area in an eerie silver light.

Toshi looked down. The shadows from the bamboo and part of his house formed a symbol in the muck that he hadn't intended. In fact, if he took a step back and included the floating bamboo leaves and swamp grass, he could clearly make out several symbols, a small group of naturally occurring kanji that his eyes had isolated from the surroundings.

Toshi sighed, then swore softly. Seeing symbols everywhere was a side-effect of mastering kanji magic, like an overly imaginative child looking up at the clouds. Toshi stared at the ground around him, not wanting to interpret the shapes but unable to prevent himself from doing so.

The shadows formed the kanji for "moon."

The leaves and grass combined to make the symbol for "unstoppable."

The oily mud kicked up by his feet spelled "disaster," or, if he squinted and cocked his head, "cataclysm."

Last, a fallen shoot of broken bamboo approximated a crude triangle, similar to the mark on his hand. As Toshi watched, the faint current caused the bamboo shoot to drift a few feet until it was partially overlapping the shadow symbol for "moon." The combined hyozan/moon symbol then burst into flame, charring the sodden ground and raising a fetid waft of gray steam.

Toshi swore again. He did not pray to any kami, but neither did he dismiss the power of the spirit world. These four symbols gave him considerable pause, because he believed that such serendipitous kanji were meant to be interpreted by those who found them. The meaning of "moon" seemed clear to him—he had a handful of angry soratami stewing on his hovel floor. The hyozan symbol pointed to his own involvement in the evening's festivities.

It was the symbols for "unstoppable" and "disaster" that were really troubling him. On their own, they didn't bode well. In taking them together with the other symbols, Toshi found a more pointed and pressing interpretation than a simple general cataclysm. Either he personally was headed for disaster, or the moonfolk were. Either the disaster was unstoppable, or the moonfolk were. He turned the potential readings over in his mind, trying to come up with something that didn't point to a conjunction of the hyozan and the moonfolk which would in turn lead to an unavoidable catastrophe for all involved.

Then, as he often did when magic showed him something he didn't want to see, Toshi became angry. It was no good going to the sea to dine on mussels if the moonfolk were going to press their complaint, if they were going to pursue him relentlessly until tragedy claimed them all.

Toshi was currently alive and healthy in large part thanks to his ability to recognize potential threats and react to them before they became dangerous. He grunted as he settled on the only sure meaning he could take from the odd collection of signs. The hyozan had come into contact with the soratami, and they were locked together until something vast and destructive happened to them all. He wouldn't be free of them without first paying a tithe of blood and fire and pain.

He felt the pressure around him change and a towering silence rose. Under his shack, the vile swamp water began to swirl, and a shapeless form began to rise. By coincidence or by the soratami's design, a kami was breaking through. Here, even in Numai, the spirits came to make war and kill a humble ochimusha in the bargain.

"Swell," Toshi said. His sense of self-preservation was one great boon that had kept him alive so long in Numai. Another was his habit of striking first. If the signs pointed to a mutually destructive event between him and the moonfolk, he would make sure that it happened on his terms and his timetable. The hyozan reckoners were in the business of revenge for hire, but sometimes they threw dice. Sometimes, like when his neck was in the noose, they were obliged to take preemptive revenge.

He tightened his pack on his shoulder, turned his back on the manifesting spirit, and disappeared into the gloom.

CHAPTER 3

By sunset on the following day, Toshi was well into the rocky foothills to the east, far away from Numai. The rugged terrain was surrounded by a series of naturally occurring stone needles that had once been broad mountains. Centuries of the cold, cutting wind had eroded them down to thin, towering mounds, their peaks invisible among the high clouds. The rest of these badlands were dotted with squat, rolling ridges and craggy bluffs, devoid of vegetation. The air was frigid here, biting and bitter, with most of the moisture concentrated above the snow line. Down here, at ground level, it was all dust and dry stone, the landscape a uniformly monotonous beige.

Normally, such a journey would have taken days even with the fastest steed and on the Daimyo's best roads. Toshi allowed himself to relax slightly. The soratami would never expect him to have come this far this quickly, even if they knew where he was headed.

Toshi patted his pack, which was lighter than it had been when he left his shack. So far, dealing with the moonfolk had forced him to reveal some of his strongest hidden assets simply to stay alive. He was thankful to keep the secret of his rapid travel for a little while longer.

Now that he was one step ahead of the soratami, Toshi concentrated on the challenges before him. He was on the fringes of

Godo's realm, and the *sanzoku* bandit king guarded his borders zealously. As the last holdout against the Daimyo's army, Godo had been leading a guerrilla campaign against Konda for almost ten years, and it was only the vastness of his inhospitable region and the Kami War's drain on the Daimyo's resources that kept the bandits alive and free.

Godo and his band were also locked in a territorial struggle with the local *akki* goblin tribes, but Toshi had never cared enough to inquire further. He himself rarely came to the badlands, and when he did he followed a safe, straight line between Godo to the south and the akki to the north. He probably could have traveled directly to his goal by the same method that had brought him this far, but that would have exposed him and his secret to the bandits. It would also attract the akki, who would have chased him until they caught it. Better to go by foot and draw less attention.

Toshi hiked until the sun went down and it became too dark to see the terrain. Rather than continue and risk stumbling into an akki warren, Toshi bundled his cloak around him and scratched a kanji into the dusty ground. The symbol would make him invisible and undetectable without direct physical contact, which was unlikely in this desolate region.

It was cold and miserable and Godo's howling war dogs woke him twice, but Toshi managed to get a few hours of much-needed rest. Dawn found him already moving, following the ridge line due east. He began to see more plants and animals as the temperature rose and the cruel wind abated. To the north was the great Jukai forest, which was a lush as the badlands were barren. But Toshi's goal was elsewhere, in a deep, jagged valley on the very edge of the region.

He knew he was close when he saw the row of heads on pikes. They were in various stages of decay, but most were overly brave or stupid bandits who had strayed too far from camp. Some were would-be apprentices who had not survived their training period. There were also a few non-human skulls that Toshi couldn't identify.

Beyond the row of heads was a huge square rock that completely blocked the well-worn footpath leading east. Alongside the rock was a giant hammer, with a handle taller than Toshi and a head as big as a palanquin. The rock had been cracked and broken in places by the hammer, but judging by the mound of sand and dust the wind had piled up on one side, the huge weapon hadn't been wielded in years.

Toshi nodded, impressed. Between the heads and the hammer, the message was clear: this is o-bakemono country, and you are not welcome. The ogre mages did not like visitors but did like eating people. For the o-bakemono, especially the one he had come to see, the warnings were a remarkably social gesture.

Toshi turned sideways to slip between the pikes and circled around the huge block of stone to get back on the path. The rear face of the stone block had two large kanji carved into it. Most people who dared to come this far would be dissuaded by the symbols on the rock, which denoted the name and status of the creature who ruled this valley: Hidetsugu the ogre, o-bakemono shaman.

Toshi continued down into the valley. As he expected, it didn't take long for a response once he was past the gruesome warnings on the path.

A tall, broad-shouldered youth in dusty red robes came out of a stone hut at the bottom of the valley. He was bald and though he walked with a slight limp, he came toward Toshi with confidence, even malice.

"Turn and run," the bald youth called. His voice was like his body, thick and burly. "Master Hidetsugu already has a student."

Toshi dropped his pack and held his arms out. "I am Toshi Umezawa, and I have business with your master. Fetch him."

The youth drew closer, and Toshi saw he was covered in scars. His forearms and chest were criss-crossed by a network of ragged slashes. His left eye was split by a gash that might have been made with an axe or one of Master Hidetsugu's fingernails. His chin was off center and his nose was flattened across his right cheek.

The hulking youth stopped and reached behind him. He drew a vicious-looking tetsubo from his back, an octagonal war club lined with sharp metal studs.

"Turn and go," he said. "Or join the other heads." He swung the heavy tetsubo as effortlessly as a willow switch. "If your skull remains solid."

"I'm not going to do either of those things," Toshi said, "because I'm so intimidated. Look, just go get Hidetsugu and say the following three things to him: Toshi, hyozan, questions. If he still doesn't want to talk to me, you can bash my brains in as much as you like."

The bald youth snarled and took a step forward, raising his club.

"Enough." Hidetsugu's voice rolled out of the stone hut like an avalanche. It was pitched so low it made Toshi's spine tingle. "Stand aside, Kobo. I recognize this one."

The bald youth lowered his club and turned his profile to Toshi, tilting his head down. His eyes were closed and Toshi heard him whispering a student's mantra.

Hidetsugu the o-bakemono pulled himself out of the hut. The door was twice as tall as Toshi, but the ogre still had to crouch and strain to force himself through. When he was clear, he rose to his feet and lumbered up the path. With each ponderous step, the ground shook and dust rose.

Hidetsugu stood over twenty-five feet tall, each of his limbs as thick as Toshi's whole body. He wore a red robe similar to his student's, only his was trimmed in black. He carried a heavy, segmented plate of burnished metal on each shoulder and a girdle of similar metal covered him from his waist to his knees. His enormous head was flat and wide like a dragon's, with a sharp crest of bone running from the center of his forehead to the back of his skull. His great slashing teeth spilled out over his lips, as if even his powerful jaws could not keep them contained. He too carried a club, but Hidetsugu's seemed to be an entire tree trunk with arm-sized nails driven through it. His deep-set eyes glowed like red stars and his tongue lolled hungrily from one side of his mouth.

Toshi quickly pulled up his sleeve and showed the tattoo. "Greetings, oath-brother Hidetsugu."

The ogre kept coming, past Kobo and right up to Toshi. He dropped the thicker end of his club to the ground and used it to support his weight as he leaned forward.

"Umezawa," he rumbled. He pulled the armor away from his left collarbone, revealing a triangle like Toshi's burned into his flesh. The hyozan kanji was seared below the triangle.

"You said 'questions,' ochimusha. Make them brief." Hidetsugu let the armor fall back into place, covering the brand.

"Can we talk inside? I'd like to get out of the cold and wash the dust from my throat."

Hidetsugu stood up and thumped his club on the ground. "Questions," he repeated. "Make them brief. I have other guests, more important than you."

"Right," Toshi said. "Because you're such a gregarious fellow."

Hidetsugu growled and tightened his grip on the club.

"Master," the bald youth said. "If this worm is distressing you—"

"Relax, lumpy," Toshi said. "I came to Hidetsugu years ago, and we formed a pact. I can annoy him, but we're oath-bound to protect and avenge each other."

Hidetsugu cocked his head. "Your memory is very selective, Toshi. I recall you coming with some of Uramon's dogs in order to kill me. As I was picking the last of them from my teeth, you offered to parley."

Toshi shrugged. "I had already devised a way out of Uramon's gang. You just gave me the opportunity."

"More like you amused me. And I was full."

"Don't make yourself sound so generous. I gave you the means to get Uramon off your back once and for all. She knows ogres, too. And demons. And monsters. Sooner or later, one of them would have come for you."

"Or all of them. Which was why I agreed to your proposition. I hate interruptions."

"Evidenced by your welcome mat of decapitated visitors."

Hidetsugu thumped his club. "Right now, oath-brother, you are an interruption. Get on with it."

"Okay, okay. Let's see. Questions, brief questions." He snapped his fingers and said, "Soratami? Kami in an uproar? Portents. Unstoppable, disaster, my neck on the block. Hyozan." He made a show of ticking off each point with his fingers. "Pact. Oath. My problems are your problems."

The ogre grunted, but did not reply. Toshi's playful smile faded.

"Something big is brewing, Hidetsugu. I've got trouble with the soratami, and the kanji don't look good. The signs say moonfolk and hyozan are bound to destroy each other. I get nervous when portents use such generalities."

Hidetsugu squinted. "That seems specific enough."

"But it doesn't mention me," Toshi said. "Or you. If the hyozan and the moonfolk disappear, what happens to the individuals in each group? I'm not planning to wait to find out if this mess will claim me in the end."

Hidetsugu grinned, exposing his tusk-like teeth.

Toshi's stomach went cold. He liked ogre mirth even less than equivocal portents.

"Hidetsugu," he said. "Oath-brother. What do you know?"

The ogre's eyes danced as the brain behind them calculated. He raised his club, and Toshi sprang back, but Hidetsugu merely lowered the weapon back down onto his own armored shoulder.

"Kobo," he said, without looking at the bald youth. "Go to the spring and fill a bucket. Toshi is our final guest today, and even I did not expect him. We will shortly have grave matters to discuss."

"Inside." Toshi added.

Hidetsugu grunted again. "Inside."

* * * * *

Hidetsugu's home was deceptively small from the outside. The stone hut covered a great sloping tunnel that led to a deep underground cavern that the ogre had excavated himself. The cavern was dimly lit and seemed to go on indefinitely. As far as Toshi could see, small patches of light created by torches and braziers were spaced unevenly across the vast expanse of darkness. Toshi's steps echoed off something hard and stony in the distance, but he had only the vaguest guess as to the room's dimensions.

Hidetsugu led him to a large, flaming brazier next to a brick furnace on the eastern wall. There was a crude wooden bench with a series of metal rods carefully laid out like cutlery at a formal dinner. The ogre began fiddling with the twisted, sooty pieces of metal.

"This is Toshi," he growled. "An *ochimusha* from the marsh." He twisted a small attachment onto one of the rods with a metallic click and tossed the contraption into the furnace with one end protruding.

"So?" The voices spoke as one from the left and right of the furnace, but the fire prevented Toshi from seeing who spoke.

"He has seen signs, portents. Tell them, Toshi."

"Tell who?"

Hidetsugu snarled and beckoned. Two identical warriors stepped into the light from each side of the furnace. Both men were exactly the same in almost every respect, size, shape, demeanor, and they moved in unison with the precision of one man and his reflection. They wore thin, dagger-like mustaches and chin whiskers and they were dressed in polished bandit armor, which Toshi had always considered incongruous. The heavy plating on their shoulders and hips rang like coins as they walked, and they kept their hands on the long, curved swords on their hips.

Toshi quickly noted that the twins wore their hair bandit-style under their loose horned helmets, braided and looped around one shoulder. The bandit on the left wore his braid around his right shoulder, the other around his left. Toshi thought they looked like barbarian bookends, but he kept this opinion to himself.

"These men represent Godo," Hidetsugu said. "And behind you is Ben-Ben, from Ichi's akki tribe. Tell them your story."

Toshi did not turn around, but he heard the crab-like scuttling of an akki goblin on the move. "What about you?" he said.

"I will also be listening."

Toshi shrugged. "I ran into some soratami in the ruins outside Konda's stronghold. They were working with a pack of nezumi. Later, they traced me back to my home, but I escaped. I saw portents that said this is not over."

"And he was attacked by kami."

Toshi started, but maintained his composure. "Hidetsugu is correct, though I don't know how."

The ogre grinned again and growled happily. He urged Toshi to continue with a wave of his hand.

"But yes, I was twice beset by angry spirits." Toshi shrugged again. "I think something big is going on, and it won't end without bad business for everyone. My problems with the soratami are tangential, but I believe all this is connected."

"Toshi is a kanji magician," Hidetsugu said. He pulled the metal rod out of the furnace and inspected the glowing end. "He and I are bound by this mark." The ogre showed them the hot end of the rod, which was bent into a triangle with the hyozan kanji beneath.

Toshi recognized the rod for what it was, a branding iron. He saw that the twins did, as well.

"What is that for?" one said.

"And what does any of this have to do with our arrangement?" said the other. "I thought we were all agreed."

"Kobo!" Hidetsugu put the branding iron back into the fire. "Bring the bucket."

From the top of the incline, Toshi saw the big bald youth's silhouette descend.

The akki behind him grumbled. "Too many humans," he said. "Hidetsugu promised, only two of Godo's men." Ben-Ben sniffed. "Left my refuge for this."

In the firelight, Toshi looked at the mountain goblin and laughed. Ben-Ben was a ridiculous figure, squat and armored like an armadillo with a long, sharp nose and a crusty, rocky carapace across his back and shoulders. He was no taller than a nezumi, but his arms were disproportionately large and powerful, his huge hands capped by long, pointed claws. He wore a small leather drum around his neck and thick-soled wooden clogs on his feet. For no reason that Toshi would ever understand, Ben-Ben wore a limp, soggy thing with multiple arms or tentacles on his head, and he carried it with all the gravity and pomp of an official's hat.

"I don't get this either, Hidetsugu. I came here for information, and maybe a place to hide out for a few days. I don't know or care what you've got brewing between Godo and the goblins."

Both twins narrowed their eyes. "Keep it that way, ochimusha."

Toshi smiled. "You say that like it's an insult. If you weren't offal-eating sanzoku dogs, I might take offense."

The twins each drew a sword, but froze when Hidetsugu growled.

"I have also seen portents," the ogre shaman said. "And as rude as Toshi is, you must know this: His success is Godo's. What you and the akki are planning will not work if Toshi dies here. This I have seen."

Kobo the apprentice lumbered into the light and dropped a wooden bucket heavily onto the stone floor. Opaque white liquid sloshed over the sides, and the bald youth quietly went to stand behind Hidetsugu.

"Besides,' Hidetsugu said, "Toshi is my oath-brother and also my guest. If you harm him, I am obliged to respond." He reached his entire arm into the fire, singing the hair off his flesh and raising a ghastly stink. Without the slightest sign of discomfort, Hidetsugu drew the glowing branding iron out of the furnace and inspected the tip. He blew on it like a choice morsel, and the tip glowed brighter.

"We were given assurances," the twins hissed.

"Promised no pain," Ben-Ben echoed.

"My bond with Toshi goes back further than any promises made to Godo and Ichi. Barely a week ago, you came seeking my help. I have given it. You came seeking my counsel. I now offer it: go forward as we have planned. But remember this man and this mark." He waved the branding iron. "Events will churn and bubble around him and his hyozan symbol."

Without another word, Hidetsugu suddenly shoved the red-hot brand into the bald monk's breast. Kobo screamed as his skin burned and his blood sizzled, but he held his ground. With fists clenched and eyes streaming, the apprentice stood firm under the ogre's onslaught. Hidetsugu leaned down on the branding iron, forcing Kobo back and plowing up a small heap of dust and pebbles behind the apprentice's heels.

With a sickening wrench, Hidetsugu withdrew and yanked the hot iron from his student's flesh. Kobo staggered, but did not fall. Slowly, he straightened back to his full height and folded his arms across his chest, his wrist just below the smoking wound. He was breathing heavily and his eyes were wet, but his face was a rigid mask of indifference.

Hidetsugu then plunged the smoking brand into the bucket, raising a small cloud of steam.

"Get out," the ogre said to the twin bandits. He turned to the akki and jerked his head toward the incline. "You, too. You asked for my blessing and my advice. I have given both. Go."

"Thank you, Hidetsugu o-bakemono." To their credit, the bandits did not let their fear show, but Toshi could tell they were rattled. As they moved to the exit, they had none of the synchronized precision that had characterized their movements before. They were simply two men in a hurry, going in the same direction.

If Toshi was reading the akki's facial expression correctly, Ben-Ben was more transparently awed but also less frightened. Maybe not all goblins lived in a constant state of confusion, but this one certainly did. He tipped his soggy fish hat and made his unsteady way toward the incline, avoiding the patches of light as best he could.

When he was alone with Hidetsugu and Kobo, Toshi snapped, "What in the rocky gray hell was that all about? There is no way I'm getting involved with their turf war. They'll never see me again if I can help it."

Hidetsugu tossed the brand aside and hooked the bucket with his smallest finger. He extended his massive arm to Toshi and waved the steaming container under the ochimusha's nose.

"Drink," he said.

"Drop dead." He glared suspiciously into the milky-white liquid. Blackened flesh floated on its surface. "I'm not swigging from a bucket of apprentice stew."

The bucket did not waver. "Drink," Hidetsugu repeated.

The ogre mage didn't have to threaten. His entire being, from his posture to his glaring expression, spoke volumes about what was in store if Toshi refused again.

Toshi swore, inhaled, and took the bucket. He held his breath, raised the bucket to his lips, and took a long, slow draught.

His throat bobbed as he swallowed, once, twice, and then Toshi dropped the bucket and staggered back.

"Gyah," he said. He spit into the brazier and wiped his mouth on his sleeve. "What have you been feeding him, Hidetsugu, yak dung? He's gamier than a nezumi pig farm."

Hidetsugu ignored Toshi and spoke to his apprentice. "Light the brazier on the south wall." As the bald youth disappeared into the darkness, Toshi could see the angry wound on his breast still smoking.

Hidetsugu turned to face him. "You saw symbols, ochimusha, portents," he said. "Come and see what I have seen."

Toshi spat out another fragment of Kobo and followed the ogre. From the sound of the echoes, they were approaching the wall of Hidetsugu's cavern. The o-bakemono's footsteps stopped and Toshi stepped around him so that they were side by side.

"You've gone soft out here, Hidetsugu," he said. "Even if things are bad, I never thought I'd see you socializing with—"

Toshi fell silent as the brazier before them lit up. The flames revealed a surprisingly elegant mosaic on the wall, composed of tiny chips of polished red and black rock. The figure in the mosaic was a nightmarish combination of teeth and jaws, topped by three malevolent eyes arranged in a triangle. The figure was surrounded by a cloud of bat-winged scavengers.

Above the figure were kanji that spelled out a title: The All-Consuming Oni of Chaos. Toshi was not sure if the kanji were the mosaic's title, or the creature's.

Below the mosaic, nailed into the rock of the cavern wall, was the motionless form of a ponderous kami. It was wet and heavy, like a deep-sea fish out of water. It was even shaped like a fish, with a thick upper body that narrowed and then expanded again in to a wide, flat tail. It had rounded, club-like appendages jutting from under its misshapen head, and a crooked vertical mouth lined with rows of triangular teeth all the way down its throat. Small, sharp, shells shaped like crescent moons floated listlessly around it. When one of these shells touched the iron spikes that pinned the kami to the wall, they cracked and fell to the cold stone floor.

"It came here looking for you," Hidetsugu said. "It called your name as it manifested. I had to put it aside quickly, but now that the meeting is over and you're here, you can tell me."

Toshi stared dumbfounded at the pinned spirit beast. In his experience, kami were either alive and mobile or dead and broken, but they were never helpless captives. The thought of what it must have taken to pin this great beast to the wall and keep it quiescent without killing it made Toshi shudder.

"Your problems are mine, oath-brother," Hidetsugu said. His rumbling voice made Toshi's spine vibrate. "So I must know."

He grabbed Toshi around the waist and lifted him to eye level, where his foul breath blew the ochimusha's hair around like a summer squall.

"What have you done, Toshi," he husked, "to bring the wrath of the spirit world upon us?"

CHAPTER 4

The rational side of Toshi's mind told him he had nothing to fear. Hidetsugu was capable of crushing him to death on a whim, but the ogre would not without great risk to himself. The oath that bound them was both a blessing and a curse—if they turned on each other, the effects would be unpredictable and disastrous. Toshi tried to think in Hidetsugu's iron grip, struggling to come up with an out that would appeal to the o-bakemono. Reason could sway an ogre sage, provided he were calm enough to listen to it.

Toshi failed to develop a convincing argument, however, because he was unable to focus on anything but Hidetsugu's awful teeth and the powerful jaw that housed them. The heat, the stench that rolled off of the o-bakemono eclipsed every other sensation. In the end, it was not Toshi's mind, but his body that determined his response.

"Can't," he rasped, "breathe."

"Whisper, then." Hidetsugu shook him gently in the air, and Toshi felt his ribs creak.

"Don't know," Toshi flared. He winced, pushing vainly against the thick fingers around his waist. Then he gulped another breath of air. "Moonfolk chased me." He grimaced. "Saw portents. Came here."

Hidetsugu rotated his wrist so that Toshi was parallel to the floor. "You didn't rob a soratami shrine? Or kill a moonfolk priest?"

"No," Toshi wheezed. His eyes narrowed and he squeezed more air into his lungs. "Put me down . . . oath-brother. You know I . . . keep clear of the kami and their stooges. I'll tell you . . . everything I know. I . . . came for help. Remember?"

Hidetsugu turned Toshi around so that they were eye to eye. He looked deep into the ochimusha's face. Toshi felt his lips swelling, and it seemed that both his eyes and eardrums were bulging out of his skull.

"Put me down," he said. "Or kill me." With as much dignity as he could muster, the red-faced rogue crossed his arms and stared angrily up at Hidetsugu.

"You're hiding something," the ogre said. "But then, I expect no less from you."

Hidetsugu opened his fist and Toshi fell heavily onto his knees. With his arms wrapped around his bent rib cage, Toshi coughed and tried to regain his breath.

The ogre waited patiently while Toshi sucked air. When the ochimusha made it up to one knee, Hidetsugu said, "You really don't know, do you?"

Toshi ran an exploring hand over his rib cage one last time. "Know what?"

"That the kami attacks are growing worse, more frequent and more dangerous than ever. They go places they should not go, places they should not be able to go." He pointed to the marine-looking kami on the wall. "Does that look like a mountain spirit to you?"

Toshi sniffed. "At the moment, it looks like a sack of something that's been pounded by your hammer out there. But to your question about the kami attacks: yes, they're getting worse. They have been for months now. Everyone knows that."

"You're aware of it," Hidetsugu said, "but you do not 'know' anything about it."

Standing up to his full height, Toshi stretched his arms out and inhaled until the pain made him stop. "Educate me, then."

Hidetsugu turned away. "I already have a student. And if I didn't, I wouldn't choose you." The ogre pointed a thick, clawed finger at the impaled kami. "That came here looking for you, right after you saw symbols that drove you here. Either you've being set up, or you're bluffing me into thinking you've being set up."

Toshi's eyes narrowed. "Well, then," he spat through clenched teeth, "That doesn't really matter, does it? You're obliged to back me up."

"And I shall. But you are being pursued by kami as well as soratami. You need a special kind of assistance, one that I cannot provide myself."

"Since when is battling kami beyond your abilities?" Toshi started to laugh, he still lacked the lung capacity. He coughed, then said, "Pursued by *a* kami. The others from the swamp were just a few more mindless spirit beasts lashing out at the real world."

Hidetsugu chuckled. "How can you wield such powerful magic with such a dismal understanding of its source? Nothing is co-incidental when it comes to kami. There are no 'mindless spirit beasts.' Everything has a purpose, and its spirit exists to fulfill that purpose."

Toshi shrugged. "I accept that." He pointed at the marine kami. "So what is that thing's purpose?"

Hidetsugu's smile revealed a row of sharp teeth. "Right now, to be an appetizer for my oni."

"You know what I mean. Why did he come here? If it was sent by the same spirits that sent me those portents, what do they want? Did you ask the big fish before you put it on the wall?"

Hidetsugu growled in annoyance. "It doesn't speak now. Or perhaps it cannot. It hasn't said anything to me since I pinned it down."

Toshi eyed the motionless kami. "I don't think it's likely to any time soon . . . or ever again. Here's a better idea. Why don't you ask your oni?"

Hidetsugu's eyes flashed. "Careful, oath-brother. Do not say his name. He is less friendly than I am—and bound by no oaths."

"Well, that's why you should ask him. He knows you, right? He's a spirit, we need information from the spirit world. It's very simple."

Hidetsugu narrowed one eye and his nostrils flared. "Oni and kami are as different as the sea is from the land. Together, they form the shore. Individually, they could not be more distinct."

"And that's that? You pray to oni and I don't pray, so we're just out of luck? There must be some ritual you can perform. You're an o-bakemono. You're supposed to be well-informed."

Hidetsugu raised his upper lip. "There are rituals I know. But instead, perhaps you could anoint your jitte with your own blood and inscribe the kanji for 'enlightenment' across your forehead. Then we'd know."

Toshi shook his head and said, "Feh. I'd rather have answers. Enlightenment breeds indolence. Even if the kanji didn't fry my brain, it'd make me all tranquil and contemplative."

"So we are back to not knowing."

"And no way of knowing."

"Not true," the ogre said. He clapped his hands together. The sharp report echoed across the cavern. "Kobo!"

Toshi stepped back as the huge bald youth lumbered forward. The smell of burning flesh was rank and powerful around the ogre's apprentice, and Toshi could see the seared and smoking mark of the fresh brand. Kobo's arm hung stiffly below the blackened mark, and he flexed his fist repeatedly as if trying to reestablish feeling or function. Other than that, a slight twinge when he spoke, and a few drops of sweat on his broad skull, the huge youth showed no outward signs that the ghastly wound was troubling him in the slightest.

Let's see how tough he is when the flies start laying eggs in him, Toshi thought. Then, aloud, he said, "If you're going to read his entrails, give me chance to get clear of the spatter."

"Silence, fool. Kobo is the finest apprentice I've had in decades. I would never waste him on simple augury." As the burly youth approached, Hidetsugu said, "Toshi, what do you know about the *budoka* fighting monks of Jukai?"

"Nothing. They're in the forest, after all. I never go there."

Hidetsugu waved Kobo closer, into the light from the brazier. "Kobo is originally from Jukai, where the kannushi priests dwell. They are holy men, especially devout in their spirit-worship. They dedicate their lives to honoring the Myojin of Life's Web."

Toshi nodded. "Morons."

Hidetsugu growled. "Some of these priests train the *budoka* warrior monks, acolytes who practice and perfect the brotherhood's ancient fighting techniques. Kobo is from a long line of budoka, but he sought to be more than his masters, more than his ancestors. He sought to become *yamabushi*, a slayer of kami. But yamabushi are of the mountains, not the forest, and so he came to the badlands looking for someone to train him.

"Those few yamabushi masters he found would not deign to mentor to a forest monk. Neither would the kannushi in the forest allow his return. They knew of his potential and turned him away. Eventually, he came to me.

"Five years in my service and he's still got all his limbs. He's still obedient, still sane. He's not even very bloodthirsty, but I still have a few years to train that into him. I cannot make him into a yamabushi. But I shall make him into something that can crush yamabushi and kami alike into boneless mush."

Toshi looked the huge bald apprentice over. "Yes, he's quite remarkable. You should be proud."

"Kobo's people in the forest are closely connected to spirits there. And I am on good terms with the local yamabushi."

"Meaning they're terrified of you and won't risk antagonizing you if they can help it."

"Precisely."

Kobo stood, stoic and silent. Toshi glanced from the apprentice to the ogre. "So you think clean-head's tribe might know something?"

"I think it will be easy to enlist the budoka monks' aid against the soratami and their kami. The spirit of the woods always move in opposition to that of the sky—it is the order of things. The warriors will be very interested in your story, Toshi. Their enemy is moving, and they might easily be roused to action.

"Great things are in motion, oath-brother, mystic and military events on a global scale. We must move carefully or be crushed by them. As you saw, the goblins and the bandits are taking their first tentative steps as allies. If you two can incite the forest monks while I bring the yamabushi into play, the moonfolk will have far more to worry about than a lone ochimusha and his freelance reckoners."

Toshi smiled. "So we're going to stir things up to draw the heat off of us? I like it." Then he reflected on what Hidetsugu had just said, and a cold sense of dread welled up in his stomach. "'You two?'" he said. "As in me and this walking slab of rock?"

"That is what I am suggesting."

"Then that is what I am refusing."

"Why? You came to find answers and assistance. Here is both in one sentence: You must seek elsewhere."

"I mean why him, why the forest monks?" Toshi was incredulous. "You said they wouldn't let him back in. What makes you think they'll listen to me if I show up with him in tow?"

Hidetsugu smiled unpleasantly. "They will listen, or he will demonstrate what a mistake they made in turning him away five years ago. Kobo," he suddenly barked at his apprentice. "Make sure to leave at least one of your former masters intact enough to answer Toshi's questions."

"Of course, master."

Toshi shook his head. "I absolutely refuse," he said. "If you want to send your boy on a revenge run, do it without me. Muscling a bunch of monks isn't going to get the soratami off my back."

"There are many monks in the forest. Some of them will be interested in your proposition. Kobo might not even find his tribe before you find budoka who are more . . . accommodating. In the meantime, you will need his protection along the way. Or do you expect to fight both kami and soratami alike by yourself?"

"I don't want to fight. I want to lie low." He looked up at Kobo. "He's not capable of low."

"You cannot rely on that luxury," Hidetsugu said gravely. "Remember, they would have been waiting for you here if their plans worked out."

Toshi opened his mouth, then closed it again.

Hidetsugu nodded encouragingly. "Think about it, Toshi. Have you ever heard of a soratami in the forest?"

The ochimusha snapped back, "I haven't heard of anything in the forest, lump-brain. I never go there."

"Careful." Hidetsugu's grip tightened on his club, but he did not raise it. "The moonfolk hate the forest at least as much as you do. Their power is tied to their home in the clouds, to the spirits of sky and moon. The forest spirits will not welcome them, cannot sustain them."

"Or me. I'm from Numai." But Toshi was faltering. The ogre made sense, though Toshi could not imagine a prospect more dismal than a prospecting jaunt into the Jukai. He glanced over at Kobo. "Can he fight?"

"He's an ex-budoka monk who has been my student for five years." Hidetsugu smiled, the sly and victorious smile of a gambler with a winning hand. "Do you think I'd send him out as your bodyguard if he wasn't capable, oath-brother?"

"You planned this all along," Toshi realized. "You've intended to shuffle your boy off to the woods with me in tow ever since that fish kami flopped into your cave." Toshi blinked. "Is this why you branded him earlier, to make him part of the hyozan oath?"

"And I did not do it lightly. But Kobo will help us solve our problem. The least we can do in return is stand ready to solve his."

"The least we can do is leave him here and not oblige me to take care of him."

Hidetsugu leaned down into Toshi's face, and once more the ochimusha felt an instinctual urge to run and hide.

"That is precisely what you will do," the ogre growled. "I have marked him with the hyozan and you have consumed his flesh. He is nearly one of us now, a reckoner. And you, Toshi, will complete the ritual, so that you are as responsible to him as we are to each other."

Toshi was unable to hold the ogre's savage glare. "And if I don't?"

"Then we have nothing more to say to each other." Hidetsugu nudged him with a finger as thick and as sharp as a spear. "Do it, Toshi, and properly. This is my price for helping you. My student will return alive, or you shall avenge him according to our pact. Swear Kobo into our brotherhood, so that I know you will defend his life like your own. Otherwise, we can all sit here and wait for the moonfolk or even another kami to come collect you." Hidetsugu stood to his full height and Toshi heard the ridge on the ogre's skull scrape against the ceiling. "Who knows when or how terrible that visit will be? It may be beyond my power to protect you. I will, of course, look forward to avenging you according to our agreement."

Toshi glared up at the o-bakemono. As much as he hated Hidetsugu being right, he hated the circumstances even more. There truly was very little choice.

He drew his jitte and said to Kobo, "Hold out your hand." With swift, practiced motions, Toshi scratched the hyozan triangle and kanji into the bald youth's palm. Kobo's hand was callused and tougher than leather, so Toshi had to trace the symbol multiple times before it was scored into the bald youth's flesh.

Then Toshi repeated the symbols on his own hand and gestured for Hidetsugu's. The jitte's sharp tip was even less effective against the ogre's palm, but Toshi patiently kept at it until he had inscribed all the symbols he needed.

He gestured, and all three of them locked hands. They stood silently for a few moments, feeling a cold flow of nameless force traveling from one to the other like water through an aqueduct. They were all completely silent.

Then Toshi said, "We are free, bound only to each other. My life is yours, yours is mine. Harm one, harm all. The survivors must avenge. Whatever is taken from the hyozan, the hyozan recovers tenfold."

Toshi dropped the apprentice's hand and jerked free of the ogre's. "It's done," he said. "When do we leave?"

Hidetsugu looked over to the oni mosaic and the kami transfixed to the wall.

"Soon," the o-bakemono said. "Right after we have made the proper obeisance to the All-Consuming."

"I'd like to do some consuming of my own. I'm already sick of trail food."

Hidetsugu's eyes gleamed. "Have you ever dined on kami flesh? You'll never get a fresher cut."

Unable to determine if the ogre was joking, Toshi shuddered.

* * * * *

Under Hidetsugu's orders, Kobo lit all the torches and braziers in the cavern. The interior of the cave was aglow with hellish orange light, and blood-red shadows danced on every wall.

The o-bakemono was kneeling before the mosaic altar to his oni. In the final stages before its death, the marine kami twitched and struggled against the crude iron nails that held it. Hidetsugu was growling in a language that Toshi did not comprehend, but he imagined its kanji were short, sharp, and vicious.

Kobo ran to and fro around his master, lighting torches and tossing them toward the altar. Sometimes Hidetsugu's chants would rise in pitch and volume, and then his apprentice would crack open a clay pot and spread the thick red liquid within across the cavern floor.

Toshi stood well back from the ritual. He had seen Hidetsugu at work before and knew it was best to have a clear path of escape. Besides, the ogre had warned him that The All-Consuming Oni of Chaos was not particular about what it consumed. Summoned to feast on a kami, it would not hesitate to wolf down any extraneous humans nearby.

The smoke thickened and the air in the cavern grew foul. Toshi heard a faint sound, like the buzzing of a swarm of locusts as it descended on a field. The buzzing grew louder, and Hidetsugu's chants rose to be heard above the din.

Firelight played across the surface of the mosaic, and white sparks leaped from the spaces between tiles. Toshi's thought his vision had fogged for a moment, but when he looked away from the altar he could see perfectly. There was some form of distortion over the image of the oni, and it was growing.

The All-Consuming Oni of Chaos thrust one of its hungry mouths into the world of substance. Ghostly images of a dozen other mouths loomed in the distorted air around it. Hovering like insects, the bat-winged scavengers screeched and hooted in the distance, far beyond the oni in the widening pool of blurry air. A second pair of voracious jaws appeared, followed by a third, and a fourth. In moments, a dozen or more of the disembodied mouths had manifested in the cavern and were sniffing the air, jostling one another, zeroing in on the helpless kami. Above this storm of angry teeth and jaws, three huge eyes opened, arranged in an upright triangle. Two massive horns began to emerge over the highest eye, which scanned the inside of the entire cavern while the lower two fixed hungrily on the dying kami.

Like a school of carnivorous fish, the floating maws descended on the maritime spirit, ripping free huge chunks of its dense, blubbery flesh. The kami squirmed against its restraints and began lowing in a deep, mournful voice that brimmed with pain. Blood, scales, and bits of meat flew out from the altar, creating a terrible cloud of sticky gore. The lower eyes of the oni rolled up in their sockets, but the third remained locked on its meal, glowing an unholy blood red as the oni exulted in gluttonous carnage.

At the center of the ghastly maelstrom, the kami finally died and began to fade away. The oni's mouths faded too, following its meal from one world to the next, unwilling to give up even a single bite. The buzzing roar died down and the air began to clear. The last thing to fade from the grisly tableau was the oni's uppermost eye.

Hidetsugu continued to chant. Then, the ogre shaman stood with his eyes closed and hands open. He brought his massive palms together with the sound of a black powder keg explosion, and every flame in the cavern went out.

Toshi stood perfectly still in the sudden darkness, sweat rolling down the back of his neck. He could hear Kobo shuffling, moving things across the floor, but he could not hear Hidetsugu.

"Now we're done," the ogre said. His voice came from behind Toshi, and the ochimusha jumped. "Get ready to leave." Then, Hidetsugu chuckled. "Kobo."

A torch burst into fiery life with the burly apprentice below. Kobo was no longer in his red and black robes, but instead had donned a simple woolen wrap that covered him from his waist to his knees. He wore spiked wire wrapped around both wrists, and Toshi saw that he had a set of metal rings embedded in his torso. A strand of animal hide stretched from the ring on one collarbone down to the one on his ribs, then back up to the other collarbone. The rough strips of hide rubbed against the raw, weeping brand on Kobo's chest.

"Let me guess," Toshi said. "You're dressed like one of the forest monks."

Kobo nodded. It occurred to Toshi that he hadn't heard the burly youth say very much since he'd arrived.

"So," he said, "that Consuming Oni back there . . . can you summon that? Because things may get rough out there, and I want to know what you're capable of."

The ogre's apprentice held Toshi's eyes but he seemed somewhat embarrassed.

"No," he said. "I am nowhere near that powerful."

"Yet," added Hidetsugu.

"Good," said Toshi. "I don't want that thing anywhere near me unless Hidetsugu is there with his club and a suitable decoy. Keep things simple and we'll get along just fine."

Kobo looked to his mentor, who nodded. He echoed the nod to Toshi and said, "As you say, oath-brother."

"And don't call me that." He gestured between Hidetsugu and himself. "When we do it, it's kind of endearing, like a playful insult between friends. When you say it, it sounds far too ominous."

"But he is your oath-brother, Toshi. I will hold you to that."

"You don't have to hold me to anything. I'm bound. I will honor the oath."

Hidetsugu brushed past Toshi and crouched down to his apprentice. "Go now. Seek as I have instructed. Follow Toshi's example—he's an expert at staying alive."

"I will not fail you, master."

Hidetsugu jerked his head toward the incline. Outside, the morning sky was just starting to exchange darkness for dawn.

Without another word, Kobo turned and started up the incline. Toshi watched him go, then turned back to Hidetsugu.

"You think this will work?"

The ogre busied himself with the embers slowly dying in the brazier. "We'll all die eventually. The trick is to die well, with your eyes open."

Toshi shook his head. "You barely make sense to me any more, old man. In a few more years, you're going to need a second apprentice to wipe the drool away from your senile lips."

Hidetsugu strode away from Toshi, disappearing into the gloom in just a few huge strides.

"Find out what threatens you, Toshi." The ogre's voice echoed from every wall, and Toshi strained to spot him. "For it threatens us all."

Despite his best efforts, Toshi did gaze around as he exited Hidetsugu's cavern. He was not eager to spy more portents that might give him an omen for what was to come. But he was a kanji adept, and he could not help but look.

To his relief and his indefinable dread, he saw nothing but Kobo as the apprentice stood waiting outside the ogre's hut. Silently, they made their way north, leaving the shadows behind as the sun rose over the ridge behind them.

CHAPTER 5

Pearl-Ear stood looking out a window from the mezzanine of the Daimyo's stronghold. With a short turn of her head, she could change her view from the rich, crowded splendor within the tower and the blasted devastation without.

Towabara had changed dramatically in the twenty years since she went up into the tower to announce the princess's birth. Then, the view from this height would have shown a horizon dotted with villages and towns, with good clear roads and vast, unbroken fields.

Now, from her window, the fox-woman could still see nearly all western Towabara, from the fortifications at the base of the tower past the skeletal villages and towns, all the way across the smoke- and mist-blanketed wasteland to the vague horizon. Campfires burned below, and sentry patrols carried lanterns out in the haze, tiny pinpricks of light struggling against a field of dismal gray.

Once, the stronghold had been the center of Konda's vast holdings, the keystone of his kingdom. Now, the tower and its immediate grounds contained virtually all Konda's domain. His lands had been devastated by the Kami War, his people dead, driven off, or crowded behind its walls like rabbits in a warren.

Daimyo Konda's stronghold still soared hundreds of stories over the rest of his domain. Where it had once crowned a gleaming and vibrant society, now it was one of the few large structures still standing. The tower was begun as the young lord's first great act as sovereign, and it had served as both fortress and palace once the outer defensive walls were complete. From this powerful seat, Konda drove the bandits out of the Araba, consolidated a dozen different local warlords under his banner, and established his nation as the greatest power in Kamigawa.

The tower's foundation was carved into the very roots of the rocky mountain. It was called a tower because it stretched up so high, but it was broader even at its midpoint than any other castle in the kingdom. It had taken a great deal of powerful magic, thirty thousand laborers, and over a decade to complete. By the time the final spire was set in place, Towabara was a nation that deserved such a grand capitol and Konda had earned his right to rule it.

Pearl-Ear looked down at the rolling clouds of dust that roamed the ruins like a predator, then up to the sun, muted and faint behind an endless ceiling of yellow clouds. Twenty years of war had bled the entire land white, draping it in despair and pallid, sickly hues.

Far below, her sharp ears caught the sound of soldiers shouting. She peered through the haze and saw a company of warriors converging, moving, circling around an indiscriminate mass. The kami had come again, as they always did. Konda's retainers and soldiers had gone out to beat them back, as they always did.

Inside the building, a loud brass gong sounded, calling all Konda's top advisors to their weekly assembly. Despite the trouble inside the gates, Konda was determined to conduct affairs of state normally.

Pearl-Ear dreaded this meeting more each passing week. The bickering between diplomats was almost as painful as the tales of akki unrest and bandit raids that poured in from around the kingdom. If she were free to do as she pleased, she would have returned to her people in the forest years ago.

Lady Pearl-Ear gathered her robes and padded down the mezzanine stairs, to the great hall where the assembly took place. She was not free. She was bound by duty to her people, her position, and her beloved friends. Her greatest joy in Eiganjo was also her greatest burden—how she wished she could simply pack up the things that mattered most and go. To the forest, to the countryside, even to Numai. Anywhere but here, in the cursed kingdom of Daimyo Konda.

As Lady Pearl-Ear reached the final step, a pair of human girls approached her. The smaller of the two was dressed in a floor-length blue robe with wide white sleeves, the traditional uniform of the Minamo Academy. The student wizard had short, straight brown hair that framed her face and accented her wide brown eyes. She was lean and ropy, with arm muscles that rippled like a soldier's. Pearl-Ear could sense an aura of varnished wood and bowstrings on her. The Minamo trained its students as *kyujutsu* archers as well as mages, and that this one, Riko-ome, was at the top of her class in both. The student archer's face and figure were both quite feminine, but compared to the young woman next to her, Pearl-Ear thought Riko seemed rather plain and boyish.

The fox-woman chided herself for unkindness. She was predisposed to think well of Princess Michiko, the Daimyo's daughter, and it was unfair to make comparisons. Further, everyone at court agreed that Michiko was blessed of divine beauty, as breathtaking and impeccable as a dove in flight. She was tall, long-limbed, and she moved with an easy grace that was almost hypnotic. Her face was wide, open, and inquisitive. Her smile was a warm reward, her tears a bitter punishment.

"Lady Pearl-Ear!" the princess whispered excitedly. "Riko says that some important delegates from her school will attend today's assembly."

"Indeed they shall, Princess." In looks, in voice, and in demeanor, Princess Michiko reminded Pearl-Ear very much of Yoshino. "I saw them arrive myself earlier this morning."

"Do you think the scholars have brought good news?"

"That I do not know. But come now, and we shall find out together." She bowed to Riko. "You must excuse us, Riko-ome. If you wait for us in your chambers, I will send word when the assembly has ended."

The student returned the bow. "Thank you, Lady Pearl-Ear. I will be waiting."

As Riko went up the stairs, Pearl-Ear took Michiko by the hand and led her down the hall.

"What have you two been studying today?" Pearl-Ear found it was easier to separate the two girls if you kept one of them talking.

"We were reading about the soratami. If I am to rule by my father's side one day, I must learn about all the tribes of Kamigawa." Even as Michiko answered, she craned her head to wave to her friend.

"That is an impressive task, Michiko-hime." Pearl-Ear tugged gently, and the princess turned to face her as they walked. "The moonfolk are a mystery unto themselves. Few outside the tower have ever seen one. My own people have had cold but cordial relations with them for generations, and even we know very little about them."

"Riko says the academy has frequent dealings with them. She thinks there may even be records in the school archives dating back a thousand years."

"The academy's resources are indeed vast."

"Someday, we will go there together and research the soratami properly."

"You and I, Princess? Or you and Riko?"

Michiko smiled. "All three, I pray."

So like her mother, Pearl-Ear thought. "Quickly now," she said. "The assembly cannot start without you."

Together, they crossed the great hall and moved into a smaller suite in the western annex. The room had high-backed chairs lining one wall and a row of tables lining the other. Though there was all manner of food and drink on the tables, no one ate and no one sat.

Instead, roughly twenty of the most esteemed members of the court all stood in small groups, talking in urgent whispers. Lady Pearl-Ear recognized General Takeno, weathered, worn, and bent from twenty years of war. The moonfolk ambassador who had been outside the Daimyo's chambers on the night of Michiko's birth was there, flanked by a robed wizard and a boy with white hair and blue eyes. Pearl-Ear recognized Choryu, another student from the academy and a friend of Riko's and Michiko's. He was older and more advanced in his studies and often attended to high-ranking academy officials on their visits to Eiganjo.

The rest of the assembly included soldiers, ministers, merchants, and other prominent humans from the Daimyo's kingdom.

Michiko suddenly pointed at one of the corners. "Look, Lady Pearl-Ear! A kitsune-bito, like you."

Pearl-Ear started and quickly scanned the corner. There was a fellow kitsune in the room, a male with a small, compact build. His gray eyes laughed as they locked onto Pearl-Ear's. Then he disappeared behind a cluster of army officers.

"Do you know him?"

Pearl-Ear nodded, not taking her eyes off the spot in the corner. "I do. But I think he has taken to using charms from the marketplace outside. I would have sensed him otherwise."

Michiko's eyes became excited and she whispered, "Who is he? Is he a spy? Is he checking up on you?"

Pearl-Ear patted her shoulder. "Nothing so furtive, Princess. My people are a playful lot, given to tricks and jests. I imagine he was sent here by my village elders to provide or obtain information. And he is hiding from me only because he is very childish."

"I think he's handsome," Michiko said. "What's his name?"

"Let's just call him *Sharp-Ear* for now."

Michiko wrinkled her nose. "I don't understand."

"My sister is indulging in a little wish fulfillment." The male kitsune spoke from behind the two women. He slid in between them and draped an arm around Pearl-Ear. "Lady Pearl-Ear is hoping that I'm not here to stay."

Pearl-Ear forced herself to speak calmly. "Princess Michiko, my brother. Bow before the princess, Sharp-Ear."

The lithe fox-man stepped back and bowed low, sweeping his arm dramatically out behind him. "Forgive me, Michiko-hime. I meant no disrespect." Still bowing, Sharp-Ear swept out his leg as well, balancing on one foot with his tail waving side to side.

Michiko laughed. "None taken. Lady Pearl-Ear never said she had a brother."

Sharp-Ear straightened up and took the princess's hand. "She has seven," he said, and then he knelt with Michiko's hand pressed to his furry gray forehead. He bobbed back up and released her hand. "And nine sisters. We kitsune go in for big families. I think I have two or three siblings that I've never even met."

"That sounds like a beautiful dream." Pearl-Ear had crossed her arms and was glaring reproachfully at Sharp-Ear.

"Lady Pearl-Ear!"

"No, Princess, pay her no mind. Sharp tongues are also a mainstay of the kitsune-bito." He leaned in and nudged Pearl-Ear's cheek with his shallow vertical muzzle. She turned her own face away, offering only her cheek.

Sharp-Ear seemed unfazed. "I have missed you, sister. The entire village plagues me incessantly for news of your exploits here at court."

"You won't have anything to tell them if we don't let Princess Michiko begin the meeting." Pearl-Ear turned to Michiko. "If you would?"

The princess nodded and made her way up to the front of the room where a small dais had been erected.

"Why have you come?" Pearl-Ear whispered.

Sharp-Ear kept his eyes forward, fixed on the princess. "I have come, like everyone else, to share news of the war."

"What news? I am special envoy to the Daimyo, and I—"

"Shhh. The princess is about to speak."

A servant rang a chime and the chatter in the room died down. Michiko raised her arms and called out, "Honored guests. Loyal retainers of the realm. Representatives of all Kamigawa. On behalf of my father, Daimyo Konda, I bid you welcome."

The room answered in unison. "Long live the Daimyo."

"He already has," Sharp-Ear whispered. Pearl-Ear elbowed him through his robes.

"This meeting," the princess continued, "is for the Daimyo's benefit, and yours. If he is to address your problems, he must know what they are. All entreaties will be heard. But first, General Takeno will speak on the recent progress he has made in defending this stronghold."

Michiko stepped down and the wizened general mounted the dais. His hair was white and thinning, his fingers trembled, but his eyes were clear and his voice strong.

"The kingdom continues to suffer intrusions from the spirit world." A rough murmur started to rise, but Takeno silenced it with a stern look. "There have been no casualties for almost a month. We have a limited area to defend and our troops can respond in a matter of seconds. We have mastered the art of containing them in these confined spaces, with only minor wounds on our side. The situation is stable."

"Forgive me, General, but that is not the case." To Lady Pearl-Ear's horror, the voice was her brother's, speaking from directly beside her. All around the room, nobles and generals and dignitaries stared and whispered behind their hands.

Takeno peered down at the kitsune-bito male. "You speak out of turn, sir. Who are you, with such dramatic pronouncements and no regard for procedure?"

Her brother winked at her before stepping forward. "I am Sharp-Ear." He bowed again, sweeping his arm back. "Of the kitsune-bito."

"The Daimyo already has a foxfolk advisor."

"Who resides in this stronghold, sir. I bring news from the edge of the forest, far to the east."

"And? Deliver your news and be done with it. This is not a theater for you to practice oration."

"Two days ago," Sharp-Ear said, "my sainted mother was praying at the family shrine. She called upon the kami of her favorite tree, an old but insignificant spirit who dwells among the cedars. She asked it for a blessing. Instead, the tree attacked her. She escaped with a nasty wound across her throat and a ruined robe.

"Later, on the other side of the village, a mother was singing a lullaby to her toddling kits. She sang of bees, and flowers, and sweet summer days. A cloud of insects appeared suddenly and swarmed over the family as a single entity, stinging some of the children until they nearly died.

"And during an elder's council, where it was being decided to send the brightest and most handsome of us to tell this sad tale, a kami shaped like a triple-headed fox with the body of a yak and the tail of a serpent appeared. He spat upon the council table, igniting it. He struck at our most revered elders, splintered a sacred stone, and tore the roof off the building."

Pearl-Ear gasped, and she was not alone.

Sharp-Ear bowed again. "That is my tale. We thought the Daimyo should be told."

Takeno stared at the fox-man, considering. "If your words are true . . ." he began.

"I have also seen it," interrupted a merchant from the floor. "My sons were in the counting house, and they claimed the coins rose up and pelted them like hailstones. When I went to see what they were screaming about, I saw the face of my fortune, sneering at me and hurling abuse."

One of the Daimyo's most decorated retainers stepped forward. "I placed my clan's ancestral blade in the hands of my infant son. The blade curled and cut him across the stomach."

Sharp-Ear raised his voice over the growing chorus. "The Kami War is no longer a matter of territorial intrusions against the Araba. It can no longer be contained within these strong walls by swift-armed response. The most common household spirits have joined the fight, and they are every bit as vicious as those who wage war against the Daimyo's people."

The moonfolk leaned and whispered to the wizard, who nodded. Then both soratami and the mage turned and headed for the exit, with Choryu the student close behind.

"Order," Takeno barked, thumping his foot on the floor to calm the nervous and increasingly loud dignitaries. "This is exactly why we gather in this way, to discover—"

A dull wave of pressure compressed Pearl-Ear's ears against her head. Silence preceded a tremendous clap of thunder that shook the entire room. Dust fell from the ceiling beams and General Takeno stumbled from the dais.

The chamber was suddenly full as a huge, symmetrical shape appeared at its center. It was as tall as the room and half as wide. A thin stem at its center connected two huge, bulbous growths that formed the bulk of its body. It was hunched slightly, looking like great mushroom on the edge of a reflective pool. Spidery limbs grew out of its center, flexing and probing like skeletal fingers, and white energy crackled along its surface.

The air around it was filled with glowing packets of light, like lanterns in a fog. Those spear-like appendages skittered across the floor and waved grotesquely in the air, and several of them straightened out and began to shudder.

Pearl-Ear sprang past the horrific kami, reaching Princess Michiko in three quick leaps. Though she was smaller than Michiko, Pearl-Ear scooped the princess up as if she were an infant, cradling her in both arms.

With a noxious puff of white smoke, the bulbous kami fired a series of its sharp fingers like a volley of arrows. Some shattered on the finely masoned walls, others became lodged in the spaces between the stones. One soared through the space beside the dais, exactly where Michiko had been standing.

Pearl-Ear curled her wiry arms around Michiko and sprang for the door, careful to keep a watchful eye on the kami's twitching limbs. She could not move at top speed while carrying the princess, but she could move far faster than Michiko could.

Then Sharp-Ear was beside her, taking half of Michiko's weight. Her brother still had a mischievous gleam in his eye, but the rest of his face was deadly serious. They locked eyes, nodded, and then dashed from the meeting chamber with the princess held aloft between them. Barely a second had passed between the time Pearl-Ear sprang forward. They carried Michiko to safety, with long, skeletal spears shattering close behind with every step.

Once clear of the chamber, the kitsune flattened themselves against the stone wall, covering Michiko with their bodies. Many of the chamber's residents flew past them in a panicked rush to safety. Some were bleeding or carried spear tips in their flesh. Two lay face-down with spreading pools of red beneath them; they were trampled without hesitation by those fleeing behind them.

Those that made it out of the room quickly ran headlong into a phalanx of soldiers rushing to get in. Sharp-Ear tightened his hold on Michiko and Pearl-Ear, and she responded in kind. In the confusion, the princess was safest where she was.

Pearl-Ear tilted her head and risked looking into the chamber. The terrible swollen kami held several of the meeting attendees in its scrabbling limbs. Its appendages were sharp, and they clicked together like knitting needles. When two or more of these limbs touched, a thin strand of silver thread shot out, snaring the wounded as well as those who had stayed to fight or were too scared to run. The silky thread crawled over its victims, muffling their screams and drawing them in. Those that weren't speared or smothered by the silk were torn open by the flailing insect arms.

Takeno and the samurai who spoke at the meeting both had their swords out, slashing at the spirit invader. They did not stop the creature, but they slowed its advance and tore long rents in its pillowy mass. More soldiers came in and, under Takeno's direction, began hacking the cocooned dignitaries free.

Slowly, the soldiers cleared the room and then drove the bulbous horror across the ichor-stained floor. The creature began to scream as the last of its arms was lopped off. It was growing new limbs as it fought, and it could not replace the arms it was losing fast enough to remain a threat. It tried to surge forward, to crush the soldiers, but they kept it at bay with *naginata* halberds and the U-shaped blades of their *sasumata* pikes.

Pearl-Ear turned back to the princess. Michiko was wide eyed, stunned, and muttering to herself. She listened closely and heard the princess praying to her father.

The fox-woman looked at her brother, and the amusement was completely gone from his eyes. Sharp-Ear shrugged helplessly.

"My father," Michiko said, her eyes suddenly alive and earnest. "My father must be told. He'll know what to do."

It was a girlish thing to say, a child's wish for her parent to make everything right. Lady Pearl-Ear wasn't sure if Daimyo Konda was capable of that, but the princess was right about the one thing: the Daimyo must be told.

"I agree, Michiko-hime. We must go to Daimyo Konda."

Michiko stopped, gaping as if she had only just noticed the foxfolk protecting her. "Yes. Let's go now."

Another hideous shriek sounded from the meeting chamber, and a bloody sword flew out the door.

"In a moment," Sharp-Ear said.

Lady Pearl-Ear nodded, and they cradled Michiko between them as the horrible hacking sounds went on, until the kami's cries were no more.

CHAPTER 6

Sharp-Ear went with Lady Pearl-Ear and Michiko as far as he could, but the upper reaches of the Daimyo's tower were off-limits to all but the most trusted of Konda's court. As the sentries stood, impassively blocking the doorway with their crossed pikes, Sharp-Ear bid his sister and the princess farewell.

"I shall be waiting for you in the great hall," he said with a wink. He bowed low and added, "Majesty."

As he stood, Sharp-Ear's eyes locked onto Pearl-Ear's and he hunched his shoulders slightly, tilting his head. Her brother was a gadabout and an idler, but she knew he was concerned for her safety and for Michiko's. If she asked him, he would stay close by to hear her when she called.

Instead, Pearl-Ear nodded almost imperceptibly and flicked her eyes toward the staircase. Sharp-Ear narrowed his eyes, nodded back, and headed down the stairs.

The sentries saluted and asked Lady Pearl-Ear to state her business.

"I must see my father," Michiko said. Her face was a sad porcelain mask, but only her wide eyes showed over her folded paper fan. "The most terrible thing has happened—"

"The princess has come fresh from the assembly," Lady Pearl-Ear broke in smoothly. "She has an urgent report for his Lordship."

The sentries grunted and parted their spears. Lady Pearl-Ear stepped through and entered the antechamber as Michiko added, "Thank you" from behind her fan.

The main chamber was lined with the Daimyo's retainers, hardened and trusted warriors all. They stood shoulder to shoulder, unmoving, their eyes hidden beneath woven wicker hats. Not a single head raised as Lady Pearl-Ear and Michiko entered the room, not a single robe rustled.

The same soratami from the assembly stood at the far end of the room, blocking the entrance to the upper chamber as he had on the night of Michiko's birth. To a casual observer, the moonfolk were all of indiscriminate age and gender, but Pearl-Ear had been watching this one for twenty years now, and her senses all told her he was male.

The moonfolk bowed before Michiko, but regarded Lady Pearl-Ear with cold, pale eyes.

"His lordship is not receiving visitors at this time."

"Perhaps." Lady Pearl-Ear's fur bristled. "However, this is no social visit, but his daughter bringing news of great importance."

The soratami sneered as if Michiko's news could not possibly merit the slightest attention from her father. This particular moonfolk was a constant obstacle to any who sought the Daimyo. In her decades of service in the tower, Pearl-Ear had never once gone straight in to see Konda, but instead had endured a long series of clipped and frustrating discussions with the sullen ambassador.

"Soratami-san." Michiko stepped forward and bowed from the waist. "I must speak to my father now."

Lady Pearl-Ear watched him weigh the situation. He had been at the assembly, so he most likely knew what Michiko was here to recount. The Daimyo had often brushed his daughter aside when the spirits were active, but she was still his daughter and a princess of the realm.

"The Daimyo is not receiving visitors," the moonfolk said at last. "But wait here, Princess, and I shall fetch him for you."

Without waiting for a reply, the moonfolk turned and ascended the stairs at the far end of the room. Pearl-Ear watched the pale, ghostly form disappear into the darkness, but she could still hear his feather-light steps on the stone.

Several long, silent moments passed. Then, the Daimyo's powerful voice rang out.

"Clear the chamber."

The retainers hesitated only for a moment, then mustered into two long lines and marched with machinelike precision out of the room.

Pearl-Ear swallowed, preparing herself for the Daimyo's arrival. Sending the soldiers away was a sign of trust and respect, but she couldn't help thinking that it also prevented anyone from witnessing any exchanges between father and daughter. If Michiko revealed any secrets, none but Pearl-Ear and the moonfolk ambassador would hear.

Konda's tread came down the darkened stairs, and then the Daimyo himself swept into the room. Lady Pearl-Ear bowed and she heard Michiko do the same beside her. The kitsune envoy centered her balance, took a deep breath, and faced the Daimyo.

Konda appeared exactly the same as he had been on the night of Michiko's birth. His face was still smooth but slightly weathered, on the verge of wrinkling. His white hair was still bright and healthy, bound into a top-knot under a skullcap. His keen almond eyes still floated insouciantly in his head, drifting from side to side and from top to bottom like blind fish in a bowl. He was surrounded by a pale nimbus of light that might have been an effect of the torchlight behind him. His face was animated, robust, alive with power and focus. Only his wandering eyes hinted at the furious churning of the Daimyo's innermost thoughts.

"Michiko," he called sharply. Lately, he bore Michiko's company with a definite sense of disinterest. Today, however, he spread his arms wide and beckoned Michiko in, his face turned toward her even as his eyes wandered about the room. Except for the expression on his face and the tilt of his head, he seemed every inch the figure of a welcoming, nurturing father.

"My Lord Daimyo." To her credit, Michiko maintained a dignity befitting a princess. Pearl-Ear knew that she would have preferred to run headlong into Konda's arms and tell him what she had seen in one long-winded rush of words and tears. Instead, she approached her father slowly and allowed herself to be enveloped by his long, sinewy arms.

As he hugged his daughter, Konda's pupils wafted up and back, as if trying to look over his own shoulder without moving his head. Lady Pearl-Ear followed his line of sight and realized he was staring at the darkened doorway and the stairway beyond. She shuddered, remembering what Konda kept at the top of those stairs.

"My dear." Konda released his daughter and held her by the shoulders. "I have already heard of the attack on the assembly. Were you harmed?"

"No, my lord. Lady Pearl-Ear and her brother were swift to protect me."

"Lady Pearl-Ear has always been swiftest when protecting you." The Daimyo glanced over at Pearl-Ear. "But this is the first I've heard of a brother."

"My lord. Sharp-Ear was here for the assembly," Pearl-Ear said.

"Hah. And I can gather he is not here to stay."

"No, my lord."

"Well, then, I shall have to reward Sharp-Ear of the kitsune-bito before he returns to his people."

"That is not necessary, my lord." Pearl-Ear thought, Nor is it wise. His head is swelled enough.

"Sharp-Ear is the reason I came to you, father." Michiko stepped forward and took her father's hand. "He says that his village on the edge of the forest is under attack. Even the most common and benign household kami are becoming hostile."

The Daimyo's face clouded. "Regrettable," he said. "But not unexpected. The kami intrusions have been growing more frequent and more violent for weeks now."

"But it's not right," Michiko said. "The people, our people and Lady Pearl-Ear's alike, have always revered the spirits. We pray to them for blessings and guidance. Why do they harm us?"

Lady Pearl-Ear shifted her balance uncomfortably. She could see flashes of Lady Yoshino in Michiko, and unless his strange new eyes didn't function at all, so could Daimyo Konda.

The lord of the tower smiled, but under his wandering eyes the expression was anything but comforting.

"Why?" He echoed gently. "That is a question we all want answered. I believe the kami are reacting to something new and powerful." He extended his hands, raising them to the roof. "This tower, this kingdom, has endured, prospered, and succeeded beyond anything Kamigawa has known before." He lowered his hands and placed them on his daughter's shoulders.

"The kami for our kingdom must be great indeed," he said. "A shining, powerful beacon of order and hope. I believe the other spirits are reacting to it, and us, as the other tribes reacted to me when I first set out to unite them. They are suspicious of this new power and attack out of unreasoning fear and a desperate need to preserve their own status.

"But do not worry, my daughter. For a time, there will be conflict and even bloodshed until the scales rebalance and the spirit world accepts our own kami's preeminence . . . just as the warlords and bandit kings came to accept our word as law.

"Until then, take heart in the support of Terashi of the Sun and The Myojin of Cleansing Fire. These spirits have already accepted the truth and will never forsake us."

The Daimyo smiled, his eyes vacillating. He held Michiko's at arm's length, where she stood with an expression of uncertainty mixed with awe.

"My lord is wise," Pearl-Ear said evenly. "To know the mind of a spirit is beyond all but the wisest and most advanced of my people."

Konda turned his face to Pearl-Ear, but he did not release his daughter. "I know what I know," he said.

"My lord," Lady Pearl-Ear said.

The Daimyo lifted his hands and folded them into his sleeves. He half-turned on the stairs and ascended a single step. "I have a kingdom to look after. If there was nothing else?"

Lady Pearl-Ear bowed. "There is one thing, my lord. My brother has brought disturbing news from my village. I would go to my people now, to reassure them of the Daimyo's conviction and dedication to our shared future."

Konda shrugged. "Of course. I will have a mounted escort—"

"Father," Michiko broke in. "Riko-one has invited me to visit the Academy and make use of their archives."

The Daimyo scowled, his brow casting a shadow over his wandering eyes. "And?"

"I wish to go."

"Out of the question."

"Why? If I am to take my place at your side someday, I must learn all I can. Lady Pearl-Ear says that on a daily basis."

"And you should listen to your teacher. There is more than enough for you to learn and be inside the tower walls."

"But—"

"Do not argue with the Daimyo," Lady Pearl-Ear cut in. "It is unseemly for a daughter and inexcusable for a princess."

Michiko's face reddened. She clenched her jaw and bowed.

"Forgive me, father."

Konda fixed his dour face on his daughter's as his eyes floated from side to side. "You may leave me now."

Lady Pearl-Ear stepped forward, took Michiko's hand, and guided the princess back. "A moment, my lord. In light of the kami attack inside the tower, I will have Princess Michiko focus on her archery training."

Konda grunted. "Very good. She should be able to defend herself, if need be. Who will be her instructor?"

"I have retained the services of a *yabusame* expert. He has been known to have novice students in the saddle and splitting targets at a full gallop in a matter of weeks."

Konda ascended another step, his face turned up into the darkness at the top of the stairs. "That is acceptable. In two weeks' time I will attend my daughter's lessons to see how she is progressing."

"We will be ready to impress you, my lord."

Without a further word or glance, the Daimyo went back up the stairs into the darkness.

Pearl-Ear squeezed Michiko's shoulder and silenced her with a sharp look. She hurried the princess out through the antechamber and into the main stairwell of the tower.

When they were several flights away from the sentries and alone on the stairs, Michiko exploded, "Why did you do that, Lady Pearl-Ear? I don't want to stay here and practice archery while you—"

"Princess," Pearl-Ear said sternly. "I have had to correct your impertinence once today. If I am obliged to do so again, your punishment will make archery practice seem like a vacation at the hot springs."

Michiko sulked down the next two flights of stairs. Finally, Pearl-Ear said, "You feel slighted, Princess?"

The Daimyo's daughter regarded Lady Pearl-Ear suspiciously. "I do. If the kami attacks are happening everywhere, then anywhere is as safe as here. Riko and Choryu said the wizard archives can help."

Pearl-Ear prodded Michiko with her elbow. "And?"

"And I wanted to see the academy. I've only heard stories and seen paintings, but Riko says it's even more breathtaking in person. All the buildings floating on the waterfall, and the clouds overhead. . . ."

"Riko," Pearl-Ear mused. "Your friend from the academy."

"Yes, Riko. My friend from the academy."

"Studying to be a wizard herself."

"Yes. She's going to be a great wizard someday."

"And in the meantime, she studies history, alchemy, artifice?"

"Sometimes. She studies lots of things. What are you getting at?"

"Potions, incantations, magical gemstones. The life of a student is full of novelty, isn't it? What else does Riko study?"

Michiko stopped and crossed her arms. "You're just avoiding the question."

"No, Princess, you are. What else does Riko study?"

"Arcane languages." Michiko leveled her eyes defiantly at Pearl-Ear. "Calligraphy. Meditation. Tidal rituals."

Pearl-Ear sighed. "Archery?"

"Riko is the best archer in her class." Michiko blinked. "Wait. . . ."

"Someone like that . . . a gifted archer, a fellow student . . . would be quite useful to the Daimyo's daughter as she studied her bow skills, wouldn't it?"

"I can train with Riko while you're gone?"

"As was always my intent. Do you think I'd leave you with no one to talk to? You'd go mad and take half the tower with you."

"But you," Michiko began. "You said you knew a yabusame expert. Riko shoots on foot."

"I do know a yabusame expert. You stood huddled between him and me while the kami attacked the assembly."

Michiko's eyes opened wide. "Sharp-Ear? Your brother trains mounted archers?"

"He does. And as I said, he can train you to competence in a very short time. Riko is there to sweeten the bargain, but she may learn something from him as well." Lady Pearl-Ear rose to her full height, bringing her eyes as close to level with Michiko's as she could manage, the effect powerful despite the difference in their sizes.

"I swore to your mother that I would always protect you. Stay here and be safe, behind your father's walls, guarded by your father's retainers, accompanied by your closest friend and my closest relative. I will not be long. And when I return, I hope to have a better idea of why the spirits have turned against us. Why they have focused their rage on your father's kingdom."

Michiko paused, then bowed deeply before Lady Pearl-Ear. "Forgive me, sensei," she said. "When you return, I shall have learned enough to impress you as well as my father."

Pearl-Ear placed her soft, furred fingers under Michiko's chin and lifted her face. "You have never disappointed me, child. Now, to your chambers. I will collect Sharp-Ear and tell him he has a new job in the tower. We will come to inspect your equipment and your attitude before supper."

Michiko smiled and went swiftly down the stairs, gathering her long robes in her fists as she ran.

Pearl-Ear watched until the princess disappeared through a doorway several stories below. Wearily, she sighed again and turned, climbing back up to the next highest landing. When she reached it, she whistled sharply.

"Come out, Sharp-Ear."

The grinning male kitsune-bito rose from the shadows behind an ornate decorative chest. "Did I hear right?" he said. "Did you just volunteer me for government work?"

"I need your help, little brother. Come with me." Pearl-Ear turned and slipped through the doorway next to the ornate chest.

Sharp-Ear chuckled. "And mother always said I was the sneaky one."

* * * * *

Pearl-Ear lit candles and chanted until her brother slipped into the room. Without a word, Sharp-Ear picked up a taper and joined in, working his way toward his sister. They met in the middle of the room, nodded to each other, and blew out their tapers.

"I am going home," Pearl-Ear said.

"So I have heard. But pray, what do you expect to learn there that will help the princess here?"

Pearl-Ear retreated to the far corner of the room and sat cross-legged in the center of a semicircle of flickering candles. "There is more at stake than just the princess."

"That's true," Sharp-Ear said, "but that isn't why you're going." He glided across the room and sat facing Pearl-Ear. "Everyone says you'd have come home to stay years ago if not for the princess. They say she's your obsession rather than your student."

Pearl-Ear closed her eyes. "And you, brother? What do you say?"

"I say she brings out a great sadness in you as well as a great joy."

Pearl-Ear nodded, her eyes still closed. "She vexes me sometimes. She is so noble, so trusting, so gentle."

Sharp-Ear waited in silence for a few moments, then said, "How does this vex you?"

Pearl-Ear opened her eyes. "Because there were omens when she was born. Conflicting omens without definite meaning."

Sharp-Ear's eyes sparkled. "Well, trot them out and give us a look. Omens are tricky things, but then so am I. If we work things out together—"

"This is no game, brother. Apart from Michiko's arrival, the year of her birth was a dark one for the Daimyo. The kami incursions began. Michiko's mother was one of the first to be killed when her caravan was attacked en route to a kitsune-bito healer."

85

Pearl-Ear turned away. "The birth was very difficult. Lady Yoshino never fully regained her strength."

Sharp-Ear's voice was soothing. "You two were close."

"I admired her greatly. And I was with her when her daughter was born. I watched Michiko carefully over the years for any sign of the horror I saw hovering over her that day. And while all the kingdom has seen little else but bloodshed and blasphemy since that day, none of it could be connected to the princess. She is a bright, beautiful, and honorable girl, but she is just a girl. She is no more blessed or cursed than anyone else. Yet I feel she is somehow tied to the Kami War, even if it's only through the coincidence of their simultaneous beginnings.

"And while I watch, and wait, and worry, the world continues to decay. The Daimyo sits in his tower and doesn't age as the spirits of Kamigawa decimate his kingdom. He believes they are jealous of his newfound power, which few have seen and none comprehend. Not even him, I fear.

"Now the kami are striking beyond his borders. Something has aroused their ire, and Michiko is involved. I know she is the key, but I can never determine to what."

Sharp-Ear tilted his head. "Why is it important? Why do you care?"

"You brought the answer to that question yourself, brother. A cedar spirit attacking those who sing to it. A monstrous fox hurling curses at the village council. This thing, this war, is growing. It has always threatened to engulf us all, and now it is making good on that threat."

Sharp-Ear narrowed one eye. "That explains the why, but not the 'why you?' The Daimyo employs the finest scholars, shaman, and wizards in the entire world. What can you learn that they cannot? What perspective can you offer that they don't already have?"

Pearl-Ear closed her eyes again, breathing deeply several times before responding. "I have held one foot in the Daimyo's world for over two decades," she said. "But the other remains firmly at home among our people. You were right to come here, Sharp-Ear. I have been too long away. Perhaps after a visit, I will rediscover the balance of mind and clarity of thought that is preventing me from seeing the truth."

Sharp-Ear stood up. "If you say so, Pearl-Ear. But I think there are things you are not telling me. Things that trouble you, which you will not share. I have spent many years deceiving people for my own amusement, sister, so I am not easily deceived."

"I have told you nothing but the truth, Sharp-Ear."

"I'm sure you have. You are no liar. But you have omitted something, Pearl-Ear, and so I rightly name you 'omitter.' "

Pearl-Ear's face curled in annoyance. "This debate is pointless. I need you to protect Michiko while I'm away. Train her in the basics of yabusame, make her proficient in the saddle and with the bow. I will not be gone more than a week. I cannot go if you do not agree."

"I will do as you ask," Sharp-Ear said. He smiled. "But you have intrigued me, sister, and you would not have done so accidentally. I shall press our young princess for information, I shall tweeze from her details about her life here in the tower. I shall ask her what she thinks of the omens around her birth."

"You will do no such thing." Pearl-Ear's eyes flashed. "She's just a girl, an innocent who has never knowingly harmed anyone. She has no malice in her, and yet the Myojin of Cleansing Fire wept on the day she was born. You tell me how to ask a simple, stainless child why the spirit world reacts to her like a sword thrust through a hornet's nest. You tell me, Sharp-Ear, and then we both shall ask her."

Sharp-Ear held Pearl-Ear's furious gaze for a moment, then bowed his head. "Forgive me, Pearl-Ear. I will do as you ask and train the princess in yabusame."

"Thank you." Pearl-Ear let her eyes drift shut and began chanting softly under her breath. When she reached the end of her mantra, she said, "I must rely on you, brother. Please, for once in your life, be reliable."

"Not to worry," Sharp-Ear said slyly. "You'll be amazed at how reliable I shall be. Just don't complain to me when I make a first-class mounted archer out of her and she wants to join the Daimyo's cavalry." He offered Pearl-Ear his hand.

With her eyes still closed, Pearl-Ear reached out to her brother. She squeezed his warm hand, then let it fall.

Then Sharp-Ear slid silently out of the chamber, leaving Pearl-Ear to chant softly among her candles.

CHAPTER 7

Just over a day into their journey together, Toshi decided Kobo was not such a bad traveling companion after all. The hulking bald monk hardly ever spoke, carried more than his share of the supplies, and kept up every step of the way. Together they made steady progress across the edge of the mountainous badlands until the road grew soft and loamy and saplings struggled to rise above the hard, beige dirt.

Toshi had dropped back behind Kobo, who was clearly more familiar with the route. Now, as the youth hesitated, Toshi urged him on with an impatient wave of his hand.

"I'm out of my element from here on," he said. "You take the lead."

Kobo grunted. He adjusted his pack and strode forward, his big feet leaving deep prints in the soggy grass.

They continued to march until midday. After they stopped for water and a chaw of jerked meat that Toshi didn't examine too closely, he said, "How much farther until we hit the tree line?"

Kobo shaded his eyes with his hand. "Not far."

"How long, then?"

"Before sundown." The big monk loped off again. Toshi choked back the rest of his canteen and hustled to catch up.

As they walked, he tested the ogre's apprentice, slowly closing the gap between them. Earlier he had established that Kobo had limited peripheral vision on his left side, probably a result of the damaged eye socket. His hearing was excellent, however, and that seemed to help compensate. The ochimusha let his foot scrape against a stone as he passed it, and Kobo's head immediately jerked to the left.

"It's just me," Toshi said.

"I know," Kobo replied. He glared at Toshi from the corner of his eye as he hiked, then turned his attention back to the trail.

Toshi didn't exactly admire Kobo, but he respected anyone who could withstand Hidetsugu's abusive training regimen for five years. Now that they were all linked by the hyozan, he wondered if the o-bakemono would ease up on the youth's physical punishment. He quickly scanned Kobo's back and shoulders, taking in the network of scars and half-healed lacerations. He smelled the still-fresh hyozan brand in angry red on Kobo's breast and decided that if anything, Hidetsugu would be an even sterner taskmaster from now on.

Hours later, they stepped through a curtain of cedar trunks and ivy into the cool, shaded interior of the forest. The sun was setting, but they still had hours of daylight left. Above them, yellow light streamed through the thick cedar branches and danced along the moss and exposed roots along the forest floor.

"Wait," Toshi hissed.

Kobo stopped. "We still have far to go—"

"Shhhh." Toshi looked up at the canopy and listened carefully. "I heard something."

Kobo shrugged impatiently. "The forest is full of noise. Hidetsugu trained me to filter out sounds that mean nothing. You will have to adjust."

"Then I smell something. Hold still a moment and trust your oath-brother."

Kobo grumbled and loosened the straps on his pack. The heavy bundle thumped loudly to the forest floor and rolled onto its side.

"I smell nothing."

"That's because Hidetsugu smeared your nose across your face. Shut up and let the handsome, smart member of our party assess the situation."

Toshi stared at the trees ahead. There was only the barest hint of a path through the thickest part of the forest, but what there was led to a small opening in the trees. The massive branches and draped moss cast deep shadows on each side of the opening. Among the ruins in the city, Toshi had seen alleyways that reminded him of the path ahead. There was usually a nezumi-bito ambush waiting inside.

"Kobo," Toshi whispered. "Are you carrying any ranged weapons?"

"Huh?"

"Ranged weapons. Bows, spears, shuriken. Even a weighted chain. Anything we can use from here to attack people over there." Toshi pointed at the opening.

Kobo shook his head.

"There's someone watching us up there." Toshi quickly scanned the ground around his feet for something to throw. "I want to flush them out."

"Yes, oath-brother." Kobo squatted down and dug his fingers into the turf. The smooth, rounded top of a large stone poked up between his hands.

"Easy," Toshi hissed. "That rock's bigger than it—"

With an explosive grunt, Kobo wrenched the barrel-sized stone halfway out of the ground. With his muscles rippling across his back and veins pulsating on his forehead, the ogre's apprentice let out a roar that echoed across the forest.

The rock came free in a cloud of dirt. Kobo staggered back, balanced the stone on one shoulder, and then positioned his hands beneath it. A low, dangerous growl started deep in his chest, and his legs swelled as they dug into the turf.

"All right then. Grab the big rock. Don't mind me," Toshi spat. He drew his jitte in one hand and his long sword in the other, stepping clear of Kobo in case the youth lost control of his burden.

But the bald monk was in his element. With a surge of brute strength and another tree-splitting roar, he heaved the small boulder across thirty feet of open space. Toshi had one second to marvel at the sight of the crude missile arcing over the grass, and then it smashed down into the shadows and moss on the right side of the path ahead.

"Look out below!" Toshi yelled. Kobo tilted his head quizzically, his face flushed and his breathing heavy.

"Ideally," Toshi explained, "you would have waited for me to say that before you threw the rock."

Cedar leaves and bits of broken wood rained down from above, but Toshi could not see the stone. He narrowed his eyes, focusing on the long, claw-fingered hand now lying limp on the edge of the path. The owner of the hand was obscured by brush and foliage.

"Use your good eye," Toshi said, as he pointed to the hand, "and look there."

Kobo squinted, then straightened up, slamming his fist into his open palm. "Akki," he said.

"Akki," Toshi agreed. He raised his voice, calling, "So anything on the right side of the path is now paste. And anything on the left side of the path is paste-to-be. Kobo . . . fetch the other rock."

Kobo looked confused and started to shrug. "No more rocks, oath—"

Two small figures suddenly sprang out from their cover on the left side of the path. One of the akki goblins turned and faced them, blocking the path as his partner scurried off into the forest. The little monster screamed defiantly, waving its too-long arms and drumming on its own carapace with clawed fingers.

"Come on," Toshi shouted as he charged. "I want to catch the other one before he brings back the rest of his clan."

Small as he was, the remaining akki managed to block the entire path. He was unarmed, but his claws were dangerous enough and the armored plate on his shoulders protected him from Toshi's swords. The ochimusha slowed as he closed on the akki, staying clear of the goblin's long reach.

"Go back, go away," the akki screeched. "Killyou, killyou, killyou dead!"

Toshi leveled his eyes at the little brute. "Kobo," he said calmly, "kick this little dungball across the forest, will you?"

A huge bald blur swept past Toshi. The comic look of surprise and fear on the akki's face was priceless. Then it disappeared behind Kobo's roaring form.

The huge, sandaled foot slammed into the akki's chest, driving it up into the air like a child's inflatable ball. The little monster screamed as he sailed off, spinning awkwardly until he slammed into the solid center of a cedar trunk.

Kobo turned. "I cannot run long distances, oath-brother."

"Then step aside," Toshi said as he sprinted past. "And try to keep up."

Toshi ran, fending off branches with his jitte and slicing through vines with his long sword. The akki were a lot like the nezumi, he thought. Small and cowardly, but numerous. Goblins were nowhere near as good at throwing off pursuit as the ratfolk were, so Toshi had little problem following the fleeing akki's trail. Behind him, he heard Kobo lumbering. Hidetsugu should have trained him for distance as well as sprints.

Maybe it wouldn't matter. If Toshi could catch the akki, all he had to do was delay him or pin him down until the ogre's apprentice came along to mop up. Hidetsugu had not been bragging about Kobo's fighting skills—the big bald lump was formidable.

He broke through into a clearing just in time to see the akki disappear into the thicker brush on the far side. Toshi sheathed his sword and sprinted across the tranquil glade, barely noticing the bright evening sun overhead. He was catching up. Another few moments and he could tackle the akki and sit on its head.

Toshi plunged back into the brush, then stifled a yelp as the ground fell away beneath him. He maintained his balance as he hurtled down the incline with branches slapping his face and torso.

Momentarily blinded, Toshi crossed his wrists in front of his face to protect it and continued to run. He was careful to watch the ground in front of him to avoid any more surprises the terrain might throw at him. He half-staggered into another clearing, and as he regained control of his own momentum, Toshi smelled smoke.

The ochimusha lowered his hands. All around him, fifty yards in every direction, the trees had been felled. Most of the lumber seemed to be piled onto a great bonfire in the center of the circle. The fire was blazing ferociously, its flames licking higher than the tallest nearby tree.

Scores of akki goblins knelt around the fire, chanting softly and hurling dirt in the air. Most were unarmed, but some carried crude clubs made of bone or makeshift spears made from broken swords tied to the ends of poles. Lit by the great fire, the dirty little creatures took on a hellish red tinge.

As one, half of the akki fell silent and turned to glare at Toshi.

"A party for me?" Toshi said, more loudly than he'd intended. "This *is* a surprise."

Near the fire, three akki stood next to two humans who had torches in their hands. Toshi didn't recognize the biggest goblin, but the others were familiar. There was the one he had been chasing, who was still panting and wild-eyed. Beside him was Ben-Ben the hermit, fresh from Hidetsugu's hut. He still wore his ridiculous squid hat proudly on his knotty little head.

The humans were likewise familiar. Dressed in bandit armor, the two men slowly turned to face Toshi, and cruel smiles formed on their identical faces.

"You," the first twin said. "The ochimusha with the mouth."

The second twin's voice rose over the goblin's chant and the roar of the fire. "Complete the ritual," he said. Then he looked to his brother. "This can't be a coincidence. He dies?"

"He dies." The first twin turned to a squad of armed akki nearby, who were eagerly stroking their weapons. "Kill him."

An akki with a crude spear whooped and let it fly. Toshi barely deflected it with his jitte as he leaped clear. As the rest of the party readied their weapons, Toshi backpedaled and scanned the smoke-filled clearing. The path behind him was all uphill. Everywhere else was full of gristly little toads with hard heads, small brains, and orders to do him harm.

He considered making a kanji that would turn the ground into damp, clinging quicksand, but it wouldn't affect the entire clearing and by the time he finished inscribing it, he'd have half a dozen akki spears stuck in him. He needed something else, a spell or a tactic that could affect a small army.

From his left, one of the other akki screeched and pounced on his back. The little monster's grubby fingers clawed at Toshi's face, and as he struggled to throw it off him, Toshi saw the armed party unleash a volley of spears.

Quickly, Toshi spun in place so that his back was to the fire. He felt a thump and the akki on his back grunted. There was another thump as the second spear bounced off the goblin's hard shell, then a third. Then Toshi heard a wet, slapping sound and felt the tip of a spear enter his own lower back. The akki riding him gurgled and went limp.

Toshi shrugged off the dead goblin with the spear sticking clear through it. He touch-inspected the wound in his own back, nodding grimly. It was minor with very little pain, but it was bleeding freely. He faced the fire again, carefully watching the armed akki party as it closed the distance between them.

All the spear-carrying goblins had already let fly. Those that remained carried cudgels and spiked clubs. He turned his body so that they could not see his wound and then dragged the tip of his jitte through the blood flowing down his back.

"I'll just be on my way now, thank you," he said. He brandished the jitte, blood dripping from its point. "You just stay back, or I'll do something you'll regret. I'll regret it, too, but you'll regret it more, I promise."

"Keep chanting," said the first twin.

"You there," said the second, gesturing to another cluster of akki. "Help see to our guest."

Twelve more akki started toward him, and Toshi clenched his jaw. Blood, tears, and other bodily humors on his jitte made the kanji he inscribed all the more potent, but the only magic he had for a group this size was difficult to control. He could strike everyone in the clearing down with a temporary plague if he didn't mind exposing himself to it, but he wasn't that desperate yet.

A leering, snaggle-toothed akki hurled a stone throwing axe. It missed, but it buried itself deep into the trunk of the tree beside Toshi.

I may be that desperate after all, he thought. He glanced down, looking for a clear patch of dirt where he could draw a symbol.

Then a huge bald figure exploded out of the forest like a cannonball. Kobo charged past Toshi with his tetsubo war club drawn and ready. The massive youth plowed straight into the pack of goblins, his roar every bit as intimidating as one of Hidetsugu's.

At first, all Toshi could do was watch as Kobo laid into the akki with his tetsubo. He may not have been fast over long distances, but he was a tornado in close quarters. The studded club was alive in his hands, smashing goblin weapons to pieces and the goblins themselves into pulp. He twirled the heavy weapon like a baton, crushing limbs, cracking skulls, and staving in the akki's natural armor like stale bread. As a traveling companion, the ogre apprentice's worth was increasing by the second.

The twins barked out another command, and another wave of akki swarmed toward Kobo. They surrounded him and literally began to scale him like a tree, even as he battered the others aside with his club. For a moment, Kobo was completely covered in squirming akki bodies, and the burly youth faltered. Then, like a dog shaking off water, Kobo rose, shuddered, and sent the vicious horde flying.

Kobo spun his tetsubo up one arm, behind his neck, and down the other, coming to rest in a position of complete readiness. He glared at the twins, beckoning them with his fingers.

"That's my oath-brother," Toshi called. "We look out for each other."

The twins both raised a hand, then simultaneously chopped down. The akki chant stopped and the only sound left in the glen was the crackle of the fire and the groans of fallen goblins.

"Impressive," said the first twin.

"But this," said the second twin, "is our patron, the Myojin of Infinite Rage. And we also look out for each other."

The second twin waved, and the bonfire expanded out past the boundaries of the clearing, engulfing the entire area in blood-red flames.

Toshi was mildly surprised to find himself alive and unbroiled. As his vision cleared, he saw that all the akki had fallen to their knees and were facing the fire. The twins were still sneering, their eyes locked on Toshi and Kobo.

An giant, ornate wooden throne floated above the pile of burning logs. It was the kind of chair a warrior king would have, once he had conquered most of the globe and built a castle from the bones of his enemies. A small jade and ruby statue sat in the center of the throne, a different weapon in each of its six arms.

The statue and the throne were surrounded by bright red flames that flickered too slowly, as if the fire was somehow heavier and denser than those of the bonfire. In these flames, Toshi could discern a kind of face above the throne and multiple arms on each side. Some of the limbs carried beads, some carried fans, but most carried swords, pikes, and other bladed weapons. These arms and items rotated around the central figure on the throne, floating like bubbles in oil.

You.

Toshi's eyes watered and his ears popped as the kami's terrible voice tore through his head. He fought the urge to look around, to pretend he didn't know the Myojin of Infinite Rage was speaking directly to him.

You are not welcome here, Toshi Umezawa. You are a tool in my enemy's hands. I shall make an example of you.

"A blessing," the first twin cried. "O Majestic Kami, we serve at your pleasure."

"Touch us with your wisdom, empower us with your rage," said the second. "Godo and his entire army stand ready."

Beside them, Ben-Ben the akki hermit prayed fervently, his fishy hat forgotten on the forest floor.

The swirling mass of the kami's body seemed to reorient on the twins.

You have my blessing. Continue your work. Leave the thug and the ogreling to me.

The second twin scowled, but both bandits lowered their torches. The scowler let out a long whistle and both twins jerked their heads to the north.

As the great kami's form flickered hypnotically overhead, the entire assembly of akki turned and began filing out of the clearing. Even those who were latched on to Kobo with claws and teeth stopped in mid-attack to join the exodus. Kobo struck down any who weren't quick enough to get out of range, but the ogre's apprentice did not pursue them. Instead, he backpedaled closer to Toshi, keeping his eyes on the kami.

You are a troublesome man, Toshi Umezawa.

"You don't know the half of it. And how do you know my name?" Toshi had never directly encountered a major kami in person before. He was surprised to find himself more annoyed than awed. "What do you spirits want from me?"

I seek the same goal of all clear-thinking sentients: an end to the Kami War.

"That's rich," Toshi said. "A fiery spirit of anger wants peace? Tell me another one."

"Careful, oath-brother."

The kami's flame rose higher and brighter. *I never said I sought peace. I seek an end to the war. An end that benefits me and mine.*

"Well, carry on then. Good luck with that."

Your kami handlers should never have sent you here, ochimu-sha. But you have come, and I cannot permit you to leave.

"I have no kami handlers," Toshi said.

No? The disembodied voice seemed amused. *Then who guides your destiny? Who answers when you call?*

"The hyozan does." Kobo stepped forward. "Do your worst, false god. We are not afraid."

The flames grew hotter. *Be silent. You serve a blasphemous brute who serves the beast of chaos. Your ogre blood will boil this night. Your master and his oni will suffer the same, in time.*

Toshi shrugged. "He's new. But he's right. If you're going to kill us, at least be quick in the attempt. We've got places to go." He tightened his grip on the handle of his jitte, his own blood still smeared across the tip. How would a spirit of rage attack them, he wondered. Force them to turn on each other? Burn them from the inside out?

As he stood waiting, Toshi heard another sound just under that of the crackling flames. It began as a dim, buzzing hum, but as it grew Toshi realized it was a distorted echo of the akki chant that summoned the great red kami.

Three balls of red flame leaped out from the bonfire, each as big as a chariot. They hovered just above the ground, spinning in place as the flames licked the air around them.

Die well, Umezawa, and be remembered. Otherwise, no one in either world will notice your passing.

"Same to you," Toshi called.

The flames around the Myojin of Infinite Rage flared. There was a blast of concussive force, and then the bonfire collapsed in upon itself in a great implosion of air.

The great kami's departure also sucked the flames away from the three fireballs, leaving three huge, grotesque shapes among the stumps and burned grass. The first resembled a tangled bale of barbed wire that had been doused with oil and set aflame. Twisted points of fiery metal floated in the air around its central mass as the kami shimmered and undulated, slashing the air with whips of sharpened wire.

The second kami was a great, barrel-shaped insect with two oversized forelegs and a scorpion's tail. It floated several feet off the ground, surrounded by a cloud of stinging flies. Its armored exoskeleton clicked as its sank its scythe-like forelegs into the turf and hauled itself forward.

The third looked like a cross between a turtle, an eagle, and a razor-tusked boar. Toshi blinked and rubbed his eyes, but the thing's true shape was lost in the cloud of heat distortion that surrounded it.

"Oath-brother," Kobo hissed. "I can summon a lesser oni to aid us, but it will take time and concentration."

Toshi scanned the three spirit beasts before them. Each was a "lesser" kami itself, and he wasn't sure one lesser oni would be enough. Besides, each of Rage's subordinate kami was only a short leap or lunge away, and time was something they didn't have.

Toshi shook his head and drew his long sword. "That's no good to us, Kobo," he said. "I think we'll have to do it ourselves."

CHAPTER 8

The lesser kami each began to stalk Toshi and Kobo, spreading out and inching closer amid a thoroughly unpleasant chorus of growls, whines, and clicks.

"Kobo," Toshi said. "You take the barbed wire and the bug. I'll deal with the . . . I'll deal with the other one."

"Yes, oath-brother."

"Kobo?"

"Yes, oath-brother?"

"The Myojin of Rage called you 'ogreling' and said you had ogre's blood. Do you?"

Kobo's back straightened and his face shone with something approximating joy. "Yes, oath-brother. I ate and drank of Hidetsugu's own flesh upon achieving—"

"I know the ritual." Toshi wrinkled his nose. "Hidetsugu has described it to me. And that's why you're even stronger than you look?"

Kobo's odd look of pride and excitement widened. "It is."

"Good." He drew his jitte and showed it to Kobo. Then he gestured at an axe wound one of the akki had made in the bald youth's bicep. "May I?"

Kobo looked suspicious for a moment, but then he shrugged. Toshi wiped the length of his jitte across Kobo's arm, coating it with the apprentice's blood.

"Now then," Toshi said. "Let's defend ourselves. And don't get killed behind my back. I don't have time to avenge you *and* figure out what's going on."

Kobo's mouth flickered as close to a smile as Toshi had seen. "Don't worry about me."

Toshi nodded. Indeed, the ogre's apprentice seemed downright eager for the coming struggle.

A single flaming tendril of sharpened wire lashed out and coiled around Kobo's club. It tried to pull the weapon from the bald youth's grip, but he tightened his fists and dug his sandals into the sod. The wire remained taut as the kami reeled it in, drawing itself closer to Kobo as the youth stood firm.

The bug kami floated over this strange tug of war, orienting on Toshi. Its stinger tail curled up over its body, but Toshi guessed it could strike from below as well as above. Best to stay out of range in either case.

He started to sidestep, keeping his sword trained on the bug, but then the third kami lunged forward. Toshi still didn't have a clear idea of its shape and that concerned him. If he couldn't tell what it was, he couldn't tell how it would attack.

As the bug kami continued to float calmly toward him, Toshi saw the third tensing for another leap. Beside him, Kobo still strained to hang onto his club without being pulled in like a fish.

In a sudden flash of inspiration, Toshi yelled, "Switch!" and then sprang forward, already swinging his sword. The blade bit into the wire between Kobo and the flaming kami, hesitated, and then broke through.

The barbed wire kami recoiled and keened in pain as thick purple ichor spattered from its severed tendril. The wire around Kobo's club withered and fell away like dried ivy.

Kobo reacted quickly, drawing his club back as soon as Toshi cut it loose. The bald youth spun himself around, swinging the tetsubo overhead and bringing it down squarely on the third kami's back, just as the monster was about to spring on Toshi. The force of Kobo's blow cracked the thing's hard shell. Its body seemed to fold in half around the club as Kobo drove it down into the dirt.

Toshi ran under the scorpion-thing, which was still making its unhurried way across the clearing. Either it could not move quickly or it was saving its speed for a death blow from its stinger. In either case, Toshi had time to close the distance between himself and the barbed wire mass while the bug thing meandered closer.

A half dozen whip-like tendrils slashed at him as he approached, but Toshi protected himself with his jitte and the flat of his blade. The closer he got, the more tendrils he fought. As he slashed and hacked his way through, the kami retreated, rolling along the ground like a boulder.

Sensing a feint, Toshi stopped his advance. The thing rolled back another few feet, then rose up like a wave about to break, towering over the ochimusha. The kami spread itself out, covering a much wider area, and threw itself over Toshi like a blanket. He rolled clear, and as the kami gathered its mass for another charge, Toshi quickly scratched a series of kanji into the ash-covered ground.

The problem of how to kill a corporeal spirit without vitals or extremities had crossed his mind, raising a cold smile on his lips. He had spent a lifetime in Numai, among the nezumi-bito and the jushi. There was no shortage of methods for killing something without a blade or a club.

Behind him, Kobo was pounding the third kami into an even more unrecognizable shape. It had one of its mouths clamped on to the youth's calf, but its small, sharp teeth could barely puncture Kobo's skin. He had tasted Hidetsugu's flesh and so shared Hidetsugu's strength. Above them, the scorpion kami hovered closer, apparently convinced that Kobo was the greater danger. Toshi almost smiled again.

Instead, he finished the last line on the last kanji and rose to his feet. The barbed wire kami was rolling toward him, but cautiously. It sent wire tendrils ahead of the main mass, probing and inspecting the ground as it went. When it reached the edge of the first kanji on the ground, it stopped and hissed menacingly, but would advance no further.

"You're not as brainless as you look," Toshi called. "But then, you couldn't be." He waggled his jitte and his sword, but the kami would come no closer.

"The thing is, you don't actually need to step on this trap to trigger it." He held out the tip of his jitte, still stained with his own blood as well as Kobo's. He tossed the weapon into the air and then drew his short sword as the jitte stabbed deep into the ground, directly in the center of the last symbol.

A small black wind rose between Toshi and the kami. As the breeze blew ash and dust into Toshi's face, the characters he had carved rose into the air. The dark current carried the kanji to Toshi, swirled them around his head, and then sent them hurtling into the center of the barbed wire beast.

The symbols disappeared as they touched the kami's body. The thing keened again, its cries growing louder and more pained as the wind drove it back.

The flames surrounding the wire kami flickered and then grew dim. The wildly flailing ends of its tendrils slowed, and Toshi heard a harsh, cracking sound like ice breaking underfoot. A blackish-red patina of flaky grime spread out from where Toshi's symbols had touched the kami's body, and within seconds it became mired in a thick coating of rusty scabs.

Toshi watched the fiery points around the barbed wire slow, stiffen, and drop. Then he stepped forward, retrieved his jitte, and thumped the handle into the stiff, motionless mass of brittle wire. The dead kami collapsed and disintegrated like a dome of spun sugar.

He nodded to himself. Ogre's blood made strong magic, even when it was mixed with a human's.

Kobo shouted a warning that snapped Toshi back to the fight just as the scorpion kami struck. Toshi easily dodged the incoming stinger, which obliterated the remainder of the barbed wire kami's corpse.

Toshi leaped clear of a second strike, then a third. He had been correct: the scorpion kami was only slow when it moved between strikes. Once you were in range, it lashed out over and over until it scored. He flipped and rolled toward Kobo until he was clear. The last remaining kami turned and floated once more in their direction.

Toshi cocked his head. "So," he said, "that minor oni you mentioned? Time enough to summon it now?"

Kobo watched the scorpion kami. "Perhaps. I don't think we need it now, though."

"Humor me. I'll keep you safe."

Without another word, Kobo dropped into a cross-legged position, steepled his fingers, and balanced his forehead on them. While the ogre's apprentice chanted softly, Toshi stepped between Kobo and the kami.

The monster's stinging fly aspects reached them first, and Toshi swatted at them with his sword. Kobo was probably right: they didn't need an oni's help to win this battle. He preferred to be extra cautious when poison was involved, however, as a single scratch from the scorpion could mean another death for the hyozan reckoners to avenge. Or worse, the toxin could paralyze Kobo, and then Toshi would have to carry him.

Toshi paused, mentally noting the position of each swiftly buzzing fly. Then he waved his sword in a continuous, curving arc that rose up, down, then doubled back on itself. At the end of his swing, Toshi held his position, sword at the ready, feet wide and balanced. Before him, seven bisected stinging flies fell to the ground.

Toshi smiled. The scorpion kami was almost in range.

"Kobo? Any time you're ready."

Kobo stood. "I summon the dogs of war," he growled. "Blood-lust, brutality, and barbarism. As ogre serves oni, as human serves ogre, so will you serve me. Rise," he clapped his hands, "and make merry."

There was a flash, and a huge, feral shape appeared beside Kobo. Toshi realized he stood between it and the kami overhead, and smoothly slid out of the way.

The oni had the expected triple eyes and forward-sweeping horns, but it was not a humanoid shape. Instead, it was four-legged and as big as a bear. It was broad and bulky through the chest and shoulders, but its hips were thin and tapered over its spindly hindquarters. It was covered in thick, tough hide and had sharp spears of bone along its spine. Its armored chin came to a savage point, and caustic foam dripped from multiple rows of sharp, gnarled teeth.

The scorpion kami struck. The first sting punched into the oni-dog's shoulder, but did not penetrate to the vulnerable areas below. The second strike deflected off the oni's polished horn, leaving a deep scratch that was filled with venom.

On the third strike, the oni caught the scorpion's tail in its jaws and clamped down with a nauseous crunch. The kami let out an ear-splitting shriek. To Toshi's bemusement, the kami's stinger broke off in the oni's mouth as the bug-like thing rose high into the air.

Before he could celebrate or taunt, however, the kami sprouted another stinger from the end of its ruined tail. In seconds it was whole and complete as if it had never been wounded.

It also seemed to have picked up speed, now hovering and darting like a hummingbird. The new stinger dripped with fresh venom as the kami searched for an opening.

"Kobo." Toshi readied his jitte, just in case. "I'm not complaining, but do you think you could summon up something that could fly? We're only targets here."

Kobo actually smirked. "Trust me, oath-brother. As I trust you."

The oni turned its head and sniffed the air. It tensed its scrawny hind legs, filled its broad chest with air, and then sprang straight up.

The oni's bulk slammed into the floating kami and the brute latched onto the bug with both its massive forepaws and its multi-layered jaws. The kami shrieked again and tore at the oni with its stinger and its scythed forelimbs. One of the blades lodged in the oni's shoulder and broke off. The other carved long strips of flesh from the oni's back and ribs. In return, the oni was cracking the kami's exoskeleton and rending huge, ragged chunks from its soft innards. It let each new piece fall to the forest floor below, spattering the area with crimson gore.

As they fought, the oni's weight slowly dragged them back down to the ground. The kami's struggles began to slow, but the oni continued to savage its foe with unabated ferocity. If it felt the damage the bug had inflicted, it did not care.

By the time the oni's legs touched the ashen ground, the kami was already dying. It had lost the scythe end of one arm, and the other was slowly being amputated by the oni's crushing jaws. Its stinger had scored on the oni's belly a dozen times or more, to no visible effect. The oni settled onto the ground, still hauling down on the bug kami. It pinned its prey with one of its heavy forelimbs and, with a powerful wrench of its huge shoulders, tore the spirit beast in half.

Toshi nodded, impressed. He sheathed his weapons and slapped Kobo on the back.

"Well done, oath-brother. I knew—" Toshi stopped there, for the sound of the slaughter rose again, louder than before. Kobo's oni had won the fight, but it was not yet through with its opponent.

The oni burrowed into the kami's corpse like a badger in a

beehive. Cloudy red blood and shards of exoskeleton flew as it tore the kami into pieces and then the pieces into scraps. For several long minutes, Toshi and Kobo watched silently as the oni dog spread the body of its enemy across half the clearing.

"Well," Toshi said at last, "you did tell it to make merry. Can you also make it stop?"

Kobo nodded. He clapped his hands again, and the oni's gore-flecked head rose out of the carnage.

"You honor me," Kobo said. "That honor will be repaid three-fold. Your task is done. I did bid you rise, and now I do bid you: Depart."

The oni raised its head and howled. It held the note as its body began to fade. Toshi kept his eyes locked on the demon dog's gore-streaked muzzle, his hand on his swords.

The oni's howl lingered long after it had gone.

"I know you'd probably never presume to ask," Toshi said, "but I feel like I should say something. I really don't have any idea why all these kami know me by name and are out to get me."

Kobo shrugged. "Perhaps they see something we don't. Something you have forgotten or haven't yet done."

"That would make some sense," Toshi said. "I've gotten away with so much over the years. I guess it's only fair I take the blame for something I didn't do." He smiled. "At least the oni are on my side."

Kobo scowled. "Never believe that, oath-brother. Not for a second."

"All right, fine. Kami or oni alike confound me. And you religious, worshiping types have absolutely no sense of humor." He thought for a moment. "Say, oni are spirits, too, like kami. Could one of your spirits tell me why the others are chasing me?"

Kobo shook his head. "Too dangerous. I would not even try without my master here to supervise the ritual. And even if they did know, they would never tell you for free."

"Completely unlike the kami, of course." Toshi sighed. "Ah, well. Hidetsugu did send us out to solve this mystery on our own, didn't he?"

"He did, oath-brother."

"Then let's collect the gear we dropped back at the top of the hill. After that, we go deeper into the woods."

They scaled back up the heavily wooded hillside, and Toshi glanced back at the clearing. The remains of three kami and a handful of akki goblins were the only proof they had ever been there.

Once more, he wondered about the kami and their growing interest in him. He didn't understand why a powerful being of pure spirit would bother to cloak itself in flesh just for a shot at him . . . or anyone else, for that matter. The Kami War was a fact of life, but he feared he would never understand why. Toshi was far from humble, but he knew that the ways of kami and the people who prayed to them were almost completely opaque to him.

Why, he thought, with no hope of an answer, didn't everyone just leave everyone else alone?

PART TWO

SPIRIT GUIDES

Princess Michiko rode confidently atop a huge white stallion, standing in the special stirrups as she had been taught. She carefully nocked an arrow onto her longbow, stretched the cord tight, and let fly, missing the target by a clear foot.

Sharp-Ear of the kitsune-bito sighed. It was bad enough that Pearl-Ear had left him to mind the children while she went off on her secret mission of self-discovery, but she had also left him to do so under an assumed name.

"Try again," he called, as Michiko rode past in the other direction. She nodded and spurred her fine steed.

Not that assumed names were a problem for the kitsune. They were a playful people, and that playfulness often concealed taciturn, even secretive personalities. Pearl-Ear herself was a good example—she had been keeping secrets from her people and the Daimyo's alike. She hadn't told any of the kitsune elders about her concerns regarding Michiko's birth. She apparently hadn't told anyone in the tower about her rare meetings with the Daimyo, though she was one of a small handful that still saw Konda face to face.

The fox-man smiled. The residents of the tower didn't even know that Pearl-Ear wasn't her real name. Still, if she could spend years as Lady Pearl-Ear for the good of human-kitsune relations, he could be Sharp-Ear for a few days for the same good cause. He just wished the princess had someone else to mind her so that he would be free to explore.

From his raised observation platform, Sharp-Ear watched as Princess Michiko exchanged a few words with the rest of her little class. Two members of the Minamo Academy stood at the far end of the courtyard, offering encouragement and advice between runs at the target. The girl, Riko, was a promising student, but she had been taught to shoot from her own two feet and would have to unlearn quite a bit before she was comfortable on horseback. The boy Choryu showed little aptitude for archery and less interest. He was quite keen on the girls, however.

Sharp-Ear dropped his hand, and Michiko began her gallop. She maintained a good stance and balance as she thundered past Sharp-Ear and sank an arrow in the target's second ring, a foot or so away from the center.

"Good enough," Sharp-Ear called. "Again."

Riko cheered and Choryu waved. Michiko treated him to one of her dazzling smiles, then reined her horse in and headed back to the starting area.

Sharp-Ear followed Michiko with his eyes, keeping the young male wizard in his peripheral vision. Choryu was the white-haired youth from the assembly, the one beside the moonfolk before the kami attacked. Relations between the soratami and the kitsune-bito were cordial, but distant. Sharp-Ear hoped he could use the boy's familiarity with the moonfolk to garner an introduction. They might have valuable information to share. Besides, he had never interacted with moonfolk personally, and he was curious.

Michiko rode by his observation platform again and scored on the outer rim of the bull's eye. Sharp-Ear nodded to himself, then waved Michiko in. He noticed that she was still standing tall in the stirrups to keep her eye and arms steady, even though she had no arrow nocked.

"I think I'm improving, sensei."

"That's because you are. How are your legs?"

"Hmm? Oh, fine." She eased herself down into the saddle, wincing slightly.

"A little stiff, perhaps?"

"A little," she admitted.

"Well, hop down then and we'll start the next exercise."

Michiko shouldered her bow and swung her legs over so that she was sitting sidesaddle. She dropped to the ground and stumbled, but she recovered her balance before she fell. She looked concerned for a moment, then she smiled up at Sharp-Ear.

"So far, so good," he said. He stepped off the platform and landed gracefully next to the princess. "Come," he said. "Let's collect the others."

Michiko took one step forward, and as Sharp-Ear expected, almost fell again. Her legs seemed half-stuck in the standing saddle position, her feet spread wide and her knees locked. She could only manage an awkward duck-like waddle, which Sharp-Ear found both amusing and endearing.

Michiko noticed his smile and stopped. She crossed her arms and said primly, "Perhaps more than a little stiff, sensei."

Sharp-Ear laughed merrily. "Don't worry, Princess. You're still a novice. To master yabusame school archery, you have to train your legs as well as your eyes and arms. Another week or so and you'll be as limber as . . . well, as this."

Sharp-Ear pressed his heels together with his toes pointed outward. He bent at the knee, lowering himself almost to the ground. He held the squat for a few moments, his arms spread wide, and then he sprang high into the air. Twisting as he went, Sharp-Ear turned a complete somersault and landed silently next to Michiko, raising little more than a puff of dust.

Michiko clapped her hands. "I don't think I'll ever be that limber, sensei."

"Then I must train you harder, Michiko-hime." He offered the princess his arm and she took it.

"Now," he said. "Let's regroup." Together, moving slowly to accommodate Michiko's stiff legs, they walked to Riko and Choryu.

Riko rushed forward to meet them. "You're doing very well," she said. "I didn't come anywhere near the center until I had been practicing for months."

"You taught me how to draw and aim long ago," Michiko said. "I'm still learning how to stand on top of a galloping horse, however." She exaggerated her gait and made a great show of how stressful each step was. "Next time, I shall ride back to the tower."

As they approached Choryu, he bowed. "Well done, Princess." The wizard straightened and fixed his ice-blue eyes on Sharp-Ear. "You are a gifted teacher, sensei."

"I have a gifted pupil," Sharp-Ear said. "Three," he added, with a nod to Riko. As he turned back to Choryu, Sharp-Ear's smile widened. "Make that two."

Choryu winked. "It's true, I am not here to learn. But don't be offended. What use are arrows to a wizard?" He cupped his hands over his chest and chanted softly. Sharp-Ear heard the phrase "your power flows through me" twice, and then Choryu looked up and opened his hands.

A stream of sapphire-blue water surged up from his palms, rising high over their heads. The stream maintained its shape and speed as it curved around and flowed back toward the ground. At eye-level, the stream bent again, orbiting Michiko's head, then Riko's, then Sharp-Ear's. Both girls laughed, and Michiko slowly raised her index finger until it was touching the water.

When all three wore halos of blue connected by sapphire streams, Choryu spread his hands, drawing the water back into his palms.

Sharp-Ear clapped politely. "Impressive," he said. "But is water a weapon?"

Choryu dusted his hands on each other. "Absolutely. You've seen how a drop of water can cut through a rock?"

"I have. With the help of gravity and several uninterrupted decades to do its work."

Michiko giggled. Choryu scowled.

"Bad example," he said. "How about, 'you've seen how a wave can smash a ship?'"

"I have seen that, as well. Point taken." Sharp-Ear bowed to the princess. "That is the end of today's lesson. I will be in my quarters if you have any questions. Otherwise, I shall see you all tomorrow morning, right here."

His students bid him farewell, and then Riko began an excited critique of Michiko's archery. Choryu stood slightly apart, watching the princess intently.

Sharp-Ear followed the narrow path out of the courtyard and around the corner of the tower's external walls. He pressed himself against the wall and disappeared into the shadows, listening to his charges. Like all students, they seemed to forget the teacher once he was out of plain sight.

As he had done for the past several days, Sharp-Ear planned to remain unnoticed as he kept close enough to hear what they were saying. If they held to their pattern, they would return to the tower, make their way to Michiko's suite of rooms, and talk about things that were important to them. Michiko's progress. Academy gossip. The state of the war. Lady Pearl-Ear at court.

Sharp-Ear excused this intrusion on the princess's privacy as part of his promise to his sister. Pearl-Ear had told him to protect Michiko as well as train her, so he had not strayed more than a stone's throw from the princess since Pearl-Ear had left. He was learning all sorts of new things, and while most of them were only useful to other twenty-year old girls, some of what Michiko said or didn't say was extremely valuable.

And his sister was correct. Michiko's aura was bright and

considerate, but it had a terrible weight behind it. There was a vague inscrutability about her that loomed like a shadow and lingered like a sharp scent. It was neither benign nor malicious, but something else . . . something powerful.

The fox man sat silently in the shadows as his students made their way to the tower. His sharp ears easily distinguished Michiko's whisper from the wizards' chatter.

"It's not safe to say more. Wait until we're inside."

Choryu and Riko continued to banter, more loudly than was necessary. The trio mounted the steps to the tower entrance and went inside, their voices becoming vague and indistinct.

Sharp-Ear's ears twitched. Ah, to be a student again, he thought. Childish secrets and minor conspiracies, all to be kept from the nearest authority figure.

A plume of smoke drifted over the battlement and Sharp-Ear caught the scent of fire and blood. The kami were restless today, and there had been several skirmishes out in the wastes.

Sharp-Ear's grin faded. Sticking close to the wall, crept up to the tower entrance and then stepped in.

As he followed their progress up and ever up, Sharp-Ear felt his heart beat quicker. He had a dire burden to bear on behalf of his sister, his people, perhaps the entire world. And he very badly wanted to know what the princess wouldn't risk discussing in public.

* * * * *

For the third time in as many days, Sharp-Ear worked his way into the rafters above the ceiling and navigated his way toward Michiko's private reception hall. Below him, through a thin layer of plaster and stiff paper, lay a room full of comfortable couches and tasteful bolts of silk. The fox-man shimmied silently out to the center of the ceiling, balancing on a narrow beam.

"We can at least agree on one thing." Choryu's voice came clearly through the plaster ceiling tiles. He sounded restless. "They're never going to let you out, and you're never going to learn anything here."

"I never agreed to that," Riko answered. "I said that it's crazy not to consult the Academy, because that's where all the information is."

Michiko's voice was hushed, troubled. "But I did agree," she said. "It is as I have seen in my dreams. Towabara suffers, and I am sequestered in this tower. All Kamigawa suffers, and I have never even seen the borders of the kingdom I must one day rule." Her voice became flinty, sharper and harder than Sharp-Ear had heard it. "I have a responsibility to my people. I cannot fulfill it here, where I am held ignorant and aloof from the world around me."

"The libraries and scholars at Minamo," Choryu said, "have access to all the knowledge that has ever been. It's there for the finding."

The fire in Michiko's voice faded. "But my father and Lady Pearl-Ear both bid me stay and learn from Sharp-Ear. Perhaps we should wait until she returns and petition my father again."

"He'll refuse again," said Choryu. "Without explanation. Just like last time."

"He is my father, and lord of this kingdom. He does not have to explain."

"Of course not. Excuse my poorly chosen words. Long live the Daimyo.

"But with respect, Princess, I think your father's armies have proven that force of arms is not the answer. The kami attack, Towabara defends, and the battlefield grows ever wider and bloodier. We need more information before we can begin to settle the war, and we're not getting it here."

" 'We,' Choryu?" Riko's words echoed Sharp-Ear's own

thoughts. "You and I have no standing here. We risk nothing, yet you ask Michiko to risk all."

"We," Choryu repeated. "I have not been Michiko's friend as long as you, Riko, but that doesn't mean I am less loyal. This problem is not just hers, it is the entire world's. The Academy has always been dedicated to the greater good. I know there is something in the archives that can help us."

"They could if we had access." Riko's voice was strong and even. "The largest and most extensive libraries are forbidden to all but the highest-ranking masters. Even if we reach the Academy, there is no guarantee that we will be allowed to find the answers we seek."

"Oh, we'll make it," Choryu said. "We all ride well. My magic is powerful enough to protect us from bandits or wild animals, and you two have your arrows. If we go quickly and quietly, without fanfare, we can be there and back before Michiko is missed."

"And once we arrive?"

"Once we arrive, we rely on Michiko to get us into the libraries. The Academy has been working quite closely with the Daimyo's stewards. If we present ourselves properly, there's no way they'll refuse a polite request from Daimyo Konda's daughter.

"Besides, it's not like we're researching powerful spells. We just want to know what's going on around us. Maybe this has happened before. Any one of a dozen history books could tell us how it ended."

Riko sighed. "I do not think it will be that simple. If the answers were so easy to acquire, why haven't they been?"

Sharp-Ear nodded silently in agreement.

The female archer continued. "What do you think, Michiko? Before we decide if this is wise, tell me: is it even possible? Would you risk so much for the real possibility of nothing in return?"

Michiko's voice was soft and hesitant. "Choryu is right. I could be gone for days before my father noticed."

Choryu pounced. "And Lady Pearl-Ear won't be back before then, either."

Riko's robe rustled as she sank into one of the couches. "And Sharp-Ear?"

Michiko responded immediately, "Sharp-Ear would notice."

The fox-man grinned in the darkness. Pearl-Ear may have doubted his reliability, but he had at least impressed Michiko as an attentive instructor.

Choryu scoffed. "He currently has no standing at court. Who would he tell? Who would listen?" Sharp-Ear's smile faded.

Riko stood up quickly. "Any fool can say, 'Where is the princess?' If no one knows the answer, someone will go and look."

"Tell Sharp-Ear you're sick," the water wizard said. "Tell him you're injured. Tell him anything that will make him look the other way for a few days. If he doesn't raise the alarm, no one else will, either."

Sharp-Ear would not have believed that Michiko would be childish enough, selfish enough, or dimwitted enough to agree to a secret jaunt into war-torn countryside simply because she was bored. But he heard her assent in her voice, sensed it on the air even as Michiko uttered the words. It was not restlessness but duty that drove her.

"I have decided. We will go to the Minamo Academy."

Riko and Choryu both reacted, the former with concern and the latter with relief, but Sharp-Ear did not stay to listen. The fox-man immediately began inching silently back across the rafter.

"When do we leave?" Riko asked.

"Before first light tomorrow."

"Excellent," Choryu said. "This is for the best, Princess, you'll see."

Sharp-Ear crept along the beam, sadly shaking his head. Perhaps he had misjudged Michiko's maturity. Perhaps he was misjudging her now, and she really did intend to make the journey as some sort of token effort to be helpful in these violent times. In either case, the princess had decided to quit the tower and slip away from his kind tutelage and expert supervision. Pearl-Ear had bid him "be responsible." Here, now, it was clearly his responsibility to do something.

* * * * *

Gaining entry to Choryu's chambers was more difficult than Sharp-Ear had expected, but it was well within his abilities. There were very few locks or charms that could keep a determined kitsune out.

So when Choryu returned to his quarters and lit the lantern, he found Sharp-Ear stretched out comfortably on his bed.

"We must talk, wizard." Sharp-Ear stretched and rolled to the foot of the bed, where he stood eye to eye with Choryu. "About this trip you have planned."

The boy's strange blue eyes betrayed nothing. Choryu stared at Sharp-Ear quizzically, his spiky white hair seeming to vibrate in the firelight.

"I'm surprised to find you here, sensei," he said. "And disappointed."

"I cannot let Princess Michiko leave the tower."

Choryu stepped back and rebarred the door to his room. "No one is asking you to, sensei. We're just need you to trust Michiko-hime's judgment and step aside."

"It is your judgment I question." Sharp-Ear flexed his ankles and bounded lightly to the floor. "What makes you think you and Riko alone can protect her all the way to your academy gates?"

Choryu smiled. "Are you offering to come along?"

"No, wizard. I am canceling the whole trip."

Choryu shook his head. "We leave in the morning, sensei. You saw that thing at the assembly. It's no safer here than anywhere else. At least at the academy, we can study the situation, research the causes, isolate a solution."

Sharp-Ear scowled, and when he spoke, his voice growled from the back of his throat. "She thinks of you as her friend," the kitsune said. "And you're going to bring her before your masters so they can study her."

"I am her friend," Choryu flared. "And my masters are as concerned for her well-being as I am."

The young wizard bowed, his tone imploring, "Please, sensei. This is what the princess wants. We all seek answers to the same questions. At the academy, we can seek them together."

"No, my young friend. This is not the way. Wait for my sister's return. Send an organized delegation, an official caravan to the school with Michiko-hime at its head. And if Konda will not let her go, I will lead another procession to the school and ask them on behalf of the kitsune-bito. But you are about to make a terrible mistake and endanger the very person you seek to assist. I will not let you do it."

"I am sorry, sensei. But you cannot stop me."

Choryu splayed his fingers wide, palms facing backward. Sharp-Ear rushed forward, confident that he could bowl the wizard over before he could summon a stream of water.

But Choryu raised not a stream, but a sheet of water that materialized like a wall between the wizard and the fox-man. Sharp-Ear splashed into the vertical curtain of blue liquid. It was thicker, denser than real water.

The kitsune dug his toes into the wooden floor and tried to surge forward. The thick blue water held him in place, however. It still flowed and burbled around him, even waving the fur on his arms back and forth like a lazy field of undersea grass. But Sharp-Ear himself was frozen in place, unrestrained but unable to make his limbs function.

"You won't drown," Choryu said. "Nor will you hunger. You

are caught in a field that represents the precise moment when ice transforms to water. You are fixed, like the crystal, but flowing, like the droplet."

Sharp-Ear had not taken a deep breath before entering the trap, but his lungs did not ache. Tentatively, he tried to let his air out, but nothing happened and nothing within him changed.

"It will preserve and protect you for weeks, months if need be. But the princess will be back in a matter of days. I will release you then, and make amends. Forgive me, sensei."

Sharp-Ear watched in silent misery as Choryu painted several powerful charms on his door. The white-haired wizard blew out the lantern, bowed to Sharp-Ear, and pulled the heavy door shut behind him.

A whitish blue light crawled around the edge of the door in the doorjamb, making a complete circuit before sputtering out like a wet candle. Sharp-Ear was left alone, helpless, and quite possibly forgotten in the darkness.

His sister would certainly kill him if this went on much longer. He had best escape and salvage what he could of his reputation for responsibility.

* * * * *

Sharp-Ear waited for several hours, until the square of sunlight from Choryu's window had crawled to the edge of his liquid prison. The sun would set in a short while, but by then he would have gotten what he needed.

Choryu had obligingly explained the nature of the trap in which Sharp-Ear now languished, but the kitsune would have escaped the same way no matter what stasis/paralysis/immobility spell he had dredged out of the academy archives.

Sharp-Ear reminded himself not to underestimate the young wizard again. He had been much faster and much more powerful than the kitsune expected. But he was still young and foolish enough to trap a defeated foe rather than finish him off, and almost every trap involved keeping the target still.

The kitsune occupied a unique position among Kamigawa's tribal society. They straddled the social world of commerce and civilization on one side and the solitary realm of harmonious nature on the other. Kitsune clerics healed using human medicines and mystic ritual alike; kitsune warriors came as disciplined samurai bushi on the battlefield and as free-roaming independent rangers in the deep woods. They were gregarious among their own kind but elusive and sometimes off-putting to outsiders.

One thing they excelled at was motion. Their minds and bodies were fast, lithe, and graceful. They lived long lives, matured slowly, and existed in near-constant motion most of the time. In a word, Sharp-Ear, thought, we are excitable.

Sharp-Ear repeated the words to a powerful mantra in his mind as he watched the sunlight slide into the edge of his prison. Sunlight had warmth, but light itself had motion, energy, vitality. He was trapped in a transitive moment when one thing becomes another . . . with a little light, energy, and motion, he could complete the transformation.

"Dance," Sharp-Ear thought to the countless drops of blue liquid that flowed through the edge of the sunlit square. His vision fogged as the water seemed to boil around him. In his mind he repeated his mantra, focusing his mind, body, and spirit on channeling the power of the Great Sun Spirit.

Sharp-Ear heard a hiss and a watery pop, and then he fell forward in a great splash of cold blue water. Coughing, sodden, his eyes alight with triumph, Sharp-Ear stretched out his hand and reached into the vertical shaft of sunlight nearby.

"Thank you, old friend." The fox-man sprang to his feet, shook himself, and went to examine the charms on the door while he planned his next move.

The water wizard was correct in that Sharp-Ear's voice did not hold much sway with the rulers of Towabara. If he tried to report the princess before she left, she could simply deny it. If he tried after she left, she would likely be returned and punished severely . . . assuming she wasn't waylaid on the road and ransomed by bandits. And then not only would Sharp-Ear himself be in the soup for letting her go, but Choryu would have succeeded in the first part of his misguided effort to help Michiko. Sharp-Ear was far too wet and far too annoyed to allow that.

His mind fairly whirred as he read the symbols on the door and traced his finger around the doorjamb. He doubted he could talk Michiko out of the trip as easily as the wizard had talked her into it. If confronted, she would most likely agree with whatever Sharp-Ear said then find some other way to get out undetected.

He could allow her to go, catch up with her himself, and chaperone the remainder of the trip. At least that way she would have a proper guardian. Pearl-Ear would tear his tail off, but Michiko would be somewhat better protected.

The lithe kitsune-bito bounced up onto Choryu's table, pushed a square of ceiling aside, and darted up into the rafters. The wise thing to do would be to quietly sabotage the outing, make the travelers think that the spirits frowned on such a journey.

Sharp-Ear scowled, wrinkling his muzzle. Short of hobbling every horse in the Daimyo's stable, he didn't see how he could prevent them from traveling. Hobbling Michiko herself did cross his mind, but he rejected the idea and decided not to tell anyone he'd had it. He could put a sleeping draught in the wizard's morning tea, but that merely delayed the problem. They would try again as soon as they were all up to it.

He tried to follow Pearl-Ear's example, to think like her. What would a proper guardian, a responsible one, do? Sadly, a huge cause of the distance between himself and his sister was the fact that they thought nothing alike. It was like asking a fish to think like a bird, and he gave up that line of thought almost as soon as he opened it.

Then the fox-man's eyes sparkled. An idea, born from pieces of all his other ideas cobbled together, was taking shape in his mind. He knew where they were going. Perhaps he couldn't stop them, but he could steer them toward the safest possible course.

Sharp-Ear nodded happily. This was an energetic solution, one worthy of a kitsune trickster. His erstwhile students might think of it as a journey, but in reality it was just another training session in Sensei Sharp-Ear's dojo.

CHAPTER 10

In the cool, dark, predawn mist, Princess Michiko rode into Eigan Town proper for the first time since she was a child. Concealed beneath one of Riko's student robes and flanked by Riko and Choryu, Michiko kept her head bowed as they rode past the sentries. Traffic was light, but there were enough merchants and pilgrims moving to and from the tower to keep anyone from taking a closer look at the three student wizards headed back to Minamo.

Her heart hammered in her chest until they cleared the north ridge and the torches on the tower walls and guard houses went out of sight. She could still see the white tower stretching high into the clouds, but to anyone looking back down, she was just another traveler.

She and Riko had planned their route very carefully. They would skirt the northwest edge of the Jukai Forest, following one of the less-traveled paths that would also keep them far from the criminals to the west and the bandits to the south. They would remain on the border between Towabara and kitsune-bito territory, where dangers were few and every citizen was a loyal supporter of Konda. If they ran into trouble and had to reveal themselves, they would find no shortage of volunteers eager to assist the Daimyo's daughter.

By sunrise they were looking at the western boundary of the

Jukai, with an almost unbroken curtain of cedar trunks and boughs that stretched into the horizon. The road was wide enough for them to ride side by side, and as they had hoped, there were no other travelers to be seen.

Riko seemed nervous and Choryu excited, which did not surprise Michiko. Of the three, Riko had been the least interested in traveling incognito. She and Michiko were closer than sisters, and the student archer was clearly concerned about the dangers they would face. Choryu, on the other hand, seemed to live for exploration and adventure. He approached this trip as a challenge to be met, a chance to experience something new. He was especially animated this morning, almost jittery as they stole away and glancing back long after they were clear of Eiganjo.

Michiko stole a glance at Choryu from beneath her hood. He was handsome, with strong features and those dazzlingly clear blue eyes. His close-cropped white hair made him look even more manic, however, as if there was too much thought energy in his skull and it had bleached the hair above it and fused it into points.

Choryu was a year ahead of Riko and close to graduating. He would soon be a full-fledged water mage and an assistant instructor at the Academy. Riko said that he had focused on his spellcraft almost exclusively, advancing higher and faster than normal at the expense of every other subject. Riko herself adopted a wider focus, unsure of where her true interests lay.

Privately, Michiko thought Riko's archery was every bit as advanced as Choryu's magic, and she had told her friend so. She had not mentioned this to Choryu for fear of offending the proud young man. She liked both of her friends from the Academy, and at times she could see herself as a combination of the two. Perhaps she should consider enrolling at Minamo. It would help her to choose a discipline to focus on and to show her father that she was competent on her own.

They rode on, stopping only for a midday meal and to water the horses. Michiko relaxed more with each passing mile. The smell of cedar and the feel of fresh air on her face nourished her—she had not realized how stale and stifling it was in the tower. She hoped they would see some wildlife on the way. Besides horses and her father's dog, the tower had very little in the way of animal life.

Michiko's brow furrowed as she rode. There was very little life of any kind in the tower these days. Her father was always locked away in the upper reaches of the tower. The survivors of kami attacks were all dour, silent, and traumatized. Even the tower staff and the armies of Towabara looked wan and drained, almost overwhelmed by the fighting and the influx of refugees.

She straightened in her saddle. She was doing the right thing. When she was little, her nurse referred to her as "Towabara's hope for the future." If that were truly her destiny, then perhaps this journey was the first step toward it. Even if she didn't find the answers she sought, merely making the attempt would change her, teach her, maybe even redefine her. Michiko the sheltered princess was of no use during a Kami War. She was resolved to becoming someone who mattered, someone who could help.

"You see?" Choryu said, when the sun started to set. "We're halfway there and we've barely seen another soul."

"Halfway is the most dangerous point," Riko replied. "Our starting point and our destination are equally far away. We're completely removed from assistance at either end."

Choryu smiled, his eyes twinkling in the dusk. "Well, don't say that. You'll jinx us."

"Worse than you did by gloating at the halfway mark?"

"My friends," Michiko interrupted. "I am pleased with our progress, but I won't be comfortable until we get where we're going. How much longer can we ride before we have to rest for the night?"

"There's plenty of daylight left," Choryu said. "If we press on and pick up the pace, we can probably make it to the edge of falls."

"And the Academy is at the top of the falls."

"Close enough," Riko said. "But reaching the edge of the falls doesn't mean we're there. It's the largest river in Kamigawa, and by far the tallest and widest waterfall. On horseback, it will take at least another day to climb the path."

"It would only take half a day by boat."

"We can't rely on a boat being available. Nor can we expect a ferryman to keep our presence a secret."

"If we can hire a ferryman," Choryu smiled, "we won't need to keep our presence a secret. I would even send word to the headmaster that Princess Michiko has arrived."

"I would prefer to arrive unannounced," Michiko said.

"Excuse me, Princess. I only meant—"

"No need to explain," Michiko cut in. "Let's just keep going and see how far we go."

"Of course. Riko?"

"Agreed. But when it gets dark, I want you to help me weave a concealment spell so we can spread out our bedrolls and get some sleep. I don't fancy someone stumbling across us in the middle of the night."

The resumed riding in silence. Michiko took in the view of the forest to the east, straining to memorize every leaf. The rich browns and deep greens of the trees were such a striking contrast to the dull, dusty gloom that hung over her father's tower. Kamigawa was so colorful, and she had seen so little of it.

On the west sat the vast plains of Towabara, once fertile but now dry and lifeless due to three years of drought and two decades of war. Far in the distance, she could see the vast, rolling dust clouds that scoured the flatlands. She had heard soldiers tell of giving their swords a mirror shine just by leaving them out to be polished by the wind-driven grit.

As she mused, Michiko followed the dust storm's movement. It rolled over the plains like a cloud, making its way steadily west.

A strong breeze kicked up, rushing from the plains toward the forest, and Michiko squinted against it. Choryu's horse coughed, and Riko pulled her hood over her face.

"It's just a squall," Choryu called, raising his voice to be heard. "It will pass."

"Let's hope so," Riko said from under her hood. "I may ask you to conjure me a jug of water when it does."

"It's coming toward us," Michiko said.

"What?"

With cold dread in her throat, Michiko pointed at the distant dust cloud. "When the wind changed, the storm changed too. It's heading right for us."

Riko spurred her horse and came up beside Michiko. "Are you sure?"

"See for yourself. It's picking up speed."

"She's right," Choryu said. He patted his nervous mount, reassuring the beast. "It's bearing down on this spot."

"I don't like this," Riko said.

Choryu laughed. "It's just a storm, I keep telling you."

"It's a storm that changed direction."

"Changed direction with the wind."

"The wind felt natural. That storm feels anything but." She turned to Michiko. "The kami attacks have been spreading, haven't they?"

The princess nodded.

"And there was one in the tower recently, wasn't there?"

"Yes," Michiko said. She grabbed her friend by the arm. "Can you and Choryu shield us?"

The student wizards looked at each other, their expressions dismal.

"No," Riko said.

Choryu looked nervous for the first time since they'd cleared the tower gates. "I could conjure a flash flood to take us away from here," he offered.

"That's more likely to kill us as the dust storm," Riko snapped. "Not to mention the horses. We're better off taking cover in the trees. Once the storm passes, we can return to the trail."

The rolling dust cloud was now a few hundred yards away. It would reach them in a matter of minutes.

"Princess?" Choryu spoke gingerly. "I would not recommend going into the trees. There are—"

"Hold." Michiko held up a finger, her eyes still fixed on the storm. The student wizards followed her gaze.

Together, they watched as the dust cloud approached a large, lone tree. It was an old cedar, as thick as a person's waist, from a time long ago when the forest reached farther into the plains. As the storm cloud approached, the wind tore each of the cedar's leaves away and tossed them into the churning cloud of dust and debris. Then the cloud engulfed the tree, and they heard a terrifyingly loud crack as fragments of the ancient cedar were hurled back into the maelstrom.

"Into the forest," Michiko said. She prodded her horse, which sprang forward.

"Michiko!"

"Princess, wait!" Riko and Choryu followed, bringing their horses into a gallop and falling in behind Michiko.

The princess called out as she rode. "Deep as we can get before the winds catch us! One tree couldn't stop it, but perhaps the entire forest can." Free from the need to stand and take aim, the princess rode like the expert she was, putting even more distance between her and her friends.

Michiko broke through the tree line, weaving her steed in between the ancient cedars. There was no trail to follow, but she was covering ground quickly, charging deeper into the Jukai.

Riko and Choryu were far behind, but she could hear them yelling after her.

Michiko ignored their cries and spurred her horse on. She could hear the roar of the wind and felt the first stinging specks of dust through her academy robes.

They were well into the forest when the dust storm caught them. Wind and grit filled Michiko's ears, blinded her eyes, and almost lifted her from her saddle. She heard Riko calling for her to wait, and Choryu simply shouting her name.

She pulled up on the reins, but the horse refused to slow down. Foam flew from its lips into Michiko's face as the fear-maddened steed ran for its life.

They had been so careful, she thought. They had prepared for sentries and bandits, but now they were in real danger from one of the most common weather phenomena in all Towabara.

The wind's fury seemed to double, and Michiko lost sight of anything but the inside of her eyelids. Dust coated her throat and nostrils. She struggled to breathe. The horse beneath her was charging at full gallop, and it was all she could do to hang on.

The horse whinnied in terror and fell away beneath her. The reins were torn from her hands and Michiko could feel herself still sailing forward, tumbling gently as she soared. With her eyes still clogged with dust and tears, she could only wait for the inevitable impact and hope that she survived it. She was amazed she had traveled this long without hitting a tree.

The roar of the wind suddenly ceased, and Michiko felt as if she were floating, carried along by tender hands. She no longer felt the wind on her flesh, but she still could not open her eyes. If Riko and Choryu still called her name, she could not hear it, nor could she feel sting of the wind-driven grit.

Uncertain if she were conscious or dreaming, Michiko felt herself slipping away, lost in a void of quiet darkness.

* * * * *

She awoke to the sound of game birds calling to each other.

Michiko started and sat upright, squinting against the slanted beams of sunlight that pierced the forest canopy. It has been dusk when the storm hit, but now it seemed like midday. How many sunrises had she missed while she was asleep?

Nearby, a horse whinnied. She spied her mount, who was absently munching on a patch of tall grass.

She could scarcely believe her luck. This animal had been in headlong flight when Michiko lost consciousness. Either her father's stables produced exceptionally clever animals, or the kami that protected Towabara were watching over her.

She rose on unsteady legs and made her way to the horse. It snorted and shook its head as she took up the reins.

Michiko paused to remember the horse's name, then whispered, "Thank you, Kaze-san."

Kaze snorted again and offered her the top of his head. Michiko obligingly scratched between his ears.

As she patted her mount, Michiko scanned the forest for any sign of Riko or Choryu. She cupped her hands and called as loudly as she could, but she got no response. She felt cold, a lonely ache in her stomach, but Michiko tried to buoy her own spirits. She had survived the storm, somehow, so they must have as well. She tried not to think of Riko lying wounded and alone, calling Michiko's name. She tried not to think of Choryu, scouring the endless woods all the way back to the tower.

The real question was what to do next. She did not recognize where she was, and she had no idea how she had gotten there. She knew they had been traveling northeast, but after her long nap she wasn't sure where she was in relation to the Academy or her father's tower.

She decided to lead the horse in an ever-widening circle until she found her friends, the road, or something else that could tell her where she was. She was carrying enough food and water for three days, so she would not starve until then. She had her bow and a full quiver of arrows, so she was not defenseless. She was alone, a condition that usually eluded her as the Daimyo's daughter. Rather than afraid, Michiko felt exhilarated by a sense of purpose and the prospect of achieving something no one expected her to attempt.

Michiko began to walk, marking the trees she passed with the short knife she carried. She walked for hours without seeing another living thing. She shouted herself almost hoarse with no reply but a ghostly echo among the trees. She felt she was moving farther away from her friends, but she kept walking, leading her docile steed behind her.

The lost princess marked more trees and expanded her circle, thinking of her friends and their joint decision to travel to the Academy. Where Riko had been passionate about Michiko's opportunity to effect change in Kamigawa, Choryu had been militant about her responsibility to do so. His eyes flashed when he spoke of it, and the sheer force of his personality was at least as powerful as his arguments.

She came to an unfamiliar clearing, paused to look around, and sighed. Her search must have covered more than a mile, and there was still no sign of the wizards. She faced northeast, orienting herself against the sun, and mounted her horse.

If Choryu and Riko were here, she could guess what they would say. They would tell her to press on for Minamo and complete the journey. To return to the tower would be worse than never having left. Her father would rage and she would have armed escorts at her heels forever after. The only thing that would make that bearable would be if she could produce something concrete for the people of Towabara.

Michiko raised her heels to prod her horse forward, but stopped in mid-kick. Across the clearing, in the shade of a giant cypress, there flashed a yellow light. It sputtered at first, like a newly lit candle, but then it shone bright and strong. The tiny glow drifted up and out of the shadows, but Michiko could still see it plainly, even in direct sunlight. It floated to the center of the clearing and hovered there, pulsating like a beacon.

The princess smiled, tears of relief in her eyes. She had been driven from the path by a rogue storm, but now the spirits had sent her a sign. Lady Pearl-Ear had often told her kitsune-bito folklore about foxfire, hovering flames that led lost travelers to safety. Perhaps this was foxfire in action. Perhaps Towabara's patron kami of Sun and Justice had taken pity on her. Perhaps they were rewarding her initiative or even encouraging her to continue.

She had never spoken of it to anyone but Riko, but Michiko had heard whispers of a dire spirit curse that hung over her father's tower. She was uplifted by the presence of the friendly light, grateful for the good will of the foxfire and the kami who sent it. She was kept hidden behind stone walls in Eiganjo Castle, but here, in the depths of the Jukai Forest, the spirit world smiled upon her.

The foxfire glow bobbed up and down, then drifted toward the far side of the clearing. Michiko prodded her horse and it trotted forward a few yards.

The orb of light glowed brighter. It withdrew further. Michiko encouraged her mount and followed another few yards.

Then the orb passed through a line of cedars, out of sight. Michiko brought her horse to a trot, and as they passed through the same trees she saw the orb ahead. It was traveling northeast, slowly enough that she could follow it but quickly enough that she had to keep moving to do so.

Michiko stared at the foxfire light as she rode, hypnotized by its soothing glow and comforted by its company. It was probably a mere spell effect, but whatever it was, it signified that someone was aware of her situation and was trying to help. Even if it hadn't been sent by Riko and Choryu, it was leading her in the right direction.

The princess guided her horse through the forest, keeping one eye on the spirit guide and one on the trees around her. As she rode forward into her future, she wanted to impress upon her memory the beauty and danger that surrounded her in the present.

CHAPTER 11

Riko was beside herself. Her anxiety showed in her face, in her body posture, in every visible aspect of her being. Choryu himself fought against a sickening chill in his guts, struggling to keep his jaw set and his eyes resolute.

He had utterly failed. Michiko was gone and he had failed her, failed Riko, failed his masters back at Minamo. If he couldn't recover the princess and escort her safely to the academy, he would be casting his own life and that of everyone he knew into the most dire peril.

"We have to keep looking," Riko said for the hundredth time. Choryu had stopped listening to her long ago. So long as the archer kept searching, she could say whatever she liked.

Where had Michiko gone? They were all within sight and sound of each other, but that cursed storm hit and seemed to swallow the princess whole. When Choryu and Riko dug out from under the dust, they found they were on the opposite side of the road—they had followed Michiko east and wound up to the west.

They retraced their steps and found the place where the storm had driven them from the road. There were three sets of hoofprints leading off the road and into the forest for a hundred yards or so, and then all three disappeared. It was like the storm lifted the horses into the air and threw them each in different directions.

Off to his right, Choryu heard Riko calling for Michiko. His fellow student was distraught about what had happened, but she didn't know half the extent of their predicament. She had no idea.

Choryu quietly slipped down into a trench and then jogged about a hundred yards until he was well clear of Riko. He glanced around, spread his open palms out wide, and began to chant.

"Ichikawa, spirit of the great river," he chanted softly. "Your power flows through me. Hear my words, kami of the rushing waves. Your power flows through me."

Be quiet, a cold, hollow voice said. It felt cold in his ears, so cold it burned.

Where is Princess Michiko?

"Lost," Choryu whispered. "I was bringing her to the school as instructed. We were driven apart by a freak storm."

Fool. Who told you to take her from the tower?

"M-my instructions came from Headmaster Hisoka himself. I saw the scroll with his seal upon it."

Hisoka takes his orders from me. From now on, you will do nothing that I did not instruct you to do.

"No," Choryu gulped. "I will obey. What must I do?"

Retrieve her and complete your assignment. Under no circumstances let her venture too deeply into the forest. The snakes are restless and their kami is poised to interfere. Keep her away from the spirits of nature and the forest-dwellers who worship them. Else all we have worked for will come undone.

Protect her, water wizard. Without her, you are less than meaningless.

"But how can I find her? Where shall I look?"

The bodiless voice sighed in exasperation. *Who were her guardians in the tower?*

"Her father?" Choryu hesitated. "Kitsune," he said, with greater conviction. "Foxfolk."

Then seek her to the north where the foxes dwell. She will most likely be drawn there. Whatever finds her will also find you. Pray that it is benevolent.

"Choryu!" Riko's voice sounded near panic even at this great distance.

"Over here," the water wizard called. "Come quick! I think I've figured out which way she went!"

Choryu waited as Riko came crashing through the underbrush. The cold, patrician voice lingered in his ears. He was afraid for Michiko. He was afraid for the future of Kamigawa.

And under the cloud of his unseen patron's ire, he feared greatly for himself.

"Michiko," he whispered. "Stay safe. We're coming for you."

* * * * *

Michiko rode throughout the day and on into the evening. The shining orb always stayed about twenty yards ahead of her, but it remained in sight at all times. She had dined on trail bread and fruit as she rode, and she'd drained half her goatskin of water. She felt rested, relaxed, and eager to ride on.

As the sun disappeared and darkness settled over the forest, Michiko was torn. The foxfire was waiting up ahead, impatiently flashing at her. She could easily follow it in the gloom, but she was not willing to ride or walk Kaze over terrain she could not see. One misstep could result in a broken leg for the horse or worse, especially if he fell on her.

"I must wait here," she called. "I must wait until morning." She slid down from the horse and began unrolling her pack.

The orb shot toward her like a bird, stopping a few yards from her mount. It circled overhead, flaring from near-blinding light to almost complete darkness.

"You must wait with me," she said. "Or go on alone." She pulled an apple from her supplies, cut off a section, and held it out for Kaze.

The glowing orb buzzed furiously, flickering among the cedar boughs overhead. When Michiko spread out her bedroll and started to build a small fire, the foxfire floated down, illuminating her efforts. Once the blaze was going strong, the ball of light seemed to fasten itself to a tree branch, hanging like a lantern over the princess's solitary bivouac.

Michiko smiled, careful to keep her back to the orb. She was still following the foxfire on faith, but she was doing so according to her schedule. It could go on with out her, but it would not.

As the campfire crackled, Michiko's thoughts drifted to the spirits. Some kami were still friendly to the citizens of Towabara, despite twenty years of strife between the human and spirit worlds. She wondered if the great kami were like the leaders of great nations, with their own individual goals and spheres of influence. If one kami attacked a village, would another come to the villagers' aid? Or were they like the tribes of Towabara, powerful in their own right but subordinate to a hierarchical leader like her father?

When it came to honoring the spirits, there were almost as many schools of thought as there were spirits to worship. She practiced the rituals and spoke the prayers that were common to her father's tribe, but her studies had exposed her to the songs of the forest druids, the group meditation of Minamo sages, and the complicated symbols of kanji magicians. Nearly everything in Kamigawa had a spirit, and it seemed that everyone had a different method for invoking those spirits.

Michiko cut herself a branch and wedged it into the ground. She hung a small pot from the end of the stick, poured more of her water into the pot, and then positioned the pot over the fire. The water quickly began to boil, and Michiko scattered a handful of tea leaves into it.

The most powerful kami, such as Towabara's patron spirits,

could be invoked to affect the physical world. Her father's generals prayed to Cleansing Fire before they rode into battle and performed rites to gain favor from the Sun. She had heard both spirits manifested when her father won the climactic battle to unify the tribes of Towabara. Also, Lady Pearl-Ear taught her that the cedar spirits worshiped by the kitsune-bito would aid some and hamper others, based on how the humans treated the forest.

But until the Kami War started, it was unheard of for a kami to attack the physical world. Absent invocation, prayer, or ritual, the kami were purely spiritual beings who were content to remain in the spirit world. It wasn't until after Michiko's birth that kami attacks became frequent and eventually commonplace.

A wave of bitter grief surged through the princess, and she shifted uncomfortably on her bedroll. She pulled the stick with the teapot out of the fire and set it on the ground to cool.

Her mother had been among the first killed by hostile spirits. Michiko had not known Yoshino, and her father would not speak of her. Daimyo Konda had ordered all Yoshino's likenesses removed from the tower after her funeral. Lady Pearl-Ear kept a small portrait of Yoshino in a golden cameo, but she rarely wore it. She had shown it to Michiko several times, however, usually on the day of the princess's birth.

Michiko had memorized every finely etched line of that portrait. She believed that she favored her father physically, but that her personality came largely from her mother. Lady Pearl-Ear had said so once, indirectly, complimenting an essay Michiko had written. When pressed, the fox-woman grew distressed and changed the subject.

As Michiko sipped her tea directly from the pot, the glowing orb suddenly swooped down to eye level. It darted left, then back in front of Michiko's face, then left again. It was buzzing excitedly and flashing on and off in succession.

Instinctively, Michiko followed the foxfire's motion with her eyes. She spit out her tea and leaped to her feet, smoothly taking the bow and quiver from the horse's back.

Several yards away, the air had grown thick and was folding in upon itself. The denser cloud slowly sculpted itself into a series of squat and burly bulbs, all emanating from a central core of lumpy, fibrous material.

Michiko nocked an arrow and took aim. She had personally seen half a dozen kami attacks, but the one in the tower was freshest. She remembered Sharp-Ear's off-the-cuff advice when he first started training her: the larger the target, the easier it is to hit, and if nothing else presents itself, go for the eye.

The gnarled, root-like shapes had no eyes that she could see, so she trained her arrow at the center of the mass. She was hesitant to fire until she had to—there was no need to antagonize the creature until it attacked. The mass was now as big as a pony, and she decided to hold her fire until it was as big as Kaze.

Perspiration formed on the princess's brow as she waited. She remembered her previous train of thought, and wondered if the bow was the proper tool for this encounter. If this was all part of her destiny, as her dreams and her spirit guide seemed to indicate, perhaps she was meant to reach out to the enraged kami instead of fighting them.

"Hear me," she told the growing mass of bulbs and roots. "I am Princess Michiko of Towabara, daughter of Daimyo Konda. I do not wish to fight you, but to understand you. We need not be enemies. Will you speak with me?"

In response, the kami continued to grow. Two of the bulbs came to a single point over the main mass. They were joined by another pair, and then another. As Michiko watched and waited for a response, a skeletal facsimile of a human rib cage formed before her, complete with a fibrous brown heart that throbbed at its center.

Then the rib cage split vertically and lunged forward at Michiko, snapping like some great pair of jaws. She released her arrow straight into the thing's heart, and it recoiled, snapping shut well clear of her. A cloud of greenish-black spores puffed out from the pseudo-organ, and Michiko covered her mouth and nose to keep from inhaling them.

More rib-cage maws formed around the original one, each with snapping jaws and a dense, beating organ within. Being pierced through the heart did not seem to affect the first one after the initial shock of the arrow sinking in. Michiko nocked another arrow as a light flashed from the corner of her eye.

She spared a glance toward the light and saw the foxfire orb hovering over Kaze's saddle. It flashed frantically, urging her to follow.

The princess looked back at the monster, growing larger all the time. It would soon have more mouths than she had arrows, and her weapons didn't seem to be doing much good in the first place. She let fly the bolt she had ready, then vaulted up onto the horse's back.

As her feet found the stirrups, the glowing orb grew brighter and more intense—so bright that she could see the ground for twenty yards in all directions. Her spirit guide had led her this far and was now capable of leading her on. She might not be able to defeat the kami, but she was certain she could outrun it.

She spurred Kaze just as three of the rib cages shot forward, snapping like hungry birds. Michiko instinctively stood upright as Kaze galloped forward, aimed back over the horse's hind end, and fired a second arrow into the creature's original heart.

The central jaws recoiled once more, blocking the others and granting Michiko time to ride clear. She heard a hideous mewling and the snapping of bony jaws behind her, but she kept her eyes fixed on the terrain as she steered Kaze through the maze of trees.

Then, the glowing guide doubled back and rushed past her like a shooting star. A cry formed on Michiko's lips, but she kept her composure and pulled back on the reins. She fumbled with another arrow for a split second and then turned, ready to fire.

The glowing orb surged straight into kami's body, blasting through multiple jaws like a cannonball through thatch. When it reached the center of the mass, the foxfire's glow became too bright to look at. Michiko shielded her eyes and smelled a horrific burning stench just as the orb exploded, sending dirt and debris hurtling across the forest.

The blast snuffed out her campfire, and the orb's light was also gone. For a moment, Michiko could only sit in the sudden darkness and comfort Kaze. She began to wonder if she could sit perfectly still until daylight, or if another kami would come for her in the night.

A glimmer of yellow light shone from the shattered remains of her campsite. It grew into a brighter glimmer, then a glow. Considerably diminished, the foxfire orb rose once more and floated toward Michiko and Kaze.

It stopped in front of the princess's face and flashed wearily.

"I am sorry," Michiko said. "From now on, I will follow until you stop."

The orb flickered and then grew brighter, recreating the shine that made travel possible. She would have to go no faster than a canter, but Michiko knew she could navigate by the orb's reduced light if she were careful . . . and no more kami attacked.

Slowly, carefully, she followed the foxfire as it lead her northeast.

* * * * *

Pearl-Ear sat meditating in the early morning mist. Merely being in her home village had a restorative effect on her, but she was no closer to the answers she sought.

Two days ago, she had met with Lady Silk-Eyes, the village

elder and one of the most respected kitsune-bito in all Kamigawa. The wise old fox had told her to sit, remain awake, and clear her mind. He said she must empty her thoughts before attempting to organize them. Since then, Pearl-Ear had spent her time sitting, chanting, and fasting, consuming only fresh water from the village well and the occasional pot of tea.

The kitsune-bito had villages scattered all along the northwestern section of the Jukai. Taken together, the foxfolk population was barely a third that in the Daimyo's tower, but they had proven their worth to Towabara as both citizens and warriors. They were a careful, circumspect people who liked visitors, but rarely invited them. Pearl-Ear was enjoying the solitude and the cleansing effect of her vigil, but her problems were too many and too pressing to be completely dismissed.

She sat with eyes closed in the doorway of her hut, provided by the elder for the duration of her stay. In the distance, she heard the careful tread of a kitsune-bito, which served to announce the foxfolk's arrival. If it had been anything but a formal visit, she would not have heard a sound until the visitor opened the gate.

"Lady Pearl-Ear of Towabara?"

Pearl-Ear opened her eyes. "I am Lady Pearl-Ear of the kitsune-bito," she corrected. "It is only of late that I have been a member of the Daimyo's court."

The visitor was another female, roughly Pearl-Ear's size but visibly younger.

"Forgive me, noble Lady Pearl-Ear. "I am called Cloud-Fur."

"Cloud-Fur. Welcome."

"The elder sent me to fetch you. You have a visitor."

"Here?" Pearl-Ear straightened and retied her robes. "Is there trouble in the tower?"

"I cannot say. I was asked to bring you around so that you might greet a traveler from Eiganjo."

"Was it a messenger? A soldier?"

"I have not seen the visitor, only the elder."

"Thank you, Cloud-Fur. I will come with you now."

Together, the two kitsune-bito made their way across the sparsely populated village. At this early hour the clerics were in prayer, the farmers hard at work, and the warriors were patrolling the woods. The foxfolk homes were spaced wide and many were partially concealed by low-hanging cedar boughs or great sheets of climbing ivy. There were larger kitsune villages, grander ones with gleaming white towers, but they were all to the south, closer to akki territory and Godo's bandit horde.

At the entrance to Lady Silk-Eyes's dwelling, Cloud-Fur stopped. Her mission complete, she bowed to Lady Pearl-Ear and headed back into the village.

Pearl-Ear watched her go and then turned to the elder's hut. Most likely the Daimyo had sent someone after her, calling her back to the tower. As she passed through the waist-high gate into the elder's yard, Pearl-Ear was mentally preparing her polite refusal. She had made progress here in the village, but she needed more time before she was ready to return to the tower.

She stopped at the doorway and called, "Sensei?"

"Come in, Lady Pearl-Ear. We have been expecting you."

The interior of the hut was dark, but Pearl-Ear's eyes quickly compensated. The elder kitsune sat at the far end of the room next to an overstuffed straw mattress. The occupant of the mattress was asleep.

"Wake, child," Lady Silk-Eyes murmured. "Lady Pearl-Ear is here."

The sleeping form stirred. The young woman sat straight up, and Pearl-Ear recognized her a heartbeat before she could speak her first breathless words.

"Lady Pearl-Ear," Michiko cried happily. "Praise the spirits, I made it!"

CHAPTER 12

A thousand thoughts churned through Pearl-Ear's mind but she remained speechless. As Lady Silk-Eyes lit a lamp and filled the room with a soft yellow glow, Michiko struggled free of the mattress.

Why had she come here? How had she managed the journey alone? What shockwaves had the princess's disappearance sent through the Daimyo's tower?

As Lady Silk-Eyes quietly left the hut, Michiko's feet found the floor. She rushed into Pearl-Ear's waiting arms.

"The spirits led me to you," Michiko said. "I was lost in the forest and the spirits sent me a guide. Foxfire brought me straight here . . . it even helped me battle a kami!"

"Breathe," Pearl-Ear whispered, hugging the child close. "Start from the beginning. What were you doing in the forest?"

Michiko hesitated, then said, "I was on my way to the Minamo Academy. I was separated from my party by an unnatural storm."

Lady Pearl-Ear pushed Michiko back and held the princess by the shoulders. "Was it a kami attack?"

"No, that came later. I lost Riko and Choryu in the woods and—"

"Riko? Choryu? What were they doing there?"

Michiko's eyes never wavered. "We were going to the Academy to look for answers."

"What? That is sheer madness."

"It is not, sensei. The kami attacks grow worse all the time. They even attacked my father's advisors in council. He would not let me seek help from the Academy, so I sought it on my own."

"You are a very foolish girl, then. There is far more at stake here than your pride or your need for the Daimyo's attention."

Michiko frowned. "I did not do this for me. Not for pride or the rare gift of my father's approval."

Lady Pearl-Ear felt her expression hardening. "But you disobeyed your father, and you disobeyed me. The Daimyo forbade you to leave the tower, and—"

"And I am the Daimyo's daughter," Michiko replied with a rebellious flip of her head. "I was acting for the good of my people and all Kamigawa."

"Sharp-Ear should have stopped you. I will tell him so when I see him."

"Sharp-Ear didn't know. And he couldn't have stopped me if he did."

"Sharp-Ear didn't know," Pearl-Ear echoed sarcastically. "And that makes everything all right?"

Michiko suddenly crossed her arms and scowled. "I thought you'd be happy to see me. I didn't expect a lecture."

"You quit your father's house in secret and exposed yourself to unimaginable danger. You dishonored my brother, and me for leaving him in charge. A lecture is the least of your worries."

"But don't you see? My journey was decreed by fate and guided by the spirits. I dreamed of taking a larger role in the Kami War. I escaped the tower as easily as crossing a room. And despite freak storms and angry kami, I am here, where you yourself came to gain better perspective on the dangers that threaten Kamigawa. Think how much I can learn here, how much I can help you learn."

Pearl-Ear paused. After the initial shock of seeing Michiko and the reflex scolding that followed, she was noticing something new about the princess. Michiko had always been lighthearted and energetic, but now she was something more. She seemed to have a purpose, something that was driving her. And she was far more confident than Pearl-Ear had seen.

"Tell me more," Pearl-Ear said, "about this journey. You were caught in a storm?"

"We were attacked by a storm. It changed direction with the wind and swept right over us."

"Describe the storm."

"It was a large, fast-moving windstorm, a spinning cloud of dust. The wind was very forceful. It tore down an ancient tree standing alone on the plains, but the forest protected us."

Pearl-Ear nodded. Some things were starting to make a little more sense. "And the spirit guide?"

"A glowing ball, about two fists wide. Like the light from a small lantern without the lantern. I thought it might be kitsune foxfire. It guided me through the Jukai and defended me from a horrible grasping kami made of roots."

"Foxfire. I see. And you went on this ill-advised trip because of a dream?"

"I have been dreaming about the horrors of war, and of me standing by, doing nothing. I took it as a message, and acted on it." She fell to her knees and grabbed the hem of Lady Pearl-Ear's robe. "Sensei, please. I was sent on this trip and guided through it by friendly spirits. Don't you see? This means that not all the kami are against my father. It is their love that sparked this journey, and their concern that got me here safely."

"It was not friendly spirits," Pearl-Ear said. "It was my foolish brother."

Michiko accepted Lady Pearl-Ear's hand and got to her feet. "Sharp-Ear? We left him back at the tower."

"Not so. The storm you describe? That image is from an old teaching story we kitsune show our kits. It demonstrates that the world is alive, interactive, and always changing—a tree grows on the flatlands, a great wind levels the tree, but the forest halts the wind.

"And the foxfire? That is an old kitsune trick many adolescents use on travelers to lead them astray. In harsher times, our samurai would use it to lead enemy forces into traps or away from populated villages. These days, it's just another prank played by tricksters."

Michiko's mouth hung open in shocked silence. "But it led me here. . . ."

"Which is where I imagine Sharp-Ear wanted you to go. This business about fighting kami supports my theory. An adolescent wouldn't be able to use foxfire as a weapon. But he can."

The princess seemed on the verge of tears. "But why would he frighten us and drive away my friends?"

"He must have figured you'd be safest with me. I'm sure he meant no harm to Riko and Choryu, it's just that he doesn't usually stop to think about all the consequences of his actions."

Michiko sagged as if all the vitality had been drained from her body. "So we have no friends among the kami. Their war against us is total."

In that moment the princess was the image of her mother, complete with Yoshino's ability to infect everyone nearby with her mood. Pearl-Ear suddenly felt so sorry for the devastated princess that her anger melted and she swept Michiko up in her arms again.

"Not so," she whispered. "Your father has powerful allies in the spirit world as well as this one, else his tower would have fallen decades ago. This is a foolish thing you have done, Michiko, but we can derive some good from it. When we return to Eiganjo Castle, I will petition your father again for a trip to the Academy. I will insist upon it. Only this time, I will go with you and we will travel with a phalanx of armed guards."

Michiko laughed, her eyes still moist. "Thank you."

"Now," Lady Pearl-Ear said. "We must find your friends. Where did you lose them?"

Michiko's eyes brightened. "We were halfway to the academy. I searched for them after the storm, but they were gone. I expect they returned to the tower, or went on to the school to wait for me."

"Very well. I will assemble a search party—"

"That is not necessary, Lady Pearl-Ear." Lady Silk-Eyes spoke from the doorway leading outside. "Our patrols picked up two Minamo students in the woods only this morning. They claimed to be lost on their way back to the school. They are being seen to on the far end of the village."

Pearl-Ear brightened. "There, you see? Your friends are safe." She turned to the elder. "And my brother?"

Lady Silk-Eyes shrugged. "That I do not know."

"Thank you, elder." To Michiko, she said, "We can travel back to the tower together, you and I and the wizards. On the way, we can work out what to tell your father."

"Then you should make haste, Lady Pearl-Ear." Lady Silk-Eyes came back into the hut. "There are powerful forces gathering all around us, and they are about to converge on this village."

"Of course, elder. We will go at once."

Lady Silk-Eyes reached out, took Pearl-Ear's hand, and squeezed. "Be careful, Lady Pearl-Ear." She nodded toward Michiko. "Some humans from Towabara think we can see the future, but in reality we are merely observant. We see the world around us clearly, which makes it easier to tell what can happen. From there, it's all down to experience and guesswork.

"I see that your trials have only begun," the kitsune elder said, squeezing Pearl-Ear's hand. She reached out with her free hand and took hold of Michiko's. "And your journey, my child, is far from over."

Lady Silk-Eyes dropped their hands and folded her arms into

the sleeves of her robe. "Off you go, my dears. If you are still in the village come midday, come see me again. We will share a meal and conversation." She looked meaningfully at Lady Pearl-Ear.

"I would be honored," Michiko said.

"Excellent. Perhaps we shall see each other again." Lady Silk-Eyes moved over to the fireplace and began assembling a pile of sticks. Whistling, she poured water into a teapot and broke out a bundle of tried tea leaves.

"They're waiting," she said, without turning.

Pearl-Ear guided Michiko from the hut, gently pushing her ahead. She hesitated for one moment after Michiko was out the door, glancing back at the elder.

The touch of Lady Silk-Eyes's hand on hers lingered. The village elder's somber prediction weighed likewise on her mind.

But the old fox did not look up from her fire building, and Pearl-Ear quickly joined her own student outside.

* * * * *

Lady Silk-Eyes had said Riko and Choryu were being attended to, but Pearl-Ear suspected they were being guarded instead of pampered. As she and Michiko approached the kitsune samurai compound, she found the sights, sounds, and scents of warriors preparing for battle.

A gleaming white kitsune male stopped them at the heavy wooden gate to the compound. He made no introduction as he held up his hand, halting Lady Pearl-Ear and Michiko.

"The elder sent us," Pearl-Ear said. "The humans you found were separated from Princess Michiko." She waved towards the princess, who bowed formally.

The kitsune samurai kept his hand on his long sword. He thumped the closed gate with his free hand, narrowed his eyes over his long snout, and then jerked his head toward the compound.

The gate creaked open. Another pair of armed kitsune rangers stood inside, each dressed for the deep woods in gray-brown robes.

"They're here for the wizards," the gate sentry said.

The new kitsune both gave Michiko a long, appraising look. Lady Pearl-Ear could tell they were drawing in the princess's aura. Apparently satisfied, they waved Lady Pearl-Ear and Michiko through the gate.

"Follow," one said.

Pearl-Ear's unease grew as they crossed the compound. The camp was not large, but there were more than thirty kitsune samurai and rangers visible . . . which meant there were far more hidden or patrolling nearby. Each of them was armed and dressed in drab colors that would serve as camouflage among the trees. Immersed in her own meditations on the far side of the village, she'd had no idea so many warriors were gathered here.

The samurai led them to a small hut near the back of the compound. Pearl-Ear counted ten more warriors as they went. This was more than a defensive force for the village—it was a small foxfolk army.

Inside, they found Riko and Choryu eating from rough wooden bowls at a long table against the wall. Riko let out a happy yelp and almost upset her meal as she sprang up.

"Michiko!" she cried. The princess went to meet her friend, and the two embraced. "We thought we'd lost you. Were did you go?"

"Where did you? I spent hours looking for you."

"Praise the spirits you're all right," Choryu said. "I would never have forgiven myself if—"

"Forgiveness is something you should seek, not grant," Pearl-Ear said. "All three of you."

Choryu defiantly held Lady Pearl-Ear's glare. "Something had to be done. We were only attempting—"

"I don't care, Choryu. I just want to get us all safely back to the tower."

Choryu scowled, but said no more. As Michiko recounted her adventure in the woods, Pearl-Ear checked the interior of the hut. Four kitsune samurai and one officer stood along the walls, silent but alert. Riko and Choryu seemed slightly haggard and distressed by their experiences, but they were largely unhurt. Each bore a series of minor cuts and bruises. The white-haired student remained at the table, sullenly stirring his soup with a wooden spoon.

"We searched," Riko was saying. "And never stopped. But we never saw your horse's tracks once we left the road. The more we searched, the deeper we went into the forest. I've never been so lost."

"How did you find your way here?"

"We didn't. The kitsune found us, perhaps half a day's walk from here. Choryu guessed you'd come this way, and here you are."

"Choryu," Michiko called. "You're awfully quiet. Don't despair, my friend. We are safe here."

"I am not despairing," Choryu said. "I am humbled by the generosity of our hosts." He fixed his penetrating eyes on Michiko's. "And I am eager to complete our journey safely."

This last remark went by without comment as the girls went over to the table, still chattering away. Pearl-Ear took a closer look at the white-haired wizard. He was sporting a deep purple bruise over one eye and his left arm hung stiffly by his side.

"Where is the leader of these warriors?" Pearl-Ear asked.

A large gray samurai officer stepped forward, accompanied by a single ranger. "Here," he said. "I am Silver-Foot."

Silver-Foot was taller and broader than the rest, with two white stripes running along the fur on top of his head. He bobbed a perfunctory bow to Lady Pearl-Ear, and the ranger followed his lead.

"I hope you weren't put to too much trouble by my charges."

The lower-ranking samurai grinned. "The boy resisted, but we reasoned with him."

Pearl-Ear traced a soft-furred finger under her eye, outlining an area as big as Choryu's bruise. She raised an eyebrow.

"He attempted to cast a spell on us." The samurai shrugged, opening his hands to the sky. "But no harm was done. Besides, he was easy to carry."

"Indeed. Please accept my thanks on behalf—"

"You are Lady Pearl-Ear from the Daimyo's land." Silver-Foot's handsome exterior disguised a brusque personality

"I am."

"We have reports of an armed and mounted party making its way up the western border of the forest. They came from the tower in Eiganjo."

"That is the path my student and her friends took. They are most likely the Daimyo's retainers, searching for Princess Michiko."

Silver-Foot's face wrinkled. "So they aren't coming here."

"I suppose they could find their way here if my charges left tracks. But no, there is no reason to expect them. What is it, Silver-Foot-san? Why are there so many warriors here, and why are you so dour?"

Silver-Foot bobbed again. "No offense intended, Lady Pearl-Ear. But your students being here is a bad thing, one that you should have prevented. They are lucky we found them when we did."

"What do you mean?"

"Two days ago, far to the south," Silver-Foot said, "we found the remains of a scouting party. One scout had had his skull cracked by a hard, blunt instrument. Another had been stabbed repeatedly with small, dirty blades. We found the third hung up in the branches of a tree with arrows through his legs and chest."

Pearl-Ear tilted her head. "Bandits? This far north?"

Silver-Foot shook his head. "Worse."

Pearl-Ear's voice dropped to a whisper. "Hostile kami?"

The officer sneered again. "Spirits don't use crude clubs and dirty knives, milady. But to continue: yesterday, before we found your wandering wizards, we came across a single felled tree. It hadn't been cut down with saw or axe, but instead had been chiseled down, bit by bit, with something small and hard. Whoever did that also carved a trench in the trunk and lit a large fire there."

Over at the table, the wizards and Michiko were done reacquainting themselves and had begun to listen to Pearl-Ear's conversation with Silver-Foot. Pearl-Ear stepped forward and bowed her head. Silver-Foot lowered his own until their foreheads touched.

"I don't understand," Pearl-Ear whispered. "What felled the tree? What does this all mean?"

Before the officer could answer, a cry came from the main gate.

"All hail Elder Lady Silk-Eyes!"

Pearl-Ear and Silver-Foot straightened up. Through the open doorway, she could see the wizened elder approaching, escorted by the same two kitsune samurai.

"I will answer you," Silver-Foot whispered, "as soon as the elder makes her wishes plain."

Lady Silk-Eyes swept into the room, and all the kitsune present fell to one knee. Michiko and Riko rose from the table and likewise genuflected in honor of the elder, but Choryu remained seated at the table. The proud youth was probably unaccustomed to being treated so roughly. Perhaps, Pearl-Ear thought, he would learn from this experience and not invite such rough treatment in the future.

Lady Silk-Eyes steadied herself on her gnarled walking stick. "Reunions complete, then? Everyone all caught up?"

Lady Pearl-Ear rose. "Yes, elder. Thanks again for the village's assistance and your own kindness."

The old fox smiled, her eyes twinkling. As the rest of the kitsune returned to their feet, she said, "And you, captain? You have made the arrangements we discussed earlier?"

At the word "captain," Silver-Foot's ears flattened. Hierarchical ranks were rarely used in kitsune society and even more rarely observed. Except for age and experience, all members of the community were roughly equal in terms of status. Silver-Foot did not seem comfortable hearing his military title on the lips of the village's spiritual leader.

"Yes, elder. I sent my fastest riders west to meet the Daimyo's men and fetch them here."

"Excellent. When will they arrive?"

Choryu looked up from his bowl. Riko seemed nauseated by this news as she nervously bunched her robe in her fist.

"That's not necessary, elder." Pearl-Ear tilted her face down and folded her hands over her stomach. "A small escort will be more than enough to take us—"

"They can be here in less than two days," Silver-Foot cut in. "Assuming they listen to my riders and respond quickly."

Lady Silk-Eyes nodded. "That gives us time to prepare. Very good." She turned to Pearl-Ear and said, "Gather your children and follow me. Leave matters of war to warriors."

"But elder," Lady Pearl-Ear said, the panic in her voice rising. "We are not at war with the Daimyo. They are only looking for the princess, and if we—"

"Less than two days," Lady Silk-Eyes mused, ignoring Pearl-Ear. She looked up at Silver-Foot. "And how far south did you find the tree and the scouting party?"

"A day's march for kitsune," the officer said.

The elder nodded. "I see. Too close to call, then. Well, this will be exciting, won't it?" She took Pearl-Ear by the hand and said, "Come, Lady Pearl-Ear, and bring the children. We have much to do and a whole village to rouse. We have two sets of visitors coming, and I want to have a proper reception ready." Lady Silk-Eyes turned back, still clutching Pearl-Ear's hand. "Tell me, Silver-Foot, which do you think will arrive first? The goblins or the Daimyo's troops?"

Pearl-Ear might have stumbled if not for the elder's firm grip. Across the room, Choryu's head sank almost into his bowl. Riko stood in open-mouthed astonishment, and she turned to Michiko just as the princess mouthed, "Goblins?"

"Come," Lady Silk-Eyes said again, tugging on Pearl-Ear's hand. "You came here for answers, and we have less than two days to find them."

CHAPTER 13

The entire village was assembled quickly, mostly due to the love and respect they held for Lady Silk-Eyes. The rest were mobilized by fear of the approaching goblin horde.

Lady Pearl-Ear watched her people filing into the village's central courtyard, enjoying a sense of belonging even as the danger approached. There were over seventy villagers that she recognized, with another score that were new to her. They came in all shapes, sizes, and ages, and each bowed before the elder before assembling in carefully arranged groups on the dry soil. Even in these tense circumstances, the kitsune-bito were bright-eyed and chatty, muttering to each other before they sat. Once in place, however, their conversations faded, replaced by the low, thrumming sound of a group chant.

There were kitsune warriors, too, more than she had ever seen in one place. They numbered as many as the villagers, if not more, each samurai armed with the traditional long and short swords, each ranger with a dagger and a long wooden staff. Some seemed to be from other villages, and while many stopped by the square to bow before Lady Silk-Eyes, none stayed. The elder sent them all to Silver-Foot to become part of the officer's impromptu army.

Shocked at first, Michiko now seemed consumed by curiosity. Whether she was being influenced by the convivial kitsune villagers around her or she was blossoming outside the confines of her father's tower, Michiko seemed much more alert and alive.

"The akki have never raided this far north, have they?"

"Not in living memory," Pearl-Ear said. "And we are a long-lived people."

"What will they do if they find us?"

"That depends on what they want. I've heard that a goblin army cannot move quietly, yet they have come this far without being noticed. They are either unusually disciplined or they have been enchanted. Either way, this is far beyond what anyone expects from them."

"Both of those options point to an outside influence," Riko said.

"Very good." Whereas the girls usually clung to one another, Riko was clearly following Michiko now. Despite her own fear and fatigue, Riko had adopted Michiko's student-like interest in the situation. "Determining what that influence is may well be a part of the elder's ritual."

"I have never seen a kitsune rite in person," Riko mused. "Will I be allowed to observe?"

"More than that," Lady Silk-Eyes cut in. "You're going to participate."

None of them had heard the elder approach, not even Pearl-Ear. Lady Silk-Eyes nodded to the fox-woman.

"Go ahead," she said. "Explain."

"The spirits of our village, our land," she said, "are not the same as the ones in Eiganjo Castle." She turned to Riko. "Or the patrons of the Minamo Academy. The white myojin, for example, is extremely rigid about who can invoke his power, and when."

"But the kitsune also pray to the white myojin and the Sun," Michiko said.

"We do. But we also call upon the cedar and other natural spirits. The kami here are less grand, but more accommodating. It's less a question of quality—how precise an invocation is—and more of quantity. The more voices we raise, the stronger the spirit magic will be."

Pearl-Ear paused to look around the courtyard. "And with that in mind, where is Choryu? We may need his voice, as well."

"He was quite miserable after the kitsune found us. He lashed out, and was subdued . . . gently," Riko added, with a bow to Lady Silk-Eyes. "I think he feels responsible for getting Michiko into this mess."

"Please go and find him," Lady Pearl-Ear said. "This is no time to sulk."

Michiko sighed. "I must make sure he understands. This is not his fault."

"Even if it were, he should be here with us."

Riko shook her head sadly. "He can be difficult when his mood is sour. Will one voice make such a difference?"

"Perhaps not," Michiko cut in. "But with goblins about and the kitsune warriors on alert, he'll only cause trouble if he's not here with us."

Riko and Pearl-Ear smiled together. Michiko cocked her head quizzically and said, "What?"

"Sometimes, princess," Riko said, "you are wiser than your years. I will go find Choryu."

Lady Silk-Eyes slid in close to Pearl-Ear. "When we find the wizard boy, keep him close to me," she said. "He has the look of a skeptic about him, and it will take careful guidance to keep him from spoiling the ritual."

"Your pardon, elder." Michiko had watched Riko go, but now she turned to face the kitsune women. "What were you saying about the ritual?"

"I said nothing about the ritual yet, child. I was talking about your headstrong friend."

"Oh."

"You see?" The elder patted Pearl-Ear's shoulder. "The princess is a capable young woman of remarkable faculties. It is not necessary to keep secrets from her."

Pearl-Ear's ears flattened and she stared at the back of Michiko's head. If the princess heard, she was not yet interested in responding.

"With respect, elder," Pearl-Ear hissed. "It sounds like you've been talking to my brother. Who should not have been talking."

Lady Silk-Eyes laughed. "I have not been in contact with your Sharp-Ear, my dear. Your student came here to find something. You came here to avoid something. I think that they are perhaps the same thing and that you should share your respective burdens rather than concealing them."

Pearl-Ear continued to stare at Michiko. "Perhaps, elder."

"And you should do so soon. After the ritual, it may be too late."

Before Pearl-Ear could reply, the elder patted her on the shoulder and glided back to the center of the square.

Lady Pearl-Ear stepped forward and stood next to Michiko.

"Have you been keeping secrets, sensei?"

"A kitsune always keeps secrets. It's our nature."

"True." Michiko continued to stare straight ahead, and Pearl-Ear did the same.

"It's odd that we have not seen your brother. He was the one who guided me here, after all."

"Not so odd, Princess. He knows that when I find him, I will cut off his tail and nail it to his forehead."

"He was an excellent yabusame instructor. I put his teachings to good use in the forest."

"I never said he was a bad teacher. Merely a careless guardian."

"I learned a great deal. But he said one thing that stuck out. He said that the art of yabusame had grown more important since I was born."

Pearl-Ear's heart grew cold. "That sounds like standard archery instructor talk to me. Comparing the good old days gone by to the more dangerous ones at hand."

"So he was merely referring to the Kami War."

"Almost certainly."

"But I have noticed it before, sensei. No one has ever said so, but the my birth coincides directly with the start of the war."

Pearl-Ear sighed. "A less self-interested student would dismiss that as mere coincidence."

"I have found, sensei, that there is very little coincidence when kami and kitsune are involved."

Lady Pearl-Ear felt tears forming in her throat. "I loved your mother very much. For her sake, let me defer my answer until a more appropriate time."

Michiko's eyes were dry and bright. "It is in her name that I ask, Lady Pearl-Ear."

Pearl-Ear faced the princess. "Your arrival changed many things in Eiganjo Castle. It provided the Daimyo with a potential help-mate and heir. It provided me a vocation. And it filled your mother with pride she could barely contain.

"You deserve to know the truth, Michiko. And I swear that I will see that you find it. But until I know the truth, I can and will say nothing. Now," she said as she took her student's hand, "let us take our places for the ritual."

They sat at the front of the growing throng. Lady Pearl-Ear began chanting along with the other kitsune, but the princess was silent for a few moments until she picked up the cadence of the chant. Then she, too joined in.

Pearl-Ear felt someone sit next to her, and she cracked an eye. Riko mouthed, "Choryu" and shrugged. Then the student archer closed her eyes and joined the chant.

They were speaking an old kitsune dialect, but Riko and Michiko both were familiar enough with the modern foxfolk tongue that they could contribute. As the throng repeated the same phrase, Pearl-Ear let time and space and all the worries she had been carrying slip away. It could have been moments or it could have been days, but Pearl-Ear had no idea and less interest in telling one from the other.

When Pearl-Ear heard was nothing but the chant in her ears and felt nothing but the vibration in her own throat, Lady Silk-Eyes spoke.

"Hear us, spirits of the plains. Spirits of the trees. Spirits of our ancestors. Your children here in the utsushiyo need your guidance. We face enemies from your realm as well as from ours. If there is a kami among you who still cares for the kitsune, answer us now."

In response, the chant grew louder and higher in pitch. On either side of her, Pearl-Ear heard Riko and Michiko matching the changes, following the elder like an orchestra follows a conductor. Pearl-Ear could feel the power coalescing above the crowd as her own voice also swelled and the group chant grew louder and more powerful. It was working.

The noise reached a crescendo. The elder's stick tapped crisply three times against a wooden bucket, and the makeshift drumbeats brought the chant to a sudden stop.

Pearl-Ear opened her eyes. She looked at Michiko, at Riko, and then up at Lady Silk-Eyes.

The kitsune elder stood in the center of the courtyard, surrounded by a hundred or more silent kitsune. She held her walking stick aloft with both hands and her face was pitched back, muzzle to the sky and her throat exposed. Lady Silk-Eyes coughed, then let out a soft, mournful howl.

Pearl-Ear and the rest echoed the howl, combining their voices with the elder's. Lady Silk-Eyes began to sway, rolling her shoulders and hips with her feet planted. Then she stepped off her mark, winding her way around the center of the square in a sinuous, hypnotic dance, softly howling all the while.

The air above them was dominated by a bank of luminescent

green mist. It glowed softly, like a lantern through gauze. The cloud was as wide and as long as the square itself, and though she could not see through it, Pearl-Ear knew that it rose higher into the evening sky than the tallest cedar.

Lady Silk-Eyes twirled her staff and herself around five times, then brought the gnarled stick's end down on the wooden bucket. The dull wooden boom sounded again and the howling stopped.

A spark flashed deep within the dull green cloud. A rolling wave of light surged across the surface of the fog bank, crackling as it went. Below, the throng waited silently, eagerly, their eyes wide open in awe and anticipation.

Slowly, an image began to take shape in the fog. Currents of mist thicker than the main body, flowed together and intertwined, climbing high into the sky. The image clarified, becoming a kit-sune watchtower.

This tower continued to expand, swelling outward and upward. Pearl-Ear recognized the Daimyo's tower even before it was complete. Above the tower, brighter fog pooled, giving the impression of a full moon over the capitol of Towabara.

A white spark leaped out of the fog-tower's highest point and sailed away from the enormous structure. It moved more slowly the farther it got from its starting point, though it strained and heaved like a fish on a line. Eventually, the tower moved toward the light, towed along by the spark's progress.

"Behold," Lady Silk-Eyes intoned. "The light of Towabara draws the Daimyo himself behind it. More, spirits. Show us where the light must go."

The misty tower dispersed, but the white light floated on. It meandered across the cloud, and as it approached the far end, a new shape began to form there. It was far smaller than the tower had been, but still gigantic compared to the spark.

The new form quickly sprouted arms, and legs, pointed ears, and a short vertical muzzle. It coalesced into the form of Lady

Silk-Eyes herself, and the cloud-elder mimicked the real elder's motion as perfectly as a mirror.

"Behold," Lady Silk-Eyes said. "Towabara's treasure seeks out the oldest and most oddly shaped among us."

Light laughter ran through the crowd and then just as quickly subsided.

"Now we see what has happened," the elder said. "Not what should happen. More, spirits. Show us where the light must go next."

Like the tower before it, the fox silhouette dissipated. The white spark continued to the edge of the cloud and then doubled back.

Two new forms took shape at the center of the fog bank. One was a smaller, brighter version of the Daimyo's tower. The other was less distinct. A dozen or more streams of thick mist flowed into one another, but maintained their own boundaries. The streams flowed over and around each other, twisting themselves into complicated free-form knot. More streams were drawn into the center of the tangle, and the knot grew wider and heavier until it actually began to sink toward the bottom of the cloud.

The white spark hesitated between the rising tower and the sinking knot. The images in the cloud shuddered, as if someone had tossed a pebble into a pond and the ripples were affecting the vision.

Then, the tower faded and the knot rose to meet the spark. The white speck of light pressed against the outermost layer of smoky streams and then sank in. When it reached the center of the still-expanding mass, the spark flared, and the vision ended.

Pearl-Ear blinked at the suddenly empty sky over the courtyard. She turned to her right and saw Michiko staring upward with tears in her eyes.

"Behold," Lady Silk-Eyes said. "There will be many distractions before the light of Towabara reaches her destination. She will be sorely tempted to return home before the journey is complete.

But she must not. Thank you, spirits. You have shown us the way."

The entire crowd replied as one. "We honor you, spirits of plain and cedar."

The elder kitsune rested her stick on the ground and leaned on it. "Michiko of Towabara," she called. "Have you seen the spirits' display?"

The princess sputtered. "I have, elder. But I do not understand it."

Lady Silk-Eyes smiled. "You left your father's house to find answers. You will find them among the snakes of the forest. Seek you the *orochi-bito*, Princess, the snakefolk of Jukai. Among the knot of serpentine bodies is where your questions will be answered."

An impressed murmur rode through the crowd. With the ritual's sudden end, the spell was broken and the kitsune-bito began to talk once more. The chatter was evenly divided into two camps: those who were amazed by the idea of the princess visiting the orochi-bito, and those who were anxious and fearful, having come for news about goblins.

Michiko turned to Lady Pearl-Ear. "What does this mean?" she asked. "What are the orochi-bito?"

Pearl-Ear hesitated. She wasn't sure how to answer Michiko's question. The orochi-bito of the deep woods were as mysterious and solitary as the moonfolk in the Daimyo's tower. They dwelled in the thickest parts of the Jukai and shunned the other tribes of Kamigawa. They had no single ruler, no ambassador to Towabara, and no documented interaction with any human civilization. Even the kitsune, with their mastery of the forest and its ways, had never encountered more than a handful of orochi—and those encounters were always fleeting.

"Look," said Riko. "There's Choryu at last."

Grateful for the distraction, Pearl-Ear turned to where Riko was pointing.

The white-haired wizard stood on the very edge of the village square, half-concealed by the stiles of a fence that encircled someone's garden. Pearl-Ear looked from Michiko to Riko to Choryu, struck by the difference in their expressions.

Michiko was still in shock, troubled by what she had seen and preoccupied with puzzling it out. Riko was caught up in the rush of energy created by the group vision, and she was waving energetically to catch Choryu's attention. Choryu himself looked pained, as if someone had stabbed him in the stomach while telling him the worst news of his young life.

Pearl-Ear felt a flutter of pity for the headstrong wizard. He had been a student longer than the girls had, with better access to the extensive libraries at Minamo. She wondered if his studies included tales of the orochi-bito, if he had read second-hand accounts of how ruthless and territorial they were and heard the campfire stories about how no one had ever returned alive and in their right mind from a trip through the snakefolk's forest.

From the look on Choryu's face, Pearl-Ear guessed that he had.

CHAPTER 14

The following morning, twenty of Daimyo Konda's finest troops rode into the kitsune village. Lady Pearl-Ear recognized their leader as her old acquaintance Captain Nagao. Behind Nagao, the mounted archers and swordsmen were a study in discipline, their oiled leather armor gleaming in the sun, their weapons sharp and ready, their horses immaculate. A single kitsune scout rode before them on a pony.

The scout raised a hand and the entire column came to a halt. He turned and saluted Captain Nagao, then trotted off to the side of the road.

Silver-Foot, Pearl-Ear, and Lady Silk-Eyes came out to meet the Towabara retainers.

"Greetings, Captain," Pearl-Ear said. "It's good that you have come. There—"

The leathery officer tilted his leather helm back, exposing his face to the morning sun. He did not look happy. "Where is Princess Michiko?"

"Safe in the village. But there is—"

"Lady Pearl-Ear of the kitsune. I am to take you and Princess Michiko back to the tower. Immediately." He craned his head and shouted, and a soldier rode up with two riderless horses. "And if your brother is present, I would like a word with him as well on behalf of the Daimyo."

Pearl-Ear cleared her throat. "We will come with you, Captain. But there is an even more pressing danger nearby."

Nagao shook his head. "The Daimyo was very clear. Nothing is to delay Michiko's return."

Silver-Foot stepped forward. "Not even an akki raiding party? There are at least two hundred goblins in the woods nearby. We have seen their tracks and found the casualties they left behind. According to the compact between the Daimyo and the kitsune, we officially request his aid."

Nagao frowned. He turned and muttered something to his lieutenant and then swung his legs around and slid down from his horse. As Nagao approached the kitsune delegation, his lieutenant issued orders to the Towabara riders. Soon the road was clear and the Daimyo's retainers were standing at attention alongside their mounts.

After they had all introduced themselves, Nagao's face was tense and haggard, but his concern was genuine. "Are you certain?"

Silver-Foot nodded. "Quite certain. I notice you don't seem very surprised."

"Strange things are happening all over," Nagao said. "I'll just add this to the list." He called to his lieutenant.

"Send two riders back to the tower," Nagao told him. "On my authority, we need a full division of infantry and another company of yabusame archers. Get them here as fast as possible. Go, and be quick about it."

The lieutenant saluted and scurried off. Nagao inhaled deeply and blew the long breath out between pursed lips.

"I can't send the princess back if there are goblins about," he said. "And I can't return without her. Nor can I ignore your official request for aid."

Silver-Foot nodded. "I have one hundred kitsune warriors under my command. Together, your troops and mine can defend this village until reinforcements arrive."

Nagao smiled without humor. "Mine is not a defensive unit. We are trained to travel light and fast, to hit the enemy hard and then withdraw."

"That will not be effective here, against the akki."

"I have battled akki before. You don't need to tell me what will work against them." Nagao composed himself. "Excuse me, noble Silver-Foot. I am at my wit's end. We didn't come for akki, we came for a runaway girl. The plan was to overtake her and bring her back swiftly, fighting only if we had to and even then, only enough to disengage without casualties." He paused, considering. "Do you know where they are based?"

"I believe they are on an extended march. No base camp. They seem to be perpetually on the move, always heading north."

"And what is to the north?"

"More trees. More kitsune. Eventually, they will reach the shores of Kamitaki Falls."

"If they make it that far, may they all drown there. Why do you think they are here? They've never come this far north before, and there are easier routes to take if they wanted to raid Eiganjo."

Silver-Foot sneered. "They are a mindless rabble. Who knows what drives them? Though, as you say, strange things are happening. Perhaps something has stirred them, called them out of their normal territory."

"Not something," a male kitsune said from within the village. "Someone."

Pearl-Ear recognized the voice and once more cursed her brother for his ability to mask his presence. She would have to learn that trick from him before he was made to pay for letting Michiko out of the tower.

"Sharp-Ear," she said. "How long have you been here?"

The small grey fox stepped out of the crowd of kitsune observers.

"Who is that?" Nagao said.

"I," Sharp-Ear said, "am Lady Pearl-Ear's brother. I am Michiko's tutor and her spirit guide. I am a kitsune scout and an expert archer. I am the reason most of you are here."

Nagao turned to Pearl-Ear. "Is this babbler your missing brother, Lady Pearl-Ear?"

"Yes," Pearl-Ear said.

"Then the Daimyo will want his head."

"That may be true," Sharp-Ear said. "But I think you all want what's in my head more. I came from the woods. I have seen the akki horde."

Nagao glared at Sharp-Ear, hand on his sword, but he did not draw. Pearl-Ear also fixed her most withering gaze on her brother, and Silver-Foot's eyes leaped back and forth between all three.

"Perhaps," Lady Silk-Eyes said," we should all adjourn to my hut for a parley and a pot of tea."

* * * * *

In the cramped confines of the elder's home, Nagao, Pearl-Ear, Silver-Foot, and Sharp-Ear all sat around a small wooden table. Princess Michiko and Lady Silk-Eyes served tea, which only Sharp-Ear drank. She kept staring intently at the kitsune trickster and he kept winking, raising a girlish giggle every time.

"There are almost three hundred akki in the woods," Sharp-Ear said. "And there are more of them each day. Don't ask me how. Maybe they breed on squalor and misery, because that's what they're marching on."

He smiled, and when no one smiled back, he continued. "All armed . . . well, armed in the sense that every last one of them has something heavy or sharp to swing. Nothing like the well-polished blades of Towabara or kitsune."

"Save your flattery," Nagao growled.

"Agreed," Silver-Foot said. "Just tell us what you know."

"They will pass through here within a day. They move under

cover of darkness. That also seems to be when their numbers increase. They do not light campfires to cook, but they do build a large bonfire every few days. They light it about an hour before dawn and perform some sort of ritual that ends when the sun comes up."

"Akki don't raid this way," Nagao said. "They're either running straight at you or fleeing as fast as they can. They make so much noise and bother when they move that it's impossible not to see them coming or know that they're gone. That's one of the reasons they're easier to contain than the bandits."

"Bandits," Sharp-Ear mused. "Sanzoku. Like the ones leading the akki raiders?"

Both Silver-Foot and Nagao fixed their eyes on Sharp-Ear.

"Bandits as well?" the kitsune asked.

"How many?" said Nagao.

"A half-dozen or less," Sharp-Ear said. "The ringleaders are a pair of twins. They tend to stay out of sight, but I got several good looks at them."

"This is bad," Nagao said. "Two of Godo's best lieutenants are twins. Were these two tall, thin, topknots looped around their shoulders?"

"That's them."

Nagao nodded. "Seitaro and Shujiro."

"Capable warriors?" Silver-Foot asked.

"Very capable. Strong leaders, too. Next to Godo himself, they're the most powerful sanzoku chiefs in the region. We've been hunting them for years." The Towabara officer paused. "But this makes even less sense than the akki alone. Godo and the goblins are notoriously quarrelsome. They engage in border disputes about once a year. Light skirmishing, nothing too dramatic, but it helps keep them in check."

"These bandits seem to have settled their differences with the akki."

"To our disadvantage." Lady Pearl-Ear reached for an empty mug. "This is getting worse by the second."

Lady Silk-Eyes sat at the table, placing her staff alongside her mug. "What will you do, Captain Nagao?"

"My orders are to keep the princess safe, and bring her back to the tower," Nagao said.

"Which you can't do with an army of goblins loose." Silver-Foot smiled a thin smile. "You said yours was not a defensive force. Could you mount an offense?"

"If we knew where they were, yes. Easily. My yabusame riders could occupy the bulk of the akki . . . if I had assurances that the princess would be kept safe."

"We were preparing to keep a whole village full of civilians safe before you arrived," Silver-Foot said. "One more human girl will not tax our defenses."

"But we don't need to attack," Pearl-Ear said. "Why not deploy all the warriors we have and dig in until the tower sends help?"

Nagao grunted. "You don't wait for akki to attack," he said. "You take the initiative. You're a diplomat, Lady Pearl-Ear, not a soldier. We must fight on our terms, not theirs."

"Besides," Silver-Foot shifted uncomfortably. "Three hundred akki is more than we can handle if they all come at once. I see three options. One: evacuate everyone and withdraw to the tower."

"That will not do," Lady Silk-Eyes said. "The moment you start rounding them up, our people will flee into the woods. We do not like to be corralled. Besides, this village is not merely a collection of huts. We are connected to this place, bound to the land itself."

Silver-Foot nodded. "Two: we set up defensive perimeters and hope we don't have to defend them against the entire horde before reinforcements arrive."

"I never follow a plan that hinges on hope," Nagao said.

"Nor I. Finally: the soldiers of Towabara and a hand-picked team of kitsune take the fight into the woods. While they harass the akki, the rest of my forces will stay here and protect the villagers and the princess."

"That sounds like a the way to go," Sharp-Ear said.

Pearl-Ear flared. "Be silent, fool."

Nagao toyed with his empty mug. "The fool is right. That is the most promising option. But I cannot leave the princess in anyone else's care." He looked up at Silver-Foot's curling lip and quickly added, "I know how capable the kitsune are in battle. I have fought beside your kind many times. But I received my orders from the Daimyo personally, and it is my responsibility to protect the princess and bring her home. I cannot delegate that role to anyone, no matter how formidable."

Lady Silk-Eyes filled Nagao's mug. "Then you have a decision to make, captain of Towabara. Your nation's leader gave you a task; your nation itself demands another. Save the princess, battle the akki. Are they mutually exclusive?"

Nagao left his steaming mug alone as his brow wrinkled. "What?"

Pearl-Ear stepped in. "She means, can you do both? First one and then the other?"

"There is nothing I would like more than to ride out and wipe the akki off the face of the map. But the princess has wandered off before while guarded. What guarantee do I have that she'll be here when I return from battle?" He turned to Sharp-Ear. "Don't say a word, tutor."

"Wouldn't dream of it."

"You have my word, Captain," Silver-Foot said. "One soldier to another. My retainers will defend her with the rest of the village, and keep her here until you return. If you do not return, I will consider it my personal obligation to return her to Eiganjo Castle."

Nagao shifted his mug back and forth in front of him. "There are conditions," he said.

"Name them."

Nagao pointed at Sharp-Ear. "He comes with me. He's supposed to be a yabusame expert and we can use all the archers we can muster."

Silver-Foot nodded. "Agreed."

"Whether I return or not, Princess Michiko goes back to the tower once the reinforcements arrive. I want Lady Pearl-Ear to go with her."

Pearl-Ear started. "I will stay by the princess's side, no matter where she goes."

"She's going to the tower. Listen, I am a fool for accepting the word of tricksters . . . no offense intended."

"None taken." Sharp-Ear's eyes sparkled.

"But I do expect you to honor your end. If we fight and die to protect your village and you let the Daimyo's daughter go, or allow her to become harmed in any way, there will be consequences."

"Understood." Lady Silk-Eyes rose, collecting the mugs.

"Very well. Captain Silver-Foot, assemble your warriors. I want to see where the princess will be protected and who will be protecting her before I ride out."

"Done."

"You've been very quiet, Princess." Pearl-Ear turned to Michiko, waiting silently in the corner. "Do you understand the difficult position you've put us all in? Especially your father."

"I am in a difficult position myself, sensei."

"To be sure. And it will become more difficult. For you, all your friends, and the whole of Kamigawa if you are not returned to the tower soon." Pearl-Ear bowed to Nagao.

The soldier stood. "Princess," he said. "I hope you realize that we are all your servants, and that we are ready to die on our behalf. But don't make me come looking for you again."

Nagao bowed. "Princess. Elder. Lady. Excuse me now." Nagao turned to Silver-Foot. "If you would, Captain, come with me and we will prepare for battle."

*   *   *   *   *

In a few short hours all was ready. The kitsune villagers along with the elder, Lady Pearl-Ear, Princess Michiko, and the two student wizards were all safely ensconced in a storehouse with half of Silver-Foot's warriors stationed outside. Another ten patrolled the village perimeter, hidden from view by their expert camouflage and fieldcraft.

Silver-Foot himself took the rest of his warriors and Sharp-Ear to Nagao's temporary campsite to take part in the offensive. Each of the kitsune brought their own horse and weapons, except for Sharp-Ear, who had to make do with what he could borrow. As they mounted up to move into the woods, Nagao placed Sharp-Ear alongside his own horse at the head of the column, both to act as guide and so he could keep an eye on the crafty kitsune.

With the sound of hoofbeats fading into the distance, Pearl-Ear sat with Michiko, Riko, and Choryu in the storehouse. The water wizard was still in a dismal mood.

"This is a disaster," he muttered. "How long must we squat like toadstools in this dank barn before we're carted off back to Eiganjo? Or worse?"

"Captain Nagao said nothing about retrieving you two," Michiko said. "You may return with us, or you may go on to the Academy."

Choryu conjured a small ball of water into the palm of his hand and made a fist, splattering the liquid in a circle around him. "It's nice to have options. If we survive to explore them."

Riko elbowed him, and Pearl-Ear said, "The brave captains know their work. We will be safe here."

"I would like to go on to Minamo," Riko said. "If I can find something of value, I will bring it back to the tower."

"In time to prevent my punishment?" Michiko smiled.

"I hope so. But if not, I at least want to prove that this was not a completely childish errand we were on."

"Ill advised, yes," Pearl-Ear said. "Childish, I am not so certain. Provided you were motivated by a real concern for the Daimyo's kingdom and not simply seeking adventures." She gazed meaningfully at Choryu.

"I suppose I should be glad we're not going deeper into the forest after all," Choryu said. "That vision was mistaken. The snakefolk would have killed us on sight and fed us to their young."

"You saw what we saw," Michiko retorted. "The elder and the entire village focused on our problem ahead of their own. Our path clearly leads to the orochi-bito."

"And certain death. The orochi don't help outsiders, Michiko-hime. To them, we don't exist until we enter their territory. And then we don't exist for long."

"What about the orochi?" Michiko turned to Lady Pearl-Ear. "The elder said we would find answers there."

"It is unlikely that we will be traveling again any time soon. But perhaps Sharp-Ear or one of the other kitsune would be willing to go on our behalf."

"If Nagao lets him out of his sight."

Pearl-Ear excused herself and circulated around the storeroom, checking on the door sentries and greeting her fellow kitsune. She was something of a minor celebrity, what with her work in the tower and the arrival of the princess, but the foxfolk were mostly concerned with the hostile goblins so close by.

Pearl-Ear was also concerned. As much as Sharp-Ear abused her good nature and failed in his duties, she did not want to see him fall in battle, especially not against akki. He was quick and clever and he was good with a bow, but he was not a maker of war.

Return to me, brother, Pearl-Ear prayed silently. *If nothing else, I would like to hear how you would explain the things you have done.*

CHAPTER 15

Sharp-Ear led the Towabara archers into the denser woods to the northeast of the village. It would have been easy for him to lead them astray, to guide them to a deserted part of the forest and lose them among the cedars.

He chuckled as he dismissed the notion. Despite Pearl-Ear's low opinion of him, he was not a completely selfish creature. Besides, the goblins were threatening his village, and the safest course was to support the Daimyo's cavalry.

All things considered, he told himself, things weren't going so badly. Oh, yes, there was a hostile force loose in the woods, the Daimyo had called for his head, and Pearl-Ear would probably skin him and wear his fur as socks. He had survived worse. On the up side, he had prevented Michiko from going to the academy, guided her safely to Pearl-Ear, and led Choryu to a minor but well-deserved beating. Things may not have improved since then, but they had definitely progressed.

He sensed something ahead and held up his hand. Beside him, Nagao nodded and repeated the gesture. When the mounted archers saw their captain move, they all responded instantly, bringing their horses to a silent stop.

"Thirty yards," Sharp-Ear whispered. "Due east."

Nagao leaned over, steadying himself on Sharp-Ear's mount. "How many?"

"Very many. Almost all, in fact."

Nagao turned his horse around and walked it back to the column. He exchanged words with his lieutenants, pointing one to the north and one to the south. The yabusame company split into three groups, one following each lieutenant and one staying with Nagao.

"Listen," the officer said. "We are the main thrust of the attack, but we are also the diversion. My men and I are going to ride straight in, right up the middle, shooting as we go. If the akki hold true to form, they'll try to close around us and mob the horses. Once they commit to that, the others will attack their flanks."

"That sounds like suicide."

"Only if you ride at less than a full gallop, or miss too many targets. Are you ready, tutor?"

Sharp-Ear smiled. "Ready, captain. And pay attention: I just might teach you something before this day is through."

Nagao's short sword was suddenly tight against Sharp-Ear's throat. "A friendly warning," the soldier said. "I'd be very careful about what you try to teach me this day. Stay in front. If you move to the side or fall behind, I'll consider you fair game. I don't trust you, kitsune, and if you don't die before I do, I'll make sure to take you with me."

"Ahem," Sharp-Ear said. "A strong point, well made. Or, I should say a sharp edge, well applied? In either case, you can rely on me."

"No, I can't." Nagao withdrew his sword. "That's why you're staying in front."

Without another word, Nagao drew his bow and nocked an arrow. He held the bolt loosely against the bowstring as he stared at Sharp-Ear expectantly.

"Oh. Of course. Sorry." Sharp-Ear likewise readied his weapon, and both archers rose in the stirrups until they were standing tall.

"For the Daimyo," Nagao said.

"For the princess," Sharp-Ear added. He slapped his horse

across the rump and galloped through the trees.

Behind him, he heard Nagao shout, "Hah!" and then the captain's huge horse digging up the turf.

For a few splendid seconds, Sharp-Ear was able to enjoy the rush of the wind in his face and the feel of a powerful war horse beneath him. The steed was unfamiliar, but he was an expert rider and the horse was well trained. Together, they were at least the equal of any other rider and mount on the battlefield.

Then Sharp-Ear was through the trees and into the goblin camp. The akki had felled another large tree and a small mob was working on it with crude tools. Dozens more were laid out in rows, resting for the upcoming ritual and night march. In the wide spaces of the artificial clearing, Sharp-Ear estimated there were at least a two hundred goblins, maybe more.

They were slow to recognize Sharp-Ear as a threat, mostly because they were too stupid to focus on more than one thing at a time. The group chipping away at the log was engrossed in their labor and the rest were drowsy, almost stuporous. It occurred to the kitsune rider that he could probably make it all the way across the clearing without engaging a single goblin. Nagao would probably shoot him if he did, however. The plan was to stir them up and focus their attention.

An akki with an axe stopped mid-chop as Sharp-Ear bore down on him. The little monster stood, eyes blank and mouth open until Sharp-Ear buried a shaft in the center of its face.

"Wake up and die, beetle-backs!" Sharp-Ear fired three quick arrows in succession, knocking three more goblins from the great log. "You've come to the wrong thrice-damned forest!"

Behind, Nagao and the other yabusame archers thundered into the clearing. They were not as eloquent as Sharp-Ear, but they were louder and just as accurate. Amid a cacophony of war cries, galloping hooves, and goblin screams, the Daimyo's men ripped into the akki raiders.

Sharp-Ear shot a bone-studded club from the hands of a large goblin and then trampled the little brute and two of his fellows under his steed. He continued to gallop and fire, but apart from that single incident, no one even raised a weapon against him until he reached the far side of the clearing.

There, Sharp-Ear turned and reined in his horse. Unwilling to ride back across the clearing for fear of winding up behind Nagao, he watched as the captain's squad cut a swath through the center of the akki horde. He was pleased to notice they were following the route he himself had taken. He was teaching Nagao already.

Sharp-Ear picked off stray goblins here and there as he waited. So far, the plan was failing only in that the akki weren't quick enough to close ranks around them.

Nagao's horse charged up to Sharp-Ear and reared.

"Turn, damn you all!" Nagao raised his bow in one hand, shouting loud enough to wake the trees. "Another pass! Turn and ride!" The captain fixed Sharp-Ear with a wild-eyed stare. "You first, fox-man! Ride!"

Sharp-Ear spurred his mount back across the clearing. The akki were slow to react, but they made up for their sluggishness with sheer numbers. By now even the drowsiest goblin was awake and reaching for his weapon. The mob on the log had all made it to the forest floor and were advancing toward the riders, chittering and clicking like mad insects.

A large goblin sprang onto Sharp-Ear's horse, locking its over-long arms around the beast's neck. It held on as the horse pounded along, struggling to dig its long claws or its jagged teeth into the mount's throat.

Sharp-Ear paused, mindful of shooting his own steed. He trusted his aim, but he didn't want the arrow to ricochet off the akki's shell. As he carried no sword of his own, Sharp-Ear's options were limited.

After a split-second, Sharp-Ear hurled himself forward, curling his small body into a tight ball and turning a half somersault as he went. When his toes touched the goblin's body, he straightened out and kicked with both feet, latching onto the horse's bridle with his hand.

The impact was enough to jar the akki loose, and it fell screaming beneath the horse's hooves. Still clinging to the bridle, Sharp-Ear swung under the horse's neck, threw his feet back over its head, and hurled himself spread-eagle onto its back. He felt the jolt all the way up his spine, but he clamped on with his thighs and wrapped his fingers into the horse's mane. Within two more strides he was fully in control once more, firing his bow at the increasingly thick mass of akki.

Sharp-Ear thought he heard a cheer from the riders behind him, but then realized it was an attack cry from the other yabusame waiting in reserve. With the goblins fully committed to the enemies among them, the attack on their flanks could begin.

More screams and battle roars filled the field as the akki slowly oriented on the newly arrived riders. Sharp-Ear's borrowed quiver held five times as many arrows as a normal one, and he had already used half of them. He began to aim more carefully, looking for kill shots instead of mere contact. The horse's hooves began to skid on the soupy mixture of loamy soil and goblin blood, but Sharp-Ear urged him on. As they forced their way through the mass of akki raiders, Sharp-Ear killed them as fast as he could aim, putting arrows in goblin eyes, goblin throats, and goblin hearts.

There was still no end in sight. The akki horde surged forward, mindlessly crushing the dead, wounded, and able-bodied alike as they squeezed into the cavalry's path. Clawed fingers closed around Sharp-Ear's ankle, and he stabbed down with the arrow he was about to load. The fox-man kicked free and leaped up onto his horse's back, balancing on the animal's spine like an acrobat. Sharp-Ear shuffled his feet, spinning in place as the horse plodded on. He fired arrow after arrow in a complete circle, dropping goblins in every direction as he passed.

Progress became easier as he reached the midpoint of the clearing. A dozen or more of Nagao's riders circled the chaotic battle, firing arrows into the center of the tumult and killing goblins at will.

Another akki launched himself at Sharp-Ear, screaming. The fox-man dropped back onto the horse's back with an arrow ready, but the flying akki's scream was cut short by five separate bolts to the chest. More akki fell all around him, each skewered through the head, but no bolts came anywhere near Sharp-Ear himself. He smiled, impressed. The Daimyo trained his archers well. In other circumstances, he would have applauded.

A soldier screamed behind him, and Sharp-Ear spun about so that he rode facing backward. A squad of akki had latched on to one of Nagao's riders, two on each leg, one on his right arm and one hanging from his neck. Before Sharp-Ear could act, their weight pulled the soldier down.

Then Nagao and two more mounted archers rode up on the pile of goblins that had engulfed the rider, firing as they came. Six arrows found six goblins as blackish-red blood filled the air. The soldier at the bottom of the pile struggled free. He wiped his own blood from his face and waved his commander on.

The chaos began to die down as the archers on the perimeter mopped up the last of the akki horde. Sharp-Ear spun back around on his horse. The forest floor was thick with corpses and blood. He counted only a handful of human bodies, some of which were still moving. He quickly scanned the entire area, calculating in his head. Five human dead or wounded compared to . . . a hundred or more akki, all dead. If the Daimyo's troops always achieved this sort of ratio, it was no wonder he had conquered Towabara.

Nagao trotted up alongside Sharp-Ear. He was covered in

brackish blood and down to his last three arrows, but he was unharmed. One of his lieutenants rode beside him.

"Well done, sir," the lieutenant said.

But Sharp-Ear saw no joy in Nagao's face, and he could guess why.

"There aren't enough," Sharp-Ear said. "Where are the rest?"

"And where are the twins?"

The sharp-eared fox heard the arrow before it hit. He opened his mouth to warn the captain, but he only had time to say the first syllable of his name.

"No—"

The arrowhead erupted from Nagao's chest, spattering Sharp-Ear and the lieutenant with rich red blood. Nagao's leathery face twisted into a grimace of pain and he slumped forward in the saddle.

Sharp-Ear's body worked faster than his mind. In the time it took Nagao's face to make contact with the horse's neck, Sharp-Ear had noted the bolt's trajectory, nocked an arrow of his own, and returned fire. He watched his missile fly, almost unaware of having fired it.

One hundred yards away, Sharp-Ear's arrow disappeared into a deadfall of dead branches and dry vines. Seconds later, a tall man with a top-knot looped around his right shoulder tumbled from the deadfall, shot through the neck.

"Captain!"

Sharp-Ear turned as Nagao fell to the blood-slick ground.

Something like an explosion boomed beyond the deadfall. Sharp-Ear readied another arrow.

A man exactly like the man he had just shot stepped into sight, careful to keep his body half-hidden by a stout tree trunk. The second twin turned and barked an order. Three goblins quickly scurried to the base of the deadfall and started hauling the fallen barbarian back into it.

Sharp-Ear killed two of them where they stood, but then he was out of arrows. The last akki dragged the motionless twin out of sight.

The lieutenant was on the ground next to Nagao, struggling to turn the officer over without breaking the arrow off inside him.

"He's alive," the lieutenant said. "Help me—"

Another explosion sounded from the far side of the clearing, and Sharp-Ear's horse reared. He regained control, but only after the steed had lunged several yards away from Nagao and the lieutenant.

A huge, two-legged creature with a goat-like upper body lumbered into the clearing. It had long, curved horns on its head and a bushy mat of fur across its shoulders. Its arms grew out of its rib cage, with a third sprouting from the center of its back. Its chest featured a large, black hole with wisps of smoke coming from it. Its entire head was encased in flame like the tip of a giant, freshly lit match.

Sharp-Ear's heart sank. Behind the monstrous kami was the rest of the goblin horde. They capered and gibbered like mad things, scratching the ground and hurling dirt into the air. There were over three hundred of them, fully twice as many as the ones that had soaked up nearly all the Daimyo's arrows. Whatever rapid recruitment or breeding program they were using, it was operating at peak efficiency.

"Regroup on me," the lieutenant called. He nocked his final arrow. "We fight our way back to the village."

The three-armed goat-thing roared. It lifted its head, threw its misplaced arms back, and the hole in its chest began to rumble.

"Don't regroup," Sharp-Ear yelled. "Split up, spread out, run!"

The creature inhaled deeply, puffing its cheeks. It screwed its eyes shut and clenched its three fists.

Something boomed deep within its chest, and then a massive red fireball erupted out of the creature's body. The burning projectile arced up over the clearing and bore down on the growing cluster of Towabara archers.

Again, Sharp-Ear moved before he thought. He spurred his horse, which charged forward. Sinking his fingers once more into the mane, Sharp-Ear slung himself down almost to ground level, hooked the collar of Nagao's leather mail shirt, and dragged the captain clear of the impact zone.

The horned kami's missile exploded on impact. Sharp-Ear heard the archers scream just before the shock wave blew him out of the saddle, Nagao still in tow. Sharp-Ear curled himself around the human as they sailed across the clearing. The fox hoped they would both survive the sudden landing in their future.

Sharp-Ear's back brushed the bloody soil and he rolled. A stray stone cracked against his elbow, numbing the lower half of his arm. Nagao slipped from his grasp as Sharp-Ear's forward momentum carried him out of the clearing and down into a small, stagnant pool at the bottom of a trench.

Dazed, the fox-man sank the fingers on his good hand into the mud and forced himself to his feet. Up over the lip of the trench, he heard the hoots and howls of blood-maddened akki. More explosions boomed and more soldiers screamed.

He prodded his numb arm and nearly fainted when the white-hot pain shot up through his brain.

"Stupid," he growled at himself. All he needed right now was to pass out because of a broken arm.

Sharp-Ear shook his head to clear it and listened to the carnage above. Half the akki were dead. The other half were in a killing frenzy, a sound that Sharp-Ear hoped to never experience firsthand again.

"Forgive me, Captain Nagao," he said solemnly. "It looks as if I shall desert you after all."

Painfully, Sharp-Ear struggled to the other end of the trench. He gingerly scaled up and out, keeping a careful eye on the entrance to the clearing.

The village must be warned, he thought. Silver-Foot, Pearl-Ear, Lady Silk-Eyes, they all needed to know what happened here. What they truly were about to face. A growing army of goblins and bandits backed by a kami with a cannon in its chest.

Sharp-Ear got to his feet and started to run as fast as his broken arm permitted.

* * * * *

Lady Pearl-Ear heard the footsteps outside and rose to her feet. She was one of the only people awake inside the crowded store-house, and she carefully made her way across the tangle of bodies on the floor. She reached the doorway just as it opened.

Sharp-Ear, Silver-Foot, and Lady Silk-Eyes stood outside. From their expressions, the sling on Sharp-Ear's arm, and the palpable feeling of tension in the air, Pearl-Ear knew something had gone horribly wrong.

"Wake your charges," the elder whispered. "It's not safe here after all."

"What happened?"

Silver-Foot's tone was grimmer than his expression. "The goblin horde is larger than we expected. Much larger. They are coming."

Pearl-Ear shook her head, unwilling to accept the news. "But the yabusame—"

"All dead," Sharp-Ear said. "Or soon to be dead. We rode out and conquered two hundred goblins. There were more than that still waiting, plus a powerful kami. We routed and then were routed."

"Captain Nagao?"

Sharp-Ear just shook his head. "I did what I could. I barely escaped myself."

"You must get the princess and her friends away from here,"

Lady Silk-Eyes said. "It would not do to have Michiko captured or killed, especially not here. Beyond what such a loss would do to us all, the Daimyo would take it even worse."

Pearl-Ear closed her eyes, her mind awash in a flurry of thoughts. "Back to Eiganjo?"

"Anywhere but here," Silver-Foot said. "The kitsune can fight or melt into the forest if need be. But without the riders or reinforcements, I can no longer guarantee the princess's safety."

Pearl-Ear glanced at Sharp-Ear, then fell to one knee before Lady Silk-Eyes. "We gave our word to Nagao. For his sake—"

"Nagao is gone," the elder said. "And we must put our trust in the spirit vision. Seek you the snakes."

"No," Choryu said. He stepped up to the doorway, alert and concerned. "The snakes are worse than the akki. We should go north to the Academy, and go quickly."

Sharp-Ear slowly turned and stared at the wizard. Pearl-Ear was grateful that her brother had captured such a perfect expression of scorn and disbelief so that she didn't have to bother.

"Hello, young wizard," he said evenly. "I'm eager to finish the conversation we started in the tower. You should be less eager for it. Stand aside and let the adults talk."

Choryu unabashedly held Sharp-Ear's steady gaze. Then the young wizard nodded and withdrew, backing away from the doorway until he was shrouded in shadows.

"You need a healing charm for that arm," Silver-Foot said to Sharp-Ear. "And I will send three kitsune samurai with you into the forest. That's all I can spare, but it will make a difference." He read Pearl-Ear's expression and added, "Everywhere is dangerous for Michiko now, Lady Pearl-Ear. Whether she goes back to the tower, on to the Academy, or deeper into the woods, she runs the same risk."

"Trust in the spirits," Lady Silk-Eyes repeated. "I know you will make the right decision. Fare well, Lady Pearl-Ear."

The elder and Captain Silver-Foot bowed to Pearl-Ear and then went into the storehouse, gently waking the kitsune villagers.

"I don't like this," Pearl-Ear said.

"There's nothing to like," Sharp-Ear replied. "But I trust Silver-Foot's warriors and our own fieldcraft to get us through the dangerous bits. The elder briefed me on the safest route to orochi-bito country. With the akki on their way here, we should be able to skirt them and head southeast without any trouble."

"And what of our village? Our family and friends?"

"That is a matter for another day. We must collect the children and go now."

Pearl-Ear bristled. "That is not your decision to make."

"Of course it is. You left me in charge of Michiko while you were away from the tower. You have not returned, and I have not ceded my responsibility back to you yet. I say we go."

Pearl-Ear's hand lashed out and caught Sharp-Ear by the scruff of the neck. She hauled him up to her face.

"You are still playing games, brother. I believe you let Michiko leave the tower, just to see what would happen. I won't let you risk her life again for personal amusement."

Sharp-Ear leveled his eyes at Pearl-Ear and deliberately plucked her hand off his neck.

"Lady Silk-Eyes said to seek the snakes, sister. I intend to do so, and if Michiko-hime wishes, I will accompany her. What will you do?"

Pearl-Ear stared hard into her brother's eyes, searching for any of the tell-tale signs he was hiding something. For the first time in a long time, her brother was completely in earnest."

"Go with Silver-Foot," she said. "Brief his warriors on the route we shall take. I will collect Michiko and the others."

Sharp-Ear bowed his head. "Thank you, sister."

"For what?"

"For trusting me."

"I don't trust you, Sharp-Ear. On this occasion, however, I believe you are correct."

Sharp-Ear took a step, then stopped. "What will you tell the princess?"

"The truth. For a change. I will tell her that the village is no longer safe and that we have decided to follow the elder's advice."

Sharp-Ear smiled sadly. "No matter what the snakes may tell us."

"Or do to us. Quickly now. The sooner we're away, the less time I'll have to change my mind."

Sharp-Ear squeezed her hand and padded off into the storehouse after Silver-Foot.

Pearl-Ear watched him go, grateful that she had been able to conceal her own deep misgivings. Once more, the portents from the spirit world were in conflict. The elder's vision showed both the Daimyo's tower and the orochi's bed as possible destinations for Michiko. Was this a sign of her father's great desire to have her back? Were the patron spirits of Towabara eager for their prized daughter's return? Or were the kami themselves in conflict, unable to decide on the proper course of action?

Pearl-Ear tied her robe and silently approached the corner where Michiko and Riko slept. Choryu stood, silent and sullen, watching from alongside the doorway.

The spirits may be wavering, but Lady Pearl-Ear had to be strong. Michiko was not safe, not here, not in the tower, perhaps not anywhere. It was time to find out why.

CHAPTER 16

The small party slipped out of the kitsune village quietly, without incident. Silver-Foot had provided three kitsune samurai that he claimed were the equal of an entire company of human retainers. They were brothers, he explained, and they had been training together with swords for fifty years. Now, at the end of their adolescence, they were both well disciplined and at their physical peak.

The brothers seemed mature, but lighthearted and full of energy. They were called Dawn-Tail, Blade-Tail, and Frost-Tail, though even Lady Pearl-Ear had trouble telling them apart. It helped that one marched up front with Sharp-Ear, one stayed in the middle with Michiko, and one brought up the rear. Pearl-Ear began to think of them according to these positions, Dawn-Tail up front, Blade-Tail in the middle, and Frost-Tail at the back.

Michiko and Riko were concerned for the villagers, but once they accepted the situation they became eager to reach the snake-folk as quickly as possible. Choryu was less sanguine. The water wizard still looked as if he were marching toward his own certain doom, and he muttered complaints with each misstep, each pang of thirst, and each rest stop. Pearl-Ear watched him closely, as his eyes rarely left Michiko and he seemed on the verge of running off at any moment.

After several hours, Sharp-Ear and the samurai finally relaxed.

They remained vigilant, but once clear of the akki horde they were able to spread themselves out and go at a much brisker pace. The brothers questioned Sharp-Ear about the battle in the forest, and he answered them in short, terse sentences.

Her brother's face clouded when Dawn-Tail asked about the fireball-shooting kami. He tossed his head and avoided Dawn-Tail's concern, but he also chanted a quick prayer of good luck for the village as they marched.

As the light of day waned, the forest became thicker and harder to navigate. The deeper they went, the more trees and less light there was. Decades of storms and kitsune colonization had thinned out the edges of the forest far more than she realized. It had been years since she had ventured into truly wild country, and despite the danger and the colossal burdens her mind carried, something deep inside Pearl-Ear responded to her surroundings.

Her sandals chafed and she felt oppressively warm in them. By the time they made their first camp for the night, she had packed them away and removed her outer layer of clothing. Barefoot, arms exposed, and dressed only in a knee-length shift, Pearl-Ear's body began to pick up on subtle changes in air temperature, soil consistency, and even the weather that lay ahead. How had she lasted so long in Towabara, where the landscape was all dry dust and dead ruins?

They dined on jerked meat and dried fruit. The samurai insisted that there be no campfire, and everyone but Choryu agreed. The wizard kept more and more to himself, eating alone, walking alone, and even dining alone despite repeated invitations from the girls.

"How far have we come?" Michiko asked.

The kitsune brothers looked at each other and shrugged.

"We measure distances differently in the deep woods," Sharp-Ear said. "Here, a journey is not a matter of miles, but of time."

"It took us all day to cover this much flat ground," Frost-Tail said. He seemed to be the oldest of the brothers, but Pearl-Ear would not place any of them more than a few years apart. "Tomorrow, we will climb hills and scramble over massive cedar roots. It will take all day, though we will not go as far in one direction."

"Hex you all," Choryu said. "At least tell her how much longer we'll be in this leafy green hell."

Sharp-Ear growled, but his tone was more questioning than angry. He nodded to the brothers, who had all turned to face him. To Lady Pearl-Ear, it seemed they were waiting for Sharp-Ear to act, like soldiers watching their captain.

"We have walked for almost a full day," Sharp-Ear said at last. "We have perhaps another three days to go."

"If you're not willing," Blade-Tail said, "we could leave you here."

"We could bind you and leave you helpless," Dawn-Tail added. "That'd be fair, wouldn't it?"

"And if you don't want to wait for something to come along and eat you," Frost-Tail added, "we could cut your hamstrings so that the blood and your cries of agony would bring a predator more quickly."

Sharp-Ear nodded again. "The more bile you vent, wizard," he said, "the more attractive that option becomes."

Choryu's eyes sparked blue. "Are you foxes threatening me?"

Frost-Tail stood and crossed his arms. "Yes," he said. "Yes we are. You can sulk in silence, stay behind, or we can render you speechless. But we're not interested in your opinion."

Sharp-Ear strode up to Choryu. He waved his hands around, indicating the entire group behind him. "We are assisting the princess." He pointed at the lone figure of Choryu in front of him. "You are little more than luggage.

"Pay attention, student, for this is a most vital lesson: You used up all my forbearance when you stranded me in the tower. We all know you don't want to be here and that you still want to pursue your ridiculous goal of researching the Kami War out of existence. That plan is gone, dried up and blown away." He dusted his hands together in front of Choryu's face. "Gone for good. Now, as Frost-Tail says: Be silent, or be gone."

Choryu stared angrily at the foxes for a moment. Then he said. "I have made grave errors in judgment. I admit that. I have overestimated myself. I admit that, too. For this, I humbly apologize.

"But I am right about this ill-advised jaunt into snake country. I am right and you are wrong. She's not safe here, none of us is safe here. Your elder's vision must have some other interpretation."

Dawn-Tail coughed. "Now he insults Lady Silk-Eyes." He stood next to Frost-Tail while behind them, Blade-Tail also rose.

"I've done no such thing. I'm only trying—"

"Choryu, " Michiko said. "Apologize and finish your meal."

The wizard evaluated the three kitsune samurai, then dropped his chin to his chest. "Excuse me, noble warriors," he muttered. "It seems my judgment has not yet improved."

Michiko nodded to the kitsune brothers. "And you would do well to remember that Choryu is with me. I will take it hard if you continue to bait and threaten my friends."

Pearl-Ear smiled inwardly, pleased. At least Michiko understood the gravity of their predicament. It was also gratifying to have someone else be the adult for a change when it came to dealing with young male kitsune.

They finished their supper in silence and the kitsune brothers worked out their sentry shifts. Pearl-Ear watched and waited for Michiko, Riko and Choryu to fall asleep, and then she herself closed her eyes.

Three more days before we're even in orochi territory, she thought. And no guarantee of the reception we'll receive once we get there.

Lady Pearl-Ear said a quick prayer to the patron kami of the cedars and drifted off to sleep.

* * * * *

The second day was much as Frost-Tail described it: a physically demanding slog through the dense woods with frequent vertical climbs. There was not enough energy for bickering over dinner that night, and everyone slept soundly.

The third day brought dryer, more level ground, but it also came with clouds of buzzing gnats. They didn't sting, but they flew into open mouths, noses, and eyes with alarming frequency. A mid-morning shower cleared the bugs from the air, and when it was over the sun warmed the trees so much that steam rose from the bark.

In the gnat-free sunlight, Sharp-Ear's mood visibly improved. He sang softly to himself as he hiked and fairly bounced from step to step. Michiko broadened her stride to catch up to Sharp-Ear, with Blade-Tail keeping pace beside her.

She tugged on Sharp-Ear's sleeve as they walked. "Sensei," she said. "How did Lady Silk-Eyes become elder?"

"By being older . . . elder-er than everyone else." Sharp-Ear continued his jaunty gait as he spoke. "You don't get to be old by being a fool. The longer you live, the more you learn. We kitsune live long, but the elder has lived loo-ooong. She has learned quite a bit more than any of us . . . perhaps more than all of us put together."

"And when she . . . steps down, who chooses the elder?"

"My money's on Lady Pearl-Ear. If you ask her, she's already right about everything and we should just leave it in her capable hands. But to answer your question, the village holds a meeting to decide. Anyone who wants the job can stand for it. Qualified candidates get a chance to make their case. Unqualified candidates are usually laughed down." He turned and winked. "Mind you, I'm speaking from a position of some authority here. Maturity and wisdom are hard to fake, and my people are expert at spotting fakers."

"That's mostly because we're all such fakers ourselves," Frost-Tail called from the rear.

Michiko laughed. "And why is that, sensei? In Towabara, we are taught to treasure the truth. At Minamo, Riko and Choryu learn to think dispassionately in order to keep their opinions from clouding the facts. This should be an obstacle in communication between our tribes, yet the kitsune are trusted allies of us humans."

Sharp-Ear did not look at Michiko, but he shrugged. "I am just an archery tutor," he said. "You should direct all civics questions to your actual sensei."

"Don't drag me into this," Pearl-Ear called. "Answer her yourself."

Sharp-Ear craned his head and winked at his sister. "Remember you said that." He turned to Michiko and said, "Governments always lie, Princess. It's part of how to govern. Your father is a noble man, a stalwart and straightforward one. But even he cannot tell everyone the entire truth all the time. Take his battle plans, for example. Wars are won largely by deceiving the enemy into thinking your strengths don't exist and your weaknesses are more important than they are. If he told everyone in the tower what he told his generals, he wouldn't ever win a single battle."

"I see," said Michiko. "But there is a difference between a secret and a lie."

"Very true. And your father knows that. So do the masters at Minamo. But a lie is often the best way to keep a secret. It's like the walls outside the Daimyo's tower—sort of a first line of defense. Without it, your tribe is much more vulnerable."

"But if people know you protect your secrets with lies, won't they work out the lie and the secret it protects?"

"Good question. We're entering into advanced territory here. Luckily, I am an expert.

"The best way to keep a secret is to let it out. Don't conceal it, but rather flood the environment with conflicting stories. If the

Daimyo is planning an attack to the north, he spreads the word. He also spreads the word that the attack will be to the south, east, and west. One of these has to be true, but among the chorus of lies, it's impossible to tell which. You can make your goals well known, as long as you also release a host of false ones so that your true intentions are lost in the competing voices."

Michiko wore a look of deep thought. "Is this how Lady Silk-Eyes runs the village?"

Sharp-Ear laughed. "Probably. Who knows? She's the oldest and craftiest of us all. No one but her knows what she knows, and she likes to keep it that way.

"For example, she knows that your father rarely leaves his tower. Does she know why?"

Michiko didn't answer, so Sharp-Ear went on.

"Probably not. Oh, she may know a few facts that could lead to an answer. She might know that the Daimyo keeps something in the tower that he won't leave alone. She doesn't know what it is, just that it exists and the Daimyo treasures it."

"Sharp-Ear," Pearl-Ear said quietly. "Do not speak to the princess of her father's secrets. They are for him to tell."

Her brother went on as if he hadn't heard. "Now, this valuable thing could be gold, or a magical scroll, or a shrine to his ancestors. It might even be his dog."

"Or his daughter." Michiko stopped. "Am I the Daimyo's secret? The thing he values most?"

Pearl-Ear's voice grew strong. "Sharp-Ear."

"I didn't say the Daimyo had a secret. I was speculating. But of course he treasures you above all things," Sharp-Ear said. "You're his daughter. He sent an entire yabusame company to retrieve you once he learned you were gone."

Mollified, Michiko nodded and resumed walking.

"But he didn't leave the tower," Sharp-Ear said. "I'm sure he has a hundred duties that keep him from traveling freely. But I can't help but speculate . . . what could keep him in the tower if you were not there?"

"That's enough, Sharp-Ear. She doesn't know. Nobody does. Why are you badgering her?"

"Now you are manipulating the truth, sister. You know what's in the tower. I'd even wager that you've seen it. Do you know what it is you saw? Can you solve this mystery?"

Michiko slowed, falling several yards behind Sharp-Ear. She turned and glanced back at Pearl-Ear, her eyes wet. Pearl-Ear's own face was hot and she fought the urge to growl at her brother.

"I cannot," she said at last. "But the next time we stop to make camp, I will tell Michiko what I do know."

"Oh, splendid. Because tomorrow, we may run into the orochi-bito. We should all pool whatever information we have, so that we ask the appropriate questions."

Pearl-Ear found herself staring at the back of Sharp-Ear's neck, imagining the feel of his scruff in her clenched fist. "You've said enough for now, brother," she said. "Save your breath for the hike."

They continued on. Michiko kept her head down as she walked.

* * * * *

The sun had gone below the horizon, but the sky was still bright pink through the forest canopy. As the kitsune samurai scouted out the area to make sure it was safe for a night's rest, Riko and Sharp-Ear rested in the shade of an ancient cedar.

Michiko followed Lady Pearl-Ear away from the group. The princess had not spoken since Sharp-Ear's provocative lesson in falsehood.

When they were out of earshot, Pearl-Ear sat on a pile of dried leaves. She bid Michiko to join her, and the princess gracefully folded her long legs and faced her teacher.

"Do you know what is in my father's tower? Because it is not me. I am not the thing that he treasures."

"Michiko. I do not know." Pearl-Ear extended her hand, and to her great relief, Michiko took it.

"On the night you were born," Lady Pearl-Ear said, "Your father performed a ritual in the highest reaches of the tower. He was attended by wizards from Minamo and some moonfolk. When I came to tell him you had been born, he already knew."

Michiko's face was pale as wax. "What was the ritual for?"

"I do not know. He claimed to have achieved something important, as important as what your mother accomplished bringing you into the world." She squeezed Michiko's hand. "As important. Not more so. That was the first time I saw his eyes as they are now."

Michiko nodded. "To me, his eyes have always been like that. That's how my father sees."

"It was not always so. That is another thing that no one speaks of in Eiganjo."

"What else changed that night?"

Pearl-Ear inhaled, gathering her courage. She had dreaded this conversation for twenty years, and she would not forget she had Sharp-Ear to thank for it.

"There was a statue," she said. "A fetal reptile or dragon, curled in on itself. It was in the space usually reserved for the shrine to Justice. But the next day it was gone, and I have not seen it since."

"What does it mean?"

Pearl-Ear was pondering an appropriate answer when footsteps interrupted her. They were heavy feet, but the tread was not clumsy. She quickly calculated the size of the walker and decided her conversation with the princess would continue at another time.

"Michiko," she said. "Get back to the campsite."

The princess quickly stood and turned, but before she could

withdraw, a smooth but obviously annoyed voice called out, "Wait for me, you great lumpy ox."

A deep, throaty voice answered. "My apologies, oath-brother. I thought you were right behind me."

Pearl-Ear relaxed somewhat, but she still motioned Michiko behind a stout tree. These wanderers were certainly not sneaking up on them, but there was no way to tell if they were hostile.

Pearl-Ear folded her hands into her robes as the footsteps approached. She looked back over her shoulder, and to her relief Sharp-Ear and two of the brothers were quickly making their way to where she and Michiko stood.

As she turned back, a huge bald man burst through the dense undergrowth. He was dressed in the manner of the budoka monks and he wore a gigantic pack across his broad shoulders.

"Greetings, traveler," Pearl-Ear said. "Have you lost your way?"

The giant looked down at Lady Pearl-Ear. His misshapen face spoke of a lifetime of abuse, though his eyes told her he was hardly more than a boy. He stood rock-still, steady on his feet as if the pack on his back was filled with feathers.

Behind him, his much smaller companion stepped into view. ". . . don't know how we're going to get out of here even if we do find—"

The smaller man stopped in mid-complaint. He was clearly an adult, but next to his massive companion he seemed small and childlike. He wore samurai swords on his belt. His long black hair was pulled back from his face and tied behind his head so she could see his face and his sharp, clear eyes.

Those eyes widened and in a flash he drew a jitte from his belt and held it out to Pearl-Ear.

"Just passing through," he said. "Don't want trouble? Don't start any."

Pearl-Ear cocked her head. He was quick to take arms and threaten, but at least the jitte was a defensive weapon. If he had meant them harm, he would have drawn his sword.

"I am Lady Pearl-Ear of the kitsune," she said. "We are travelers, like yourselves." She spread her arms out, and the samurai brothers stepped out on either side of her, hands on their blades. "We do not want trouble. But as you can see, we are prepared for it."

Actual mirth crossed the man's face, as if two armed kitsune were amusing to him.

"Hello, Lady Pearl-Ear. I'm Toshi," he said, twirling his jitte around his finger. "And this is Kobo." He sheathed his weapon and smiled dazzlingly. "We seem to be a bit lost. Seen any budoka tribes lately?"

CHAPTER 17

Toshi wasn't sure exactly what to make of the kitsune party. He knew the foxfolk straddled the line between the forest and Towabara, two places he himself tried to avoid. They were little people, all in all, but he never took armed strangers lightly.

He kept one eye on the three warrior foxes because he understood the kitsune to be fast and agile. The other two, Pearl-Ear and the unarmed male, barely warranted a second glance. Their group was traveling light, food and weapons only, but it was clear that the foxes were there to guide and protect the humans. The tall girl in white was gorgeous, but she looked as nervous as a bird. The other girl wore student's robes, but Toshi spotted ropy muscles rippling on her bow arm. She stayed close by the pretty one, staring daggers at Toshi and Kobo both. Boss Uramon often employed female bodyguards and assassins—perhaps the student outfit was a disguise.

Toshi fought back a sneer when he spotted the white-haired boy. Something about the student's expression put Toshi on edge. He recognized the look of anxiety and distress that only comes from privilege. The fact that it was draped in student's robes made it all the more galling. Here was an elitist, an academic, no less, who was put out by a hard day's slog and having to carry his own bedroll. Toshi's usual reaction to this sort of person was to dream of taking them into the depths of Numai and leaving them there.

They would experience more real life in ten minutes than they would in a year's worth of academic lectures.

"What are you sneering at, friend?" The male student was clearly not happy with the two new arrivals.

"Not much," Toshi admitted.

Still, they were an unthreatening lot, albeit somewhat aloof and guarded. They offered to share their food, and while they did not invite them to use their campsite, they did propose to extend their night watch to include him and Kobo.

"Thanks," Toshi said, "but that's not necessary. No offense, but I think Kobo could eat the lot of you for breakfast and still be hungry. We'll take our chances on our own."

The fox party seemed relieved by Toshi's announcement, but also offended by his reasoning. Part of him wanted to dig a little deeper, find out why this odd little group was delving so deep into the forest. Their adventure might be profitable to a pair of rough-and-tumble hyozan reckoners, if it wouldn't take too much time away from their pointless quest to find monks in the forest.

He rejected the idea of tailing them when the smallest of the kitsune, the unarmed male, said, "And you? Have you seen any snakes?"

Pearl-Ear swatted the little male with the back of her hand. The samurai grew tense while they waited for Toshi to respond. Interesting, he thought. But ultimately, not compelling.

"No," he said. "And I intend to keep it that way. If you are headed for orochi country, I wish you luck. You couldn't drag me there at swordpoint."

The little male shrugged. "We are forest folk," he said breezily. "We are not afraid."

Toshi pointed at the wizard boy. "He is."

The white-haired student reacted as if struck. "What did you say, lowlife?"

"Choryu," the student girl/possible bodyguard warned.

"I said you look as if you're about to foul yourself," Toshi said. "Or perhaps you already have. Good luck with the snakes, snowcap. I hear they love the taste of soft muscles, unspoiled by hard work."

The boy rose, blue light flickering in his eyes. He opened his hands, but before he could do more, two of the fox samurai appeared, one on each side.

"We don't have time for this," one said.

"Why are you defending him? Look at the big one! He's dressed like a budoka monk, but he can't find any others? How do we know he's not leading us into an orochi-bito ambush?"

Toshi watched in mild amusement as Choryu the boy wizard's cheeks colored. Excitable fellow, he thought. Must have been spoiling for a fight.

"Settle down," a fox said. "He said he was going. Just sit still until he's gone."

Choryu was still struggling, almost frothy. "No mere ochimusha filth can talk to me that way."

"This one does." Toshi smiled. "No offense, foxes and ladies, but your friend here is one short push away from panicking. Cut him loose before he drags you down."

"Not a bad idea," muttered the fox on the boy's left. Toshi waggled his eyebrows at him as the wizard fumed.

"Sir," the fox woman said. "You are abusing our hospitality."

"Not at all. I'm abusing that cowardly streak of piss over there."

"I may be frightened," the wizard flared. "But at least I'm going. One mention of orochi-bito and you're ready to rabbit. You're just wandering bits of trash that gets blown about by the wind. Why don't you and that bloated, tree-hugging freak blow away now and leave us alone?"

Toshi's eye flicked over to Kobo, seated on the ground with his back against a sturdy tree. He looked back at Choryu and grinned.

"You're even dumber than you look. And with that hairstyle, that's not easy."

Toshi stepped back as Kobo set aside his meal and rose to his full height. He wrapped one meaty hand around the other clenched fist and squeezed until all his knuckles cracked. The muscles in his arms and shoulders bulged.

"Did you say something to me and my oath-brother?" Kobo asked quietly. "Little man?"

Toshi could tell that the kitsune did not want this to turn in to a fight, especially not over the boy wizard. But all he had to do was clear his throat and Kobo would pounce. Toshi paused, drinking in the delicious pre-brawl tension.

"Stop this." The knockout in white stepped in between the newcomers and her own party. Toshi liked the way her hair fell across her shoulders, and the starry sparkle in her strange, bright eyes.

"It's hard enough to survive in this wild and unfamiliar place," she said. "Without us all trying to kill each other. Why don't we all just part company now and go our own ways?"

"Ahh, she's right," Toshi said. He nudged Kobo and said, "Let it go."

The huge youth grunted and slid back down against his tree. "I'm not done eating." As Kobo settled into the loose soil, the kitsune relaxed their grip on their swords.

"You know," Toshi said casually, "you really are heading the wrong way. The orochi aren't as friendly as I am, if the tales are true. Unless you've got something they want, they'll probably just skin you alive and prop you up as a warning. You've been so kind to us, I'd hate to think of that happening to you." He leaned around the pretty girl and made eye contact with the boy wizard. "You, I hope they get."

Choryu merely grumbled and gestured dismissively.

"Listen, friend," the unarmed fox-man said. "Actually, we're not friends and we don't have to be. But we don't have to be enemies, either. If you keep needling the grumpy members of our troop, we're never going to be free of each other."

"Troupe? So you're performers, then?"

"You could say that. Every one of us has a role to play," the fox-man said. His eyes twinkled. "What about you?"

"Me? I'm an independent operator. Right now, I'm partnered with him," he tilted his head at Kobo. "It's an arrangement that suits us both."

"Independents are very rare these days. So you're, what . . . searching for his budoka brothers? What happened, was he expelled?"

Toshi blinked. The little one was sharp. "Not really. He took a better job."

The fox-man made a high-pitched whistling sound. "Oooh, they hate that," he said. "Are you sure you're looking for them and not the other way around?"

"Tell you what," Toshi said. "If you find any monks, send them our way. We'll do the same with the orochi. Let's see who lives longer."

"That's no fun," the fox countered. "How will we tell who won?"

Now Pearl-Ear stepped in between the groups, alongside the looker.

"Enough," she said.

"Oh, let us boys have our fun," the fox-man said. "I just wanted to see if our new friend can take it as well as dish it out."

"This is getting us nowhere." The gorgeous girl tossed her head fetchingly.

Toshi cocked his head to one side. He liked her. She had a patrician air about her, but she wasn't afraid to step into the thick of things. If only he could convince her to drop this whole orochi business and come a-wandering with him and Kobo. Or better still, without Kobo.

As he mused, the girl wizard, the female fox, and all the armed samurai stepped closer to the knockout. Perhaps they didn't like the look of Toshi's leer. Perhaps, he corrected himself, he should learn to mask his thoughts better when looking at a pretty girl.

The mercenary part of Toshi's brain began to whir. She was important to this group, the central figure. Rich? Ransomable? He eyed the tall girl some more, trying to gauge her weight. He was sure Kobo could carry her, but he wasn't sure if there was room in the bald brute's pack.

Kobo shoved the last of the jerked meat into his mouth with a loud smacking sound.

He spotted the hyozan brand on Kobo's breast and wondered if the angry red character would ever heal properly. Then Toshi sighed. Kidnapping rich girls would get the hyozan no closer to solving his soratami problems.

"Thanks for the food," Toshi said. "We'll be—"

Kobo suddenly sprang to his feet. His tetsubo club appeared in his hands, and all three kitsune samurai drew their swords, stepping in front of the tall girl.

Toshi opened his hands to show how unthreatening he was. "One step behind, Kobo, as usual. No more fighting. I was just—"

"They're all around us," said the ogre's apprentice.

"Who is? Who's around what?"

"He's right," said one of the samurai. "Something's out there. We're surrounded."

The little fox growled angrily. "How did we miss their approach?"

A low, menacing hiss rose up from the ground nearby. It was echoed on the opposite side of the camp. More hissing came, joining the chorus, until it was the only sound in Toshi's ears.

"Orochi-bito," Choryu muttered darkly. "The snakes are upon us."

Toshi looked at each of their faces, with expressions ranging from shock to fear to steely resolve.

"Great," he said. "Just great."

CHAPTER 18

The first orochi attacker fell out of the trees onto Kobo. Toshi saw only a wild tangle of reed-thin arms and legs clad in green scales before Kobo threw himself back and crushed the orochi-bito between himself and the trunk of his sitting tree.

Then the woods around the campsite exploded into violent action as the snakefolk attacked en masse. Toshi drew his jitte with one hand and his long sword with the other, spinning in place as the blade cleared the sheath. The tip sliced across the outstretched hand of an orochi behind him, and the snake-man fell back, hissing.

Toshi looked the orochi up and down as it circled to his left, its long forked tongue flickering between its dripping fangs. It was almost as tall as Kobo, but narrower around than either of the bald youth's legs. Even with its four arms held tight to its sides and its legs pressed together, the orochi was thinner by far than a human being. Its face was a broad, flattened parody of a human-serpent hybrid, with eyes of solid red that gleamed over a sheet of smooth green and brown scales. It was so well camouflaged against the forest background that Toshi could barely tell where the orochi's limbs ended and the underbrush began. When it was in the shadows, all he could see was a glimmer of scaly motion and those terrible red eyes.

The orochi-bito he had slashed undulated back. It kept two

more of its arms out in front and the last curled protectively over its stomach. The fourth hung down past its knobby knees, a trickle of greenish blood dripping from between its fingers where Toshi had cut it.

He heard an ear-shattering shriek and ducked just as another orochi sailed over his head, smashing the one Toshi had cut back into the underbrush. Without turning, Toshi said, "Thanks, oath-brother."

Kobo grunted in reply. From the sounds, he was hard at work.

Toshi pressed his back to a tree and quickly scanned the camp-site. A dozen or more orochi were grappling with the kitsune party. The unarmed fox-man was getting the worst of it—his enemy had both his arms and both his legs clamped in its long-fingered hands and was preparing to bite. The sharp little fox thrashed and flailed to get free, which didn't actually work, but it did force the orochi to hang on instead of strike.

The three kitsune samurai had formed a small circle with the tall girl in the center. They hardly seemed to move, but every time a snake came close, there was a blur of polished steel and a spatter of reptile blood. They weren't going to win in the long run, but they were keeping their foes at bay.

The wizard boy's eyes were full of blue light and he wore a halo of water. An orochi snapped at him, extending its long neck, and he blasted it out of the campsite with a geyser of water from his hands.

The wizard girl, on the other hand, had broken out a bow and fired into the pair of orochi slither-walking toward her. The first snake took the bolt on its top shoulder, but barely slowed its charge. The second flowed over the first and fell on the wizard, splintering her bow and crashing into her like a wave.

"Lady Pearl-Ear!"

The tall girl's shout turned everyone's head. She was yelling for the fox-woman, who had one orochi by the back of the neck and was forcing its face into the soil. A second snakefolk, a female, had fastened herself mouth-first onto the fox-woman's shoulder from behind. As the orochi clamped down, Toshi could see the glands in her throat pumping venom into Pearl-Ear's body.

Lady Pearl-Ear's eyes opened wider than Toshi would have believed. She swooned and crumpled to the ground.

One of the kitsune swordsmen skewered the female orochi before she could slither clear. The snake-woman's death rattle was like wind-driven sand in Toshi's ears.

In turn, another orochi clamped onto the samurai's arm. He was able to transfer his weapon to his free hand and cut the snake-man's throat, but his eyes rolled back and he fell on top of his dying foe's body.

The confusion intensified around the tall girl, and soon the entire kitsune party had closed ranks around her. A half-dozen orochi corpses littered the campsite, but there were dozens, perhaps scores, slither-walking in. Toshi looked around, noticing that no one seemed to care about him, where Kobo was fairly covered in snakes.

Like the akki, the orochi-bito had swarmed over the huge ogre's apprentice and covered him from head to toe with their bodies. Toshi estimated that Kobo had engaged at least as many snakes as the rest of the both groups combined. If not for him, they all would have been overwhelmed and bodily carried off long ago.

The bald youth's tetsubo lay at his feet, buried in the skull of a large orochi. Deprived of his weapon, Kobo was continuing to break their bones between his enormous hands. Without the hideous grinding and grating sound, it looked as if Kobo was merely grabbing the snakes and hurling them off. Whenever he touched an orochi-bito, however, the snake hissed in agony. When they landed, their limbs, spines, or skulls had lost any semblance of rigidity.

They bit him repeatedly, but their fangs were not strong enough to penetrate his skin. Clear venom dripped from his biceps and forehead, and the occasional broken tooth shook loose when he struck. He punched his massive fist into a pair of orochi and they folded around his knuckles like wet paper. The blow continued until it struck a cedar sapling, which exploded into a shower of splinters and bark. Kobo shook the crushed pieces of dead snake from his fist, then crushed another orochi to the ground with his huge right foot.

Toshi suddenly had a clear line of sight to the white-haired boy. He was staring at Kobo with undisguised astonishment, eyes wide, head shaking in disbelief. Toshi took a split-second to enjoy that expression, then turned back to parry an incoming orochi's clawed hands.

Across the clearing, the littlest fox-man succumbed as the orochi holding him finally pinned him long enough to strike. As Toshi took a reflexive half-step forward, another kitsune samurai fell to a bite on the leg.

There were now four orochi for each member of the party and a dozen or more for Kobo. The tall girl, her wizard friend, and the last samurai were surrounded by a cluster of snakes. The wizard boy was gone—perhaps he had reverted to type and run screaming for his life. Kobo continued to bear the brunt of orochi attacks, but he was still largely unharmed.

But now there were so many snakefolk in the camp now that there weren't enough targets for them. A half-dozen of the leftovers turned and slithered toward Toshi on their long, flexible legs.

Kobo let out a muffled curse. Toshi turned and saw that the venom on his head had run down into his unmarred eye, painfully blinding the ogre's apprentice. Sensing his weakness, the orochi slithered across his body and folded themselves around his chest, linking their multiple arms to completely encircle their prey. More orochi wound themselves around Kobo, and the entire mass cinched tight and began to squeeze.

Kobo held his ground for a moment, and then a huge rush of air blew past his lips. Toshi saw him struggling to inhale but the pressure on his chest prevented his lungs from drawing air. His face reddened, then grew purple. His eyes bulged wide as they locked on Toshi.

The triangle tattooed on Toshi's hand began to burn, and the ochimusha snarled. The first of the approaching orochi caught Toshi's blade square between the eyes, and Toshi rolled under the second's grasping fingers, driving his short sword between the snake's ribs as he went. He kicked the third in its broad, flat nose and slashed an arm off the fourth.

Charging past the final two, Toshi sprinted to Kobo and struck the head from one of the constricting snakes. The pressure on Kobo's chest eased, but the other orochi closed the circle quickly enough to keep any air from entering the giant's lungs.

Toshi raised his sword again just as a stinging pair of needles injected liquid fire into his back. He reversed his blade's tip and shoved it back and up, under his own arm. The snake behind him died even as it injected venom into Toshi's body.

Toshi staggered, then fell to one knee. His throat closed. His vision doubled. The muscles around the bite cramped and spasmed. He felt the swords falling from his numb fingers.

The campsite spun before him and he heard the tall girl scream. She sounded a hundred miles away.

The last thing Toshi saw before falling to the ground was a flash of the tall girl's hair, almost lost among a wall of grasping hands and scaly skin.

* * * * *

In a painful black void, Toshi drifted. He was cold, but he could not actually feel his surroundings. His arms and legs tingled as if he had slept on all four at once, and his forehead burned with fever, though cold sweat poured down his face and back. Blind, he struggled to turn his head, searching for the barest glimmer of light. He saw nothing, a vast nothing that was darker than the space behind his own eyelids.

I'm dead, he thought dimly. The stony gray hell has finally claimed me.

His throat felt clogged, and his breath wheezed through it. No. That wasn't his breath. Something else was wheezing.

Hissing, he corrected himself. There was a constant, droning hiss all around him. That should mean something to him. He ought to remember why hissing was important, but all he wanted to do was rest . . . to rest and not to think.

The numbness in his limbs continued, but Toshi also became aware of a stinging, burning sensation across the back of his left hand.

His back still felt wet, but there was resistance. The void became more solid beneath him. Was he floating on water? It felt now as if he were spinning lazily like a leaf in a stream. He began to swirl faster, and a drop of something wet splashed across his forehead.

The burning on his hand grew worse. The fingers seemed thick and swollen, and searing agony came with each attempt to move them. Another drop splattered on his cheek.

His stomach lurched, and the muscles throughout his torso convulsed. Another drop hit him on the tip of the nose. As the water ran into his sinuses, Toshi coughed.

His hand seemed to explode on the end of his wrist. Toshi bolted upright from his supine position on the forest floor, clutching his left hand with his right. He tried to cry out, but his throat was too narrow and produced only an anguished wheeze.

It was dark. Soft, misty drizzle was falling, but larger drops had collected on the broad cedar leaves and were dripping down all around him. It had been raining, hard, from the dampness of the soil and the soaking wet bark on the trees. Moonlight illuminated the sky above the canopy overhead, but only pinpricks of silver light shone through. He was in some sort of natural enclosure, a room with walls made of live cedar.

The motionless bodies of the kitsune party lay strewn about the area—mostly those of the foxfolk themselves. The boy wizard, the tall girl, and Kobo were not here. Toshi himself and the wizard girl were the only humans in the pen.

He crouched down beside the female, Lady Pearl-Ear. She stirred when Toshi shook her, but did not wake.

"Michiko," she groaned.

Toshi turned his attention to his hand, which still throbbed and ached. Through dull, clouded eyes, he stared at himself, turning the wrist so he could see the surface of the entire fist. They had taken his weapons and his leather mail shirt. He sat for a moment, naked to the waist with one hand clutched in the other, shivering in the rain.

He staggered to his feet. Toshi wiped the moisture from his brow and took a tentative step toward the nearest wall of trees. It was a good cell, he thought. There wasn't a door to jimmy or a lock to pick.

Mechanically, with his eyes fixed on the wall before him, Toshi's hand drifted down to his hip. He picked absently at the exterior seam of his leather breeches. When the end of a thin, shining thread came loose, he wrapped it around his index finger and lifted his arm up.

A length of metallic wire pulled free of the seam. Toshi wrapped the free end around his aching hand and scanned the ground until he found two stones that were roughly the size of his fist. He tied the stones to the end of the wire with precise, tight knots and then placed them far enough apart to stretch the wire tight. Then Toshi ran his finger across the wire, slicing open the tip and producing a slow, steady flow of red drops.

Toshi quickly inscribed the same kanji on both stones, then connected them with a line of blood along the wire. The symbols puffed out a jet of dark smoke, and the entire apparatus tarnished to a dull, flat black.

Toshi picked up both stones in one hand, drew back, and hurled them at the nearest tree. The stones separated as they flew, drawing the wire taut. When the makeshift bolo made contact with the tree trunk, the stones and the wire shimmered, passing through the tree like a phantom.

The device's patina of dull black spread outward from where it struck the tree, withering the healthy cedar as it went. Toshi watched blankly as the entire tree became coated in a layer of flaky grime. He continued to stare as the tree withered in on itself, contracting down to less than a third of its original size.

Toshi turned sideways and slid through the gap he had created. Once outside the walls of the pen, he found and retrieved the stone-and-wire device.

There were no sentries he could see. Toshi turned south and shuffled like a sleepwalker through the dense woods. He still felt drugged, like part of him was back on that aimless sea of black.

Slick with drizzle and sweat, Toshi lurched through the trees, climbing a small rise to a rocky ridge. There was a hole in the canopy here, and as he looked down Toshi could see an open space with two identical trees growing on a raised platform of dirt. They were planted several yards apart. Tough hemp rope stretched between them, meeting at the center on the extremities of a large human figure.

Toshi's slack face did not change, but the terrible dread of recognition punched through his stomach like a cold fist. Slowly, deliberately, he climbed down the ravine and up onto the dirt platform.

Kobo hung between the two trees, thick ropes wound multiple times around both wrists and ankles. A wide, livid bruise stretched across his breastbone and disappeared under each arm. His head was tilted straight back, his eyes and mouth wide open. Rainwater had collected in the bald youth's jagged features, filling his eye sockets and nostrils, running continuously from the corner of his lips. The pools of liquid helped smooth out the rough terrain of Kobo's face, leveling out his scars, gashes, and badly healed bone.

The hyozan mark on Toshi's hand throbbed. He stretched that hand forward and placed the palm on Kobo's breast, where the ragged, raw outline of the same symbol had been seared into the great youth's skin.

The giant was cold and his heart was silent. Toshi lowered his hand. The ogre's apprentice was dead.

Toshi closed his eyes, rage crowding all other thoughts from his mind. His hand throbbed anew, but he merely clenched it into a fist. His eyes lost their drowsy sheen and his vision became clear, cold, and precise.

He reached out, holding his hand over the mark on Kobo's breast without touching. Both hyozan symbols burst into red flame that quickly faded into a seething black glow.

"Farewell, Kobo, oath-brother of the hyozan," Toshi said softly. "Rest now. But there is no rest for us until the job is done and you are avenged."

Toshi carefully reached forward and tilted Kobo's head forward, releasing a small deluge from his face. He placed his hand on the bald youth's sternum and pressed in. More water burbled from Kobo's open mouth and splashed down his chest. Toshi stared at the rivulets running to the ground and he nodded grimly.

"Your apprentice is gone, Hidetsugu," he whispered. "But I am still here. And there will be a reckoning."

PART THREE

CRESCENT MOON SMILE

Toshi worked quickly. Now that he was fully awake, he appreciated how vulnerable he was in the open. He untied the knots holding the stones to the wire, tied little loops in each end, and wound the thin metallic cord around his wrist.

Every living thing that had a hand in Kobo's death would be made to suffer, but not if Toshi himself remained unarmed and outnumbered. It was one of the pillars of the hyozan reckoners he had crafted—complete vengeance was more important than quick vengeance, and totality required careful planning. He could probably take quite a few of the orochi-bito with him if he attacked all-out right now, but they would certainly kill him as well. Then Hidetsugu would have to come, and the cycle of escalation would continue. The hyozan was designed to end vendettas, not perpetuate them.

Toshi squeezed another drop of blood from his finger and drew the kanji for "messenger" on a fallen leaf. As he completed the character, the leaf crumpled as if being crushed by an unseen hand. The pulpy mass churned and rolled, slowly reshaping itself into a small winged form with eyes of yellow fire.

"Return to Hidetsugu," Toshi said. "Tell him that Kobo is dead and that I will honor the oath we swore. Tell him . . . tell him he will be more than satisfied with the doom I have planned."

The dark shadow of a bird bobbed its paper-thin head and

fluttered up through the canopy. The ochimusha watched it go and ground his teeth as he prepared for what came next. It would require more than a few drops of blood.

He unwound the wire from his wrist and rewound it once around his forearm. In the scattered moonlight, Toshi could have counted the ladder of straight, sharp scars that ran up the length of that arm. He clutched both ends of the wire in one hand, pulled it down so that his flesh bent under the metallic cord and then turned his arm until the wire bit through.

Blood spit up from the wound as the sharp cord sliced into Toshi's arm. He caught the red stream in his cupped hand, quickly smearing kanji across his forehead, chest, and opposite palm. Power surged and the heat of this magic burned him, but he kept collecting and smearing until all three marks were complete. He then slapped a wet leaf over the wound and held his arm up over his head to slow the bleeding.

As he waited, Toshi watched the air around his body shimmer. The concealment kanji on his forehead would make him almost impossible to see, but he didn't imagine that would protect him from the snakes for long. The symbol on his chest was for that.

However, near-invisibility would allow him the freedom to move around the orochi-bito encampment. He needed to find his gear, his swords and his jitte and the pack he'd retrieved from his home in Numai.

He coldly approached Kobo's body and leaned into it again, pressing down on the dead youth's broad chest. More liquid burbled from between Kobo's lips, and Toshi caught it in his palm. The water mixed with the blood already on Toshi's hand, and he smeared the mixture on the trees beside Kobo.

On one, he made the hyozan triangle and kanji. On the other, he left a message for the actual killer, the person who had done the deed.

Hidden within his shroud of darkness, Toshi scaled back up the ridge and followed the hissing sound to the east.

He heard the sounds of movement, of people milling around in the same area. Creeping through the underbrush, he wriggled up behind a large tree and carefully peered around. Four orochi were standing in a circle, hissing in excited tones.

They talked about things he didn't recognize or didn't care about until his legs started to stiffen, and then the subject changed.

"How long until the ritual?"

"Not long."

"And the intruders?"

"Almost all of them accounted for. Still searching for one or two."

"The forest myojin will decide. It wants them all together."

"The princess, too?"

"Definitely. The spirit will insist she die first, you wait and see."

"All of them will die. You wait and see."

"Princess?" Toshi stood and stepped out from behind the tree. "You boys are fascinating, but let's turn back to the princess you mentioned, all right?"

The snakes all peered at the shadowy form, their red pupils shining.

"Outsider," hissed one orochi.

"Thug," hissed the other. "Escaped."

The tallest orochi, the one who had been doing most of the talking, wore a headdress made of wood and bone. "Kill him now," he said.

"Can you worms read this symbol?" Toshi spread his arms wide, displaying the mark on his chest. "Can you even understand what I'm saying?"

Two of the orochi rushed forward, an angry rasping sound their only reply. Their jaws distended as they came, displaying fangs that dripped horrid yellow venom.

"Guess not," Toshi said. Both snakes hit him at the same time, clamping on to his right shoulder and the left side of his ribs.

The reflection kanji on his chest flashed and both orochi recoiled in shock. They coughed and hissed, blood streaming from their lips, as their own venom dissolved their bodies from the inside.

The third snake, a female, shot forward on all six limbs. She feinted at Toshi with her fangs, but she knew enough not to bite.

"Symbol won't last," she said. "It fades, you die."

Toshi shook his head. "I'll be using your hide for a pair of boots before that happens." He extended his hand, which bore the kanji for the second trial of the stone gray hell, ice. A stream of cold white crystals surged from the mark to the orochi's face.

The female snake's breath hitched in mid-hiss, and cold white vapor streamed from her nostrils. She made a small, insignificant cry and then toppled headlong like a tree. When she struck the ground, her body was hard and cold like frozen stone.

Toshi turned to the last orochi, who was slowly backing away.

"I'm guessing that fancy hat means you're important." Toshi held his hand out again, and the last orochi's eyes glazed over as his breath turned white.

Toshi sprang forward, looping the wire filament around the orochi chief's throat. He sawed the wire through the incapacitated snake-man's tough outer scales. With a brutal jerk, he hauled the orochi off his feet and rammed him face-first into a tree.

Toshi tightened the wire. "Now," he whispered savagely. "We're going to have a talk. I'm going to ask you questions. If I don't like your answers, I'll use your blood to paint this symbol," he opened his palm in front of the orochi chief's eye, "on every tree for acres in all directions. By morning, you'll all be asleep in the snow, well on your way to dying from the cold." He jerked the wire again. "Savvy?"

"It won't help you," the chief said listlessly. "Great forest spirit is on the way."

Toshi spun the orochi away, snapping the wire out of the snake's throat and spinning him back into the tree. The chief sank to the ground, clutching feebly with his four arms.

"You let me worry about that," Toshi said. He walked deliberately over to one of the fallen orochi, kneeled, and pried open the snake's mouth. After manipulating the dead creature's throat, Toshi squeezed a few drops of yellow venom into his cupped hand.

Careful not to spill, Toshi went back across to the fallen chief and smeared the venom across the orochi's face. He drew and connected a series of curves and lines until the snake's entire face was contained by a ring of kanji symbols.

"You'll tell me now," Toshi said. "That's not a threat, by the way, it's a fact. We'll start small and work our way up," he said. "Where are my weapons?"

The orochi chief's mouth opened inadvertently, and he struggled to close it again. The harder he worked his jaw, the more the kanji on his face steamed and burned.

"And after that," Toshi said, "you can tell me about the princess. Tall girl, dressed in white? I believe her name is Michiko."

The orochi chief hissed in agony. Toshi merely watched and waited.

* * * * *

Fully armed and dressed, Toshi crept once more through the woods. He left the orochi chief alive but temporarily paralyzed, spitting foam between his fangs. The snake had eventually described a large clearing to the east where the orochi-bito were planning a special ritual to summon their patron kami. There would be guards on the princess, but the other prisoners were thought to be safely stashed in the cedar pen. The chief didn't seem to understand how Toshi had woken so quickly, as the entire party had been dosed with enough venom to keep them unconscious until morning.

Toshi rubbed the hyozan mark on his hand. He knew what had woken him. Let the snakes think he was immune to the venom, however. It would make them more fearful when he returned.

Toshi crawled away from the clearing, which was slowly filling with scores of snakes. There was also a small group of humans, bald, dressed in waist sashes, with the same sort of metal torso piercings Kobo had.

Toshi almost spat in contempt. These budoka monks were working in league with the orochi-bito. They would never have found help here. Hidetsugu's information was tragically out of date.

He stole away and followed the chief's information to a small hut not far from the ritual clearing. Princess Michiko was inside. There were three orochi lurking outside the small, thatched hut, but Toshi had anointed his weapons with orochi blood and venom in anticipation of this obstacle. Toshi quietly scratched a small kanji into the bark of a willow tree.

He waited until the moon slid behind a cloud, and then he stabbed his jitte into the center of the symbol. In response, three whips of tough willow vine lashed out and tightened around the orochi's throats. They clawed at the nooses and tried to break the vines, but the tree slowly pulled them off the ground and their struggles died away. Toshi strode through the orchard of dead snakes and into the thatch hut.

Inside, he found the tall girl, bound and sleeping on a pile of straw. She was pale and still, but her chest rose and fell in a slow, almost glacial rhythm.

"Princess Michiko," he said. "We haven't been properly introduced. Please come with me."

It was definitely the Daimyo's daughter. He dimly recalled seeing her image on official proclamations, but they didn't do her beauty justice. He never would have recognized her if the orochi hadn't let her identity slip . . . which raised the question, how did they know?

Toshi hooked his fingers over the vines binding her hands and hauled her up onto his shoulders. Casting spells for the past hour had burned away the last of his post-poisoning lethargy, and he felt as if he could carry the tall girl for quite a while. Fortunately, he knew he wouldn't have to.

He stood, bearing her weight until the concealing shroud began to affect her. When she was as faded and diffuse to the eye as he was, Toshi carried her out of the hut and into the deep woods due south.

He would honor his oath with Kobo, but he would do so carefully. He would pool his available assets and bring as much power as he could muster to bear.

Toshi hiked up a hill, easily balancing Michiko as he went.

He hadn't counted on the Daimyo's daughter being one of his assets, but now that he had her, he intended to make the most of it.

CHAPTER 20

Pearl-Ear woke to the distant sound of an urgent voice and the unpleasant sensation of being shaken.

"Lady Pearl-Ear! Open your eyes! She's gone! We have to find her!"

Pearl-Ear groaned and pushed the clutching hand from her shoulder. She cracked one eye and saw Choryu kneeling over her as water dripped from the trees overhead.

"Michiko," she said.

"That's right, Michiko. She's not here with you. Where did they take her?"

Pearl-Ear's eyes opened wide. "Orochi-bito," she said. "Is everyone all right?" She struggled to sit up, and Choryu roughly pulled her onto her knees.

"Everyone's alive," he said, "but we're not out of danger. They seem to be preparing a major ritual. I think they plan to sacrifice us to their patron spirit."

"Of course they won't," Pearl-Ear said. "Lady Silk-Eyes sent us here."

"That vision came from a kami, probably the same one that wants to consume her at the orochi ritual."

She blinked, her brain still fuzzy and uncomprehending. "Did you say Michiko is not here?"

"I did, and she isn't. That ochimusha scum is gone, too." He pointed to the withered cedar, now little more than a tower of ash held together by a skin of diseased bark. "That looks like his handiwork to me. He might be dead, though. I found the body of the budoka giant he was with—the orochi had him strung up between two trees."

"No, he escaped." Pearl-Ear looked up. "I remember his face," she said. "The ochimusha. He was standing over me. It felt like a dream."

"You've been poisoned," Choryu said. "You're lucky to be alive. Why wasn't he affected?"

"Maybe he's a poisoner himself," Pearl-Ear said. "Maybe he's built up a tolerance."

"Or maybe he's working for the orochi. They did attack right after he showed up."

Pearl-Ear rose to her feet, wobbling slightly. "No, that's not right. He fought with us when the snakes came," she said.

"He fought against them at the same time we did. I don't think he even noticed we were there. I think he and the giant were fighting for the right to take Michiko themselves." Choryu turned away. "Now I wish it was the lowlife's body I found."

"Wake the others," Pearl-Ear said. "We're all getting out of here, now. We must find Michiko."

"That's what I've been yelling in your face for the past ten minutes," Choryu groused. He went to Riko and shook her, sternly calling her name.

Pearl-Ear bent at the waist and examined the ground near the withered tree. He had been here. His aura scent was different than before, smokier, more tinged with magic. She realized she had underestimated the sharp-tongued traveler. He was a powerful mage, though she did not yet understand his methods.

Behind her, Choryu had succeeded in waking the rest of the party. They were all stiff and confused, but their heads were clearing. There was no fear on any of their faces as they came to understand their predicament, only anger and determination. Even Sharp-Ear looked enraged, something Pearl-Ear hadn't seen since they both were kits.

"Michiko is missing," Pearl-Ear told them. "The orochi-bito are preparing a kami ritual. We must not be here when it occurs, and we must make sure that Michiko isn't either."

"She's not missing," Choryu said. "She's *gone*. I saw them put her in a hut just over the ridge to the east. I went by there before I came here, and the hut is empty. Someone killed the guards and took her."

"Who, Toshi?" Sharp-Ear craned his neck, stretching the vertebrae. "The ochimusha?"

"Who else?"

"Well, there's you," Sharp-Ear said. "How is it that you weren't captured with us?"

"Choryu came back for us," Riko said. "How dare you—"

"Comes with being a trickster," Sharp-Ear said. "The unfortunate habit of seeking hidden motives and ascribing them to unexplained occurrences." He smiled disarmingly. "I think my vocabulary is returning. So," he spoke to Choryu, "why weren't *you* captured?"

Choryu simply glared at Sharp-Ear, almost sputtering with rage.

"Well?" Frost-Tail said. The brothers had all been disarmed, but they flexed their fingers menacingly.

"I am a water wizard." Choryu spoke slowly, with as much dignity as he could summon. "I defended myself with magic. When the snakes overwhelmed the group, I conjured a swift stream to carry me away. I stayed out of sight and watched until it was safe to wake you, and then I did. You'd still be in a stuporous sleep, dreaming of clever word games, if not for me."

"I am satisfied Choryu is no coward," Pearl-Ear said.

"As am I," Riko added.

Sharp-Ear nodded. "Fair enough. It's a good thing you were able to remain out of sight, Choryu. It would have been dangerous to act alone.

"Now, if your pride will allow it, wizard: take us to this hut where you last saw Michiko."

* * * * *

Toshi set the princess down on the crest of a gradual incline. There were no trees here and he had a clear view of the cloudy night sky.

From this vantage point he could see the small ring of fires the orochi had lit for their ritual. By now, he reasoned they had discovered his abduction of the princess. Judging by the sounds of an angry snake mob that filtered up through the cedars, they were no longer interested in stealth and were hot for his blood. He had perhaps half an hour before they caught up to him.

Toshi fished in his pack and broke out his good jitte and a small cloth parcel. He undid the string and peeled back the cloth, setting three drab, rectangular objects on the ground. He placed a small vial of bluish-white liquid on top of the soft bricks and wrapped his hand around the jitte, feeling its comfortable heft and testing its balance.

It was the finest weapon he had, forged from an alloy of steel, silver, and magic. Normally, the strength of the spell lay in the kanji he cast, the medium he used, and his own will power. This jitte acted like a mystical filter, clarifying and concentrating his spellwork to its purest and most powerful essence.

Toshi opened the vial and carefully poured the liquid along the length of the jitte's central tine. He crouched and traced three large kanji in the dirt at the top of the hill. When he was through he retrieved the soft, gray bricks from the parcel and stood over the princess, watching the sky.

The wind kicked up while he waited. It raised goosebumps on his wet skin, but the breeze was also moving the rain clouds. Good. That would make the journey easier.

Toshi waited patiently until a flicker of motion caught his eye. Far in the distance, a huge flying shape materialized between the clouds, glowing softly under the reflected light of the crescent moon.

The great moths of Towabara were rare and hard to train, and thus prized among the elite retainers in the Daimyo's service. A capable rider could use a moth to cover an entire day's march in a few hours. An expert could ride the great insects into battle and rain terror down on his enemies at speeds faster than the mightiest horse. The Daimyo's moth riders were the elite warriors of all Kamigawa. There was nowhere they could not go, no enemy they could not best.

The great silver-white moth sailed on, drawing closer. It began to circle Toshi's hilltop, gradually decreasing its altitude until it was making circles around Toshi himself. Then, it gently came to rest on the soil, delicately balanced on its six legs, its shimmering powdered wings rising and falling in the moonlight.

Toshi had encountered this moth after a pitched battle between sanzoku bandits and the Daimyo's forces. Its rider had been shot out of the saddle, and his dead weight dragged the moth itself down to the ground. Its reins became hopelessly tangled in branches of a fallen tree that had been set alight by a flaming arrow. Toshi approached the panicked insect out of curiosity, but he was soon startled to find that the beast was semi-intelligent. It understood its predicament and it wanted him to help.

Toshi had beat back the flames but did not extinguish the fire. Always best to negotiate from a position of strength. The proud beast refused to be bound for life, but Toshi was able to strike a bargain with it. If it agreed to carry him when he called, the moth could do whatever it wanted in the meantime, free from the Daimyo's endless campaigning. Five rides on demand, and the moth would both survive and regain the freedom of the skies. In the end, it agreed to be bound according to their compact, and he coated his good jitte with the dust from its wings before scratching a kanji onto its back.

The soft bricks were part of the rider's kit, composed of soft vegetable matter that would never spoil. There were eight bricks in the rider's pack when Toshi found the moth. To symbolize their deal, Toshi destroyed all but five before he let it go, keeping these as markers to be exchanged for transport.

The moth made no sound but for the gentle wind stirred by its wings. Toshi approached it now, holding out the parcel of three food bricks out before him with both hands.

"I've got another deal," Toshi said.

The moth's antennae twitched. It was listening.

"I've got three rides left," Toshi said. "And there's two of us here." He pointed back to the unconscious Michiko. "You take her and me together, now, and I will consider your end of the bargain fulfilled." He laid the bricks in front of the moth and stepped back. He pointed to Michiko, then himself.

"Me and her," Toshi said. "Then you're done."

The moth lowered its head and lapped at the first brick with its tubular tongue. It punched through the outer skin and drew in a mouthful of the soggy interior. Then it turned and tasted each of the two remaining bricks.

"So," Toshi said. "We have a deal?"

The moth's legs rose and fell like a wave as it turned its back to Toshi. It lowered its wings almost to the soil and kept them there.

"Done and done," Toshi said. He turned around, lifted Michiko up, and placed her on the moth's back. He climbed on behind her, marveling for perhaps the last time at how such a seemingly delicate creature could carry so much weight so far, so fast, and so high.

It took almost a minute of steady beats before the moth's wings were able to lift both riders off the ground. In the distance, Toshi heard the orochi-bito rabble drawing ever closer. He smiled cruelly and spit towards the sound.

"West," he told his steed. "I'll tell you when to stop."

The moth rose high into their, through the clouds, and then over them. Toshi held the reins tightly in his fists, but he gave the moth plenty of slack. It had never liked to be steered, and with its freedom so close, he imagined it would be even less tolerant.

Michiko moaned slightly and slumped back against Toshi's chest. He tightened his arms around her, keeping the reins clear of her fluttering robe, and rested his chin on her shoulder.

As they soared through the moonlight, Toshi huddled against Michiko for warmth and took in the cold, stark splendor of the nighttime sky.

* * * * *

The snakes stayed on the incline until the moon was low over the horizon. Pearl-Ear and her party had followed Toshi's well-hidden tracks this far, but the agitated mass of orochi-bito kept them from climbing higher. Sharp-Ear observed that at least everyone was looking for Michiko and not guarding them, but Pearl-Ear took no comfort from this.

Now the orochi were slithering back down the incline, heading for their ritual clearing. Pearl-Ear, Riko, and Choryu sat huddled under a camouflage of twigs and wet leaves. It was uncomfortable, but it kept them safe from the orochi. Dawn-Tail was hidden nearby in case they were discovered, but Sharp-Ear, Frost-Tail, and Blade-Tail had all stolen off to reconnoiter.

They waited until the last orochi came down, then for another long stretch to make sure there were no more. Then, Frost-Tail returned from the crest.

"The trail dies all at once," he said. "Michiko is definitely with him, and she's very much alive."

Riko closed her eyes. "At least there's that."

Pearl-Ear was less encouraged. "Which way did they go?"

"No idea. The trail stops cold. It just disappears. You think that ochimusha knows teleportation?"

"I don't know what he knows," Pearl-Ear said in frustration. "That's what makes him dangerous."

Blade-Tail materialized out of the shadows. "The orochi are performing the ritual anyway. There's several hundred of them, all hissing and chanting to the Myojin of Life's Web." The kitsune warrior scowled. "Such a grand name makes me nervous."

"The spirit's followers concern me more," Pearl-Ear said.

Sharp-Ear emerged from the woods a few moments later. He had lost some of his vivacious spark.

"I found something," he said. "Come with me."

"Is it safe?" Choryu was holding Riko's hand in the gloom.

"Everyone but us is at the ritual," Sharp-Ear said. "I think they've written us off. If they were ever interested in the first place."

The group collected themselves and followed Sharp-Ear back toward the pen that had held them. As they drew closer, he veered off and led them up a short, rocky ridge.

From the summit, Pearl-Ear looked down. "Who is that?"

"That," Sharp-Ear said, "is Toshi's friend. The big lad with the studded club."

"They killed him," Riko said. "Choryu saw it."

"I saw what you're seeing right now," the wizard added quickly. "I haven't been any closer than this, but I assumed he was dead."

"He's dead all right," Sharp-Ear agreed. "I'd offer to let you stay here, Michiko-hime, but the situation does not allow it. Don't look if the body upsets you."

Sharp-Ear motioned with his head. "Come on. You all need to see this."

They went down into the glen silently. At the foot of the soil platform, Pearl-Ear took in the wretched site.

"I believe," Sharp-Ear said, "they were trying to keep him immobile. That's why he was separated from us and brought here. They were afraid he might know enough forest magic to escape."

"There's not a mark on him," Blade-Tail said. "Except for that bruise around his chest. You think they smothered him?"

"That's one way to kill a giant," Sharp-Ear said.

From the edge of the clearing, Choryu stepped away from Riko and peered at the marks on the trees. "What do those mean?"

Sharp-Ear leaped up and landed next to one of the trees.

"This," he said, "is the same symbol our thug friend had tattooed on his hand. The giant has the same symbol branded on his chest."

"It says, 'hyozan,' " Riko called. "Iceberg."

Blade-Tail looked at Frost-Tail. "Reckoners?"

His brother nodded.

Choryu came to the edge of the platform. "What's that, then?"

"Vendetta gangs from the Takenuma Swamp," Blade-Tail said. "Tightly knit, fiercely loyal. They mark themselves so their enemies will know: strike at one, and the entire group responds."

Choryu's brow wrinkled. "Didn't do much good as a deterrent, did it?"

Dawn-Tail shook his head. "Most reckoners would rather avenge than deter. They're like fighting dogs without an arena."

Choryu nodded to the second tree. "And that? What do those symbols mean?"

Sharp-Ear cocked his head, his mouth working as he tried to sound out the words. "Not entirely sure," he said. "It's some kind of a poem, or a warning."

"A poem? How is that supposed to frighten people?"

"'The iceberg travels upstream,' " Riko intoned. She was squinting in the moonlight and reciting the words as she read them. "'Choking it off at its source. The river runs dry, dead and forsaken, yet the iceberg endures. The river has made a terrible mistake, and the hyozan now rises to destroy it.'"

"'We will kill you,'" Riko said quietly. She was staring intently at the characters on the tree, taking longer pauses between phrases as she translated in her head.

"'We will burn your fields, steal your treasure, destroy your house, and enslave your children. We will murder your spouse, poison your pets, and . . . blaspheme on the graves of your ancestors. We will do all this, and the only way to avoid it is if we never find you.'

Riko swallowed. She looked at the group, her wide, frightened eyes moving from face to face.

"'We've already found you,'" she concluded.

They all stood silent and daunted as the rain began anew.

"Who's that meant for?" Choryu asked. "The snakes?"

Frost-Tail replied. "It's meant for whoever killed the giant."

"Yes, but what's the point? Is he trying to intimidate them?"

"In part. But it's more like a minor charm, or hex," Dawn-Tail said. "The power of suggestion plays on the mind of the person responsible. If you tell someone they're being hunted, it distracts them, makes them easier prey."

"Especially if they're guilty," Blade-Tail said. "The thugs and brigands in the marsh have a terrible fear of revenge magic. Part of it's superstition and part of it's experience . . . they know how far some reckoners will take these vendettas. Sometimes all it takes to make your enemy disappear is to scare them off."

Choryu nodded. "So he's just trying to rattle the orochi-bito."

"No," the three kitsune brother said together.

Blade-Tail went on. "I've never seen a reckoner's warning as complex as this. I think he earnestly means to get even."

"Very well," Pearl-Ear said. "We could wait here for the ochi-musha to come back and exact his revenge, but I submit we must pursue him. Whatever else is true and whomever he has sworn to kill, he has Michiko."

"But how do we know where he went?"

"He is from the Takenuma Swamp. The marsh lies almost due west from here, but Towabara lies in between. He will not take the Daimyo's captive daughter anywhere near the Daimyo's tower. Nor will he go north, nor east, because those only lead to more forest."

Sharp-Ear nodded. "South, then? To the edge of the Sokenzan Mountains, on to Numai?"

"South," Pearl-Ear said. "You and Riko will have to keep up, Choryu. Once we are clear of orochi territory, we kitsune will move with all available speed. We cannot wait for you."

"We will not lag far behind."

"Good. We are unarmed and traveling through hostile country. When we reach our goal, we will face a powerful and ruthless mage. And we will strike him down. Princess Michiko must be recovered safely."

"How do we know she's still alive?" Riko asked. "He might have killed her already."

"If he has," Pearl-Ear felt real steel in her voice, and it both frightened and fortified her. "Then he will face our reckoning, and it will be more terrible than any even he can imagine."

CHAPTER 21

Michiko awoke from a dream about flying, laughing a little.

She was flying, soaring high above the clouds on a moonlit night. She was on a beautiful tour of Kamigawa on the back of one of her father's exquisite battle moths.

The cold wind fluttered her hair across her face, and Michiko frowned behind it. Her hands were bound. Her right shoulder was one massive ache. What had she been doing before the dream?

"Lady Pearl-Ear," she sat upright, but a pair of lean, strong arms clamped around her, holding her in place.

"Careful, Princess." The ochimusha's smooth, warm voice felt good in her ear. "We're too high up to risk a fall."

"Lady Pearl-Ear," Michiko said. She tossed her head to clear the hair from her face. "Where is my sensei? Where are my friends?"

"Safe, Princess, safe. We had to get you out of there in a hurry. You might say this moth owed me a favor. He rescued us on my request." The tough tugged gently on the reins, easing the moth down. "Now you owe me a favor."

"I appreciate your help and your kindness," Michiko said. "But I must see the other members of my party. Where are they?"

He hooked his thumb back over his shoulder, almost brushing Michiko's cheek. "About a thousand yards back and a hundred feet down."

Michiko stiffened in his embrace, pushing away with her elbows. "I saw them fall," she said. "I watched the orochi-bito bite them." She turned her head as far as she could, but still only caught a glimpse of Toshi's face. "I saw them bite you, too."

"We were all bit," Toshi said. "Some of us just recovered faster."

The moth continued to descend, bringing them through a thick layer of white clouds.

"Where are we?" Michiko said. "Where are you taking me?"

"To a safe place."

"Where?" she persisted. "Where is this safe place?"

"Near Towabara."

"Everything is near Towabara. It lies at the center of Kamigawa."

"Quiet, now, Princess," Toshi said. "I need to steer the moth."

Michiko's eyes narrowed as she watched the clouds flow by. "Who told you I was a princess?"

Toshi paused, then chuckled. "Oddly enough, it was the orochi-bito. But I don't think they meant to."

"Land this animal at once," Michiko said. "Or take me to my father. I will not go any further with you."

"I'm afraid that's not up to you, Princess." Toshi's soothing voice hardened. "My partner was murdered tonight. Do you remember Kobo? Large fellow, bald, build like a mountain? He was younger than you, and now he's dead. I am oath-bound to avenge him."

"I am sorry about your friend. But why do you need me?" Michiko asked. "What has any of this to do with me?"

"I knew you'd ask that. I've been working on a succinct answer. Ready?"

Michiko huffed in exasperation. "Yes, yes, just answer my question."

"Whoever killed my partner also wants you. I need to keep you close until they catch up. When they do, I'll be ready."

"You're a liar," Michiko said evenly. "You intend to ransom me for profit."

"Absolutely. But that doesn't make me a liar."

Michiko decided to say no more. She worked her wrists inside her bonds, straining to create some slack. The sturdy vines were cinched tight, however, and she accomplished nothing.

A hilly section of dense forest below was quickly rising to meet them. She could see some of the tallest Sokenzan peaks in the distance.

Lady Pearl-Ear will find me, she thought. She closed her eyes and said a silent prayer to the white myojin, for her salvation, and to the Sun, that she might be found quickly under its all-seeing eye.

Her prayers finished, Michiko began working the bonds on her wrist once more, just in case.

* * * * *

The main gates to the Daimyo's castle in Eiganjo were flung wide. Mere days ago, General Takeno had ordered a mixed punitive force of infantry and cavalry north to the Jukai border to engage the akki army that was raiding there. He had heard nothing from Captain Nagao or the kitsune village since the riders came bearing news of an akki-bandit incursion into the Jukai.

From his position at one of the highest chambers in the tower, Takeno looked down on the courtyard. Things were coming apart, just as had been predicted, just as the Daimyo had warned. It was a taxing time for the nation and their people, but Konda had not unified a nation by wilting in the face of hard decisions. The Daimyo believed true victory was in sight, if they only had the strength to endure the journey. If he had purity of purpose to earn it.

The general turned back to face Daimyo Konda, who was staring up at his beloved statue. It still sizzled and smoked as it had on the night it had come. The proof of Konda's divine right to rule, the essence of his power made manifest. So long as it was his, neither he nor his kingdom could be diminished.

The surface of the statue seethed, throwing off waves of heat distortion. Konda grinned, but Takeno was worried. The Daimyo loved to be close by when the stone figure showed signs of life. In his more lucid and talkative moments, Konda likened it to basking in the light of a perfect sunset—the light improved him, inside and out.

The statue suddenly blinked out, light and radiant motion alike severed in mid-revel. The temperature in the room plummeted, and to Takeno's horror, the statue toppled onto its face.

The Daimyo cried out incoherently as he ran to the stone pedestal. He called for Takeno to come help him reposition the stone.

But the general was old, and unlike his lord, Takeno was feeling the effects of his age. He was able to ride and shoot a bow better than any of his subordinates, but his knees ached and he had trouble walking quickly.

Impatiently, Konda crouched and wrapped his fingers around the statue. The Daimyo tensed, and then Konda's body began to glow. Pale white light surrounded his body, creating a barrier between the ruler's hands and the statue's surface. To Takeno, it seemed as if the glow was doing the work while the Daimyo controlled it from within the envelope of light.

Alone, Konda hauled the rough chunk of stone onto its side. He dropped to his knees and inspected the statue's face. It was undamaged, the markings still sharp, crisp, and unbroken. The Daimyo hung his head for a moment, whispered a prayer of thanks to himself, and then climbed to his feet.

Takeno stood where he was, hesitant to draw the Daimyo's attention. Konda's rapture-fueled strength came infrequently, but always when the ruler had been communing with his stone. Takeno had seen Konda accidentally crush the bones and stave in the armor of his own soldiers, unaware or unconcerned about his surges of devastating strength.

Now, the Daimyo bent his back once more and guided the great stone up. Again, he seemed to be lifting it, but the glow grew brighter and more distinct as it actually did the work.

When Konda was done, the monarch slumped to the floor with his back to the pedestal. He tilted his head back, allowed his eyes to wander across the ceiling, and then slowly lowered his eyelids.

As if in a dream, Takeno saw clear flashes of Princess Michiko. She was riding on the back of a battle moth, she was being led into a sheltered cave in the woods. Her hands were bound. Her face was anxious.

Konda roared and bolted upright. "My daughter!" he boomed. "Has she been returned to the tower?"

"No, my lord. She is still missing."

"Unacceptable! Where is Captain Nagao?"

"He was sent to retrieve the princess. He is also missing."

The Daimyo's wandering eyes drifted past the boundaries of their own sockets. A swirl of wind lifted Konda's hair and mustache as a strange, liquid light gathered around his head.

"Where is Michiko? Is she truly being held prisoner in the hinterlands as my vision portrayed?"

Takeno bowed. "I do not understand the power of your vision, my lord. But I saw it, too. I believe it is worth exploring."

"This will not do!" The Daimyo leaped to his feet and stormed to the chamber door. He opened it and bellowed, "Takeno! Bring me General Takeno!"

"I am here, my lord."

Konda closed the door and pressed his back against it. He stared at the statue, looking right past the general. Takeno followed Konda's eyes, to where the stone disk floated, smoking and steaming once more as strange lights played across its surface.

"Takeno is here, my lord. What do you require of me?"

"Stay where you are." Konda pulled the door open just enough to squeeze through, then descended the stairs slowly, regally.

Takeno hurried as fast as he could, catching up with Konda on the second stair down.

"My lord." The old soldier kept his head bowed as they continued down the stairs.

"My daughter," Konda said. "Has been taken hostage."

They had come to the bottom of the stairs. Takeno straightened and placed his hand on his sword. "What must I do, my lord?"

Konda took him by the shoulders. "Gather a cavalry division. Gather two. In fact, General, assemble three full divisions of mounted retainers. The gates are open. I want them riding out at dawn tomorrow."

"It will be done, my lord. Where is the battle?"

Konda snapped his fingers and called, "Map." Takeno's aide stepped forward from the corner of the room and unfurled a long paper tube, kneeling as he held it up for the Daimyo to read.

"There," Konda pointed to a spot in the hinterlands. "She's being held there. Whoever has her will probably ransom her to bandits rather than deal with us directly. I want those divisions to be very visible, General. Anyone who dares meet with her abductors will see the full force of Towabara's rage poised to come down on them like lightning from the sky.

"Search every inch of this quadrant until you find her. Check every cave; open every rotted log; drag every pond. There will be no trial for her captors. Bring me their heads and bring me my daughter. That is what you must do."

"I shall, my lord."

"You have all my trust, General. Do as I have bid you."

Takeno saluted again and marched from the room, his aides trailing behind.

* * * * *

Toshi kept expecting Michiko to try to escape, but all she did was sit in his hideout and stare at the wall. Maybe princesses were above petty concerns like being held captive.

He was pleased that she kept trying to wriggle out of the bonds around her wrists. As long as she was doing that, she wasn't doing anything that might actually help her escape. He had explained to her that even if she got loose, subdued him, and made it out of the cave, she was more than a day's walk from anywhere. She would die of thirst in the badlands, and if she went back into the forest looking for food, something would eat her instead.

She listened when he talked, but she never agreed and she continued to work on freeing her hands when she thought he couldn't see. Oh, well, he thought, and resigned himself to another pretty face that would never trust him again.

He had been sad to see the moth fly away for the last time, but he felt like theirs had been a mutually beneficial arrangement. He had also been satisfied with the distance they had put between themselves and orochi country, but they had been stationary for several hours and he was growing uneasy. The cave had seemed quite safe when he was on the moth's back. Now that he was here, it felt like another cell.

Part of it was the boredom. With nothing to do but wait, the magnitude of what he had done started to overwhelm him. He had snatched the Daimyo's daughter. Who besides Konda would even touch a ransom deal? Boss Uramon would have no part of it—she did too much business on the Towabara border. Godo would love to get his hands on Konda's offspring, but the bandit chief would certainly cut Toshi out of the deal . . . probably by cutting Toshi's head from his body.

He even considered making a run for Hidetsugu's, but even though he knew he could hold out there indefinitely, he didn't relish the idea of explaining how he had forestalled vengeance for Kobo so he could parley the Daimyo's daughter into something for himself. Hidetsugu was bound to be very emotional about the loss of his apprentice, and it didn't pay to be too close to an angry o-bakemono.

Toshi stood, keeping his head low so as to avoid the low ceiling, and walked to the mouth of the cave. He remembered how persecuted he felt with the soratami hounding him out of Numai. Now, just about every species in the world was after him or the princess.

"My boy," an amiable voice said. "You don't know the half of it."

Toshi spun around. The voice seemed to come from right behind him, but there was no one in the cave but Michiko. He turned again and looked out into the dim pre-dawn sky.

The moon was still up, a vertical crescent of silver. It hung just over the tops of the trees, seemingly close enough to reach out and touch.

"I knew you'd spot me eventually."

Toshi gaped as the moon tilted, slowly bringing one end of the crescent up until it resembled a broad parody of a grin.

The grinning moon descended, drifting down past the trees until it hovered just above the ground a few yards from where Toshi stood. Then it dwindled and a small, boyish figure took shape behind it. He was smaller than an akki, blue in color, and his body seemed to be composed of circles. His head was round, his cheeks were fat and full, his belly was soft and protruding. His fat little fingers hung under a tiny swollen hand on the end of a sausage-shaped forearm. He looked human, but the little blue man and his outrageous proportions struck Toshi as the comic result of a spell gone wrong.

"What," Toshi said loudly, "are you supposed to be?"

The little man smiled, and his cheeks wrinkled up so much that his eyes nearly disappeared. His teeth shone silver like moonlight in a cloudless sky, and particles of sparkling ice glittered in the air around his head.

"I am the Smiling Kami of the Crescent Moon," he said. "But you can call me Mochi."

Toshi drew his jitte in one hand and his long sword in the other. "You're a kami? I've been having trouble with kami lately."

"I'm a friendly kami, my boy. A cheerful and helpful one."

"You don't look like a kami."

"Oh? And how did you become an expert? Come on, then. What's a kami look like?"

"Not like overfed blue imps. Not like you."

"I swear to you that I am of the kakuriyo. I am of the spirit world, from the spirit world, and for the spirit world. I am a facet of one of the oldest and most revered kami your world has ever acknowledged." Mochi smiled encouragingly. "And I'm here to help."

"I'm sorry. Do I need your help?"

"Oh my, yes. You need my help. Believe me. You have no idea how much." He waved his hand, creating a trail of silver-blue vapor. In this wake, Toshi saw jumbled images . . . snakes in a frenzy, slithering across one another in a huge, wriggling ball . . . savage-looking kitsune rushing through the forest . . . hundreds of mounted soldiers riding out from the gates of Eiganjo. The scenes all had a sense of motion and each was coming straight at Toshi.

"When I sent you those portents outside your home in Numai, I was trying to simplify your life," Mochi said. "I never imagined you'd make such a complete pudding of it all."

The little blue man was still smiling. "So, do you want to listen? Or do you want to make fun of my appearance?"

CHAPTER 22

General Takeno addressed the tower courtyard, where over a thousand retainers waited on horseback. They were an inspiring sight, arranged in perfect lines under the Daimyo's flowing moon-and-sun standard. Their lacquered armor was dazzling in the morning light and the sun glinted off their helms. This was Konda's army, the strongest fighting force in the entire world. Other lords used magicians and giant creatures to dominate the battlefield, but Konda had done it through sheer force of personality and discipline. No tribe or nation had ever bested Towabara in battle: not armies, not mages, and not the false kami who plagued his land like a pack of spirit wolves.

Nourished by his pride, Takeno raised his sword. The old soldier's war cry rolled over the courtyard, and the retainers picked it up. The first division mounted, Takeno slashed down with his sword, and they streamed from the courtyard at full gallop.

Takeno slashed again, and the second division surged out like a great armored tide. He slashed once more, and the final division rode out through the gates.

Above, Takeno could see the Daimyo's tower window, where the great ruler watched. Together, the three divisions created a single mass of men and horses that rode ten to a row, side by side, filling the road from the gate to the hills in the distance.

Let the bandits quail, Takeno thought. Let the akki hide in their holes. The full force of a father's love for his daughter would mow them down like wheat.

Takeno watched wistfully as they last of the horsemen vanished over the hill. If his lord could have spared him, he would have been right there at the head of the charge, leading his yabusame on perhaps the most personal mission the Daimyo had ever assigned. But Takeno was a general, and Towabara was at war.

Sadly, slowly, the general turned and shuffled back into the tower to await the news of the cavalry's success.

* * * * *

In the ritual clearing of the orochi-bito, countless snakes intertwined as they danced and writhed by torchlight. With the sun struggling to clear the tops of the trees, a score of human kannushi priests knelt together in the center of the writhing snakes, chanting and hissing in the orochi's native language.

A large pile of soil and mulch stood at the center of the clearing. When the first ray of sunlight stabbed through the leaves and struck the pile, a shoot poked out. The shoot sprouted a leaf as it stretched upward, then another. It grew taller and broader, maturing from a sapling into an ancient cedar giant in a matter of moments.

A woman's face formed in the center of the new tree's trunk, a woman with smooth, brown skin and wild, leafy hair. More shoots sprouted around the face, and these also grew until there was a series of gracefully curving boughs encircling the central trunk. These boughs in turn sprouted more growth, until it seemed as if the entire forest had been compressed into this single clearing, but continued to grow in and over and around itself. Huge circular grains floated among the tangle of branches and vines, glowing a soft yellowish-green.

The frenzied chanting grew louder and more intense. The birds nearby took flight, and some of the dead and dying trees simply fell, their roots jarred loose by the rhythmic pounding of the worshippers' feet.

She was taken from us.

The priests howled and screeched, the snakes growled and hissed.

We had the means to end this nightmare once and for all. But it was taken from us.

The noise grew agonized, painful, the outraged screams of a tortured innocent.

Take it back. I am the forest, and it is me. There is no hiding. I will show you the way.

A green mist seeped through the manifested kami's limbs, flowing out and filling the ritual space. The kannushi ceased their noise to breathe deep the blessing from their patron spirit. The snakes continued to hiss as they drew in and blew out, and the sound from their throats sent the birds flying once more.

You will find her here. Go. We have the power to end this. By your love, by your devotion, we can end it today.

The clearing exploded into wild noise as the rampant worshippers overflowed the confines of the clearing and spilled out into the denser forest. Fully half of the assembled snakes melted away into the woods. All but a handful of the priests stayed to chant, preserving the manifestation of their patron spirit. When they had reclaimed the princess, their kami would grow even larger, and reward them all with the bounty of her love.

Go, my children. Go and take back what was stolen.

* * * * *

High above the Minamo Academy, floating on a cloud over the falls, the soratami reigned. Their capital city was the grandest city in the world, but no human had ever set foot there. It took powerful magic or one of the moonfolk's own cloud chariots to come and go from the city's majestic spires. Hisoka the headmaster once rode such a chariot to the gates of the city, but he was not invited in. He counted himself lucky to have seen it at all.

Among the gleaming towers of steel and glass was a huge central structure bigger than most of the human cities on the ground. This edifice was the seat of the soratami power structure, the home to its leaders and the most accomplished of their kind.

In an ornate chamber in the upper reaches of this palace in the sky, the samurai Eitoku and his shinobi partner were arguing.

"This has already gone too far, Chiyo," Eitoku said heatedly. His partner nodded.

The woman Chiyo smiled at them. "That is not for you to decide."

"You've heard our agent's report. The orochi-bito have been roused and the princess has been taken."

"Yes. Yes they have. Is this the same agent who lost her on the road to the academy?"

Eitoku looked down. "Yes. That was the headmaster's idea. We would not have approved it."

"So you failed to stop your agent from his folly. And he failed to deliver the princess to the school. You two have failed remarkably often lately."

Eitoku glared down at the woman. "You may be Uyo's right hand," he said, "but you go too far."

"I think that you do not go far enough. Like that ochimusha in the alley. Like when he trapped us all in his hovel." Her cold smile stayed fixed as her voice continued in Eitoku's head.

If not for my training, we might still be there.

Then Chiyo spoke aloud once more. "Setbacks are part of the game, Eitoku. If you panic every time things don't go exactly as planned, you won't recognize victory when it's staring you in the face."

"We should intervene directly. We should kill them all and—"

"You are too impetuous, Eitoku, too direct. You should learn to move slowly, with your eyes open. There are subtleties within subtleties to be considered. The kami are as inscrutable to us as we are to the academics at Minamo, but they make themselves plain to your superiors."

"Subtleties? The entire endeavor is unraveling as we speak."

"Hardly. We still have access and we still have control."

"But we do not have the princess. She is with that lowlife thug who—"

Chiyo cleared her throat. "Perhaps you didn't hear. We still have access. We still have control." She fluttered her eyes. "At least, some of us do. Perhaps you should stick to organizing the rats."

Eitoku's face went slack. "I am not used to being spoken to this way."

"That's because you're my junior. This is the most important endeavor the soratami have ever attempted, one that is being managed and overseen by the highest levels of our culture. You don't move in those circles. I do.

"I have better information than you. I am older, wiser, and crueler than you. You will stop harboring this fantasy that you have the power to affect our leaders' decisions. They know everything you know already and have rejected any half-baked notion you might suggest."

Eitoku turned away, cowed. "Yes, ma'am."

"Indeed. Now. Send word to your agent. We need to be ready in case the orochi-bito rabble try something unforeseen."

"Yes, ma'am."

"And listen well, Eitoku. The stakes we are gambling for are beyond your feeble comprehension. This has been in motion for decades, and you are but one small part of the process."

Chiyo smiled at the tall samurai, daring him to comment on her glib inspirational speech.

But Eitoku just nodded. "Yes, ma'am."

Chiyo gazed out the window while the warriors shuffled off. They really were such children. She had concerns of her own about the handling of this situation, but she kept them to herself. Unlike Eitoku, she did not need to be reminded to trust the soratami leadership. She was part of it, after all.

Chiyo paused, sending her thoughts to her master, who dwelled in the most secret recesses of the city. Uyo the prophet replied, and Chiyo smiled at her master's confidence.

Things were growing more complicated, more dangerous. But they were far from out of control.

* * * * *

In any other circumstances, Pearl-Ear would have been pleased with their progress. The kitsune were moving as quickly as they could and Choryu kept himself and Riko reasonably close behind, but they were all still too far away to do Michiko any good.

She had lost sight of the wizards hours ago, but she kept track of their progress as best she could. Pearl-Ear herself was the slowest of the kitsune—Sharp-Ear and the brothers did not wait, pulling a little further ahead with each acre they covered. The party was in danger of spreading out too much, but Pearl-Ear could not bring herself to slow down the group's fastest members.

The hours blurred together as they crossed meadow, thicket, and stream with the same driving, inexorable pace. They slowed only to get their bearings, check the trail, and hunt.

Without their rations, they were forced to live on whatever they could find or catch. The brothers were especially good at running prey to ground, so there was no shortage of meat—wild pigs, game birds, and weasels were numerous. The rough lifestyle left them all looking lean and wild, robes in tatters, fur tangled and muddy, muzzles smeared with blood.

Pearl-Ear's own senses had become sharper, and these more vivid sights and smells raised almost irresistible passions in her. She helped corral the game they caught, but she longed to take it down herself. A freshwater spring five hundred yards away called to her, fairly demanding that she come and drink. She had been so long among the cities of Towabara, and here was the chance to run free once more.

But Pearl-Ear was not enslaved to her instincts. Michiko was always central to her thoughts. She was the reason for this taxing survival run, and as wild as Pearl-Ear was, she focused the bulk of her energy on finding the ochimusha's trail. Whenever the brothers grew too fervid during the hunt, Pearl-Ear and Sharp-Ear brought them back to their real quarry: the princess and the man who took her.

The trail had recently grown much warmer. They had seen a great moth flying away to the north, and the creatures were so rare and concentrated in Towabara that there couldn't be two flying loose in this area. They backtracked in the direction the moth had come, and within hours Sharp-Ear had caught a familiar trace. Michiko and the ochimusha had been through here recently.

The brothers began to pant like hungry dogs when Sharp-Ear shared his find. Pearl-Ear felt the same anticipation but kept her mouth closed. Toshi was close. And with him, Michiko.

Choryu and Riko were still bringing up the rear, out of sight but well within earshot for a kitsune. The brothers carved another trail marker into the bark of a tree for the wizards, and all five kitsune spread out to form a skirmish line. Pearl-Ear nodded, and they began to run, spreading out as they went with their backs bent and their muzzles near the ground.

CHAPTER 23

"So," Toshi said carefully. "You sent me those symbols, little smiling kami?"

"Mochi," the little man said.

"Whatever." Toshi stepped between Mochi and Michiko, who had risen and was coming to the mouth of the cave.

"And you are Toshi Umezawa." The blue cherub bowed. When he rose, he turned to the princess and sank to one knee. "And Princess Michiko, daughter of the Daimyo. An honor, Princess."

Michiko bowed reflexively, then shook her head in irritation. She glared at Toshi and said, "What is going on?"

"Your guess is as good as mine. He says he's a kami." Toshi squinted down at the little blue figure. "You don't look like any kami I've ever seen."

"And you've seen a lot of them lately, haven't you?"

"As a matter of fact, I have."

"As have I," Michiko said. "But I have never seen a kami that walked and talked so much like a man."

"Each spirit is unique," Mochi said with a friendly smile. "You see, our minds are quite different from yours. What you know of us in this world is part what we are, part what you make us out to be." He held his arms out, offering them a clear view of his entire body. "The utsushiyo is your realm, made for beings like you. This form I wear is an echo of what I truly am in the kakuriyo—and echoes are often distorted, misinterpreted by mortal ears. But I am a kami, believe that. There are people who call to me and upon me all the time. They've even given me a grand name so that I might be on par with the most exalted of spirits."

"Sure," Toshi said. "I believe you completely. There's no way you could just be an imp or a kappa with delusions of grandeur. Let me fall down and start praying."

"Ah, Toshi. I can see I'm going to have to give you a demonstration."

"I think you should give me a fond farewell and leave before I tie you up and gag you."

Mochi grinned again, dazzling them with his shining silver teeth.

One demonstration, coming right up.

Toshi became blinded, staring at an endless field of white. The glare started to fade, from the edges of his vision inward. He blinked repeatedly as the scene clarified before him.

He'd thought the view from the moth's back was spectacular, but he was so high up now that he could see the edge of the world itself curving along the horizon. Continental landmasses shifted below him as the globe turned, but even here he could hear hundreds of tiny voices calling out, begging to be noticed and blessed.

Then Toshi was a ray of light, hurtling down through the clouds and illuminating a patch of sea. The white foam reflected his silver glow, and around him Toshi saw an ocean of light dancing on the surface of the water.

A strange, alien joy overcame him and he tried to shout. Overhead, the crescent moon sent down more light to play among the waves, and Toshi felt an inexplicable yearning to rise and rejoin the glow that had spawned him.

The world went white again. When his eyes cleared, Toshi's legs went rubbery and he collapsed to the cave floor.

He rolled over on to his back and struggled to a sitting position. Michiko was also down on the ground, lying on her side with her eyes blank and her mouth moving.

"The sea," she muttered. "The light."

Toshi struggled to clear his head. He climbed to his feet and drew his jitte, holding it in front of him.

Mochi still stood by the mouth of the cave, his arms spread and his teeth shining.

I am an aspect of the moon. Mochi's smile did not change; his lips did not move. *There is one moon spirit, but there are many phases. We are distinct, we are one. I am one of many, yet I am unique in all the spirit realm. We are the feasting rabbit, we are the eye of the spirit world—wide open, fully closed, and all points in between. I am Mochi, the eye squinted almost shut in mirth, the sharp silver crescent of a joyous smile.*

The voice sounded directly in Toshi's ears. From the way Michiko was wincing, Toshi guessed she was hearing it, too.

Our minds are different from yours. What one kami does cannot long be kept from the others. Those of us who can act often choose not to. But for you, Michiko, and you, Toshi, I shall act.

"All right," Toshi grunted. "You win. Just go back to talking, because this is splitting the princess's head wide open. I'm not enjoying it, either."

"Suits me." Mochi hopped up on a stone so that he was at eye level with Toshi. Beside them, Michiko stood and leaned against the cave wall.

"Mochi." Michiko stepped forward. "If I believe you are what you say, will you take me from here and help me find Lady Pearl-Ear?" She offered him her bound wrists. "I am being held here against my will."

"Touch her," Toshi called, "and we'll have a problem."

"I'm not going to free you yet, Princess. For now, I think this is the safest place you can be. While you're with me, you're under my protection."

Mochi clasped his hands behind his back and paced around the top of the stone. "Now then. Lately, you've been driven back and forth across the country by kami and their agents."

"Who has?" Toshi said. "Me, or her?"

"Both of you."

Toshi shook his head. "My trouble started with moonfolk. The kami didn't start popping up until after that." He narrowed his eyes and took a step back. "You wouldn't know anything about the moonfolk who are after me, would you, Mr. Smiling Moon Spirit?"

Mochi grinned guiltily. "I do, a little. But trust me, those snobs wouldn't deign to scheme with me. They pray to the larger spirit, the moon in all its guises."

"And I've been seeing a lot of crescent moons lately. In the sky, on the scales of angry kami, around the necks of soratami. You'd better come clean, little spirit, because you're not very convincing."

"The moonfolk are actively attempting to colonize the nezumi under their control. You interrupted one of their initial outings. Apart from trying to warn you after they surprised you at home, I've had nothing to do with your current list of troubles."

"Then what do we have to talk about? My problem is with soratami."

"I'm getting to it. You have to start at the beginning. Stop interrupting." The little kami resumed pacing. "Where was I?"

"You were talking about the kami attacks." Michiko stepped away from the wall.

"Ah, yes. Something you have become keenly interested in lately."

"I am seeking the cause of the Kami War, Mochi. If you answer no other questions for me today, answer that one. The killing and strife must stop."

Princess Michiko continued to impress and amuse Toshi with her innocence and drive. You had to be rich and pure of heart to be so concerned about others. He surreptitiously checked her wrists. Another few days and she'd work free of those ropes.

"Patience, Princess. Right. Now, the soratami have been working to expand their influence over the rest of Kamigawa. They've also become increasingly active in your father's kingdom. Twenty years ago, your father did something terrible. Me and the soratami . . . my soratami, who have nothing to do with Toshi . . . have been working to undo it ever since."

"On the night I was born," Michiko said haltingly, "they say my father performed a ritual."

"Indeed. And the ritual performed in conjunction with your birth made a great crime possible."

"Was he going to sacrifice her?" Toshi heard his question bounce around the inside of the cave as Michiko and Mochi stared at him.

"What? That would be terrible, wouldn't it? That's all I'm saying."

"The crime was my birth," Michiko said bitterly. "I was an event to him, not a child. I might as well have been a solstice or an eclipse."

"No, Princess." Mochi's face was earnest. "Never. You are as important to Konda as anything in this world."

"You are kind, but that is simply untrue. He keeps the most important thing behind locked doors and never strays from it."

"There is so much you do not understand, Michiko. Here. Let me show you."

"How can you—"

But Michiko never finished her question. Instead, Mochi opened his mouth wide and the interior of the cave once more disappeared in a blinding flash of moonlight.

* * * * *

The light receded and Michiko found herself floating below a mass of yellow clouds. Below her, the Daimyo's tower sulked like a tombstone. She was not light, as she had been in Mochi's previous vision, but possessed her own shape. She could feel her arms and legs, the weight of her robe against her skin, but she could not see herself, not even her eyelids.

A break in the clouds formed, and Michiko heard Mochi's voice whispering in her mind.

Behold the night of your birth. I regret that I cannot show you your mother one last time. Our opportunity is limited and there is something you must see.

Michiko agreed, and though she did not speak or think the assent, her phantom form was drawn to the top of the tower all the same.

She passed through the heavy white stone and a dozen or more retainers without resistance. The men and women of the tower did not register her presence in the slightest. Ghost-like, she drifted down the halls, up the stairs and into the locked chamber where twenty years hence, Daimyo Konda would spend all his time.

Her father was there, looking as he always had. His face was slick with sweat and he was grinning victoriously. A bearded man in Minamo robes was kneeling beside a brazier of blue fire. Takeno kneeled beside the brazier, chanting and hurling gold dust into the fire. A soratami stood opposite the wizard, striding back and forth as he chanted. His ears were loose and trailed behind him, the strange markings on his flesh migrating from his skull to the tips of his lobes.

Why is there a moonfolk here? Michiko wondered.

As I said, Mochi's voice answered. *We've been trying to undo this since it was done. Your father would not be dissuaded, so we decided to participate in order to keep the situation manageable, and in case something went wrong.*

"Come," Konda intoned. "Come to me now, my child."

The air above the brazier split and a thin seam of energy seeped through. The dazzling blue-white line intensified. The ends of the line withdrew into the center and formed a blazing spot of blinding energy.

"Come!"

The light crackled, contracted, and then burst, flooding the room with a sheet of luminous white. Michiko blinked reflexively, but she maintained a clear and interrupted view.

Her father and his cohorts were frozen, statues on a field of white. The center of the white void was open and swirling like a rapidly draining basin. Through the hole, Michiko could see something vast, glimpses of an alien world.

This is a window into the spirit realm, Mochi's voice said. *No mortal, not even the ones in this room on this night, has ever seen what you now see.*

Michiko floated forward, hypnotized, intoxicated by the swirling vortex. She reached out a phantom hand and broke the plane between the kami's realm and her father's.

Watch closely, Princess. And don't forget to come back.

Spirits swam and soared across the colorful emptiness, not in shapes but in vectors. There was a clear sense of motion, but no sign of bodies in motion. Michiko sensed action, but she could not distinguish any actors. It was like a thousand gusts of wind across a shapeless expanse of clouds and wavering light.

Then, the entire churning mass trembled. She had the oddest sensation of being a fish in a bowl while someone was tapping the glass. The fabric of the world around her seemed to stretch and collide with itself, trembling from to some tremendous external impact.

"Come!" her father's roar rippled across the surface of the spirit world. A million strands of force flowed back toward the rift behind Michiko, gathering from every direction into a funnel shape.

The funnel continued to swirl and collect strands of motion to itself. Michiko was reminded of the dregs in the bottom of a teapot—the bits of leaf and stem were a part of the brew, but if you stirred fast enough, you could easily separate them into a column at the center.

The swirling funnel grew thicker, more dense. It had accreted so much spirit energy that it was becoming physically solid. Michiko saw parts of the spinning mass harden, break off, and be churned back into to vortex. Soon the entire thing would congeal like cooling wax, set forever in the shape of a disk.

"Come!"

The disk turned on its axis. It oriented on the portal and drifted toward it.

Everything but the disk stopped, as if the kami had together abandoned their own pursuits and had paused to watch. There was resistance between the disk and the portal, a current of force that flowed to keep the disk in place. Her father's call was too powerful, however, and the disk surged on like a fish against the current.

A terrifying, outraged growl rumbled across the entire realm. Michiko had never imagined any sound could be so primal, so threatening. Terrified, she tried vainly to turn away, to flee before whatever made that sound appeared before her.

The substance of the spirit realm changed. The disk was now almost at the gleaming portal, but the air, the light, the very space around it had changed. It expanded and contracted like a lung, squeezing the world and Michiko too.

On the horizon, a new sun flared to life. It was joined by a second fiery orb, then a third and fourth. Stars began bursting to life in pairs, and when they had formed a line that reached all the way across the realm, they began to blink.

Eyes, Michiko realized. The paired stars were eyes in some vast and unknowable field of faces.

In the terrible light from those eyes, she saw the edges and outlines of nostrils, lips, and huge, savage teeth. Her heart froze. Whatever her father was doing had roused something unimaginably old and incomprehensibly vast. As multiple pairs of eyes surged forward to the portal, Michiko saw that their fire would fill the entire spirit realm long before the heads came close enough to touch the disk. A single one of those stars was enough to char an entire world, and there were more than a dozen coming for her now.

A pair of hands plunged through the portal and sank into the substance of the whirling disk. Michiko recognized the thin, powerful hands of her father as they dug in and hauled the disk halfway through the portal.

Michiko turned back and saw that all the visible horizon was now filled with star fire. It was drawing closer all the time.

Go, now, little Princess. You've seen what you came to see. To stay longer is to invite real danger.

Michiko's paralysis broke and though she had no sense of control over her motion, she willed herself to the portal as hard and as fast as she could. Behind her, the wave of fire was picking up speed, and she heard a louder version of the outraged growl, now a chorus of six or more snarling together.

She hit the portal just as the last edge of the disk vanished through it. Michiko was blinded once more by the trip from spirit realm to her world, and the star-eyed horror's furious sounds lingered in her ears.

How had her father summoned this much power? Even with the moonfolk and the Minamo master, it seemed impossible that the Daimyo could change the rhythm of the spirit world and distill part of it down to a form he could manipulate.

Then she was back in the chamber, listening to her father exult. He clapped Takeno on the back, he clasped the wizard's hand, he bowed to moonfolk on the other side of the brazier.

The blue flame had gone out. In the air above the smoking

metal bowl hung a circular mass of roughly carved stone. The form of a small, scaled creature was etched onto the stone disk's face, curled and stunted in the fetal position.

"Gentlemen," her father said. "We have just changed the future."

"Long live the Daimyo!" Takeno erupted. "Long live Konda!"

The wizard took up the chant, and after a few rounds the moonfolk joined in as well. Konda himself stood below the smoking statue, staring up at it intently through wide eyes. As Michiko watched, her father's pupils grew fuzzy and diffuse. They began to migrate back and forth across his eye sockets like a pair of searchlights searching for a ship in distress.

Michiko felt like she ought to scream. Instead, she said a small prayer to Justice, pleading with Towabara's patron spirit to spare her people from the consequences of Konda's crime.

On the wall of the chamber, the mural depicting Justice began to weep. Unable to close her eyes, unable to shed tears herself, Michiko could only stare as the Daimyo's men celebrated, Konda himself gaped in awe, and a princess's love for her father faltered under the weight of his actions.

* * * * *

Toshi started, almost losing his balance. He steadied himself against the cave wall. Mochi had trapped him in Michiko's point of view, so he felt everything she felt and learned what she learned. Disoriented, he focused on sorting his thoughts out from hers.

Michiko stood, eyes downcast, her arms clenched around herself. Her eyes were dry, but her expression was beyond sadness.

Mochi was next to her. He placed a comforting hand on her shoulder. "I am sorry, Princess. But that is the answer you seek. Your father dared to do what could not be done: he invaded the spirit world and captured a kami. And not just an everyday kami, but a major one. No simple well spirit or household benefactor here. He has imprisoned an essential being and is harnessing its power for his own ends."

Michiko dully raised her head. "And this is the secret of the tower." There was no inquiry to the princess's voice, only resignation. "The thing that he values most of all."

"He values you, too Princess, even if it's only because you are tied to that thing. It was created on the same night you were, born into this world only because you were. You are not the cause of the Kami War, Michiko. You are not the crime. Your birth was merely the opportunity."

Toshi's ears perked up. "What do you mean she's 'tied to' it?"

"Through the ritual. Her birth helped create sympathetic magic that brought the kami into this world. She's like the counterweight on a pan scale. The other side is only balanced, only stable, because Michiko exists as its opposite."

"And what happens to the kami statue if something happens to Michiko?"

Mochi shrugged. "I don't rightly know. Opinion is divided on the subject."

"The snakes said their kami want her dead."

Mochi wrinkled his nose. "Yes. That fits with their patron spirit's attitude. It sees the crime as a terrible imbalance in the natural order. To restore that order, it would gladly sacrifice an innocent life."

Toshi crouched down and pulled a handful of straw from his sleeping mat. "What about you, Mochi? Where do you stand?" As he spoke, the ochimusha folded pieces of straw into the same kanji character and dropped them one by one to the floor.

"I am here to help, as I said. I do not support action against the Princess."

"And what do you get out of it?"

"I am a lighthearted spirit, by nature." Mochi smiled his

dazzling smile. "The strife of the war is painfully ugly to me. I prefer to be invoked by lovers and drunkards on a fine night out, not by soldiers cursing me for more light to kill by."

Toshi glanced at Michiko, who still wore the same shocked expression.

"What a pant-load," Toshi said. "Are you buying any of this, Princess? Because I don't believe the kami do anything for purely altruistic reasons. Nobody does. Right now, all we've got is a convincing illusion and this swollen little bladder's word. I say we make him give us some straight answers before we trust him."

"We?" Mochi raised an eyebrow. "But if it's straight answers you want, I stand ready. Ask away."

"Why'd you send me those portents? They led me to danger, not out of it."

"I was trying to get you to go into hiding. How was I to know the ogre would send you right out again, straight to the place I wanted you to avoid?"

Toshi paused, unmollified. "Why are the moonfolk after me?"

"They hate for anyone to know what they're doing. It pierces the veil of mystery they've spent so long building up. When you stumbled onto them, and then escaped, it became more than an insult. They're looking to get even on behalf of the whole species."

The ochimusha casually inspected his fingernails. "How did Kobo die?"

"You already know. And if that's not the truth, I'll eat your sword with a spoon."

"Who can I trust?" Michiko stepped forward, drawing both Mochi and Toshi's attention. The small blue kami smiled.

"Him," he pointed at Toshi. "So long as you choose your words carefully and get a solemn promise out of him."

"Who can't she trust?"

Mochi turned back to Toshi. "Anyone who tries to take her to the Minamo Academy. There is far more going on this world than

I could ever explain or you could ever grasp. There are plots within plots, conspiracies within conspiracies. Many of the wizards are close to panic now that the Kami War has spilled out of the Araba. They know what happened on the night of her birth. They will do anything to study her in the hopes of determining a way to nullify that act."

Michiko became angry. "How do you know this?"

"Because some of them work for me. I admit that."

Toshi crossed his arms. "And your boys had nothing to do with focusing the other kami on me and the princess."

"Not a thing. Recently, there were conflicting opinions among soratami and the academy about what to do with you. The majority opinion was to get you to the school and learn what they could. I feared that they would then come to agree with the forest kami—that Michiko must die to restore what was lost. I reject that option. So I acted." He sighed. "Things rarely go according to plan, even for kami."

"What of Riko-ome? Does she work for you?"

"Riko-ome is your friend, Princess, and always has been."

Toshi folded another straw kanji. "And the boy?"

"Choryu is a better student than he is a friend. If he had listened to my party's counsel and left Michiko at home, perhaps none of this would have happened."

"And what about that thing in the kakuriyo?" Toshi asked. "What owns those eyes that burned up half the spirit world?"

"Don't take everything you saw literally," Mochi said. "The spirit world doesn't actually burn."

"Answer my question. What was that thing?"

Mochi's face grew dark and somber. "Something," he said, "that must never be allowed into your world." The little blue kami locked eyes with Toshi. "Such an event would put both our realms in danger."

Toshi held Mochi's gaze and nodded. "Including you."

"Including me." The feckless grin returned, but briefly. "That's the other reason I'm helping her and trying to undo what Konda has done."

Toshi turned. "Hey, Princess."

Michiko continued to stare for a moment, but then her eyes glanced up. "Yes?"

"If half of what this guy says is true, we're both in for a rough night. And I do think only half of what he says really applies to us."

Mochi raised an eyebrow. "I'm hurt."

"What makes you think I trust you any more than I trust him?" Michiko said to Toshi. "You have caused me and my friends nothing but hardship and grief since I met you."

Toshi pulled back his sleeve and showed Michiko the triangle tattoo. "Let me put it this way," he said. "I'm an ochimusha lowlife. I do dirty jobs for hire. Right now, holding you prisoner is my job. But I'm a freelancer, and I'll drop this in a heartbeat if something better comes along." He held out his hand. "Take me into your service," he said. "Make it worth my while and I'll not only let you go, I'll protect you from everyone that's coming for you. What do you say?"

"Of course not. Half the people coming here are doing so to rescue me. And I would be a fool to bargain for my safety with you. I am no fool, Toshi."

"Hear, hear."

"Quiet, chubby." Toshi looked Michiko up and down, shaking his head. "You're wrong, Princess. Time isn't on anyone's side. The first group to get here will claim you, but there's no guarantee they'll keep you. And when the fighting starts, how will you protect yourself? The snakes had you at their mercy despite your fox friends and your water wizard."

"You were there," Michiko said. "And you fell just as quickly." She drew herself up to her full height. "The only service you could offer that would sway me would be the one to join the Towabara infantry. Serve my people for two years as a soldier if you want to earn my trust. Unless you're read to take *that* oath, I will wait here with Mochi."

Toshi nodded. "Not exactly what I had in mind, but not too far afield. I wasn't thinking of an oath to your nation, Michiko, but to you. Personally."

"Toshi," Mochi said quietly. "This is a bad idea."

"And when I care what you think, I'll ask. Michiko," he stepped across the cave to the princess. "He's shown us things that you believe. Maybe I believe them, too."

Toshi watched her face. Those big eyes, those stern, set lips. She was so earnest, so innocent. Her entire world kept getting pulled out from under her. Surely all she wanted now was a rock to lean on. Toshi knew she was close to agreeing with him.

He drew his short blade, placed it blade-up between her wrists, and sliced through the vines binding her. He turned, stepped away from the mouth of the cave, sheathed his sword.

"You can go now," he said. "Take your chances on your own. Or, you can stay here with me and listen to what I have planned to keep us both alive."

Toshi drew his good jitte and twirled it around his finger before catching it in his hand. "So," he said. "Are you with me?"

CHAPTER 24

Three full companies of the Daimyo's finest mounted archers thundered south on the main route to the mountains. They moved as a single, massive entity rather than a thousand different individuals, and the merchants and farmers and villagers along the way all stared in awe as the great force of men and beasts rode by.

They were half a day's ride out of the tower, which was still visible behind them as they powered their way through the countryside. None of the men looked back, but many thought of their lord and master Daimyo Konda watching them from the highest levels of his mighty castle. He would watch them until they disappeared from view, and he would wait until they came triumphantly back with Princess Michiko leading them home.

The trees along the road began to shudder and shake. Some of the riders laughed and pointed. Look, they cried, even the soil trembles to see us pass!

The rumbling continued, growing longer and stronger until it had become a full-fledged tremor. The leader of the yabusame column reined in his horse, gradually slowing. Behind him, the rest of the great mounted entity kept pace, easing their horses from a full gallop to a moderate trot. They were still under orders to travel with all due speed, but it was foolish to risk men and horses when the ground kicked back.

But the tremor continued, soon becoming a quake that forced the Daimyo's horsemen to stop completely. Century cedars tore themselves from the ground and hurled themselves across the roadway. A great sinkhole opened a hundred feet east of the road, swallowing a rice paddy and a farmer's hut. The nearby hillside split down the middle, releasing massive rolling clods of soil and rough-hewn chunks of granite.

The horses began to scream and rear, lashing out with their hooves. Dozens fell over on one side and were quickly trampled by their skittish peers. The company captains shouted and cursed at their units, struggling to be heard over the din of shattering earth and dying horses.

Above the remains of the sundered hill, a huge yellow sphere ignited. The heat and the light were so intense that it boiled the closest retainers' eyes in their sockets and burned their hard, lacquered armor to fine ash on their bodies.

Another fireball ignited across the road from the first. Trapped between two suns, the outermost columns of soldiers and their horses withered into charred, smoking skeletons of black ash and carbonized bone. Those that survived the inferno screamed with one agonized voice.

A stentorian roar split the air, drawing blood from every human ear on the road. The two blazing orbs spun in place, and the outer layer of flames peeled back like the skin from an orange, revealing two sharp, black irises that widened vertically as they gazed down at the soldiers.

The armed men of Towabara fell quiet under the terrible gaze of those two great eyes. Their breath ceased in mid-prayer, mid-curse, or mid-dying moan. Every living thing below those eyes looked up into them in pure, devastating awe.

The titanic spirit beast roared again. A great shadow rose up past the eyes, casting the area below into almost total darkness. Reptilian fangs as big as grain silos materialized as the shadow descended, simultaneously stretching down from above and erupting up from the soil below.

The great jaws slammed shut, consuming the road and the entire valley at once. The soldiers' screams were silenced in the cacophonous blast of sundered earth and mangled stone. The entire kingdom of Towabara felt the shock, as did every kitsune village and akki warren in the wilds.

The monstrous head, never fully formed, began to fade as the last of the bordering pave-stones along the road tumbled into the gaping wound it had torn in the world. In its wake, a huge jagged canyon lay where there had once been a road. The edges of the canyon smoked and collapsed down into the pit, the land itself partially liquefied by intense heat and unimaginable force.

The ground continue to rumble menacingly for a full day and night, waves of force radiating outward from the titanic bite the spirit beast had ripped from the world.

* * * * *

Dust shook from the stone ceiling of Toshi's cave, and he waved his arms to maintain his balance. "What was that?"

Mochi looked pale. "That was the worst news I've had all day. Luckily, it doesn't seem more pressing than what we already have on our plate."

"Fair enough."

Michiko sat cross-legged on the floor, busily folding stalks of hay into the same kanji shape. Toshi nodded, glad she had at least agreed to that much. The pile on the floor of the cave was almost big enough.

"So, we've got the princess squared away."

"You mean you tricked her into thinking she's squared away." He called out to Michiko, "When this ruffian here fails, Princess, I want you to know you can still count on me."

"Yeah, yeah. So, enough about her. Back to me,' Toshi said.

Mochi sighed. "I like you, Toshi. But you're just not the most important person in the cave right now."

"I am to me." He bent, picked up a handful of straw, and started forming kanji.

Mochi watched him. "What are those?"

"Razor birds." Toshi held up a straw kanji. "Or rather, the symbol for creating a razor bird. They're mostly mindless, but they know enough to keep from cutting the person who made them." He tossed the straw figure onto the pile. "Good for when you're woefully outnumbered. They'll come in handy quite soon." Toshi started on another piece of straw.

"Hey," Mochi said. "You still don't believe I'm who I say I am, do you?"

"I don't know what you are. You've got some power. But so do I. I prefer to rely on myself."

"Power," Mochi mused. "Where do you think that power comes from?"

"Hmm? Oh, I don't know. Kappa shells? Pixies?"

"When you make a symbol and it turns something invisible or sets it on fire, what do you think causes it?"

Toshi paused. "Never thought about it much. As long as it works, I don't need to know how."

"So you deny the power of the spirit world."

"I know there's power in the spirit world. I use it all the time. I just don't think I owe anyone because of it. I figured out how to make kanji work—me. Not some spirit guide. Anyone can do what I do if they're willing to learn the symbols."

Mochi hopped up on a stone so that he was level with Toshi. "So you don't pray."

"Who would listen?"

"And there's nothing larger than yourself . . . nothing you value that you can't get on your own."

"You've got a great perspective from up there in the sky," Toshi said. He tossed another kanji onto the pile and stared at Mochi, their faces almost touching. "But I have to live here on the ground. When something larger and more valuable than me comes along, I'll pay it the proper respect. But it'll have to convince me first."

Mochi grinned, displaying his teeth. "Done."

"What?"

At the rear of the cave, a shadow separated from the rest of the gloom. It was darker, more solid, and it rolled forward like a dense, heavy mist.

Toshi stood and drew his blade. "What is that thing?" Michiko dropped her pile of straw and moved behind Toshi, ready to dash out of the cave if she had to.

"That," Mochi said, "is larger and more valuable than you. And it's going to convince you."

The black curtain of shadow crept forward until it was a few yards away from Toshi at the front of the cave. The center of the black sheet rose up, forming a hood around a pale, expressionless face. Her delicate bones and polished skin said "female" to Toshi, but she also looked human, and that couldn't possibly be true. The air had become so cold and alien since she arrived that he was starting to think her very presence was harmful.

Slender red horns grew from her porcelain forehead and curved down past her cheekbones on each side of her face. She continued to rise, filling out the black curtain with a humanoid upper body that trailed off into the darkness beneath the black material. She stood tall, her head brushing the cave ceiling, shrouded in the fabric of shadow. Pale, cadaverous hands appeared in the gloom around her, grasping from the tattered edges of her robes, and something huge but withered squatted behind her, a dried and emaciated giant holding aloft a banner made from the same fabric as her robes. The bearer's head, if it had one, was tucked down behind the central figure, so that only its arms and its wan, sinewy shoulders were visible.

"She has many names, many supplicants. The nezumi call to her for inspiration and for a bountiful year's looting. Boss Uramon keeps a shrine to her in the basement of her manor. The jushi make offerings to her twice a year, including a gold coin, a black ram, and the blood of a friend, freely given.

"You are a mercenary and a thief, Toshi Umezawa, a creature of the dark. So your whole life has been a celebration of her, despite the fact that you have never even acknowledged her existence. Behold, the Myojin of Night's Reach. This spirit is larger than you, Toshi, this kami holds you in her sway. Deny her if you can. But it will be better for all of us if you embrace her.

"Fall to your knees, ochimusha, and solemnly ask her for whatever you desire most. Share in her gifts. Thrive under her protection. There is no other way for you to survive the night."

The dire spirit made no sound, save for a distant, hollow moaning that seemed to come from behind her. Toshi was unable to tear his gaze away from that porcelain face, even as sweat beaded on his brow and ran into his open eyes.

"Ochimusha!" The voice from without was sharp and high-pitched, crackling with anger. "Send Michiko out now. We will not ask again."

"Lady Pearl-Ear?" Michiko turned, but Mochi caught her by the arm before she could step from the cave.

"It's about to become very dangerous out there, Princess, one way or the other. You should stay put for the time being."

Mochi turned to Toshi. "It has begun," he said. He extended one arm outside the cave and the other back in, toward the dark figure. "The foxes are here, and the snakes are coming. Can you defeat them all, or will you openly call on the power you've been assuming was your own?"

Toshi's paralysis finally broke. He jerked his head from Michiko to Mochi to the frightening figure at the rear of the cave.

The crescent moon kami planted his hands on his hips, smiling confidently. He tilted his head and stared hard at Toshi.

"Choose."

CHAPTER 25

They found Michiko's trail just before the ground shuddered, rolling underfoot like a ship on rough water.

They rode out the quake and then stood together, facing a single point at their feet. Michiko's trail started here, clear and strong, as if she had stepped straight from the sky to this patch of hilly, forested ground.

The kitsune said nothing. The brothers whined a bit in anticipation. Pearl-Ear growled, and Sharp-Ear responded. The ochimusha's scent was here, too.

She lifted her head and listened. Riko and Choryu were close behind, but she doubted her ability to keep the pack in check, even if she had the interest.

Pearl-Ear growled again, and the foxes all lit out at once, tearing through the rolling meadows as they followed Michiko's trail. In this, Pearl-Ear matched the speed and stamina of the males, even outdistancing them by a few strides.

She was the first to see the cave, and once more her intellect overrode her instinct. They must not charge in and try to battle Toshi in close quarters. She wanted to punish the ochimusha for what he had put them through, but Michiko was the real reason for their journeys. As always, she came first.

Pearl-Ear waved the others down. Through a soft series of grunts and gestures, she sent Dawn-Tail and Blade-Tail around either side of the cave to search for another access point. If they could get in behind the thug, they could take him down in the blink of an eye. More important, she didn't want to leave him an escape route by committing all their efforts to the front.

The brothers soon signaled her from the far side of the cave. There was no way out save the main entrance. Pearl-Ear waved them back to her and hunkered down with Sharp-Ear and Frost-Tail while she waited.

"We give him one chance," she said. "He's desperate, but he's not stupid. He'll try to bargain his way out."

Frost-Tail growled.

"Of course not. We just want to get him away from Michiko. I will get him talking. I will agree to his demands. And when we see an opening, we split them apart. I'll take Michiko away. You all subdue the ochimusha."

"What about . . ." Sharp-Ear's question trailed off as Choryu and Riko came bustling through the woods. "What about those two?"

"They are Michiko's friends. They will come with me."

The student wizards lumbered up. Pearl-Ear had a soft spot in her heart for each of them on Michiko's behalf, but compared to the light- and fleet-footed kitsune, Choryu and Riko were a handicap.

"Is she in there?" Choryu said. He was red-faced and out of breath, his white-blonde hair plastered to his skull.

Sharp-Ear nodded. "First we must get her away from Toshi."

"Then let us do so, now." His face looked panicked as well as flushed. "There are orochi-bito coming up quickly behind us. We cannot let her fall into their hands again."

"That will not happen," Pearl-Ear said. "We will move as soon as the others return." She raised a finger to keep Choryu quiet as Dawn-Tail and Blade-Tail crept in.

"Lady Pearl-Ear lures them out," Frost-Tail told them. "We get in between them and take the ochimusha. Lady Pearl-Ear and you wizards go for Michiko."

The scouts nodded. Sharp-Ear took hold of his sister's hand and squeezed. She returned the gesture, then jerked her head toward the cave. The three brothers and Sharp-Ear quickly positioned themselves around the cave entrance, far enough away to be concealed but close enough to rush in.

"Choryu," she spoke sharply to cut through the wizard's glassy stare. "Are you up to this?"

The young man's jaw tightened. "After all my mistakes," he said, "I'm ready to do this right."

"Riko?"

"I am ready, Lady Pearl-Ear, but I will hang back. Without my bow, I will just get in your way."

"Very well. Say nothing, do nothing, until I say." The wizards nodded. Pearl-Ear scanned the area outside the cave, spotting each hidden kitsune in turn. Then, Pearl-Ear rose and cupped a hand next to her mouth.

"Ochimusha! Send Michiko out now. We will not ask again."

She thought she heard Michiko's voice, but there was no way to be sure. Her people often played games with travelers, mimicking their own voices. She would not be drawn in by a ruse.

Toshi's voice rolled out of the cave, as smooth and as full of bluster as ever. "Is that you, Lady Pearl-Ear of the kitsune?"

"You know it is," she replied. "You have our thanks for taking Michiko away from the orochi-bito. For that we will not kill you on sight. But if you do not surrender her, now, we shall forget that kindness."

"A pleasant fantasy, but highly unlikely," Toshi said. His banter took on a slightly strained edge. Perhaps his wild journey had affected him as much as theirs affected her.

"But here's what I will do. I'm going to sit in here and fold hay for a while. Michiko has agreed to help me. If you're still alive when we're done, I'll bring her out. How does that sound?"

"It sounds like you're stalling. Let me hear Michiko unharmed and we'll see about waiting." She coughed lightly, drawing Sharp-Ear's and the samurai's attention. She held up four fingers, one for each of them, and stabbed them into her open palm. Each of her fellow kitsune nodded, ready to go on her signal.

"Lady Pearl-Ear," Riko whispered. "The orochi-bito."

"I hear them." The snakes were very close now, their rampant hissing audible on the wind.

"We have to get her out now," Choryu said.

"Settle down, wizard. You're going to put her in more danger, not less."

On a nearby ridge, the first orochi-bito appeared through the trees. Its tongue flashed in and out, and then it turned toward Toshi's cave.

"They're here," Choryu said.

"Quiet." Pearl-Ear's attention was on Sharp-Ear and the brothers. She stole a glance at the hilltop, where more orochi were slithering into view.

The wizard stood. "Go, go now!" Energy flared from his eyes. Thick streams of water formed and circulated around his arms. "For the princess!"

Pearl-Ear hit him in the side of the head with her closed fist. Choryu groaned, staggered, and collapsed.

Nearby, a reptile screamed. Pearl-Ear saw Frost-Tail with a dead orochi in his grip. In the brush, among the trees, and near the cave, fox grappled with snake and all dissolved into confusion.

"Riko," Pearl-Ear said. "You can stay here with Choryu, or you can come with me. But I am going to rescue Michiko." She stood and let out a high-pitched cry from the back of her throat.

Riko glanced at Choryu's unconscious body, then rose to stand beside Pearl-Ear. Together, the two women charged for the cave.

* * * * *

Toshi heard the sounds of snakes battling foxes. He looked back at the Myojin of Night's Reach. Mochi was probably right—she was a source of great power among Numai and he'd probably been tapping into her reserves his whole life.

Unlike the moon kami, however, she was classy enough not to mention it or demand restitution.

Outside, a kitsune snarled in pain. Mochi clasped his hands behind his back and began to rock back and forth on his feet.

"They're dying out there," Mochi said. "One thug and a pile of razor birds won't be enough and you know it."

Michiko tried once more to step past Mochi, but the little blue kami blocked her exit. "You're not going out there. Not until your protector there admits he needs our help."

Michiko turned her pleading eyes to Toshi. "Don't just stand there," she said. "We need to act, to get out there, even if it's only to run again."

"Ask us for help," Mochi said. "And we'll help. Don't do it for the foxes, or the princess, or even the word. Do it for yourself. Ask the kami for her blessing. Accept her, and me, as your patrons. You will be protected."

"I'm not taking anything from you," Toshi said. "You smile too much."

"From her alone, then. Power can take many forms, Toshi. Pray for a blessing that will aid you now, and for the rest of your life. What does a man in your position need? What makes your life worth living? She can give it to you. She can give you anything. All you have to do is ask."

"Toshi, please."

The ochimusha rubbed his temple, fighting back a headache. Between the noise outside and the chatter in here, he could barely gather his thoughts. He lowered his hand, catching sight of the hyozan tattoo.

Perfect, he thought. Another burden to bear. He couldn't keep fighting such overwhelming odds, he couldn't escape through the mob of enemies outside, and he couldn't even walk away—there was hyozan business to settle.

Toshi glanced back at Michiko, who no longer had the guile to conceal her emotions. She looked tired, frightened, and almost ready to surrender. He wished Kobo were here. Not just to simplify his options, but because the big ox was useful. Strong, obedient, good in a fight, and most of all, he kept his mouth shut.

"Well?" Mochi said. "Another few moments and this discussion will be moot. I will defend the princess myself if I have to. Michiko must survive this night. You have no such imperative."

"So you'll just leave me here to rot."

"Basically."

"Unless I tell you what I want from you kami."

"Exactly. Ask, and it shall be granted. Join us, Toshi. You can't do everything alone."

Thoughts of Kobo bubbled through Toshi's mind. He turned to the Myojin of Night's Reach.

"Hey," he called. "Let me hear it from you. You will give me what I want, when I want it, and all I have to do is ask."

The dire figure did not reply, but instead simply stared with her cold, vacant mask. Slowly, the alabaster chin dipped and then rose again.

Michiko finally broke, tears streaming from her eyes. "Do it, Toshi. Please. You don't have to save me, but please . . . help my friends."

Toshi watched her tears fall. A cold smile turned up the corners of his lips.

"I know what I want from the kami," Toshi said. "And I will call for it, humbly, when and if I need it."

Mochi cocked his head. "If?"

"If," Toshi confirmed. "I may not require a kami blessing after all, Mochi. Not when I have all the power I need right here."

With a smooth, sudden motion, Toshi drew his sword and lunged, sending the point toward Michiko's throat.

* * * * *

Pearl-Ear tore a long strip of flesh from an orochi's arm as she grappled with it. There must have been over twenty of the snakes outside the cave, but they were finding the kitsune more formidable than before. The lack of weapons made the foxes more alert, quicker and more savage. The kitsune quickly formed a line with their back to the cave and repulsed wave after wave of the snakefolk's attack.

Pearl-Ear and Riko were likewise unable to gain access to the cave, but they were poised to do so as soon as the steady flow of orochi broke. They seemed endless, but the snakes had not endured the days-long sprint that brought them here anywhere near as well as the kitsune had. Outnumbered five-to-one, Pearl-Ear and her kin were easily holding their own.

Something sharp whistled past her ear, and the orochi charging toward her screamed. The snake fell, holding a bleeding gash on its neck. Pearl-Ear silenced his struggles with a heel to the back of his skull. Three more solid whispers shot out of the cave, glancing off orochi and leaving long, gaping wounds.

Pearl-Ear concentrated, and she was able to see the fast-moving blades. They were small and black, shaped like two-dimensional birds. They had no eyes, and their entire bodies were the color of dull coal, with no differentiation among beaks, feet, and wings. The mock-birds sliced whatever they touched, swarming around the snakes like hornets, slashing them open and driving them back from the cave.

"Hey, you kitsune," Toshi yelled. "Duck."

Pearl-Ear heard a flurry of razor wings as she tackled Riko to the ground. Sharp-Ear and the brothers also took cover as a cloud of the sharp bird-things surged out of the cave and began flaying the snakes alive.

It was a terrible sight, one that would have shocked Lady Pearl-Ear a short time ago. She had been inured to blood and violence over the past few days, however, and the awful cloud of screaming snakes and spattering blood barely horrified her at all. Riko, blessed child, turned her face away.

The storm of razor birds was brief but spectacular. When it died away, not a snake was left standing outside the cave. Pearl-Ear's keen ears heard more orochi approaching in the distance, but for now she had a moment's respite.

The flock of false birds retreated back to the cave entrance and hovered there, blocking the entrance. Pearl-Ear heard the sharp snap of human fingers, and then the curtain of sharp wings split down the middle, separating as Toshi emerged with sword in hand.

The curtain closed behind him. He looked around, spotting Pearl-Ear and Riko and the rest of the kitsune. He looked confident and strong, but the mischievous grin was belied by the stern glare in his eyes.

He nodded to Lady Pearl-Ear. "Where's the wizard boy?"

She didn't answer him immediately. All she could see was the man who had taken Michiko. "Nearby," she growled at last. "Where is Michiko?"

Toshi pointed over his shoulder. "In there. We'll have our reunion once the orochi are dealt with."

Indeed, Sharp-Ear and the others were already engaging the second wave of snakes. This one was larger than the first, and Pearl-Ear guessed that the word was spreading among the snakefolk: our quarry is here. She briefly wondered how many of them had come after Michiko, and how many they'd have to subdue before they could take the princess home.

Toshi strode forward. As he passed Lady Pearl-Ear, she sprang to her feet and dug her claws into his arm. "Take me to Michiko."

Toshi shrugged, and a powerful jolt of force tossed Pearl-Ear back onto her rear.

"If it's all the same to you foxes," he said, "I'll handle this."

He drew his sword, and Pearl-Ear shielded her eyes. The weapon's edge was glowing white, not hot but brighter than the midday sun. The glow spread down the length of the blade and spilled over onto Toshi himself. It ran up his arms, over his shoulders, and across the rest of his body until he was surrounded by a nimbus of brilliant purplish light. When he moved, there seemed to be several of him at once as he flickered around the battle site.

And move he did. Pearl-Ear's sharp eyes were barely able to follow as Toshi darted around the area. She took in a series of strobe images: Toshi with his sword through an orochi's chest; Toshi standing next to a beheaded snake; Toshi cutting three throats with a single stroke. In each attack, he was gone before the blood could flow, flashing to a new target as soon as he'd struck the current one.

As the ochimusha flashed around the forest like a mad hummingbird, the kitsune all stared in amazement. They didn't need to defend themselves, as every snake in the area was focused on stopping Toshi. Scaled body parts continued to fly and orochi continued to drop as Toshi became a blur even to their keen eyes.

Lady Pearl-Ear recognized magical enhancement when she saw it, but she didn't understand how Toshi had become so dangerous. She watched him pursue a small group of orochi to the far side of the glen and then rolled to her feet and charged the cave entrance.

The razor birds across the entrance were so thick they appeared as a solid mass. Pearl-Ear felt a hundred pinpricks and slashes on her skin as she covered her face and plunged into the blockage. The pain was manageable so long as she didn't slow down. The birds didn't seem to be attacking her as they had the orochi, but they were numerous enough to cause her real harm if she wasn't careful.

A powerful hand caught her by the scruff of the neck and hauled her free from the wall of birds, back out to the forest glen.

"That's a terrible idea," Toshi said. "I made it very tough to get in there, and you wouldn't like what you saw anyway." He was still shining brightly, but not as brightly as before. Whatever he had used to enchant himself seemed to be wearing off.

Pearl-Ear slapped his glowing hand off her. "I will see Michiko now."

"Not a chance." Toshi pointed back to the hill that kept spawning orochi. "The grunts have been dealt with. But the generals are still to come."

Pearl-Ear followed his hand and saw a half-dozen kannushi priests on the hillside. They had clasped hands and were chanting. They alternated between hisses, shouts, and groans, but the rhythm was clearly that of a summoning ritual. Lady Pearl-Ear understood enough of the words to make her heart sink.

Riko had been standing next to the entrance of the cave, gingerly testing the wall of birds, but now she called anxiously to Pearl-Ear. "They're summoning their kami," she said.

"I hear." Pearl-Ear stepped in front of Toshi. "Can your birds deflect a major spirit?"

"Maybe. I've never tried. Probably not."

"Then let us take her from here. It's not safe."

Toshi's glow was almost completely gone. "It will be," he said. He sheathed his sword and drew a finely crafted silver jitte.

"Stand back," he said. "And watch how we deal with rogue spirits in Numai."

CHAPTER 26

Toshi strode toward the priests on the hill with his jitte out and ready. He trusted the razor birds to keep the foxes clear of his cave until he was ready to let them in . . . which might never happen. He would worry about that after he survived the next few moments.

A thin green shoot rose out of the ground a short distance from the chanting priests. As the first grew and thickened, a second rose from the soil. A third formed, and a fourth. More of the leafy tendrils climbed toward the sky and braided themselves together.

When the vertical shoots were tall and thick enough to be counted as small trees, the lateral growth began. Branches jetted out from the central mass, perpendicular to the ground. In turn, more growth flowed from these horizontal limbs, and the entire mass of living wood grew heavier, stronger, and harder as the ground compressed beneath its burgeoning weight.

A woman's face formed near the top of the construct, one not unlike the Myojin of Night's Reach. It was a similar mask of a woman's face, but this one seemed to be made of smooth, polished wood. Where the black kami was surrounded by a dark shroud and pale hands, the orochi's kami was draped in leaves and moss. Her "hair" was in fact another stand of miniature trees, and her arms curved around her body as they grew and thickened. The more the kannushi priests chanted, the more wood growth occurred.

You have done much damage here, the wood spirit droned. *Too much. Surrender the child. The balance must be restored.*

Toshi stopped a mere ten yards from the kami. "Why did you tie Kobo to those trees?"

The spirit's growth continued. Her face tilted down as if noticing Toshi for the first time.

"I asked you a question. None of this would be happening if you'd left my partner alone."

You're referring to the apostate. The one who turned his back on his own tribe.

"I'm referring to my oath-bound brother, yes. Kobo."

My children hung him out for the monks to see. He was dressed as they were. We left him to his own kind. Later, he died in the rain.

Toshi stroked his chin with the tip of his jitte. "Not good enough. Not by a long shot." He pointed the jitte at the wooden mask. "I'm going to have to punish you now."

Thick, ripe vines erupted out of the ground and coiled around Toshi's wrists. He strained against them, but they held fast. Two more leafy ropes crawled from the soil and wrapped around his ankles.

Punish me? Little man, you have a very high opinion of yourself.

"I do, at that. But you'll find me worthy of it."

The kannushi on the hill continued to chant. Behind him, Toshi could hear the kitsune attempting to storm through the cave entrance, but the birds repulsed them time and again.

What will you do, then, little conjurer? Poison me? Burn me? I am the life force of the forest itself. Fell every tree, and I emerge from the roots unscathed. Plow up the roots, and I shall return when the first seed blooms. Raze all the Jukai down to the bare rock, and I shall survive in the grass, in the moss, in farmer's fields and the city's gardens. I am the essence of life itself, of unbridled growth and unrestricted vigor. What weapon can you bring to bear that would harm me?

The vines tightened on Toshi's wrists and ankles. He felt the rough texture biting into his flesh. He looked up into the wood kami's expressionless face.

The ochimusha smiled. He closed his eyes and said, "Myojin of Night's Reach. I seek your blessing . . . now."

* * * * *

Michiko stood frozen as Toshi's sword sang toward her throat. She was off her guard, exhausted, and overwhelmed by the things she had seen and experienced. It was all she could do to watch as her death homed in.

But Toshi brought the blade up short, stopping it less than finger's width from her neck. Mochi cried out angrily. The ochimusha was oblivious, focused exclusively on the tip of his weapon.

Michiko stood perfectly still, staring down the long blade at Toshi's intent face. They maintained this stance for agonizingly long, until Michiko could no longer hold her breath. She exhaled, and this slight motion sent a cascade of tears falling from the paths they had forged down her face.

The tears struck the end of Toshi's sword, clear saltwater sparkling and steaming on the blade. Michiko took a half-step back so that she was touching the cave wall, and Toshi followed her, keeping the blade steady and almost touching her throat. More droplets fell from her face to the edge of his weapon.

"The tears of a princess," Toshi said. "That ought to give me a boost."

He pulled the sword back and pointed the tip up. Michiko's tears ran down the length, but before they could spill over onto the hilt, Toshi spun and flicked his weapon toward the pile of hay kanji. The symbols hissed and crackled where the tears touched them, and the pile began to rustle, eager to achieve full animation and take flight.

"*And that will pep them up, once I turn them loose.*" *The sword had begun to glow softly, a gentle white sheen. Toshi ran the blade along the top of his forearm, then sheathed it, subduing the light.*

Mochi was no longer smiling. "*You are very clever, Toshi Umezawa.*"

"*Yes, I am.*" *He turned his back on the moon kami and faced the towering dark figure at the rear of the cave.*

"*I have just about everything I need,*" *he said to her.* "*And what I don't have, I can steal. But there is one thing that want. One gift you can grant that I have never been able to capture.*"

"*What about me?*" *Mochi interjected.* "*I can grant blessings, too.*"

Toshi paused, casting a glance over his shoulder. "*One at a time.*" *He turned back to the black kami and sighed. With a great show of resignation, Toshi lowered himself to one knee.*

"*Lady,*" *he said.* "*I have led a tumultuous life. Everywhere I go, I am braced by the chattering of nezumi, the shrieks of akki, and the hissing of snakes. They threaten; they demand; they ask endless questions. What I want now, and for the rest of my life upon demand, is silence. I yearn for it. And if I get it, I will hoard it and savor it more completely than any miser's treasure.*"

Mochi began scoffing instantly. "*What good will that do? It may help you gain entry to a rich man's house, thief, but it's of no use here.*"

Toshi did not turn. "*I am ready to accept your blessing if you are ready to bestow it. Become my patron, Lady.*" *He waved back at Mochi.* "*Let's start with him.*"

The Myojin of Night's Reach drifted forward, bending so that her alabaster face was a mere foot from Toshi's. Her flowing shroud filled the cave from wall to wall, from floor to ceiling.

Done. The mournful, hollow voice rang in Toshi's ears, though the kami's pale, frozen lips did not move.

The white mask rose and withdrew. The kami's black robes

retracted back into the center of her being; the banner behind her folded and sank like a foundered ship. All the while, the wan face watched Toshi impassively. At last, it too disappeared into the shadows that spawned it.

Toshi turned. Michiko was still staring at him, shock-still against the wall of the cave. He winked.

"That's not what I had in mind at all," Mochi said. "But you may yet surprise me, ochimusha." He stepped closer to Michiko. "Come, Princess. Let's see if his scheme will work as well as the one I had. If not, you can always call on me."

Toshi grinned and tapped his ear. "Didn't catch any of that, actually," he said. "Michiko, say something."

"What?" She looked in helpless confusion from Mochi to Toshi. "What can I say that will make sense of this madness?"

"I heard that," Toshi said. "You may have been right, fat boy. This kami blessing stuff is a real boon."

Mochi smiled again, but his eyes were cold and challenging.

Toshi drew his jitte and gave the pile of hay figures a stir.

"Rise up, my beauties," he said. "It's time to play."

* * * * *

Held fast in the forest kami's grip, Toshi reopened his eyes. He felt something cold and vast piling up behind him, like a stiff wind on a winter night. Mochi had been correct about one thing at least: calling on the spirits' power directly was more intense and exhilarating than channeling it through kanji. He could see why so many people were so devout in their prayers. It felt too good—addictively so.

He actually felt the quiet building up inside him as if it were a totally new thing instead of the absence of one. It was like pressure in his ears and throat, pressure that threatened to spill out of his head from every orifice.

Toshi saw the manifest spirit of the forest before him. He imagined the orochi stronghold where he'd been held, picturing the large, ritual clearing in his mind. Like the akki, these forest dwellers were chanters, and they were probably gathered there by the score to combine their prayers, to call upon their patron spirit and focus its power.

A vine lashed out from the forest spirit's body and coiled around Toshi's neck. It choked him only slightly as it forced his face up.

Now you die, the forest kami said. *And all those that stand with you. The balance must be restored.*

"Milady," Toshi croaked. "Grant me your blessing. I call . . . for silence."

Then the power did explode from him, a black stream of liquid light that gushed from his eyes, nose, and mouth. Blind, deaf, and dumb at the epicenter of this storm, Toshi nonetheless saw the countless thousands of pale white hands grasping in the black river that rushed from his face to the great forest kami's.

Then Toshi's mind seized up and the world disappeared from his senses. He lost all sensation of time and place, not drifting in a void but part of that void, indistinguishable from it. His body was a portal, a lens through which the great patron spirit of the Takenuma Swamp now focused its power.

Unsure if he were alive or dead, unconcerned in either case, Toshi laughed. It was a huge, rolling blast of joy, but it came with no sound. Not even Toshi heard his own throaty roar as the geyser of black force slammed into the Myojin of Life's Web, obscuring her under a tide of darkness.

* * * * *

Far to the north, in the ritual clearing of the orochi-bito, the frenzied rite continued. The priests and snakes had been chanting for days without interruption, and the figure of their patron kami had grown almost as large as the clearing itself. Her smooth wooden face had dried and fallen like an autumn leaf, signifying her mind had traveled elsewhere.

This did nothing to diminish the supplicant's fervor, for they knew where she had gone. Soon, the child of blasphemy would be excised and the proper order of things could be restored.

Here, she was supreme. From here, she could go anywhere in the Jukai, perhaps anywhere in the world. She was Nature, unrestrained and rampant. She was Life itself, vast and complex. Her ultimate designs were inscrutable, and her full power was irresistible. There was no denying her grandeur, no escaping her influence. All hail the Myojin of Life's Web.

A strange new sound rose over the ruckus. The revelers' noise dimmed for a moment but then rose again, louder than before, determined to drown out the competing voice. It was a male voice, a human voice. It was laughing.

A dark shadow formed on the kami's body at the point where her face had been. The shadow became a cloud, and the cloud spread out across the living wooden mass, groping and testing the air like a spider in the dark. The kami's body shuddered as if struck and then groaned as it tried to contain an awesome force that swelled it like an overfull wineskin.

A sheet of black light streamed out from the center of the kami, covering the entire clearing and everything in it. As the veneer of shadow touched the kannushi and the orochi-bito gathered there, their voices stilled. Ponderous, palpable silence descended on the clearing as every shout, hiss, and prayer died in the throats that uttered them.

Deprived of its spiritual sustenance, the kami's form began to dry and crack. The thinnest branches on its outer layers split and fell away; the broad trunks that looped and curved around the central mass now sloughed bark, littering the ground with brittle wooden flakes. The wood under that bark was not live, fragrant cedar, but cold, gray deadwood. More of the kami's body collapsed in on itself, and the central tree began to sway.

The black sheet vanished from the revelers, but they were still struck dumb. Some fled, while others simply watched, but none of them could stop the horror as their patron spirit, their god, was diminished before their very eyes.

* * * * *

The vines around Toshi's body went slack. He gulped air and wrenched his hands and feet free. The tendrils creaked as they tried to hold on, but their force was spent and they would grow no more.

Toshi stepped clear of the disintegrating wood and locked eyes with the kami's wooden mask. For once, he offered no barb, jibe, or taunt. He simply watched as the great forest spirit withered, dying as quickly as it had grown.

It was as if the seasons were passing in a matter of moments. The summertime vitality of a healthy tree faded into the muted colors and dormancy of autumn, then declined into the dry and apparent lifelessness of winter. Leaves fell, shriveled, and vanished on the wind. The branches sagged and cracked, and when they broke they shattered into splinters and dust.

Behind the dying form of the kami, her monks continued to chant with their hands locked. No sound passed their lips, but they refused to stop.

Their orochi associates were either smarter or more superstitious. The snakes screamed when they saw what Toshi had done. Alone or in small groups, the orochi-bito turned and ran, fleeing the horror outside the cave.

Toshi waited until the kami's body looked more like an ancient, fragile deadfall than a hearty forest grove. Then, he turned back to the mouth of the cave, put his fingers to his lips, and blew a shrill whistle.

The razor birds responded instantly. They rushed from the cave and swarmed around the collapsing pile of dry wood, accelerating its demise by chopping it into tiny pieces. The cloud of savage creatures buzzed and completely enveloped the kami's remains. They continued to swoop and strike until there was nothing left but a wide pile of what appeared to be mulch mixed with ashes.

Toshi whistled again. He pointed over the hill where the kannushi priests still stood.

"Snakes and monks," Toshi called. "Chase them home and kill any who stop to rest."

The flock flew faster and faster in a circle over the fallen kami. Then, pairs and trios began to peel off, surging north through the forest. Some descended on the hilltop, and as they raised bleeding slashes on the monks' exposed arms, the staid priests at last abandoning their ritual and running for cover among the trees. The razor birds followed, whirring and clattering as they flew.

Toshi looked at his jitte as the power of the kami faded from him. He hadn't even needed to carve a kanji. Smiling, he twirled his weapon and sheathed it on his hip.

He turned in time to see the backs of Lady Pearl-Ear, the wizard girl, and the smallest kitsune male hurrying into the cave. His smile faded and he cocked his head.

"Hello?" he called. "I just saved us all? Anyone care to thank me?"

Tough, unyielding hands seized him and pinned his arms behind him. Toshi smelled blood and fresh meat, felt coarse, muddy fur against his skin. Someone kicked his feet out from under him.

"Thank you," one of the kitsune warriors said. Two of the foxfolk held him down while the third relieved him of his weapons.

Toshi struggled, but they held him fast. He craned his neck to view the entrance to the cave, but no one was emerging yet. The foxes holding him growled, and Toshi bared his teeth, smiling savagely.

"Here," he said. "is where things get interesting."

CHAPTER 27

Michiko hardly dared to believe her eyes when her friends came rushing into Toshi's cave. Pearl-Ear, Riko, and Sharp-Ear all looked as if they'd spent a month in the woods and they stank of meat and musk. How long had they been searching, and what trials had they endured?

Before she could say a word, Michiko was swept up in Lady Pearl-Ear's arms. Her teacher's embrace almost brought them both to the floor of the cave, but then Riko and Sharp-Ear were there, propping her up as they joined the embrace.

"You're alive," Sharp-Ear said happily. "I'm really quite relieved."

"Is this real, my friends? Have you truly found me?" Michiko muttered.

"You're safe now." Pearl-Ear pushed back and peered into Michiko's face. "Are you hurt? Did he harm you in any way?"

Michiko paused before replying, daunted by the intensity in Lady Pearl-Ear's eyes. Was that blood on the sensei?

"No," she said at last. "He had a great deal to contend with. He was too preoccupied to pay me much mind." Michiko realized that Riko was still clinging to her.

"Riko?" she said, gently pushing her friend back.

"Sorry. I'm just so glad to see you. Choryu will be delighted." She put her hand on Michiko's shoulder. "I am delighted. I'm very glad you're safe, Princess."

Michiko nodded. She turned to Lady Pearl-Ear and said, "I know what my father did. I know why the spirits make war."

Sadness crept across Pearl-Ear's joyful face. "Hush now, my child. There will be time for such things later. But first, we must get you away from here."

Michiko peered over Lady Pearl-Ear's shoulder toward the mouth of the cave. "The snakes are gone?"

The fox-woman nodded. "And their kami with them. Your abductor managed to beat them back almost single-handedly. Where did he acquire such power? He didn't have it when the orochi attacked before."

Riko added, "And if he did, he chose not to employ it."

Michiko reddened. "He and I came to an arrangement while we waited. We agreed to help each other." She shrugged. "We were both at risk, so we put aside our differences."

Sharp-Ear laughed. "Fair enough. Why don't we ask him ourselves?"

Michiko nodded. "Yes. Take me to him."

The sunlight outside the cave stung her eyes, but Michiko adjusted quickly. She noticed the bodies of many orochi-bito, but she did not dwell on them. In the tower, she had rarely seen violence and death up close. Since she'd left, she seemed to see nothing else.

They led her to the bottom of a hillside, where two muddy kitsune warriors held Toshi pinned to the ground. A third stood over the struggling ochimusha, wielding Toshi's own sword.

"Princess," the sword-bearer called. "I am Frost-Tail. My brothers and I welcome you and pledge our service."

"Thank you, Frost-Tail." She bowed curtly. "Let him up."

"Hear, hear," Toshi grunted.

"I think not," Pearl-Ear said. "He will return with us to Eiganjo, bound if necessary. He has done you a great service today, but he also—"

"I said let him up." Michiko strode forward and planted her feet as she glowered down at the kitsune. "He works for me now."

"Michiko," Pearl-Ear said gently. "I understand that you're grateful to the outlaw. But he must—"

"I am Princess Michiko Konda," she said. "The Daimyo's daughter and heir to the throne of Towabara. But I am also in league with this man. For my life, for the answers I seek, and for the foreseeable future, I have retained the services of his hyozan reckoners."

Pearl-Ear started to speak, then was silent. Sharp-Ear's face showed surprise, but his eyes sparkled with mischief and mirth. Riko stood as if pole-axed.

"Michiko?" she squeaked. "You didn't join a reckoner gang."

"No," Michiko said. "But I am hiring the services of this one."

"If you'll let me up now," Toshi said from underneath Dawn-Tail, "I still have business to conduct."

* * * * *

Toshi knew it had been a long shot, but successfully soliciting a commission from the princess was worth it, just for the look on the kitsune party's faces.

"How could you agree to this?" Lady Pearl-Ear demanded. Her maternal demeanor and warm tones had given way to the cold, sharp voice of a disappointed mentor.

"I didn't trust him," Michiko said. "In fact, I feared him. This was the only way I could think of to ensure he wouldn't harm me before you arrived."

"But he's a criminal. These hyozan, they're all criminals. What will you do when they come knocking and tell you you're obliged to go a-thieving with them?"

"Doesn't work like that," Toshi said. "What we have is a for-hire arrangement. A business deal between enlightened individuals."

"Is that what they're calling murder gangs these days? Enlightened individuals?" The largest kitsune sneered. Each of the foxes looked as if he'd like to get his arm around Toshi's throat one last time.

"He is using you, Michiko, using your good nature and trust to exploit—"

"My father used me," Michiko said evenly. "The orochi tried to use me. The kami want to use me. Everyone seems to want me for something. Toshi is the only one who offered to be of use in return.

"I have much to tell you Lady Pearl-Ear . . . Riko . . . all of you. I have seen the cause of the Kami War. I am more committed than ever to stopping it. And I will use . . . yes, use . . . whatever and whomever I can to make this happen: my father's trust, the knowledge archived at Minamo, and the services of hyozan criminals. They are all my tools, and I will make the most of them. It is no different than what every leader does for the sake of her people."

Pearl-Ear stared at Michiko, then sadly shook her head. "I think you have made a terrible mistake," she said. "But I will be there to help you survive it."

"Thank you, Lady Pearl-Ear."

The fox-woman turned to Toshi and said, "And you, ochimusha? What will you do now?"

Toshi had been waiting for this. While he had been pinned by the kitsune, the white-haired wizard had come out of the brush. He had stayed to the rear of the group, saying little. Toshi had not taken his eyes off him.

"First," he said, pointing at the wizard boy, "I'm going to settle up with your friend there."

Choryu blinked. "Me? What are you talking about now, you cutthroat?"

Michiko stepped up to him. "What do you mean by this?"

Toshi raised his voice, loud enough for everyone to hear. "Kobo . . . my partner . . . wasn't killed by the orochi. He was killed by that waste of space right there."

Choryu's face went slack. "No," he said. "You all saw. The snakes tied him up and smothered him."

"They smothered him enough to subdue him," Toshi agreed. "And they tied him up. But they didn't kill him.

"Kobo had water in his lungs. He drowned. It would take more than a rainstorm to force liquid down the throat of an ogre's apprentice. It would take a river, or an ocean tide, focused right at his face. The orochi don't conjure powerful streams of water, as a rule, do they? But I know someone who does."

"It's a lie," Choryu said. He looked pleadingly at the faces all turned toward him. "Why would I kill the big man?"

"Because you couldn't find me. Because you saw him fight and feared what he could do if he stood against you." Toshi looked from face to face, challenging anyone to refute his accusation. "Because you panicked when you thought you might not lure Michiko to the Academy." Toshi gestured impatiently. "Come on, kitsune forest-folk. Tell me you didn't smell his scent on Kobo's body."

Sharp-Ear glanced at the brothers. "We don't smell like that. There is no way to be sure."

"I'm sure. You're a dead man, wizard.

"'The only way to avoid it is if we can't find you,'" Toshi intoned. His eyes grew cold and hard. "I've already found you."

"There will be no killing here," Lady Pearl-Ear said. The kitsune foxes formed up behind her, screening Choryu from Toshi.

Michiko nodded. "Choryu is my friend. If he has done what you say he has, I shall—"

"Sorry," Toshi said. "But you're the last person who should be in my way. Weren't you there when Mochi told us not to trust anyone who tries to bring you to the Academy? This little stain is from the academy. And he killed Kobo."

"I mourn the loss of your partner, sincerely. But under no circumstances will I . . ."

She went on, but Toshi had stopped listening. He casually reached inside the waistband of his trousers and drew out a kanji formed of woven hay. It was a different character than the one that created the razor birds, one with the hyozan triangle as its central motif. The kanji for "guilty" was contained within the triangle.

"Sorry," Toshi said again, and tossed the kanji over their heads. All eyes followed its arc as Toshi called, "Kobo is dead. Mark his killer and take him back to the beginning."

The small folded character shifted in flight, becoming less brittle and acquiring a dull red glow. It maintained its shape, though it squirmed like a living thing.

The kanji floated for a moment, then streaked down at Choryu. The white-haired wizard yelped and sent a stream of thick blue water surging at the kanji, but the character splashed through almost unhindered.

It flew straight into Choryu's face and fixed itself to his forehead. Choryu screamed as the symbol burned into his flesh, burrowing down through the layers of skin until it hit bone.

"Spirits of Minamo," he cried. "Help me!"

Water shot from his hands as the kanji magic took hold. It lifted him off the ground, rotating him slightly, and Choryu screamed. He clawed at his face, his feet flailing wildly, all the while continuing to ascend.

"Lady Pearl-Ear, Riko, anybody," he wailed. "Stop him! Save me!"

The kitsune bore Toshi to the ground again, but he did not resist. He stared at Choryu and Choryu alone.

"Michiko," the wizard wailed. "Forgive me."

The wizard held that final syllable as the kanji picked up speed, hauling him high into the sky. His voice became a distant echo on the wind as he vanished into the clouds.

Toshi exhaled deeply. "That's that, then."

The foxes tightened their grip. Riko and Lady Pearl-Ear were glaring at him with expressions that changed from shock to horror to murderous intent and back again. The beautiful princess had fixed him with her dazzling eyes, her lips trembling.

The disappointment on her face raised something like regret in Toshi's mind. Close to regret, but not quite.

"He murdered my partner," he reminded them all.

Michiko shook her head and then bowed it low. Riko joined her, and one by one, the others followed her example.

Praying for a cowardly, murdering worm, Toshi thought. I should be so lucky.

"Shall we bind him for the trip back to the tower," Sharp-Ear called. "Or should we just hang him here?"

Toshi barked out a rough laugh. "You know something, boys? Our business here is concluded. Michiko-hime," he called. "You can contact me in any of the Spire's elegant public houses. Send a message or a messenger with the hyozan mark."

The littlest kitsune's voice growled from right next to Toshi's ear. "And how will you get there, outlaw?"

Toshi glanced back, but he was unable to see.

"There's a fresh kanji bleeding on my right arm," Toshi said. "You can't see it, but it's there. Want to see how well it works with a great kami's blessing? All I have to do is pronounce it, like this: Fade."

"Hold him!" The fox's voice was furious, but it faded like a waking dream as Toshi disappeared.

He slipped through the kitsune's grip like a ghost: silent, intangible, invisible. He could not be seen nor heard, but he was there, watching as they stamped their feet and cursed his name in frustration.

Through it all, the tall, elegant form of Michiko stood impassive. When the foxes had worn themselves out and exhausted their vocabularies, the princess strode to the spot where Toshi had escaped them all.

"I may yet call upon you, reckoner," the princess said severely. "Or I may send soldiers for you in the night. Until then, wait. Wait and worry."

Without another word, Michiko turned and walked away. She gathered Riko under one arm and Lady Pearl-Ear under the other, and the women supported each other as they went. The three kit-sune samurai fell in behind them. The tallest turned, glanced into Toshi's cave, and spat on the ground.

"See you soon," Toshi called, though his words made no sound that anyone else could hear.

He watched them go, waiting patiently for the opportunity to move. As an intangible phantom, he was not yet fluent in the basic mechanics of moving around. It was harder with no friction and no ground, and it took him almost an hour to complete a single step.

He sighed, relaxing for the first time in weeks. He could barely move, so he might as well lie back and rest.

As the tension drained from his body, Toshi slowly faded back into view. His feet settled back onto the bloody ground, and he quickly withdrew back into the shelter of the cave.

A breeze stirred the leaves on the trees, and a pair of birds exchanged mating calls. Somewhere in the distance, dog howled. Thunder rumbled overhead, and the powerful vibrations echoed across the ground.

Toshi looked up. He cleared his throat and said, "Shh."

The world around him went dead as if his ears had been stuffed with wax. Perfect.

The Kami War raged on, the soratami were out to get him, and he had made a whole lot of new enemies besides. On the bright side, he had sold his services to a princess and he had honored his debt to Kobo. Toshi pondered for a moment, then decided he would allow Hidetsugu a few days to settle down before returning to the ogre's hut to plan his next move. Until then, he thought, I need to rest.

The ochimusha headed for the deepest recesses of his cave where he hoped to find solitude to complement the silence.

The sun was setting over the hinterlands near the Sokenzan Mountains. The landscape was dull and beige and hard, as always, but a threatening bank of black clouds was gathering overhead. Soon it would rain and the badlands would become a temporary lake, making all travel impossible.

Hidetsugu the o-bakemono trudged along the path from his hut. He carried a small sack in his great jagged hand.

It had been days since Toshi's messenger had arrived with the news of Kobo's death. He didn't trust Toshi as such, but he knew that their oath was still in place. The ochimusha could not have caused Kobo's death by action or inaction while the pact was still valid.

Toshi had been clever not to send more information than he did. The slightest extra detail, the barest hint telling where Kobo fell would have been enough. Nothing would have stopped Hidetsugu from traveling to his apprentice's body and killing every living thing he found there. He might have killed every living thing on his way there and his way back, for good measure, and that's probably why Toshi had kept the message so brief.

Hidetsugu reached the garden of spikes where he displayed the heads to scare off visitors. He reached into the sack, drew out two akki and one bandit, and arranged them evenly among the empty spikes. The human's head was still fresh, and the smell of blood and brains brought a growl from his stomach.

The ogre shaman lumbered back to his hut, sticking to the precise center of the path. Just beyond the garden was a vast pile of dust and gravel. Days ago, it had been the great stone block he had set as a test for his apprentice. When Kobo could split the rock down the center with a single blow, he would be ready to leave Hidetsugu's service.

Hidetsugu looked around until he spotted the smashed and ruined hammer. Under his own fury, the testing stone had proven more durable than the testing hammer. Hidetsugu had been forced to create the rest of the gravel pile with his bare hands. The knuckles on his left hand were still bleeding.

He came closer to his hut, and then Hidetsugu stopped. He lifted his massive snout and sniffed the air. Visitors? he wondered. Better now than tomorrow, he reasoned. The rain would keep even the most suicidally curious away, and he was swiftly growing hungrier.

Hidetsugu was patient for an ogre. He simply stood, staring, until the visitor came hurtling down from the clouds. From the screams, Hidetsugu took him for a female, but as the figure drew closer, he saw that it was a human male.

The white-haired wizard in student's robes sailed in like some unruly bird, slamming hard into the dusty ground at Hidetsugu's feet. Even in his hunger and his lingering rage, Hidetsugu could barely muster the interest to deal with this intruder. He was clearly not in control of his own flight. Maybe the bandits had sent the o-bakemono a gift.

The mark on Hidetsugu's shoulder throbbed, and the ogre became instantly more alert. It occurred to him that someone else may have sent him this gift.

Hidetsugu reached out to where the exhausted, coughing youth lay. He pinched the back of the young man's robe between his fingers and lifted him to eye level.

The student's eyes cleared, and he screamed. He flailed and

thrashed in Hidetsugu's hand, clawing and hammering at the ogre's fingers. Hidetsugu stared at the wizard without seeing him, staring only at the mark burned into the flesh below his white shock of hair.

"I see you know Toshi," Hidetsugu growled. The wizard's wet face froze and his throat hitched. He opened his mouth, but only a wet squeak came out.

"I also see you are a student. I recently lost my student. But you already know that."

"Please," the wizard croaked. "In the name of the holiest kami—"

"You can pray to kami here if you like," Hidetsugu said. "But I know that my oni has eaten them all." He lifted the wizard high over his own head, and the youth screamed. His robe started to tear, and Hidetsugu opened his gaping mouth wide, jagged teeth the size of swords glistening in the dusk.

The wizard stopped struggling, fearful of tearing loose and falling.

"No. Please, no."

"From this point forward, you may call me 'master,' and I will call you 'excrement.' Most of my apprentices don't survive the first week. But you will be more than my apprentice. You will be my hobby."

The wizard screamed again as Hidetsugu tossed him into the air like a shelled nut. He spun end over end until he came down lengthwise across Hidetsugu's open jaw.

The ogre chomped down, hard enough to bruise bones but not to break them. Not yet. The wizard shouted, vomited, and went limp, moaning as Hidetsugu's jaws held him fast.

"Lesson one." Hidetsugu's voice was muffled as he spoke around the human in his mouth. "You will call me 'master.' "

"Master," the wizard moaned.

"Good." With the semi-conscious wizard in his teeth, Hidetsugu stomped toward the doorway to his hut. With each new step, the wizard winced and wept.

Hidetsugu ducked his head and disappeared inside his hut. A short time later, the screams began.

Long, long before they stopped, it began to rain.

What is Magic: The Gathering®?

It's the game that started the trading card game industry.

It's also the world's premier trading card game.

It's enjoyed by over 6 million players worldwide.

It's got the biggest Organized Play program, with annual prizes topping $3 million every year.

It's local game nights and global tournaments.

It's prizes for every level of player - from premier cards to cash, including the $1 million Pro Tour.

It's got the deadliest creatures and literally unlimited strategies.

It's online too.

Getting started is easy.
Your connection is waiting.

magicthegathering.com

FROM *NEW YORK TIMES*

BEST-SELLING AUTHOR

R.A. SALVATORE

In taverns, around campfires, and in the loftiest council chambers of Faerûn, people whisper the tales of a lone dark elf who stumbled out of the merciless Underdark to the no less unforgiving wilderness of the World Above and carved a life for himself, then lived a legend...

THE LEGEND OF DRIZZT

For the first time in deluxe hardcover editions, all three volumes of the Dark Elf Trilogy take their rightful place at the beginning of one of the greatest fantasy epics of all time. Each title contains striking new cover art and portions of an all-new author interview, with the questions posed by none other than the readers themselves.

HOMELAND

Being born in Menzoberranzan means a hard life surrounded by evil.

March 2004

EXILE

But the only thing worse is being driven from the city with hunters on your trail.

June 2004

SOJOURN

Unless you can find your way out, never to return.

December 2004